The Best of
The Missouri Review

The Best of
The
Missouri
Review

Fiction, 1978–1990

Edited by

Speer Morgan
Greg Michalson
Jo Sapp

University of Missouri Press

COLUMBIA AND LONDON

Copyright © 1991 Curators of the University of Missouri
University of Missouri Press, Columbia, Missouri 65201
Printed and bound in the United States of America
All rights reserved

5 4 3 2 1   95 94 93 92 91

Library of Congress Cataloging-in-Publication Data

The Best of the Missouri review: fiction, 1978–1990 / edited by
    Speer Morgan, Greg Michalson, Jo Sapp.
        p.   cm.
    ISBN 0-8262-0773-1. — ISBN 0-8262-0784-7 (pbk.)
    1. Short stories, American.   2. American fiction—20th century.
I. Morgan, Speer, 1949–   . II. Michalson, Greg.   III. Sapp, Jo.
IV. Missouri review.
PS648.S5B47   1991
813'.5'08—dc20   90–47743
                                                                      CIP

∞™ This paper meets the minimum requirements of
the American National Standard for Permanence of Paper
for Printed Library Materials, Z39.48, 1984.

Designer: Liz Fett
Typesetter: Connell-Zeko Type & Graphics
Printer: Thomson-Shore, Inc.
Binder: Thomson-Shore, Inc.
Typeface: Palatino

CONTENTS

PREFACE

The Missouri Review was born in 1978, at a time when the short story was on the tail end of a prolonged slump. The short story had achieved robust maturity before the turn of the century and had long been a popular presence in general interest magazines, but with the contraction of the mass market it began to fade. By the fifties and sixties audiences were looking elsewhere for entertainment, and the short story seemed to be evolving from popular to academic endorsement, from enjoyment to instruction, from pleasure to duty. As recently as 1984 John Updike was able to write that "short fiction . . . has gone from being a popular to a fine art, an art preserved in a kind of floating museum made up of many little superfluous magazines."

Yet a resurgence fueled by those "little" magazines, along with the university and small presses, led ultimately to what *Newsweek* termed a "Silver Age" of short fiction. The claim may be exaggerated, but it is undeniably true that talented writers and editors began to embrace the form with renewed interest.

The Missouri Review began prior to this so-called Silver Age, and from the outset we resisted becoming one of Updike's "floating museums." We did not subscribe to the notion that good fiction was the province of any particular group or school or theory of writing. We looked not for a certain sort of story, but for certain, original talent. The editors wanted to provide an open stage for those who deserved it, regardless of style or type, regardless of the current reputation of the writer. The tale *itself* was the thing. We cared about a good read, liveliness, a story that had some "juice" to it.

The editors, with one exception—Bill Peden, *MR*'s spiritual father—were young and without credentials. We had one thing in common, the fact that we were all writers or aspiring writers. We had a natural sympathy for others who were at a point early in their careers, and we consciously looked for those new writers. We shared certain preferences in fiction: for styles based on an authoritative voice, for variety of subject matter, for characters engaged in situations with real consequences, and for something that Bill called "memorableness." In many an editorial meeting, one could hear Bill say, "It's an entirely competent story. But I won't remember it next week."

This collection of twenty-five stories is from the first dozen years of *The Missouri Review*. Some of them, of course, are consensus choices. Others are favorites of one or another of the editors. We decided early on that if a story had a champion, someone willing to go to the wall for it, that story should be published. The committee method of deciding on stories has severe limitations, particularly when seeking memorableness. We found that strong disagreement about a story often was a promising sign—dull stories inspire boredom, not anger. Over the years, the practice of occasionally allowing editors to "cash chips" in the face of opposition to a favored story has produced some of the most exciting and well-received fiction *The Missouri Review* has published. We have used the same advocacy system in choosing this collection.

Many of these stories have been anthologized elsewhere, finding berths in such collections as *The Best American Short Stories* and *The Pushcart Prizes*. A half dozen represent the first published story for their authors. Several are early stories by writers who have now achieved significant reputations and received major awards, including American Book Awards and even the Nobel Prize. Other authors in this collection are well known but not yet so honored, some are still finding their voices, and a couple apparently have for now laid down the pen after a brilliant start.

Those looking for a common element of style, theme, or critical stance will doubtless find it. *The Missouri Review* has never shied from publishing writers who are under the influence of a movement or trend. After all, writers are always under the influence of something. Good writing arises from a complex of unforeseeable individual circumstances; we are finally concerned only with what the authors manage to forge in the creative act. To our mind, what these stories have in common is simple vitality and love of a tale artfully told for its own sake.

Speer Morgan
Greg Michalson
Jo Sapp

The Best of
*The
Missouri
Review*

SARAH COLE: A TYPE OF LOVE STORY

Russell Banks

1

To begin, then, here is a scene in which I am the man and my friend Sarah Cole is the woman. I don't mind describing it now, because I'm a decade older and don't look the same now as I did then, and Sarah is dead. That is to say, on hearing this story you might think me vain if I looked the same now as I did then, because I must tell you that I was extremely handsome then. And if Sarah were not dead, you'd think I was cruel, for I must tell you that Sarah was very homely. In fact, she was the homeliest woman I have ever known. Personally, I mean. I've *seen* a few women who were more unattractive than Sarah, but they were clearly freaks of nature or had been badly injured or had been victimized by some grotesque, disfiguring disease. Sarah, however, was quite normal, and I knew her well, because for three and a half months we were lovers.

Here is the scene. You can put it in the present, even though it took place ten years ago, because nothing that matters to the story depends on when it took place, and you can put it in Concord, New Hampshire, even though that is indeed where it took place, because it doesn't matter where it took place, so it might as well be Concord, New Hampshire, a place I happen to know well and can therefore describe with sufficient detail to make the story believable. Around six o'clock on a Wednesday evening in late May a man enters a bar. The place, a cocktail lounge at street level with a restaurant up-stairs, is decorated with hanging plants and unfinished wood pan-eling, butcherblock tables and captain's chairs, with a half-dozen darkened, thickly upholstered booths along one wall. Three or four men between the ages of twenty-five and thirty-five are drinking at the bar, and they, like the man who has just entered, wear three-piece suits and loosened neckties. They are probably lawyers, young, unmarried lawyers gossiping with their brethren over mar-tinis so as to postpone arriving home alone at their whitewashed townhouse apartments, where they will fix their evening meals in

1

radar ranges, and afterwards, while their TVs chuckle quietly in front of them, sit on their couches and do a little extra work for tomorrow. They are, for the most part, honorable, educated, hard-working, shallow, and moderately unhappy young men. Our man, call him Ronald, Ron, in most ways is like these men, except that he is unusually good-looking, and that makes him a little less unhappy than they. Ron is effortlessly attractive, a genetic wonder—tall, slender, symmetrical, and clean. His flaws, a small mole on the left corner of his square but not-too-prominent chin, a slight excess of blond hair on the tops of his tanned hands, and somewhat under-developed buttocks, insofar as they keep him from resembling too closely a men's store mannequin, only contribute to his beauty, for he is beautiful, the way we usually think of a woman as being beautiful. And he is nice, too, the consequence, perhaps, of his seeming not to know how beautiful he is, to men as well as women, to young people, even children, as well as old, to attractive people, who realize immediately that he is so much more attractive than they as not to be competitive with them, as well as unattractive people, who see him and gain thereby a comforting perspective on those they have heretofore envied for their good looks.

Ron takes a seat at the bar, unfolds the evening paper in front of him, and before he can start reading, the bartender asks to help him, calling him "Sir," even though Ron has come into this bar numerous times at this time of day, especially since his divorce last fall. Ron got divorced because, after three years of marriage, his wife had chosen to pursue the career that his had interrupted, that of a fashion designer, which meant that she had to live in New York City while he had to continue to live in New Hampshire, where his career had got its start. They agreed to live apart until he could continue his career near New York City, but after a few months, between conjugal visits, he started sleeping with other women, and she started sleeping with other men, and that was that. "No big deal," he explained to friends, who liked both Ron and his wife, even though he was slightly more beautiful than she. "We really were too young when we got married, college sweethearts. But we're still best friends," he assured them. They understood. Most of Ron's friends were divorced by then too.

Ron orders a Scotch and soda, with a twist, and goes back to reading his paper. When his drink comes, before he takes a sip of it, he first carefully finishes reading an article about the recent reappearance of coyotes in northern New Hampshire and Vermont. He lights a cigarette. He goes on reading. He takes a second sip of his drink. Everyone in the room—the three or four men scattered along the bar, the tall, thin bartender, and several people in the booths at the back—watches him do these ordinary things.

He has got to the classified section, is perhaps searching for someone willing to come in once a week and clean his apartment, when the woman who will turn out to be Sarah Cole leaves a booth in the back and approaches him. She comes up from the side and sits next to him. She's wearing heavy, tan cowboy boots and a dark brown, suede cowboy hat, lumpy jeans and a yellow T-shirt that clings to her arms, breasts, and round belly like the skin of a sausage. Though he will later learn that she is thirty-eight years old, she looks older by about ten years, which makes her look about twenty years older than he actually is. (It's difficult to guess accurately how old Ron is, he looks anywhere from a mature twenty-five to a youthful forty, so his actual age doesn't seem to matter.)

"It's not bad here at the bar," she says, looking around. "More light, anyhow. Whatcha readin'?" she asks brightly, planting both elbows on the bar.

Ron looks up from his paper with a slight smile on his lips, sees the face of a woman homelier than any he has ever seen or imagined before, and goes on smiling lightly. He feels himself falling into her tiny, slightly crossed, dark brown eyes, pulls himself back, and studies for a few seconds her mottled, pocked complexion, bulbous nose, loose mouth, twisted and gapped teeth, and heavy but receding chin. He casts a glance over her thatch of dun-colored hair and along her neck and throat, where acne burns against gray skin, and returns to her eyes, and again feels himself falling into her.

"What did you say?" he asks.

She knocks a mentholated cigarette from her pack, and Ron swiftly lights it. Blowing smoke from her large, wing-shaped nostrils, she speaks again. Her voice is thick and nasal, a chocolate-colored voice. "I asked you watcha readin', but I can see now." She belts out a single, loud laugh. "The paper!"

Ron laughs, too. "The paper! *The Concord Monitor*!" He is not hallucinating, he clearly sees what is before him and admits—no, he asserts—to himself that he is speaking to the most unattractive woman he has ever seen, a fact which fascinates him, as if instead he were speaking to the most beautiful woman he has ever seen or perhaps ever will see, so he treasures the moment, attempts to hold it as if it were a golden ball, a disproportionately heavy object which—if he doesn't hold it lightly yet with precision and firmness—will slip from his hand and roll across the lawn to the lip of the well and down, down to the bottom of the well, lost to him forever. It will be merely a memory, something to speak of wistfully and with wonder as over the years the image fades and comes in the end to exist only in the telling. His mind and body waken from their sleepy self-absorption, and all his attention focuses on the woman, Sarah Cole, her ugly face, like a warthog's, her thick, rapid voice, her dumpy, off-center wreck of a body, and to keep this moment here before him, he begins to ask questions of her, he buys her a drink, he smiles, until soon it seems, even to him, that he is taking her and her life, its vicissitudes and woe, quite seriously.

He learns her name, of course, and she volunteers the information that she spoke to him on a dare from one of the two women still sitting in the booth behind her. She turns on her stool and smiles brazenly, triumphantly, at her friends, two women, also homely (though nowhere as homely as she) and dressed, like her, in cowboy boots, hats and jeans. One of the women, a blond with an under-slung jaw and wearing heavy eye makeup, flips a little wave at her, and as if embarrassed, she and the other woman at the booth turn back to their drinks and sip fiercely at straws.

Sarah returns to Ron and goes on telling him what he wants to know, about her job at the Rumford Press, about her divorced hus-band who was a bastard and stupid and "sick," she says, as if filling suddenly with sympathy for the man. She tells Ron about her three children, the youngest, a girl, in junior high school and boy-crazy, the other two, boys, in high school and almost never at home any-more. She speaks of her children with genuine tenderness and concern, and Ron is touched. He can see with what pleasure and pain she speaks of her children; he watches her tiny eyes light up and water over when he asks their names.

"You're a nice woman," he informs her.

She smiles, looks at her empty glass. "No. No, I'm not. But you're a nice man, to tell me that."

Ron, with a gesture, asks the bartender to refill Sarah's glass. She is drinking white Russians. Perhaps she has been drinking them for an hour or two, for she seems very relaxed, more relaxed than women usually do when they come up and without introduction or invitation speak to him.

She asks him about himself, his job, his divorce, how long he has lived in Concord, but he finds that he is not at all interested in telling her about himself. He wants to know about her, even though what she has to tell him about herself is predictable and ordinary and the way she tells it unadorned and clichéd. He wonders about her husband. What kind of man would fall in love with Sarah Cole?

2

That scene, at Osgood's Lounge in Concord, ended with Ron's departure, alone, after having bought Sarah's second drink, and Sarah's return to her friends in the booth. I don't know what she told them, but it's not hard to imagine. The three women were not close friends, merely fellow workers at Rumford Press, where they stood at the end of a long conveyor belt day after day packing *TV Guides* into cartons. They all hated their jobs, and frequently after work, when they worked the day shift, they would put on their cowboy hats and boots, which they kept all day in their lockers, and stop for a drink or two on their way home. This had been their first visit to Osgood's, a place that, prior to this, they had avoided out of a sneering belief that no one went there but lawyers and insurance men. It had been Sarah who had asked the others why that should keep them away, and when they had no answer for her, the three had decided to stop at Osgood's. Ron was right, they had been there over an hour when he came in, and Sarah was a little drunk. "We'll hafta come in here again," she said to her friends, her voice rising slightly.

Which they did, that Friday, and once again Ron appeared with his evening newspaper. He put his briefcase down next to his stool and ordered a drink and proceeded to read the front page, slowly, deliberately, clearly a weary, unhurried, solitary man. He did not notice the three women in cowboy hats and boots in the booth in back, but they saw him, and after a few minutes Sarah was once again at his side.

"Hi."

He turned, saw her, and instantly regained the moment he had lost when, Wednesday night, once outside the bar, he had forgotten about the ugliest woman he had ever seen. She seemed even more grotesque to him now than before, which made the moment all the more precious to him, and so once again he held the moment as if in his hands and began to speak with her, to ask questions, to offer his opinions and solicit hers.

I said earlier that I am the man in this story and my friend Sarah Cole, now dead, is the woman. I think back to that night, the second time I had seen Sarah, and I tremble, not with fear but in shame. My concern then, when I was first becoming involved with Sarah, was merely with the moment, holding onto it, grasping it wholly as if its beginning did not grow out of some other prior moment in her life and my life separately and at the same time did not lead into future moments of our separate lives. She talked more easily than she had the night before, and I listened as eagerly and carefully as I had before, again, with the same motives, to keep her in front of me, to draw her forward from the context of her life and place her, as if she were an object, into the context of mine. I did not know how cruel this was. When you have never done a thing before and that thing is not simply and clearly right or wrong, you frequently do not know if it is a cruel thing, you just go ahead and do it, and maybe later you'll be able to determine whether you acted cruelly. That way you'll know if it was right or wrong of you to have done it in the first place.

While we drank, Sarah told me that she hated her ex-husband because of the way he treated the children. "It's not so much the money," she said, nervously wagging her booted feet from her perch on the high barstool. "I mean, I get by, barely, but I get them fed and clothed on my own okay. It's because he won't even write them a letter or anything. He won't call them on the phone, all he calls for is to bitch at me because I'm trying to get the state to take him to court so I can get some of the money he's s'posed to be paying for child support. And he won't even think to talk to the kids when he calls. Won't even ask about them."

"He sounds like a bastard," I said.

"He is, he is," she said. "I don't know why I married him. Or stayed married. Fourteen years, for Christ's sake. He put a spell over me or something, I don't know," she said with a note of wistfulness in her voice. "He wasn't what you'd call good-looking."

After her second drink, she decided she had to leave. Her children were at home, it was Friday night and she liked to make sure she ate supper with them and knew where they were going and who they were with when they went out on their dates. "No dates on school nights," she said to me. "I mean, you gotta have rules, you know."

I agreed, and we left together, everyone in the place following us with his or her gaze. I was aware of that, I knew what they were thinking, and I didn't care, because I was simply walking her to her car.

It was a cool evening, dusk settling onto the lot like a gray blanket. Her car, a huge, dark green Buick sedan at least ten years old, was battered, scratched, and almost beyond use. She reached for the door handle on the driver's side and yanked. Nothing. The door wouldn't open. She tried again. Then I tried. Still nothing.

Then I saw it, a V-shaped dent in the left front fender creasing the fender where the door joined it, binding the metal of the door against the metal of the fender in a large crimp that held the door fast. "Someone must've backed into you while you were inside," I said to her.

She came forward and studied the crimp for a few seconds, and when she looked back at me, she was weeping. "Jesus, Jesus, Jesus!" she wailed, her large, froglike mouth wide open and wet with spit, her red tongue flopping loosely over gapped teeth. "I can't pay for this! I *can't!*" Her face was red, and even in the dusky light I could see it puff out with weeping, her tiny eyes seeming almost to disappear behind her wet cheeks. Her shoulders slumped, her hands fell limply to her sides.

Placing my briefcase on the ground, I reached out to her and put my arms around her body and held her close to me, while she cried wetly into my shoulder. After a few seconds, she started pulling herself back together and her weeping got reduced to sniffling. Her cowboy hat had been pushed back and now clung to her head at a precarious, absurdly jaunty angle. She took a step away from me and said, "I'll get in the other side."

"Okay," I said almost in a whisper. "That's fine."

Slowly, she walked around the front of the huge, ugly vehicle and opened the door on the passenger's side and slid awkwardly across the seat until she had positioned herself behind the steering wheel. Then she started the motor, which came to life with a roar. The muffler was shot. Without saying another word to me, or even waving, she dropped the car into reverse gear and backed it loudly out of the parking space and headed out the lot to the street.

I turned and started for my car, when I happened to glance toward the door of the bar, and there, staring after me, were the bartender, the two women who had come in with Sarah, and two of the men who had been sitting at the bar. They were lawyers, and I knew them slightly. They were grinning at me. I grinned back and got into my car, and then, without looking at them again, I left the place and drove straight to my apartment.

3

One night several weeks later, Ron meets Sarah at Osgood's, and after buying her three white Russians and drinking three Scotches himself, he takes her back to his apartment in his car—a Datsun fastback coupe that she says she admires—for the sole purpose of making love to her.

I'm still the man in this story, and Sarah is still the woman, but I'm telling it this way because what I have to tell you now confuses me, embarrasses me, and makes me sad, and consequently, I'm likely to tell it falsely. I'm likely to cover the truth by making Sarah a better woman than she actually was, while making myself appear worse than I actually was or am; or else I'll do the opposite, make Sarah worse than she was and me better. The truth is, I was pretty, extremely so, and she was not, extremely so, and I knew it and she knew it. She walked out the door of Osgood's determined to make love to a man much prettier than any she had seen up close before, and I walked out determined to make love to a woman much homelier than any I had made love to before. We were, in a sense, equals.

No, that's not exactly true. (You see? This is why I have to tell the story the way I'm telling it.) I'm not at all sure she feels as Ron does. That is to say, perhaps she genuinely likes the man, in spite of his being the most physically attractive man she has ever known. Perhaps she is more aware of her homeliness than of his beauty, just as he is more aware of her homeliness than of his beauty, for Ron, despite what I may have implied, does not think of himself as especially beautiful. He merely knows that other people think of him that way. As I said before, he is a nice man.

Ron unlocks the door to his apartment, walks in ahead of her, and flicks on the lamp beside the couch. It's a small, single-bedroom, modern apartment, one of thirty identical apartments in a large brick building on the heights just east of downtown Concord. Sarah stands nervously at the door, peering in.

"Come in, come in," he says.

She steps timidly in and closes the door behind her. She removes her cowboy hat, then quickly puts it back on, crosses the living room, and plops down in a blond easy chair, seeming to shrink in its hug out of sight to safety. Ron, behind her, at the entry to the kitchen, places one hand on her shoulder, and she stiffens. He removes his hand.

"Would you like a drink?"

"No . . . I guess not," she says, staring straight ahead at the wall opposite, where a large framed photograph of a bicyclist advertises in French the Tour de France. Around a corner, in an alcove off the living room, a silver-gray ten-speed bicycle leans casually against the wall, glistening and posed, slender as a thoroughbred racehorse.

"I don't know," she says. Ron is in the kitchen now, making himself a drink. "I don't know . . . I don't know."

"What? Change your mind? I can make a white Russian for you. Vodka, cream, kahlua, and ice, right?"

Sarah tries to cross her legs, but she is sitting too low in the chair and her legs are too thick at the thigh, so she ends, after a struggle, with one leg in the air and the other twisted on its side. She looks as if she has fallen from a great height.

Ron steps out from the kitchen, peers over the back of the chair, and watches her untangle herself, then ducks back into the kitchen. After a few seconds, he returns. "Seriously. Want me to fix you a white Russian?"

"No."

Ron, again from behind, places one hand onto Sarah's shoulder, and this time she does not stiffen, though she does not exactly relax, either. She sits there, a block of wood, staring straight ahead.

"Are you scared?" he asked gently. Then he adds, "*I* am."

"Well, no, I'm not scared." She remains silent for a moment. "You're scared? Of what?" She turns to face him but avoids his eyes.

"Well . . . I don't do this all the time, you know. Bring home a woman I . . ." He trails off.

"Picked up in a bar."

"No. I mean, I like you, Sarah, I really do. And I didn't just pick you up in a bar, you know that. We've gotten to be friends, you and me."

"You want to sleep with me?" she asks, still not meeting his steady gaze.

"Yes." He seems to mean it. He does not take a gulp or even a sip from his drink. He just says, "Yes," straight out, and cleanly, not too quickly, either, and not after a hesitant delay. A simple statement of a simple fact. The man wants to make love to the woman. She asked him, and he told her. What could be simpler?

"Do you want to sleep with *me*?" he asks.

She turns around in the chair, faces the wall again, and says in a low voice, "Sure I do, but . . . it's hard to explain."

"What? But what?" Placing his glass down on the table between the chair and the sofa, he puts both hands on her shoulders and lightly kneads them. He knows he can be discouraged from pursuing this, but he is not sure how easily. Having got this far without bumping against obstacles (except the ones he has placed in his way himself), he is not sure what it will take to turn him back. He does not know, therefore, how assertive or how seductive he should be with her. He suspects that he can be stopped very easily, so he is reluctant to give her a chance to try. He goes on kneading her doughy shoulders.

"You and me . . . we're real different." She glances at the bicycle in the corner.

"A man . . . and a woman," he says.

"No, not that. I mean, different. That's all. Real different. More than you . . . you're nice, but you don't know what I mean, and that's one of the things that makes you so nice. But we're different. Listen," she says, "I gotta go. I gotta leave now."

The man removes his hands and retrieves his glass, takes a sip, and watches her over the rim of the glass, as, not without difficulty, she rises from the chair and moves swiftly toward the door. She stops at the door, squares her hat on her head, and glances back at him.

"We can be friends. Okay?"

"Okay. Friends."

"I'll see you again down at Osgood's, right?"

"Oh, yeah, sure."

"Good. See you," she says, opening the door.

The door closes. The man walks around the sofa, snaps on the television set, and sits down in front of it. He picks up a *TV Guide* from the coffee table and flips through it, stops, runs a finger down the listings, stops, puts down the magazine and changes the channel. He does not once connect the magazine in his hand to the woman who has just left his apartment, even though he knows she spends her days packing *TV Guides* into cartons that get shipped to warehouses in distant parts of New England. He'll think of the connection some other night, but by then the connection will be merely sentimental. It'll be too late for him to understand what she meant by "different."

4

But that's not the point of my story. Certainly it's an aspect of the story, the political aspect, if you want, but it's not the reason I'm trying to tell the story in the first place. I'm trying to tell the story so that I can understand what happened between me and Sarah Cole that summer and early autumn ten years ago. To say we were lovers says very little about what happened; to say we were friends says even less. No, if I'm to understand the whole thing, I have to say the whole thing, for, in the end, what I need to know is whether what happened between me and Sarah Cole was right or wrong. Character is fate, which suggests that if a man can know and then to some degree control his character, he can know and to that same degree control his fate.

But let me go on with my story. The next time Sarah and I were together we were at her apartment in the south end of Concord, a second-floor flat in a tenement building on Perley Street. I had stayed away from Osgood's for several weeks, deliberately trying to avoid running into Sarah there, though I never quite put it that way to myself. I found excuses and generated interest in and reasons for going elsewhere after work. Yet I was obsessed with Sarah by then, obsessed with the idea of making love to her, which, because it was not an actual *desire* to make love to her, was an unusually complex obsession. Passion without desire, if it gets expressed, may in fact be a kind of rape, and perhaps I sensed the danger that lay behind my obsession and for that reason went out of my way to avoid meeting Sarah again.

Yet I did meet her, inadvertently, of course. After picking up shirts at the cleaner's on South Main and Perley Streets, I'd gone down Perley on my way to South State and the post office. It was a Saturday morning, and this trip on my bicycle was part of my regular Saturday routine. I did not remember that Sarah lived on Perley Street, although she had told me several times in a complaining way—it's a rough neighborhood, packed dirt yards, shabby apartment buildings, the carcasses of old, half-stripped cars on cinderblocks in the driveways, broken red and yellow plastic tricycles on the cracked sidewalks—but as soon as I saw her, I remembered. It was too late to avoid meeting her. I was riding my bike, wearing shorts and T-shirt, the package containing my folded and starched shirts hooked to the carrier behind me, and she was walking toward me along the sidewalk, lugging two large bags of groceries. She saw me, and I stopped. We talked, and I offered to carry her groceries for her. I took the bags while she led the bike, handling it carefully as if she were afraid she might break it.

At the stoop we came to a halt. The wooden steps were cluttered with half-opened garbage bags spilling egg shells, coffee grounds, and old food wrappers to the walkway. "I can't get the people downstairs to take care of their garbage," she explained. She leaned the bike against the bannister and reached for her groceries.

"I'll carry them up for you," I said. I directed her to loop the chain lock from the bike to the bannister rail and snap it shut and told her to bring my shirts up with her.

"Maybe you'd like a beer?" she said as she opened the door to the darkened hallway. Narrow stairs disappeared in front of me into heavy, damp darkness, and the air smelled like old newspapers.

"Sure," I said and followed her up.

"Sorry there's no light. I can't get them to fix it."

"No matter. I can see you and follow along," I said, and even in the dim light of the hall I could see the large, dark blue veins that cascaded thickly down the backs of her legs. She wore tight, white-duck bermuda shorts, rubber shower sandals, and a pink sleeveless sweater. I pictured her in the cashier's line at the supermarket. I would have been behind her, a stranger, and on seeing her, I would have turned away and studied the covers of the magazines, *TV Guide, People, The National Enquirer*, for there was nothing of interest in her appearance that in the hard light of day would not have slightly embarrassed me. Yet here I was inviting myself into her home, eagerly staring at the backs of her ravaged legs, her sad, tasteless clothing, her poverty. I was not detached, however, was not staring at her with scientific curiosity, and because of my passion, did not feel or believe that what I was doing was perverse. I felt warmed by her presence and was flirtatious and bold, a little pushy, even.

Picture this. The man, tanned, limber, wearing red jogging shorts, Italian leather sandals, a clinging net T-shirt of Scandinavian design and manufacture, enters the apartment behind the woman, whose dough colored skin, thick, short body, and homely, uncomfortable face all try, but fail, to hide themselves. She waves him toward the table in the kitchen, where he sets down the bags and looks good-naturedly around the room. "What about the beer you bribed me with?" he asks. The apartment is dark and cluttered with old, over-sized furniture, yard sale and secondhand stuff bought originally for a large house in the country or a spacious apartment on a boule-vard forty or fifty years ago, passed down from antique dealer to used furniture store to yard sale to thrift shop, where it finally gets purchased by Sarah Cole and gets lugged over to Perley Street and shoved up the narrow stairs, she and her children grunting and sweating in the darkness of the hallway—overstuffed armchairs and couch, huge, ungainly dressers, upholstered rocking chairs, and in the kitchen, an old maple desk for a table, a half-dozen heavy oak dining room chairs, a high, glass-fronted cabinet, all peeling, stained, chipped and squatting heavily on a dark green linoleum floor.

The place is neat and arranged in a more or less orderly way, however, and the man seems comfortable there. He strolls from the kitchen to the living room and peeks into the three small bedrooms that branch off a hallway behind the living room. "Nice place!" he calls to the woman. He is studying the framed pictures of her three children arranged like an altar atop the buffet. "Nice looking kids!" he calls out. They are. Blond, round-faced, clean, and utterly ordi-nary-looking, their pleasant faces glance, as instructed, slightly off camera and down to the right, as if they are trying to remember the name of the capital of Montana.

When he returns to the kitchen, the woman is putting away her groceries, her back to him. "Where's that beer you bribed me with?" he asks again. He takes a position against the doorframe, his weight on one hip, like a dancer resting. "You sure are quiet today, Sarah," he says in a low voice. "Everything okay?"

Silently, she turns away from the grocery bags, crosses the room to the man, reaches up to him, and holding him by the head, kisses his mouth, rolls her torso against his, drops her hands to his hips and yanks him tightly to her, and goes on kissing him, eyes closed, working her face furiously against his. The man places his hands on her shoulders and pulls away, and they face each other, wide-eyed, as if amazed and frightened. The man drops his hands, and the woman lets go of his hips. Then, after a few seconds, the man silently turns, goes to the door, and leaves. The last thing he sees as he closes the door behind him is the woman standing in the kitchen doorframe, her face looking down and slightly to one side, wearing the same pleasant expression on her face as her children in their photographs, trying to remember the capital of Montana.

5

Sarah appeared at my apartment door the following morning, a Sunday, cool and rainy. She had brought me the package of freshly laundered shirts I'd left in her kitchen, and when I opened the door to her, she simply held the package out to me as if it were a penitent's gift. She wore a yellow rain slicker and cap and looked more like a disconsolate schoolgirl facing an angry teacher than a grown woman dropping a package off at a friend's apartment. After all, she had nothing to be ashamed of.

I invited her inside, and she accepted my invitation. I had been reading the Sunday *New York Times* on the couch and drinking coffee, lounging through the gray morning in bathrobe and pajamas. I told her to take off her wet raincoat and hat and hang them in the closet by the door and started for the kitchen to get her a cup of coffee, when I stopped, turned, and looked at her. She closed the closet door on her yellow raincoat and hat, turned around, and faced me.

What else can I do? I must describe it. I remember that moment of ten years ago as if it occurred ten minutes ago, the package of shirts on the table behind her, the newspapers scattered over the couch and floor, the sound of windblown rain washing the sides of the building outside, and the silence of the room, as we stood across

from one another and watched, while we each simultaneously removed our own clothing, my robe, her blouse and skirt, my pajama
top, her slip and bra, my pajama bottom, her underpants, until we
were both standing naked in the harsh, gray light, two naked members of the same species, a male and a female, the male somewhat
younger and less scarred than the female, the female somewhat less
delicately constructed than the male, both individuals pale-skinned
with dark thatches of hair in the area of their genitals, both individuals standing slackly, as if a great, protracted tension between
them had at last been released.

6

We made love that morning in my bed for long hours that drifted
easily into afternoon. And we talked, as people usually do when
they spend half a day or half a night in bed together. I told her
of my past, named and described people I had loved and had loved
me, my ex-wife in New York, my brother in the Air Force, my father
and mother in their condominium in Florida, and I told her of
my ambitions and dreams and even confessed some of my fears.
She listened patiently and intelligently throughout and talked
much less than I. She had already told me many of these things
about herself, and perhaps whatever she had to say to me now lay
on the next inner circle of intimacy or else could not be spoken of
at all.

During the next few weeks we met and made love often and
always at my apartment. On arriving home from work, I would
phone her, or if not, she would phone me, and after a few feints and
dodges, one would suggest to the other that we get together tonight, and a half hour later she'd be at my door. Our lovemaking
was passionate, skillful, kindly, and deeply satisfying. We didn't
often speak of it to one another or brag about it, the way some
couples do when they are surprised by the ease with which they
have become contented lovers. We did occasionally joke and tease
each other, however, playfully acknowledging that the only thing
we did together was make love but that we did it so frequently there
was no time for anything else.

Then one hot night, a Saturday night in August, we were lying in
bed atop the tangled sheets, smoking cigarettes and chatting idly,
and Sarah suggested we go out for a drink.

"Now?"

"Sure. It's early. What time is it?"

I scanned the digital clock next to the bed. "Nine-forty-nine."

"There. See?"

"That's not so early. You usually go home before eleven, you know. It's almost ten."

"No, it's only a little after nine. Depends on how you look at things. Besides, Ron, it's Saturday night. Don't you want to go out and dance or something? Or is this the only thing you know how to do?" she teased and poked me in the ribs. "You know how to dance? You like to dance?"

"Yeah, sure . . . sure, but not tonight. It's too hot. And I'm tired."

But she persisted, happily pointing out that an air-conditioned bar would be cooler than my apartment, and we didn't have to go to a dance bar, we could go to Osgood's. "As a compromise," she said.

I suggested a place called the El Rancho, a restaurant with a large, dark cocktail lounge and dance bar located several miles from town on the old Portsmouth highway. Around nine the restaurant closed and the bar became something of a roadhouse, with a small country-western house band and a clientele drawn from the four or five villages that adjoined Concord on the north and east. I had eaten at the restaurant once but had never gone to the bar, and I didn't know anyone who had.

Sarah was silent for a moment. Then she lit a cigarette and drew the sheet over her naked body. "You don't want anybody to know about us, do you? Do you?"

"That's not it . . . I just don't like gossip, and I work with a lot of people who show up sometimes at Osgood's. On a Saturday night especially."

"No," she said firmly. "You're ashamed of being seen with me. You'll sleep with me, but you won't go out in public with me."

"That's not true, Sarah."

She was silent again. Relieved, I reached across her to the bed table and got my cigarettes and lighter.

"You owe me, Ron," she said suddenly, as I passed over her. "You owe me."

"What?" I lay back, lit a cigarette, and covered my body with the sheet.

"I said, 'You owe me.' "

"I don't know what you're talking about, Sarah. I just don't like a lot of gossip going around, that's all. I like keeping my private life private, that's all. I don't *owe* you anything."

"Friendship you owe me. And respect. Friendship and respect. A person can't do what you've done with me without owing them friendship and respect."

"Sarah, I really don't know what you're talking about," I said. "I am your friend, you know that. And I respect you. I really do."

"You really think so, don't you?"

"Yes."

She said nothing for several long moments. Then she sighed and in a low, almost inaudible voice said, "Then you'll have to go out in public with me. I don't care about Osgood's or the people you work with, we don't have to go there or see any of them," she said. "But you're gonna have to go to places like the El Rancho with me, and a few other places I know, too, where there's people *I* work with, people *I* know, and maybe we'll even go to a couple of parties, because *I* get invited to parties sometimes, you know. I have friends, and I have some family, too, and you're gonna have to meet my family. My kids think I'm just going around bar-hopping when I'm over here with you, and I don't like that, so you're gonna have to meet them so I can tell them where I am when I'm not at home nights. And sometimes you're gonna come over and spend the evening at my place!" Her voice had risen as she heard her demands and felt their rightness, until now she was almost shouting at me. "You *owe* that to me. Or else you're a bad man. It's that simple."

It was.

7

The handsome man is overdressed. He is wearing a navy blue blazer, taupe shirt open at the throat, white slacks, white loafers. Everyone else, including the homely woman with the handsome man, is dressed appropriately, dressed, that is, like everyone else—jeans and cowboy boots, blouses or cowboy shirts or T-shirts with catchy sayings printed across the front, and many of the women are wearing cowboy hats pushed back and tied under their chins. The man doesn't know anyone at the bar or, if they're at a party, in the room, but the woman knows most of the people there, and she gladly introduces him. The men grin and shake his hand, slap him on his jacketed shoulder, ask him where he works, what's his line, after which they lapse into silence. The women flirt briefly with their faces, but they lapse into silence even before the men do. The woman with the man in the blazer does most of the talking for everyone. She talks for the man in the blazer, for the men standing around the refrigerator, or if they're at a bar, for the other men at the table, and for the other women, too. She chats and rambles aimlessly through loud monologues, laughs uproariously at trivial jokes, and drinks too much, until soon she is drunk, thick-tongued, clumsy, and the man has to say her goodbyes and ease her out the door to his car and drive her home to her apartment on Perley Street.

This happens twice in one week, and then three times the next—at the El Rancho, at the Ox Bow in Northwood, at Rita's and Jimmy's apartment on Thorndike Street, out in Warner at Betsy Beeler's new house, and, the last time, at a cottage on Lake Sunapee rented by some kids in shipping at Rumford Press. Ron no longer calls Sarah when he gets home from work; he waits for her call, and sometimes, when he knows it's she, he doesn't answer the phone. Usually, he lets it ring five or six times, and then he reaches down and picks up the receiver. He has taken his jacket vest off and loosened his tie and is about to put supper, frozen manicotti, into the radar range.

"Hello?"

"Hi."

"How're you doing?"

"Okay, I guess. A little tired."

"Still hung over?"

"No. Not really. Just tired. I hate Mondays."

"You have fun last night?"

"Well, yeah, sorta. It's nice out there, at the lake. Listen," she says, brightening. *"Whyn't you come over here tonight? The kids're all going out later, but if you come over before eight, you can meet them. They really want to meet you."*

"You told them about me?"

"Sure. Long time ago. I'm not supposed to tell my own kids?"

Ron is silent.

"You don't want to come over here tonight. You don't want to meet my kids. No, you don't want my kids to meet you, that's it."

"No, no, it's just . . . I've got a lot of work to do . . ."

"We should talk," she announces in a flat voice.

"Yes," he says, "we should talk."

They agree that she will meet him at his apartment, and they'll talk, and they say goodbye and hang up.

While Ron is heating his supper and then eating alone at his kitchen table and Sarah is feeding her children, perhaps I should admit, since we are nearing the end of my story, that I don't actually know that Sarah Cole is dead. A few years ago I happened to run into one of her friends from the press, a blond woman with an underslung jaw. Her name, she reminded me, was Glenda, she had seen me at Osgood's a couple of times and we had met at the El Rancho once when I had gone there with Sarah. I was amazed that she could remember me and a little embarrassed that I did not recognize her at all, and she laughed at that and said, "You haven't changed much, mister!" I pretended to recognize her, but I think she knew she was a stranger to me. We were standing outside the Sears store on South Main Street, where I had gone to buy paint. I had recently remarried, and my wife and I were redecorating my apartment.

"Whatever happened to Sarah?" I asked Glenda. "Is she still down at the press?"

"Jeez, no! She left a long time ago. Way back. I heard she went back with her ex-husband. I can't remember his name. Something Cole."

I asked her if she was sure of that, and she said no, she had only heard it around the bars and down at the press, but she had assumed it was true. People said Sarah had moved back with her ex-husband and was living in a trailer in a park near Hooksett, and the whole family had moved down to Florida that winter because he was out of work. He was a carpenter, she said.

"I thought he was mean to her. I thought he beat her up and everything. I thought she hated him," I said.

"Oh, well, yeah, he was a bastard, all right. I met him a couple of times, and I didn't like him. Short, ugly, and mean when he got drunk. But you know what they say."

"What do they say?"

"Oh, you know, about water seeking its own level."

"Sarah wasn't mean when she was drunk."

The woman laughed. "Naw, but she sure was short and ugly!"

I said nothing.

"Hey, don't get me wrong, I liked Sarah. But you and her . . . well, you sure made a funny-looking couple. She probably didn't feel so self-conscious and all with her husband," the woman said seriously. "I mean, with you . . . all tall and blond, and poor old Sarah . . . I mean, the way them kids in the press room used to kid her about her looks, it was embarrassing just to hear it."

"Well . . . I loved her," I said.

The woman raised her plucked eyebrows in disbelief. She smiled. "Sure, you did, honey," she said, and she patted me on the arm. "Sure, you did." Then she let the smile drift off her face, turned and walked away.

When someone you have loved dies, you accept the fact of his or her death, but then the person goes on living in your memory, dreams, and reveries. You have imaginary conversations with him or her, you see something striking and remind yourself to tell your loved one about it and then get brought up short by the knowledge of the fact of his or her death, and at night, in your sleep, the dead person visits you. With Sarah, none of that happened. When she was gone from my life, she was gone absolutely, as if she had never existed in the first place. It was only later, when I could think of her as dead and could come out and say it, my friend Sarah Cole is dead, that I was able to tell this story, for that is when she began to enter my memories, my dreams, and my reveries. In that way I learned that I truly did love her, and now I have begun to grieve over her death, to wish her alive again, so that I can say to her the things I could not know or say when she was alive, when I did not know that I loved her.

8

The woman arrives at Ron's apartment around eight. He hears her car, because of the broken muffler, blat and rumble into the parking lot below, and he crosses quickly from the kitchen and peers out the living room window and, as if through a telescope, watches her shove herself across the seat to the passenger's side to get out of the car, then walk slowly in the dusky light toward the apartment building. It's a warm evening, and she's wearing her white bermuda shorts, pink sleeveless sweater, and shower sandals. Ron hates those clothes. He hates the way the shorts cut into her flesh at the crotch and thigh, hates the large, dark caves below her arms that get exposed by the sweater, hates the flapping noise made by the sandals.

Shortly, there is a soft knock at his door. He opens it, turns away and crosses to the kitchen, where he turns back, lights a cigarette, and watches her. She closes the door. He offers her a drink, which she declines, and somewhat formally, he invites her to sit down. She sits carefully on the sofa, in the middle, with her feet close together on the floor, as if she were being interviewed for a job. Then he comes around and sits in the easy chair, relaxed, one leg slung over the other at the knee, as if he were interviewing her for the job.

"Well," he says, "you wanted to talk."

"Yes. But now you're mad at me. I can see that. I didn't do anything, Ron."

"I'm not mad at you."

They are silent for a moment. Ron goes on smoking his cigarette.

Finally, she sighs and says, "You don't want to see me anymore, do you?"

He waits a few seconds and answers, "Yes. That's right." Getting up from the chair, he walks to the silver-gray bicycle and stands before it, running a fingertip along the slender crossbar from the saddle to the chrome-plated handlebars.

"You're a son of a bitch," she says in a low voice. "You're worse than my ex-husband." Then she smiles meanly, almost sneers, and soon he realizes that she is telling him that she won't leave. He's stuck with her, she informs him with cold precision. "You think I'm just so much meat, and all you got to do is call up the butcher shop and cancel your order. Well, now you're going to find out different. You *can't* cancel your order. I'm not meat, I'm not one of your pretty little girlfriends who come running when you want them and go away when you get tired of them. I'm *different*. I got nothing to lose, Ron. Nothing. You're stuck with me, Ron."

He continues stroking his bicycle. "No, I'm not."

She sits back in the couch and crosses her legs at the ankles. "I think I *will* have that drink you offered."

"Look, Sarah, it would be better if you go now."

"No," she says flatly. "You offered me a drink when I came in. Nothing's changed since I've been here. Not for me, and not for you. I'd like that drink you offered," she says haughtily.

Ron turns away from the bicycle and takes a step toward her. His face has stiffened into a mask. "Enough is enough," he says through clenched teeth. "I've given you enough."

"Fix me a drink, will you, honey?" she says with a phony smile.

Ron orders her to leave.

She refuses.

He grabs her by the arm and yanks her to her feet.

She starts crying lightly. She stands there and looks up into his face and weeps, but she does not move toward the door, so he pushes her. She regains her balance and goes on weeping.

He stands back and places his fists on his hips and looks at her. "Go on and leave, you ugly bitch," he says to her, and as he says the words, as one by one they leave his mouth, she's transformed into the most beautiful woman he has ever seen. He says the words again, almost tenderly. "Leave, you ugly bitch." Her hair is golden, her brown eyes deep and sad, her mouth full and affectionate, her tears the tears of love and loss, and her pleading, outstretched arms, her entire body, the arms and body of a devoted woman's cruelly rejected love. A third time he says the words. "Leave me, you disgusting, ugly bitch." She is wrapped in an envelope of golden light, a warm, dense haze that she seems to have stepped into, as into a carriage. And then she is gone, and he is alone again.

He looks around the room, as if searching for her. Sitting down in the easy chair, he places his face in his hands. It's not as if she has died; it's as if he has killed her.

THE EYE

Paul Bowles

Ten or twelve years ago there came to live in Tangier a man who would have done better to stay away. What happened to him was in no way his fault, notwithstanding the whispered innuendos of the English-speaking residents. These people often have reactions similar to those of certain primitive groups: when misfortune overtakes one of their number, the others by mutual consent refrain from offering him aid, and merely sit back to watch, certain that he has called his suffering down upon himself. He has become taboo, and is incapable of receiving help. In the case of this particular man, I suppose no one could have been of much comfort; still, the tacit disapproval called forth by his bad luck must have made the last months of his life harder to bear.

His name was Duncan Marsh, and he was said to have come from Vancouver. I never saw him, nor do I know anyone who claims to have seen him. By the time his story reached the cocktail-party circuit he was dead, and the more irresponsible residents felt at liberty to indulge their taste for myth-making.

He came alone to Tangier, rented a furnished house on the slopes of Djamaa el Mokra—they were easy enough to find in those days, and correspondingly inexpensive—and presently installed a teen-age Moroccan on the premises to act as night-watchman. The house provided a resident cook and gardener, but both of these were discharged from their duties, the cook being replaced by a woman brought in at the suggestion of the watchman. It was not long after this that Marsh felt the first symptoms of a digestive illness which over the months grew steadily worse. The doctors in Tangier advised him to go to London. Two months in hospital there helped him somewhat. No clear diagnosis was made, however, and he returned here only to become bedridden. Eventually he was flown back to Canada on a stretcher, and succumbed there shortly after his arrival.

In all this there was nothing extraordinary; it was assumed that

Marsh had been one more victim of slow poisoning by native employees. There have been several such cases during my five decades in Tangier. On each occasion it has been said that the European victim had only himself (or herself) to blame, having encouraged familiarity on the part of a servant. What strikes the outsider as strange is that no one ever takes the matter in hand and inaugurates a search for the culprit, but in the total absence of proof there is no point in attempting an investigation.

Two details complete the story. At some point during his illness, Marsh told an acquaintance of the arrangements he had made to provide financial aid for his night-watchman in the event that he himself should be obliged to leave Morocco; he had given him a notarized letter to that effect, but apparently the boy never tried to press his claim. The other report came from Dr. Halsey, the physician who arranged for Marsh's removal from the house to the airport. It was this last bit of information which, for me at least, made the story take on life. According to the doctor, the soles of Marsh's feet had been systematically marked with deep incisions in the form of crude patterns; the cuts were recent, but there was some infection. Dr. Halsey called in the cook and the watchman: they showed astonishment and dismay at the sight of their employer's feet, but were unable to account for the mutilations. Within a few days after Marsh's departure, the original cook and gardener returned to take up residence, the other two having already left the house.

The slow poisoning was classical enough, particularly in the light of Marsh's remark about his provision for the boy's well-being, but the knife-drawn designs on the feet somehow got in the way of whatever combinations of motive one could invent. I thought about it. There could be little doubt that the boy was guilty. He had persuaded Marsh to get rid of the cook that came with the house, even though her wages had to continue to be paid, and to hire another woman (very likely from his own family) to do the cooking. The poisoning process lasts many months if it is to be undetectable, and no one is in a better position to take charge of it than the cook herself. Clearly she knew about the financial arrangement that had been made for the boy, and expected to share in it. At the same time, the crosses and circles slashed in the feet were inexplicable. The slow poisoner is patient, careful, methodical; his principal concerns are to keep the dosage effective and to avoid leaving any visible marks. Bravado is unknown to him.

The time came when people no longer told the story of Duncan Marsh. I myself thought of it less often, having no more feasible hypotheses to supply. One evening perhaps five years ago, an American resident here came to me with the news that he had discovered a Moroccan who claimed to have been Marsh's night-watchman. The man's name was Larbi; he was a waiter at Le Fin Bec, a small back-street restaurant. Apparently he spoke poor English, but understood it without difficulty. This information was handed me for what it was worth, said the American, in the event that I felt inclined to make use of it.

I turned it over in my mind, and one night a few weeks later I went down to the restaurant to see Larbi for myself. The place was dimly lit and full of Europeans. I studied the three waiters. They were interchangeable, with wide black moustaches, blue jeans and sport shirts. A menu was handed me; I could scarcely read it, even directly under the glow of the little table lamp. When the man who had brought it returned, I asked for Larbi.

He pulled the menu from my hand and left the table. A moment later another of the triumvirate came up beside me and handed me the menu he carried under his arm. I ordered in Spanish. When he brought the soup I murmured that I was surprised to find him working there. This brought him up short; I could see him trying to remember me.

"Why wouldn't I be working here?" His voice was level, without inflection.

"Of course! Why not? It was just that I thought by now you'd have a bazaar or some sort of shop."

His laugh was a snort. "Bazaar!"

When he arrived with the next course, I begged his pardon for meddling in his affairs. But I was interested, I said, because for several years I had been under the impression that he had received a legacy from an English gentleman.

"You mean Señor Marsh?" His eyes were at last wide open.

"Yes, that was his name. Didn't he give you a letter? He told his friends he had."

He looked over my head as he said: "He gave me a letter."

"Have you ever showed it to anyone?" This was tactless, but sometimes it is better to drive straight at the target.

"Why? What good is it? Señor Marsh is dead." He shook his head with an air of finality, and moved off to another table. By the time I had finished my crème caramel, most of the diners had left, and the place seemed even darker. He came over to the table to see if I wanted coffee. I asked for the check. When he brought it I told him I should like very much to see the letter if he still had it.

"You can come tomorrow night or any night, and I'll show it to you. I have it at home."

I thanked him and promised to return in two or three days. I was confused as I left the restaurant. It seemed clear that the waiter did not consider himself to be incriminated in Duncan Marsh's troubles. When, a few nights later, I saw the document, I no longer understood anything.

It was not a letter; it was a *papier timbré* of the kind on sale at tobacconists. It read, simply: *To Whom It May Concern: I, Duncan Whitelow Marsh, do hereby agree to deposit the sum of One Hundred Pounds to the account of Larbi Lairini, on the first of each month, for as long as I live.* It was signed and notarized in the presence of two Moroccan witnesses and bore the date June 11, 1966. As I handed it back to him I said: "And it never did you any good."

He shrugged and slipped the paper into his wallet. "How was it going to? The man died."

"It's too bad."

"*Suerte.*" In the Moroccan usage of the word, it means *fate*, rather than simple luck.

At that moment I could have pressed on, and asked him if he had any idea as to the cause of Marsh's illness, but I wanted time for considering what I had just learned. As I rose to leave I said: "I'm sorry it turned out that way. I'll be back in a few days." He held out his hand and I shook it. I had no intentions then. I might return soon or I might never go back.

For as long as I live. The phrase echoed in my mind for several weeks. Possibly Marsh had worded it that way so it would be readily understandable to the *adoul* of Tangier who had affixed their florid signatures to the sheet; yet I could not help interpreting the words in a more melodramatic fashion. To me the document represented the officializing of a covenant already in existence between master and servant: Marsh wanted the watchman's help, and the watchman had agreed to give it. There was nothing upon which to base such an assumption, nevertheless I thought I was on the right track. Slowly I came to believe that if only I could talk to the watchman, in Arabic and inside the house itself, I might be in a position to see things more clearly.

One evening I walked to Le Fin Bec and without taking a seat motioned to Larbi to step outside for a moment. There I asked him if he could find out whether the house Señor Marsh had lived in was occupied at the moment or not.

"There's nobody living there now." He paused and added: "It's empty. I know the guardian."

I had decided, in spite of my deficient Arabic, to speak to him in his own language, so I said: "Look. I'd like to go with you to the house and see where everything happened. I'll give you fifteen thousand francs for your trouble."

He was startled to hear the Arabic; then his expression shifted to one of satisfaction. "He's not supposed to let anyone in," he said.

I handed him three thousand francs. "You arrange that with him. And fifteen for you when we leave the house. Could we do it Thursday?"

The house had been built, I should say, in the fifties, when good construction was still possible. It was solidly embedded in the hillside, with the forest towering behind it. We had to climb three flights of stairs through the garden to get to the entrance. The guardian, a squinting Djibli in a brown djellaba, followed close on our footsteps, eyeing me with mistrust.

There was a wide terrace above, with a view to the southeast over the town and the mountains. Behind the terrace a shadowed lawn ended where the forest began. The living room was large and bright, with French doors giving onto the lawn. Odors of damp walls and mildew weighted the air. The absurd conviction that I was about to understand everything had taken possession of me; I noticed that I was breathing more quickly. We wandered into the dining room. There was a corridor beyond, and the room where Marsh had slept, shuttered and dark. A wide, curving stairway led down to a level where there were two more bedrooms and continued its spiral to the kitchen and servants' rooms below. The kitchen door opened onto a small flagstoned patio where high philodendron covered the walls.

Larbi looked out and shook his head. "That's the place where all the trouble began," he said glumly.

I pushed through the doorway and sat down on a wrought-iron bench in the sun. "It's damp inside. Why don't we stay out here?"

The guardian left us and locked up the house. Larbi squatted comfortably on his heels near the bench.

There would have been no trouble at all, he said, if only Marsh had been satisfied with Yasmina, the cook whose wages were included in the rent. But she was a careless worker and the food was bad. He asked Larbi to find him another cook.

"I told him ahead of time that this woman Meriam had a little girl, and some days she could leave her with friends and some days she would have to bring her with her when she came to work. He said it didn't matter, but he wanted her to be quiet."

The woman was hired. Two or three days a week she came accompanied by the child, who would play in the patio where she could watch her. From the beginning Marsh complained that she was noisy. Repeatedly he sent messages down to Meriam, asking her to make the child be still. And one day he went quietly around the outside of the house and down to the patio. He got on all fours, put his face close to the little girl's face, and frowned at her so fiercely that she began to scream. When Meriam rushed out of the kitchen he stood up smiling and walked off. The little girl continued to scream and wail in a corner of kitchen until Meriam took her home. That night, still sobbing, she came down with a high fever. For several weeks she hovered between life and death, and when she was finally out of danger she could no longer walk.

Meriam, who was earning relatively high wages, consulted one *faqih* after another. They agreed that "the eye" had been put on the child; it was equally clear that the Nazarene for whom she worked had done it. What they told her she must do, Larbi explained, was to administer certain substances to Marsh which eventually would make it possible to counteract the spell. This was absolutely necessary, he said, staring at me gravely. Even if the señor had agreed to remove it (and of course she never would have mentioned it to him) he would not have been able to. What she gave him could not harm him; it was merely medicine to relax him so that when the time came to undo the spell he would not make any objections.

At some point Marsh confided to Larbi that he suspected Meriam of slipping soporifics into his food, and begged him to be vigilant. The provision for Larbi's well-being was signed as an inducement to enlisting his active support. Since to Larbi the mixtures Meriam was feeding her master were relatively harmless, he reassured him and let her continue to dose him with her concoctions.

Tired of squatting, Larbi suddenly stood up and began to walk back and forth, stepping carefully in the center of each flagstone. "When he had to go to the hospital in London, I told her, 'Now you've made him sick. Suppose he doesn't come back? You'll never break it.' She was worried about it. 'I've done what I could,' she said. 'It's in the hands of Allah.'"

When Marsh did return to Tangier, Larbi urged her to be quick about bringing things to a head, now that she had been fortunate enough to get him back. He was thinking, he said, that it might be better for the señor's health if her treatment were not continued for too long a time.

I asked no questions while he talked; I made a point of keeping my face entirely expressionless, thinking that if he noticed the least flicker of disapproval he might stop. The sun had gone behind the trees and the patio was chilly. I had a strong desire to get up and walk back and forth as he was doing, but I thought even that might interrupt him. Once stopped, the flow might not resume.

Soon Marsh was worse than ever, with racking pains in his abdomen and kidneys. He remained in bed then, and Larbi brought him his food. When Meriam saw that he was no longer able to leave the bed, even to go into the bathroom, she decided that the time had come to get rid of the spell. On the same night that a *faqih* held a ceremony at her house in the presence of the crippled child, four men from Meriam's family came up to Djamaa el Mokra.

"When I saw them coming, I got onto my motorcycle and went into the city. I didn't want to be here when they did it. It had nothing to do with me."

He stood still and rubbed his hands together. I heard the southwest wind beginning to sound in the trees; it was that time of afternoon. "Come. I'll show you something," he said.

We climbed steps around the back of the house and came out onto a terrace with a pergola over it. Beyond this lay the lawn and the wall of trees.

"He was very sick for the next two days. He kept asking me to telephone the English doctor."

"Didn't you do it?"

Larbi stopped walking and looked at me. "I had to clean everything up first. Meriam wouldn't touch him. It was during the rains. He had mud and blood all over him when I got back here and found him. The next day I gave him a bath and changed the sheets and blankets. And I cleaned the house, because they got mud everywhere when they brought him back in. Come on. You'll see where they had to take him."

We had crossed the lawn and were walking in the long grass that skirted the edge of the woods. A path led off to the right through the tangle of undergrowth, and we followed it, climbing across boulders and fallen tree trunks until we came to an old stone well. I leaned over the wall of rocks around it and saw the small circle of sky far below.

"They had to drag him all the way here, you see, and hold him steady right over the well while they made the signs on his feet, so the blood would fall into the water. It's no good if it falls on the side of the well. And they had to make the same signs the *faqih* drew on paper for the little girl. That's hard to do in the dark and in the rain. But they did it. I saw the cuts when I bathed him."

Cautiously I asked him if he saw any connection between all this and Marsh's death. He ceased staring into the well and turned around. We started to walk back toward the house.

"He died because his hour had come."

And had the spell been broken? I asked him. Could the child walk afterward? But he had never heard, for Meriam had gone to Kenitra not much later to live with her sister.

When we were in the car, driving back down to the city, I handed him the money. He stared at it for several seconds before slipping it into his pocket.

I let him off in town with a vague sense of disappointment, and I saw that I had not only expected, but actually hoped, to find someone on whom the guilt might be fixed. What constitutes a crime? There was no criminal intent—only a mother moving in the darkness of ancient ignorance. I thought about it on my way home in the taxi.

TODAY WILL BE A QUIET DAY

Amy Hempel

I think it's the other way around," the boy said. "I think if the quake hit now the *bridge* would collapse and the *ramps* would be left."

He looked at his sister with satisfaction.

"You are just trying to scare your sister," the father said. "You know that is not true."

"No, really," the boy insisted, "and I heard birds in the middle of the night. Isn't that a warning?"

The girl gave her brother a toxic look and ate a handful of Raisinets. The three of them were stalled in traffic on the Golden Gate Bridge.

That morning, before waking his children, the father had canceled their music lessons and decided to make a day of it. He wanted to know how they were, is all. Just—how were they. He thought his kids were as self-contained as one of those dogs you sometimes see carrying home its own leash. But you could read things wrong.

Could you ever.

The boy had a friend who jumped from a floor of Langley Porter. The friend had been there for two weeks, mostly playing ping-pong. All the friend said the day the boy visited and lost every game was never play ping-pong with a mental patient because it's all we do and we'll kill you. That night the friend had cut the red belt he wore in two and left the other half on his bed. That was this time last year when the boy was twelve years old.

You think you're safe, the father thought, but it's thinking you're invisible because you closed your eyes.

* * *

This day they were headed for Petaluma—the chicken, egg, and arm-wrestling capital of the nation—for lunch. The father had offered to take them to the men's arm-wrestling semifinals. But it was

30

said that arm wrestling wasn't so interesting since the new safety precautions, that hardly anyone broke an arm or a wrist any more. The best anyone could hope to see would be dislocation, so they said they would rather go to Pete's. Pete's was a gas station turned into a place to eat. The hamburgers there were named after cars, and the gas pumps in front still pumped gas.

"Can I have one?" the boy asked, meaning the Raisinets.

"No," his sister said.

"Can I have two?"

"Neither of you should be eating candy before lunch," the father said. He said it with the good sport of a father who enjoys his kids and gets a kick out of saying Dad things.

"You mean dinner," said the girl. "It will be dinner before we get to Pete's."

*   *   *

Only the northbound lanes were stopped. Southbound traffic flashed past at the normal speed.

"Check it out," the boy said from the back seat. "Did you see the bumper sticker on that Porsche? 'If you don't like the way I drive, stay off the sidewalk.'"

He spoke directly to his sister. "I've just solved my Christmas shopping."

"I got the highest score in my class in Driver's Ed," she said.

"I thought I would let your sister drive home today," the father said.

From the back seat came sirens, screams for help, and then a dirge.

The girl spoke to her father in a voice rich with complicity. "Don't people make you want to give up?"

"Don't the two of you know any jokes? I haven't laughed all day," the father said.

"Did I tell you the guillotine joke?" the girl said.

"He hasn't laughed all day, so you must've," her brother said.

The girl gave her brother a look you could iron clothes with. Then her gaze dropped down. "Oh-oh," she said, "Johnny's out of jail."

Her brother zipped his pants back up. He said, "Tell the joke."

*   *   *

"Two Frenchmen and a Belgian were about to be beheaded," the girl began. "The first Frenchman was led to the block and blind-folded. The executioner let the blade go. But it stopped a quarter inch above the Frenchman's neck. So he was allowed to go free, and ran off shouting, 'C'est un miracle! C'est un miracle!' "

"It's a miracle," the father said.

"Then the second Frenchman was led to the block, and same thing—the blade stopped just before cutting off his head. So *he* got to go free, and ran off shouting, 'C'est un miracle!'

"Finally the Belgian was led to the block. But before they could blindfold him, he looked up, pointed to the top of the guillotine, and cried, 'Voilà la difficulté!' "

She doubled over.

"Maybe I would be wetting *my* pants if I knew what that meant," the boy said.

"You can't explain after the punchline," the girl said, "and have it still be funny."

"There's the problem," said the father.

*   *   *

The waitress handed out menus to the party of three seated in the corner booth of what used to be the lube bay. She told them the specialty of the day was Moroccan chicken.

"That's what I want," the boy said. "Morerotten chicken."

But he changed his order to a Studeburger and fries after his father and sister had ordered.

"So," the father said, "who misses music lessons?"

"I'm serious about what I asked you last week," the girl said. "About switching to piano? My teacher says a real flutist only breathes with the stomach, and I can't."

"The real reason she wants to change," said the boy, "is her waist will get two inches bigger when she learns to stomach-breathe. That's what *else* her teacher said."

The boy buttered a piece of sourdough bread and flipped a chunk of cold butter onto his sister's sleeve.

"Jeezo-beezo," the girl said, "why don't they skip the knife and fork and just set his place with a slingshot!"

"Who will ever adopt you if you don't mind your manners?" the father said. "Maybe we could try a little quiet today."

"You sound like your tombstone," the girl said. "Remember what you wanted it to say?"

Her brother joined in with his mouth full: "Today will be a quiet day."

"Because it never is with us around," the boy said.

"You guys," said the father.

*   *   *

The waitress brought plates. The father passed sugar to the boy and salt to the girl without being asked. He watched the girl shake out salt onto the fries.

"If I had a sore throat, I would gargle those," he said.

"Looks like she's trying to melt a driveway," the boy offered.

The father watched his children eat. They ate fast. They called it Hoovering. He finished while they sucked at straws in empty drinks.

"Funny," he said thoughtfully, "I'm not hungry any more."

Every meal ended this way. It was his benediction, one of the Dad things they expected him to say.

"That reminds me," the girl said. "Did you feed Rocky before we left?"

"Uh-uh," her brother said. "I fed him yesterday."

"*I* fed him yesterday!" the girl said.

"Okay, we'll compromise," the boy said. "We won't feed the cat today."

"I'd say you are out of bounds on that one," his father said.

He meant you could not tease her about animals. Once, during dinner, that cat ran into the dining room shot from guns. He ran around the table at top speed, then spun out on the parquet floor into a leg of the table. He fell over onto his side and made short coughing sounds.

"Isn't he smart?" the girl had crooned, kneeling beside him. "He knows he's hurt."

*   *   *

For years, her father had to say that the animals seen on shoulders of roads were napping.

"He never would have not fed Homer," she said to her father.

"Homer was a dog," the boy said. "If I forgot to feed him, he could just go into the hills and bite a deer."

"Or a Campfire Girl selling mints at the front door," their father reminded them.

"Homer," the girl sighed. "I hope he likes chasing sheep on that ranch in the mountains."

The boy looked at her, incredulous.

"You *believed* that? You actually *believed* that?"

In her head, a clumsy magician yanked the cloth and the dishes all crashed to the floor. She took air into her lungs until they filled, and then she filled her stomach, too.

"I thought she knew," the boy said.

The dog was five years ago.

"The girl's parents insisted," the father said. "It's the law in California."

"Then I hate California," she said. "I hate its guts."

The boy said he would wait for them in the car, and left the table.

"What would help?" the father asked.

"For Homer to be alive," she said.

"What would help?"

"Nothing."

"Help."

She pinched a trail of salt on her plate.

"A ride," she said. "I'll drive."

*   *   *

The girl started the car and screamed, "Goddammit."

With the power off, the boy had tuned in the Spanish station. Mariachis exploded on ignition.

"Dammit isn't God's last name," the boy said, quoting another bumper sticker.

"Don't people make you want to give up?" the father said.

"No talking," the girl said to the rearview mirror, and put the car in gear.

She drove for hours. Through groves of eucalyptus with their damp, peeling bark, past acacia bushes with yellow flowers pulsing off their stems. She cut over to the coast route and the stony, grey-green tones of Inverness.

"What you'd call scenic," the boy tried.

Otherwise they were quiet.

*   *   *

No one said anything else until the sky started to close, and then it was the boy again, asking shouldn't they be going home.

"No, no," the father said, and made a show of looking out the window, up at the sky and back at his watch. "No," he said, "keep driving—it's getting earlier."

But the sky spilled rain, and the girl headed south towards the bridge. She turned on the headlights and the dashboard lit up green. She read off the odometer on the way home: "Twenty-six thousand, three hundred eighty three and eight-tenths miles."

"Today?" the boy said.

*   *   *

The boy got to Rocky first. "Let's play the cat," he said, and carried the Siamese to the upright piano. He sat on the bench holding the cat in his lap and pressed its paws to the keys. Rocky played "Born Free." He tried to twist away.

"Come on, Rocky, ten more minutes and we'll break."

"Give him to me," the girl said.

She puckered up and gave the cat a five-lipper.

"Bring the Rock upstairs," the father called. "Bring sleeping bags, too."

Pretty soon three sleeping bags formed a triangle in the master bedroom. The father was the hypotenuse. The girl asked him to brush out her hair, which he did while the boy ate a tangerine, peeling it up close to his face, inhaling the mist. Then he held each segment to the light to find seeds. In his lap, cat paws fluttered like dreaming eyes.

"What are you thinking?" the father asked.

"Me?" the girl said. "Fifty-seven T-bird, white with red interior, convertible. I drive it to Texas and wear skirts with rick-rack. I'm changing my name to Ruby," she said, "or else Easy."

The father considered her dream of a checkered future.

"Early ripe, early rot," he warned.

A wet wind slammed the window in its warped sash, and the boy jumped.

"I hate rain," he said. "I hate its guts."

The father got up and closed the window tighter against the storm.

"It's a real frog-choker," he said.

In darkness, lying still, it was no less camplike than if they had been under the stars singing to a stone-ringed fire burned down to embers.

They had already said good night some minutes earlier when the boy and girl heard their father's voice in the dark.

"Kids, I just remembered—I have some good news and some bad news. Which do you want first?"

It was his daughter who spoke. "Let's get it over with," she said. "Let's get the bad news over with."

The father smiled. They were all right, he decided. My kids are as right as this rain. He smiled at the exact spots he knew their heads were turned to his, and doubted he would ever feel—not better, but *more* than he did now.

"I lied," he said. "There is no bad news."

HUNGER

Bob Shacochis

The darkness completed itself around them, bringing the horizon to their feet. The sea was only a short walk in any direction and contained the same dimension as the night, edgeless except for where it began for the men on the small circle of shore. The black sky, the black water, closed them in, running on boundlessly, never reaching another landfall that was real or that was anything more than sun-flooded imagery. Here away from Providence and the villages, there was a brotherhood among the fishermen in their isolation. They did not mind that they were utterly alone and apart from the world; this was their life.

Among them only Bowen, a white man and an outsider, did not share their history, and so the solitude was more powerful for him. The sea had turned invisible, losing the interference of horizon and joining to the sky in a cliff of darkness. From where he stood on the cay that was like a shallow china bowl turned upside down on the water, the sea was still in his hair, in his eyes, everywhere, unchallenged. It pushed in when he opened his mouth to speak, and swept out again when he exhaled, stinging his tongue. It blew against him in the breeze and was a living part of his salt-encrusted clothes. Air and water and the scab of land wrapped into each other and floated the men deep in the middle of darkness. Not even his grave held such magnitude for Bowen, not even that seemed so empty as this darkness. This was Bowen's feeling. It didn't exactly worry him; it made him hungry.

On the *Orion*, anchored in the lagoon, a light in the galley flickered on: the extreme density of the night atomized the pocket of radiance produced by the bulb. The light weakened and broke into particles only a short distance from the ship, a globe of fuzzy color suspended in moisture. The silhouette of a man in a straw panama passed across the yellow moon of the porthole. The moon blinked. On the cay, matches were struck and placed to wood. A line of cooking fires wavered on the sand, but the light revealed nothing other than the shapes of men crouched close to the auras of slow, lambent flames.

Bowen brought up more firewood from the beached catboat. He noticed that each arm of flame played with hundreds of grape-sized hermit crabs that clicked and tumbled and clutched and rolled over onto their shells in exodus from the heat and illumination.

The crabs provoked Gabriel. He grabbed any he could between his thumb and index finger and snapped them into the fire. He didn't want them crawling on his face at night, he said; he didn't want to awake to one of them picking its way across his cheeks or down his neck. In the flames, the tiny animals shrank in their red-white shells, burst and bubbled from the heat. It was a game Gabriel liked, but he was not a malicious man, not like Sterling, the murderer, who shot his mother's lover in the head with a speargun and raped the younger boys who were his cellmates in prison. Or Ezekiel, who was drunk all the time and let his wife and children go hungry. Everybody found it easier to forgive Sterling than to forgive Ezekiel. No one cared that Gabriel burned the little crabs.

The night ran up the long shadows of the boatmen, merging with their black outlines as they tended the fires. Heavy iron cauldrons and sooty dutch ovens were shoved down into the coals as the flames waned. Into each pot was placed something different to cook. Men moved in and out of the shadows joyously, with clear purpose, racing back and forth to the boats from light to darkness to light again, carrying calabash shells brimming with portions of the first day's catch. The work they had done after setting up camp at the banks that afternoon was for themselves alone. No unseen white man could put a short price on the fish; no sprat had to be ferried aboard the *Orion* tonight and packed in the ice holds. The real work would come tomorrow when the Dutchman brought his scales ashore, and his tally book. But tonight was jubilation. Tonight every man was free to eat as much as he wanted. It was a spree, an eating fete; everybody was happy. *We feedin weselves, mahn. Nobody else!* Bowen listened politely for a moment and then went about his business. *No dahmn bean big wife makin babies in she belly, five, six, sevahn kids cryin "poppa," no grahnmuddah, uncle, ahntie or cousing John Robinson ten times removed ahnd livin in de mountain so a boy must be sent up wit a dish fah de guy. No coolie mahn stockin de freezah in he shop, no tourist place on de mainlahnd, no big goddahmn Texahn cowboy. We eatin everyting we got.*

Sterling's boys fixed the birds' eggs. They had pilfered them from the nests on Southwest Cay when the *Orion* stopped there earlier in the day to report to the four lonely soldiers sent to guard the fishing grounds from Jamaican poachers, invaders from Nicaragua. With perverse confidence the mainland government dropped off young recruits here for their first duty, left them with a sack of rice, fishing line and hooks, no boat and no short wave radio, hundreds of miles from the shores of their home, for six, eight, sometimes nine or ten months to guard over the skeleton of a freighter locked onto Pearl Henry's Reef.

It was this freighter, the *Betty B*, that the men on the *Orion* first sighted after their long passage from Providence. The massive wreck perched on the bleak, sun-scarred horizon like something ripped away from a city and dropped out of the sky to crumble and rust secretly, away from mankind. Sangre anchored the *Orion* in water as transparent as coconut oil, over a sandy bottom dotted with thousands of conchs five fathoms below. One of the fishermen's catboats was unlashed from the deck and lowered over the side. The captain was rowed ashore to deliver the government permit, a laughable formality. Sterling and his boys went along to collect the eggs from the stick and pebble nests of the boobies, the frigate birds, the gulls and terns. The soldiers insisted that the eggs were under their protection and the fishermen couldn't touch them unless they paid a tax. After quick, stone-faced negotiation, a bottle of rum, a *Playboy* magazine, and twenty pounds of cassava were handed over to the military.

From the rookery Sterling had gathered perhaps two hundred of the eggs, speckled pink and blue and brown. After leveling the bed of embers, the boys boiled a ten-gallon can of seawater and threw in the eggs. The Bottom Town men stewed fish heads: triangular jaws opening wide and senseless as the cartilage that held them melted, poking through the steaming surface of the liquid among an archipelago of eyeballs and flat discs of severed brain and bone. At another fire one man tossed spiny lobster backs and thick antennae into the vapor of his pot. The tails got the best money and were handed over to the Dutchman immediately. All of the fishermen agreed the meat of the lobster, except for the fatty parts, was too rich for tasting anyway.

White gleaming wings of mashed up conch simmered in another stew. Hot lard splattered and sizzled as it foamed over dark orange sacks of roe. Turtle eggs that looked exactly like ping-pong balls boiled in the pot at the center of several men who poked a wire leader through the shells of uncooked ones and sucked out the raw yolk. Bowen was given one as he passed cautiously by in the dark-

ness on his way from scrubbing and washing the fish slime from his
hands in the wet sand at the water. He sucked the shell hollow but it
felt syrupy and inedible in his mouth and tasted like something that
shouldn't be swallowed. He spit it out in his hand to examine what
was there, squatting down near the light of the fire. It was all bright
viscid yolk threaded with a design of red capillaries. He slung the
mess out into the night for the crabs.

"Dis stuff make yah seed grow straight, mahn."

Bowen returned to his own fire. Gabriel was watching intently as
Mundo pitched a row of oval fish steaks into their pot: yellowtail
and red snapper, hogfish, amberjack, grey vertical sections of bar-
racuda. Bowen was surprised at the amount of fish being cooked,
but he did not doubt the three of them would consume all of it.
Mundo pulled plantains, brown and soft, and a giant yam from a
burlap bag, cleaned and sliced these vegetables, added them to the
stew with lime juice, salt, cornmeal dumplings, a handful of garlic
cloves, and small green cooking peppers. Bowen took a mouthful of
stale water from a jerrycan to wash the gobs of albumen gel from his
teeth.

"It's beginning to smell too good, Mundo. I'm dying from the
smell."

"Doan turn to dyin in dis place, Mistah Bone. Nobody to help
you here, mahn, so if you must staht to die, you must finish too."

The overpowering aroma of the cooking, as distinct and potent
and wonderful as the smell of water in the desert, rose from the pots
and encircled Bowen, a warm, copious, life-giving atmosphere. As
quickly as that, the sea that had wracked him all day and all of last
night, the presence that seemed to be a second skin he must learn to
move in, abated. Freed from one sensation, he was enslaved to
another. The sea was now part of his viscera, part of his strength,
and Bowen kneeled down to limit the pressure of hunger in his
stomach, cloistering the force of it with crossed forearms. It was, he
thought, the perfect gesture.

Mundo leaned behind himself into the darkness and reemerged
with a young hawksbill turtle, its eyes already shining with martyr-
dom, the flippers lashed together like hands in prayer with palm
fronds weaved through cuts in the leathery skin. He held it by the
tail over the pot and cut its pale extended neck with an easy pull of
his machete. Black blood squirted into the stew. The act disgusted
Bowen, but he couldn't prevent the hunger from swelling up inside
him, so foreign and portentous, unlike any feeling ever stimulated
in him by food. It stunned Bowen to realize he had not learned that

hunger was the pure voice of the body, of being alive. He did not know what had insulated him against this knowledge. He would rather have seen Mundo kill a worthless man like Ezekiel, the drunkard and child-beater, than butcher the magnificent sea creature near extinction, but he imagined the blood hot and salty as the brine that nourished it, the blood spilling from the opened neck of the turtle into his own mouth, seeping under his tongue, filling his mouth completely, gulping it down too fast to breathe until whatever was there that demanded so much was satisfied.

Gabriel turned on his heels, calling out, "Who de hell burnin mahnchineel tree?" Mundo clamped a lid down on the cooking pot and the three of them moved away to investigate the source of the smoke from the poisonous manchineel wood. Bowen's face and arms had begun to itch and his eyes sting. The search ended at Sterling's fire. His younger boy Jambo was responsible for the fire and mistakenly put a piece of manchineel on the coals. He should have known better, but nobody expected very much from Jambo. The can of eggs was pulled off and the water poured on the fire until the eggs drained. A column of smoke, spreading out like a thunderhead ready to explode, drove everyone upwind, rubbing their eyes, cursing and scratching.

"You a dahmn monkey, Jahmbo."

"How daht boy chop daht wood ahnd cahrry it to de ship witout blisterin he hands?"

"How you get a boy like dis, Sterlin?"

"Take ahn egg, mahn."

"Dey finish up cookin?"

"Dey feelin too hot."

"No, look. Dis one too juicy."

"Look here. Dis one nice."

"Dem eggs no good anyway. Dey too old, mahn."

"Dis one makin a bird."

"Teach it to fly, boy."

The man studied his egg for a moment and then tossed it onto the ground. Bowen bent over to look at it and saw the well-developed embryo of a man-of-war cooked white, almost plastic. Some men were tearing the shells off and popping the eggs down their throats without looking if the meat was bad or not. The close, wet air began to smell faintly rancid.

"Lord, dis guy nevah eat egg before. Sylvestah eatin de shell too."

"He mahd."

"How many eggs daht make, Sylvie boy?"

"Twenty-two." Crumbs and drips of brown gold stuck to his chin and fingers. "I ready fah someting new." But Ulysses said he had eaten twenty-three, so Sylvester ate one more out of pride.

Most of them had no desire to eat the eggs since there was an abundance of food at hand to reward their patient stomachs after the sail aboard the *Orion*. If the eggs were nice, they agreed, that was one thing, but they weren't: they were rotten. Watching Sylvester and Ulysses gobble the malodorous, runny eggs was good entertainment, but their own suppers were waiting. The group wandered back to their own fires, stirred their pots and began to eat. Sterling was the only one who hadn't fished that afternoon. He thought everybody would appreciate the eggs and eat some and then share their own food with him. Mundo called him over to take a piece of fish. His two boys, Ulysses and Jambo, went with the Bottom Town men because they wanted to smoke ganja while they ate.

Sterling, a tall, lean mulatto with stark eyes, sat down in the sand crosslegged, enamel dish in one hand, spoon in the other, stoically waiting to be served. With an empty oatmeal can, Mundo scooped into the pot and overfilled Sterling's dish until sauce oozed across the rim. Sterling's thanks were harshly whispered; the man seemed obligated to quiet gratitude. To Bowen, the relationship between Mundo and Sterling was a mystery. He watched them closely ever since Gabriel had told him it was Mundo's first fishing partner, Gabriel's predecessor, whom Sterling had killed. *Dis guy was real dahrk ahnd Sterlin crazy from his momma sleepin wit such a blahck blahck mahn so he shoot him in de face ahnd den take a stone ahnd bahng him. Sterlin young ahnd foolish den, mahn.* At the time of the murder, Mundo himself turned deadly and swore he would avenge his mate, but the army police reacted swiftly, and now Mundo treated Sterling like an older brother would. Frequently they competed against each other in the water to see who was the best sailor, the best diver, the better shot underwater. But never on land. On land Sterling was most often deferential, even helpful. He knew that Mundo's white friend collected seashells, and so the mulatto gathered them when he was working on the reefs, offering them shyly in his cupped hands to Bowen. Bowen was glad Sterling would rarely look straight at him. There was an exclusive intensity in the fisherman's eyes, a dangerous fascination. When their eyes met for the first time, it made Bowen apprehensive, and now that he knew what Sterling had done, he could tell in his resinous, never blinking eyes that

Sterling had killed a man, that Sterling had watched a man die by his own hand and for a moment had believed completely in his own power and will. It was like a brand.

With his spoon Sterling poked through the food on his dish, ostensibly waiting for it to cool, but he would not eat until Mundo had served himself. For everyone the first taste was an immense relief, a reassurance that life was good and not only hard work uninterrupted day after day. They ate from old cans or held tin bowls between their splayed knees, gouging the sand with their heels to make a trough for the bones and fat, rubbery skin. Mundo was the most serious eater. He had a big family—Gullie, his wife, and her seven children, his wife's parents and his own half-Chinese grandfather to support in his house, plus a scattering of outside children, and though he fed them well, he always needed more to eat than he could get at home. He passionately sucked the grouper head he held catlike between both hands—it was bigger than his bowl—licking the delicate flesh of the cheeks and digging out the brain cavity with his fingers. The marble eyes were relished, the bones cleaned diligently: not a speck of meat eluded him. Gabriel would take a handful of snow-white steak and squeeze it into his mouth, chewing until it was all mashed up and half swallowed, and spit out as best he could the needle sharp bones. He didn't bother that he lost large chunks of meat in the sand by doing this. Bowen was more methodical. Somewhat self-consciously, he picked the flesh free of bones before he took a bite. When invariably he missed one of them, he rearranged his mouthful with his tongue so that the bone was pushed to the forefront and then extracted; or failing this, he dropped whatever was in his mouth into the palm of his hand and pinched around until he found the damn thing. Judged by the pile of offal in front of him, knobs of vertebrae, spiny ribs, long rows of dorsal bones like serrated knives, flaps of mottled skin, Bowen was eating the most, but the opposite was true.

Sterling talked a lot to himself while he ate, sometimes only moving his lips silently, seldom spit, and hacked without concern when a bone stuck in his throat until it blasted out. Sterling behaved like this occasionally—chattered away like an old woman and then slipped back abruptly into his diffidence, embarrassed when he realized what he was doing. Like everyone else, he took second and third helpings and curled over his dish to slurp up the spicy gravy of the stew. Even Bowen, as careful as he was, had stains all over the front of his shirt, and his fingers and lips were sticky with the paste of boiled cartilage.

The men ate on and on. The darkness no longer seemed bleak, but was comfortable and intimate, its vastness a barrier against any force that might seek to disturb the eaters. The fires dwindled to passive ruby clusters of coals, mystical, beguiling, as though something other than wood and fire created them. Stars began to drop through the black canopy of haze. The men did not so much decide to stop eating as they did fall thoughtlessly away from the pots exhausted, collapsing as athletes do after their greatest effort and concentration. They were stupefied by the degree they had expanded their stomachs and patted themselves delicately, croaking with gratification. For a moment Bowen experienced a release, an awakening of something sublime, but he told himself that this was nonsense, he had misinterpreted the dull contentment for insight or oneness that follows the unrestrained stuffing of food into a clamoring gut. He let gravity take over and set him back into the broken coral that the sea had released to form the cairn of land where they camped. His dirty hands became gloved with flakes of cool sand. All around the cay the prone lengths of the fishermen groaned peacefully; with the increasing quiet, the hiss of the ocean surge on the reefs became audible, absolute energy leaching through the night from the interface of living earth and crashing, merciless water, ghost-white, somewhere in the distance.

One shadow still danced among the cooking pots, a faceless ebony *obeah* shape that seemed intent on searching everywhere. It jumped from group to group like a *loup-garou*, grunting and devilizing, throwing narcotic spells into the unprotected men, its rasping steps circling closer to where Mundo and the other three sprawled around the remains of their dinner, not talking much, staring without expression into the sky. The spirit rose out of the darkness before them, but nobody paid much attention. It was Ulysses, Sterling's oldest boy, a burly young man.

"Ahlright dere."

Sterling shifted, nodding to his son.

"Okay Mundo."

"Ahlright."

"Mundo," Ulysses asked with quick, deep words that were almost unintelligible. "You got more to eat here?" The features of his round face were knotted together by a big ganja smile.

"Go look in de kettle," Mundo said with some annoyance. "Sterling, what's wrong wit dis boy? How's daht he doan get enough to eat?"

Sterling shrugged. Somebody was always asking him what was

wrong with the boys. Ulysses eagerly removed the lid from the pot and peered in. From under his white cotton T-shirt, his black hairless belly humped downward like the hull of a boat. He dredged the bottom of the pot but found only a few bones there and sucked them dry.

"I still hungry," he announced.

"Go beg a piece ah fish from Mistah Dawkin."

"Him finish up."

"Go ahsk Henry."

"Dey ahll finish."

Sterling said to his boy, "Go eat dem eggs. Lots ah dem left."

"Dem eggs bahd."

"What de hell, mahn," Mundo said sternly to put an end to it. "Eggs still eggs, even if dey bahd."

This logic appealed to Ulysses' sense of gluttony. He retreated back into the darkness headed for the eggs, driven to clear the hunger out of his mind, for surely it already had been buried in his stomach. From where they lay, the four of them half-listened to Ulysses bumping into the gear, clanking over pots like a bear in his blind hunt for the eggs.

With his head back facing the stars, Gabriel sighed. "I like it like dis," he said. After a pause he continued. "But dis a lonely place. Dis place doan even smell like lahnd."

"I nevah been lonely. Not once," Mundo said, as though the matter was unimportant.

"Give me a cigahrette, Mistah Bone," said Sterling quietly. There was no need for politeness, for manners rooted in terra firma. Among the fishermen, all requests were straightforward and a man either helped another or he didn't. Anchored by satiation and fatigue, Bowen did not want to move. He invited Sterling to reach over and take the pack of Pielrojas from his pants pocket. Earlier he had been afraid that the men would not accept him in close quarters, but now he didn't care. Mundo and Gabriel were no problem because he worked with them, but back on Providence the others watched him cautiously, suspicious of his whiteness, never speaking to him. Mundo's own mother-in-law looked at Bowen as if he had come to steal the toes from her feet.

Sterling never took the cigarette from his mouth when he smoked. He rested back on his elbows and the ashes sprinkled down his bare chest. "Mistah Bone," he said tonelessly. "Why a white mahn like you come to de cays?"

The question amused Mundo. He answered, "Mistah Bone come

fah experiahnce. He wahnt to study how hahd de blahck mahn work." He winked at Bowen and Gabriel as he said this and tugged his red baseball cap down clownishly over his eyes to indicate the absurdity and the sufficiency of this reply. They did not pretend to understand why the world was the way it was, but amongst themselves they assumed that a man had good reasons, however offensive, for his actions. That was enough. Sterling's public showing of curiosity was easily dismissed, for Sterling was a strange man, a man who sometimes couldn't control himself. The fact was Bowen was there; he and Mundo had befriended each other. That was enough. The others were disconcerted by the enigma of a white man working with them; always and always black men had worked for clear-skinned people. That the pattern was disrupted was easy to see, but only Mundo accepted it casually as a natural course.

"I watch Mistah Bone takin notes," Gabriel spoofed, referring to Bowen's letter writing. "He comes to write history of de cay in a big big book. He writin: 'Dese bunch ah blahck men sail up to Serrana, go ashore ahnd eat like hogs!' "

Bowen laughed halfheartedly, satisfied that he didn't have to say anything. He was convinced there was nothing to look back to, for once in his life no use for the past. Secretly, he trembled from a sense of awesome freedom, not prepared for the truth of it, faithless but full of modest expectation like a baptized sinner, carried to the river by force.

A shot of light, vanishing and then reappearing more brilliantly, drew their lazy attention to the camp of the Bottom Town men, where a rag had been twisted into the neck of a soda bottle filled with kerosene and ignited, creating a phantasmagoria of gleaming skin, light sparking from eyes and angles of metal, the choppy flash of a single thick flame, orange and greasy. The men could not relax for long. They had found their second wind, were standing and stretching and beginning to talk loudly.

"Sterlin, come play *pedro*, mahn. You got money to lose? Mundo, come play wit Sterlin."

Sterling yelled over, "I smokin dis cigahrette. You wait." The cigarette was only a nub of ash stuck to his fat lower lip. More kerosene torches flared from the camps of the other fishermen.

Ulysses came back clutching his stomach. He went to the white man first.

"Mistah Bone," he pleaded, "you got some medicine?"

"What sort of medicine?"

"Stomahch powdahs."

Bowen said he didn't bring anything like that with him on the trip. He was concerned though because Ulysses' stomach was making duck sounds.

"Where'd you find that duck?" Bowen asked.

The boy began to wail. "Oh Christ. Oh me ahss, me ahss."

He turned to the other men for aid but they shook their heads unsympathetically. Mundo said mockingly, "Dem eggs real good, eh?" And Gabriel turned to Bowen and asked, "You evah see a mahn eat like dis?" Bowen had no answer because he was fascinated by the noise coming from inside Ulysses.

Now Ulysses' indulgence was a big joke. He stumbled toward the slick black ocean, stomach quacking hysterically, and Mundo hailed the others to come witness the boy's trouble. The digestive storm at his center doubled Ulysses over and he crawled the final yard to the water, set his face into the glinting surface of the lagoon and drank like a horse, sucking the water into his mouth. The fishermen banded around him, chiding his folly; their hooting chorus of laughter escaped out across the immensity of the sea, a wave of communal mirthfulness that broke against the austerity of the fishing grounds. Ulysses jerked his head out of the salt water and roared.

"Look, look, him got enough food in he belly to feed ahll of Cuba."

"Hey, Ulysses boy, you doan has to feed dem fish. Dey got plenty."

"Maybe he gonna be like a dog ahnd eat daht mess right bahck up."

When Ulysses had finished purging himself, he rolled over and smiled weakly up at the men, not like a fool, and not with shame, but like a man whose relief is genuine, a man reconciled past a moment of bad judgment. His father knelt down beside him and gently lifted his son.

"You bettah?" Sterling asked. "You ahlright now?"

"I eat too much of dose dahmn eggs," Ulysses explained without much regret. "Mundo says eggs still eggs even when dey snotty ahnd stink, but I eat too much. De first one taste good ahnd I must keep eatin dem."

Bowen stared at the boy and discovered himself gagging reflexively. He felt his eyes squeeze tight with convulsion, his jaw tearing away from his skull, his insides closing in upon him as though he too had collapsed on his hands and knees to gulp seawater the way a dog will chew grass to make itself heave. The sensation passed into a weightlessness, a rough freshness, and he turned away from the sea and walked back to the camp.

The men scattered to play *pedro*, to wash the cooking pots, to listen to Gabriel tell a story about a Providence boat that disappeared in Serrana with his father aboard. The wind fell off completely. A small piece of moon rose and gelled the sea. Out in the darkness the coral reefs relented and let the tide pass over them unbroken. Bowen lay on his blanket in the sand, waiting for sleep. The cards ticked loudly against the *pedro* players' soft conversation. The words spread entropically out into the night and somewhere, far out to the black sea, slipped underwater and were lost, flying like sea turtles through the perfect silence.

AT THE HOP

Ron Carlson

I'm trying to sing the most popular song of the year, "The Hop," by Danny and the Juniors, as I whip the towel around my arms and legs. I'm not much at grooming. It's hard to sing it for more than a minute without stopping and thinking you're silly. *At the ha-ha-ha-hop! At the ha-ha-ha-hop! At the hop! You can rock it! You can roll it! You can really start to stroll it at the hop! hop! hop! hop!* But on the radio it's a pretty strong song and has me hooked. I never listened to the radio before, except for the goof songs which my brother Bobby likes, such as "Please Mr. Custer, I Don't Wanna Go!" Now, I listen to the radio all the time. My dad framed it in the wall when he built our basement. After I switch it on I fall back on the bed and do a backward somersault naked to dry my back.

Hopping up to grab some underwear, I find something different on my bureau. Oh I've been finding these clippings out of *Ladies Home Journal* for a while now. My mother cuts them out and puts them on my bureau. They're about things like "Surviving the Troublesome Teens" and "The Six Teenage Dangers." I try not to touch them. I don't move them or go near my bureau top while they're up there. After four or five days they disappear. My mother and I have never talked about them, nor have I ever seen her place them or take them away. The last one was titled: "What Teenagers Want to Know About SEX." The word "SEX" was stencilled in red block letters on a picture of a big wooden crate, the kind they must keep dynamite in. It scares the shit out of me that they print things like that in magazines; what are they trying to do, embarrass everybody in the whole world? For that week, I gave my bureau plenty of room. I didn't change my underwear for three days and when the article disappeared, I finally felt free to sleep late the next day.

Standing there with one leg in my shorts I see something new on the old bureau. A pamphlet. Picking it up, I read: *Understanding Puberty*. Oh my God. I drop it like a firecracker. What a word: *puberty*. It should be in the pledge of allegiance: "with puberty and

48

justice for all." The truth is: I don't even know exactly what it is. They showed a film last year to all the girls while the boys were kept in Mr. Donaldson's class. Mr. Donaldson wouldn't tell us what the film was about, and I remember walking home with Fenn that I felt hurt and kind of sad that we'd been dealt with unfairly. Something was going on and no one would tell us what it was. Mrs. Talbot had been our teacher all year and then they show a film; and without a word to us, she and all the girls go into the auditorium leaving us with Mr. D., the fool.

And now, my mother is leaving pamphlets on my bureau. Next, I can already see it: she'll start leaving whole books and stacks of books. It's all not quite working.

Well, I've touched the pamphlet, moved it, and I snap on my undershorts and go back to it. *Understanding Puberty.* It could be a travel brochure. Inside I see the diagram of the male reproductive organs. It all looks a lot like Florida, the capital of which is Tallahassee. Two pages later are the female reproductive organs, the side view, internal. It looks like nothing, like lines. I try to imagine Linda Aikens or Carol Wilkes with one of these. And the truth is: my imagination won't work. If I saw some girl naked and she looked like this I would scream and tear my eyes out. No wonder sex is such a big secret: it's brutal. And this is just the puberty part. A couple of pages later there is the bold print phrase: "adolescents are torn by the violent distractions of puberty. . . ." As I'm looking at it, my mother yells down the stairs to me: "Larry, don't be late!" I drop the pamphlet again as my heart explodes and my face heats up. She knows I'm down here reading this dirty pamphlet!

"I won't be! I'm coming!" I call back, but my voice is changed, all throaty, so now she knows for sure.

I spend the next five or ten minutes trying to remember exactly how the little book was originally sitting on the bureau. I adjust it around an eighth of an inch at a time trying to get it just right. Then I pick it up again and wipe my fingerprints off the glossy cover, but the towel is wet and leaves a little smear, so I toss it back up on the dresser and try again to turn it around and around so it looks untouched. Then I take it down and check out the female reproductive organs again. I can see the buttocks, but the rest is a terrible puzzle. This time, when I replace it, I see that the cover is bent, so I leave it there all wrong and sit on my bed, sick right through the heart. By this time I don't even want to go to the party.

The song on the radio now is, *Who put the bop in the bop-she-bop, she bop? Who put the ram in the ram-a-ram-a ding-dong?* I sit on my bed and

pull on the first pair of long pants I've worn all summer, not counting my baseball uniform. They are one of the strangest pair of pants
I've ever worn: my first pair of corduroys. My mother bought them
for me as part of my school clothes. The pants are chocolate brown,
and when I stand up in them and brush my hand on the leg, they
feel wonderful. I run my new belt with the modest brass C-shaped
buckle through the loops. Tucking in my white shirt, rolling up the
sleeves, and buckling the belt, I feel better. I actually feel mature.
Maybe that was puberty I just passed through. In the mirror, I look
like any twelve-year-old lawyer. My hair is too short to comb, but I
comb it anyway, just to see if I look right doing it.

Who was that man? the song cries. *I'd like to shake his ha-a-and; He
made my baby fall in love with me!*

I slip right out of my room and head up the stairs and then go
back to my room and then go back again to the stairs and finally
stop and look at my new shoes. They are slip-ons and have little
tassels instead of laces. I return to my room. The pamphlet glows in
the dark. Finally I take it up and fold it right in half and stuff it in the
back pocket of my new trousers. I button the pocket.

Upstairs in the kitchen, my mother looks at me and says "Well!"

"Yeah," I say. "Fenn and I are going to walk over to the class
party."

"Vic, come in here," my mother calls.

My father comes in the kitchen. He is carrying my baby brother,
Regan. "Say, you look pretty good, Larry. What is this, a party?"

"Yeah, Fenn and I are going to walk over to the class party."

"Isn't Butch going?"

"Naw. He doesn't go to many things like this."

"Butch is dropping out of school," my little brother Bobby says.
He's sneaked up behind me and rubs the leg of my corduroys.

"He is?"

"No, he's not!" I say to my mother. "Bobby doesn't know anything."

"Roto said so!"

"Roto's a dope."

*   *   *

"Is Butch dropping out of school?"

"I don't know anything about Butch. He's confused me all summer," Fenn says. Fenn is wearing his glasses again. They're not his
old glasses but new ones he bought for school. The frames are little
chrome girders and they make Fenn look ready for the new age. I

don't know if he ever found out the cardboard baseball goggles we gave him were made using his old lenses; I doubt it. The goggles now dangled from the nose of the B-52 suspended from the ceiling in his room. And I don't actually know what made him decide on wearing glasses again after his wild summer of banging his head against things.

It might have been when we went downtown on Butch's birthday to see *The Sinking of the Bismarck*, which wasn't as good as the song, and then Fenn talked us into going across the street to the Gem to see *Love Me Tender* again. We actually saw it twice in a row that afternoon, and the second time through, when Elvis gets shot and his face is superimposed over the scene of the little house, Fenn rose before the song was even over and said, "Well, that's enough of that." The next day he put on his new glasses.

"Don't you want to look like Elvis anymore?" we had asked him.

"It's all over. Rock and roll has six months to live. I'm going to save my money so that when I'm fifteen and a half, I can buy a car."

"A car?" It was the first time anyone had mentioned a car that way to me. Ever.

Later, Butch had said to me quietly: "Fenn's a goner."

And he may be. Now, as we walk toward the class party, he seems a lot different from the blind kid I swindled all summer. He's wearing a red shirt, short sleeves, and chinos. I haven't seen him in a button shirt in my whole life.

Linda Aikens lives just across the river from our new school: the junior high. It's a good walk because most of the way you can stay by the river and throw rocks at the passing debris. It's just getting dark when we step down the flagstone steps into the junior high schoolyard. The asphalt yard is crisscrossed by a complicated series of lines painted in yellow paint which has swollen from seventy coats and the weather. The track and the dash marks and the baseball diamond and the basketball courts are all printed on top of each other on the old blacktop. There are several gigantic intersecting circles. I hate not knowing what those circles are for. The entire yard is, in fact, just a scary diagram of our futures, and it makes my stomach feel the same way that the diagram of the female reproductive organs did. I feel my pocket and take the pamphlet out and hand it to Fenn.

"Check this out."

He takes it and turns a few pages, still walking. It's funny to see him read without holding the paper against his nose. He hands it back. "Wonderfully informative."

"My mother left it for me."

"Your mother! What for?"

"I don't know." We walked by the huge brick siding of the gymnasium. Someone has thrown a bottle of ink against it and a blue stain flashes dead center. The whole school scares me. In four days I'll come here as a student.

"You ever jack off?" Fenn asks.

"Yeahnn," I say automatically.

"What? Do you?"

"Not exactly." I try to say it as if I know what I am saying *exactly*. Jacking off is something I've heard about. Lannie and Cling are always telling the little kids to jack off. They take the kids' nickels and then say, "Now, why don't you go soap it up in the tub and jack off." Then Cling makes an ape stance and grasps his crotch and laughs.

I have soaped it up in the tub, but I know that I have not jacked off. I still have two toy boats that I keep by the tub. That's a fact. Well, one's a submarine. I bought it at Woolworth's the day we saw *The Sinking of the Bismarck*. I don't know. I look around at the trees, swelling in the late summer dusk, and I think that: I don't know.

"You haven't have you? Have you? Do you know about it?"

It's becoming a long day for me. I try to keep walking.

"Hey. It's okay. I just learned."

"You went over to Lannie's club."

"Yeah, I went over to Lannie's club. They go up there and jack off. He's got some magazines."

"I know all about it." And I kind of do. I gave Lannie the magazines over a year ago. I found them in the vacant lot. Somebody had thrown them out of a car and they were blown into Roto's fort, which was nothing but a hole with a car battery sitting on a dirt shelf. In war, that was the radio. I remember one picture from all three magazines. It showed a woman sitting at a glass table as if she was about to eat a bowl of peaches. She had huge, featureless breasts that fell over onto the table in two piles. At that time it had seemed the most hilarious photograph I had ever seen. And, even in retrospect, it seemed that someone had been out to make fun of the woman. I could hear the photographer pleading, "Come on, now lean forward and flop your tits up on the table and take a rest."

"They showed me how to do it. They did it for me the first time. It's great; it makes you feel all lit up."

"I'll bet."

"And then you can go back whenever you want and see the magazines."

"If you join."

"Yeah, you have to join, but it's great."

We're about to step off the asphalt playground and go down the grassy slope to the walkbridge across the river, when there's a friction noise and a bicycle slips by in front of us. There is no rider. It runs in a slowing curl and finally clatters to the pavement. I already know that it's Butch's bike because the front wheel is smaller than the other, but Fenn calls, "What the hell?" Then I see Butch clear back across the painted asphalt, hanging by his hands on the chinning bar where he dismounted like a cowboy on a branch, sending his bike after us. I can barely see him; he looks like a brown flag.

"Hey, Butch!" I call.

"Better get on to the party, boys!" he cries back. Then I see that he's not coming over as he lifts a knee through his hanging arms, and swings himself up onto the bar.

"The kid's got a problem," Fenn says. He's walked on ahead. "Butch is beyond help."

I look at Fenn in his new glasses and that red shirt and I hardly know him. This kid used to be a friend of mine, I think. And now I spot another difference: this Fenn is two inches taller than I am. That wasn't true at the beginning of the summer. His face is different too in a way I can't describe except to say it seems to have more separate parts. And his eyebrows have grown together over his nose.

On the walkbridge we stop and lean on the rail and look upstream. Cling and some of his punky pals from the junior high are upriver swinging on a rope. We can see the orange stars of their cigarettes in the dark, and the ape-form Cling is outlined clearly against the river as he swings back and forth on the rope. Each time he swings back, his pals won't let him land, and eventually he ends up, slower and slower, hanging there straight over the river.

"You dirty bastards!" he says the twenty feet across to the group, and he drops into the water.

We hear the splash, and I lean over the rail and fold "Understanding Puberty" in half again and again and then twist it into a fat cigar and release it over the river. It hits the water right alongside a white quart bottle which glints once coming out from under the bridge, and we hurry and ramble after it along the ruined river trail, throwing rocks as fast as we can find them. Fenn finally swamps the bottle by heaving a boulder the size of a skull right next to it. It's not as satisfying as hearing the muffled crash and watching a bottle really go down, but we stand there in the thicket, breathing, and for a moment, it's just like old times; we're just dressed differently.

"Hey," Fenn says, pointing: "Check that!" There across the river, high in a tree, which is dead from the waist up like so many of the giant trees in the river vines, hangs a bra, a brassiere. Fenn laughs. The bra is outlined perfectly against the last yellow tinge in the purple sky. "Think of that," he says. "Think of what went in that."

"I can imagine." I lie. I can't imagine. I can't imagine how it ever got up there. I've never seen anything so wrong, so out of place.

On the way back to the bridge, Fenn asks, "Are you going to dance?"

"I don't know. Are you?"

"You kidding? Name one girl in our class who isn't a skagg."

*   *   *

Linda's house is a long, low brick house, much nicer than anything in our neighborhood. I've seen pictures of houses like this in magazines and they are called "Ranch Houses" for some reason. The brick walkway up to her front door is curved, and they have a miniature streetlamp in the front yard. It's a stupid idea because it ruins what could have been a decent sockball field. The front door has an *A* in it, and Mrs. Aikens opens the door and welcomes us in.

There are a bunch of kids in the kitchen, who spill out a large sliding glass door onto a patio. The kids in the kitchen are mainly girls and the kids on the patio are mainly boys. Lannie is out there nodding at Mr. Aikens over the barbecue grill. Lannie can con anybody. Standing there with his black hair combed out of his face and his hands in his pockets, nodding at Mr. Aikens, he looks as if he's never punched little kids in the throat for a nickel. Cling won't be here; he dropped out of school "in the first grade!" he says. Behind Lannie, I see Keith Gurber talking to the Starkey twins. They're all drinking orange soda pop. Max has one hand in the air, flattened as a plane, turning real slow figure eights. Keith is transfixed. Before I can get out of the kitchen, Carol Wilkes turns from where she's been filling bowls with potato chips and says, "Larry! What have you been doing all summer?"

I look in her face, and it is a beautiful face, my favorite face in the whole grade school. Her eyes are taller than they are wide and her upper lip flips up a little. It makes her look like she's always about to flirt. "Not much, Carol," I say. I remember everything I've ever said to her. "Playing baseball." A strange impulse rises in me to say to her, "Carol, you know you're one of my favorite people," or some such silly thing, but I will never be able to. Girls are always older than you; you can never catch up enough to know them well. Before

I can embarrass myself, Mrs. Aikens takes my arm and says she wants to show me where the soft drinks are. She takes me in the bright yellow utility room right across from the kitchen.

"Well?" Mrs. Aikens says.

"It's a nice room."

"No, Larry, do you know where the soft drinks are?"

"In the fridge?"

"No!" she laughs and laughs as if I'd said "in the hedge." I kind of smile while she has a good time laughing. She recovers and says, "No, no, no. Here they are!" She opens the washing machine lid and I see that it's full of ice. "What would you like?"

"Is there any creme soda?" I'm just going along with her all the way.

She reaches into the washing machine and extracts a tall bottle of Nehi Creme Soda. "And here's the opener." It's dangling on a string above the washer. "I read about this party trick in 'Party Hints' in the paper. Of course, you have to unplug the washer to be safe!" She bends and shows me the three prong washer plug as proof that we're safe.

"That's a great party idea, Mrs. Aikens," I say, hoping she'll just hand me the soda and let me go. "I certainly wouldn't have thought of that."

"Yes, well, a good party starts with good planning!" Finally, she awards me the creme soda and we step back into the kitchen, and I'm able to fade out into the backyard. Linda Aikens is in the corner of the patio, fiddling with her hi-fi. She has a wire rack full of 45s, and she's arranging and rearranging them.

"Hi, Linda."

"Larry!" She turns to smile at me. There's a record on every one of her fingers. "Oh, I'm glad you came." And you know, the way she says it is right: she means it. She's parted her dark hair in a new way, right down the middle, real tight and shiny, and the rest of her hair is pinned up in two braids. She kind of looks like Heidi in the movie.

I hold up my soda. "In the washer. You want one?"

"No, I want to get the records ready. Will you dance with me later?"

The backyard is hard to figure out. There is another lamppost on one side gathering bugs in a busy halo, above four wrought iron chairs, and instead of a fence a tall hedge surrounds the whole thing. The lawn is great; it just make you want to practice a few slides. They're not storing anything out here, any lumber, a wheelbarrow or even an old boat, and it doesn't look like anything is *played* out here. The yard is filling up with kids from Edison, but it still seems like such a waste, all that thick lawn. It's a hard yard to figure. I say hello to Mr. Aikens who looks pretty young to be somebody's father. He's got freckles on his forehead. "You guys all know each other?" he says to us and I say yes, we do. Lannie gives me a sly look. I'm mainly trying to do the three things my mother told me: stand straight up; not drink my soda in four gulps; not hang around the potato chips. Fenn is hanging around the potato chips. Evidently, his mother didn't talk to him.

Then for a while Mr. Aikens is serving hotdogs and Mrs. Aikens is showing everybody the washing machine. Then Linda puts on a record, "Stagger Lee," a song I never could understand, and kids start dancing on the cement patio. It's mainly the bigger kids, Howell and Kidder, kids who aren't afraid of having girlfriends.

I watch the group dance for a while and then between "Twenty-Six Miles" and "Who Wrote the Book of Love" I stand up and take my paper plate back into the kitchen. Though I made my soda last longer than any in the history of my life, it has been empty for half an hour. The bottle's warm. No one is in the kitchen except two girls who are leaning over the sink to look out the window at the dancers. Turning into the utility room, I bump into Mrs. Aikens. I show her the empty bottle and make a friendly gesture toward the washer, saying, "Unplugged, right?" But she's taking another bag of chips outside, and so I am spared a second tour and simply help myself to another cold bottle of creme soda.

When they play "At the Hop" about a dozen kids do the Hop, a dance I can't master, and it looks pretty neat the way they raise one heel over the other toe and then slip into the opposite position by just lifting their shoulders. Something like that. Now Keith Gurber is handling all the records. He runs the projector at school sometimes, and he's good at those technical things, only occasionally snagging his dangling belt in the mechanism.

"I haven't seen you dance yet." Linda has come up behind me on the lawn. "Are you ready?"

"Sure, I'm ready." The party has continued easily through the evening. I've mainly been experimenting with new ways to hold my soda so as not to warm it up so much with my hand. I've watched Fenn move to three stations, each beside a recently filled potato chip bowl, and stuff his face. Tomorrow there's going to be a triangular trail in the lawn from his feeding pattern. For a few minutes Grant and Max and some guys started having chicken fights, riding piggyback all over the yard, but Mrs. Aikens stopped that. She rushed out and asked Max, who was riding on Grant's shoulders, if he was all right. It took the spirit out of it for them, I guess, because they all settled down and headed for the washing machine.

But mostly it has been couples dancing, doing the Twist and the Hop and a little of the Pony, and once Linda and Carol led four other girls in the Stroll, which looked real smooth and ancient, like a dance they'd known forever. I thought: how do they know how to do these things? And now, I stand with Linda Aikens, one arm on her hip, the other in her hand, as the next record drops. I look over at Keith and he smiles at me. He's a kid just happy to be playing records. He hasn't had to drop any pamphlets in the river or have his friends ask if he jacks off. The song is "Earth Angel," and as it starts I commence the two-step as taught by Mr. Donaldson, but instead of it becoming the stepping and steering activity I'd known last year, this dance changes. First, Linda's head collapses against my chin. For a minute I think I might have to carry her to a chair. But no, she's moving, she's all right, she's just moving slowly in microscopic shuffle steps. I can do this. I can do this. I think: I can do this. For a while I concentrate hard on not kicking her over as I stare out on the lawn where my half bottle of creme soda stands alone. Then, without trying, I've got it. Linda's forehead, the very start of her part, is against the corner of my mouth, and though I try to stand up straight, I soon find my head against her head that way as we dance. It is the easiest thing I have ever done.

As the song ends, I peel my face from Linda's forehead; sweat has stuck us together. Linda says, "Just a minute," to me and goes over to give Keith some help. While I'm standing on the edge of the patio, Fenn calls my name and I watch him walk over and gently toe my soda over onto its side. He smiles at me as if he's just done a classic party stunt. At this distance, I look at his new chrome glasses and red shirt and I swear I don't know him anymore. I don't really even know where I am or what I'm doing, but Linda is back at my hand, pulling me through the dancers, off the patio, around the redwood trellis, into the darkness of the side yard. We can hear the music start: "Poetry in Motion." When Linda stops, I almost run into her. The sweat in the fringe of her hair is reflected in the starlight.

"Did you get my note?"

"Yeah," I say. She is still holding my hand. "I did." She doesn't say anything, just looks up at me, so I add: "I found it in my book."

I hear the part of the song I like: the neat rhyme: "motion" and "ocean." Linda looks up at me with a look I've never seen anybody make, not even in movies, and she lifts her arms around my neck and pulls herself up as I reach down and we kiss. I don't know if it is a long or a short kiss, just that she is against me, her lips against mine, and when I place my arms around her back one of my hands flattens on her bra and I move that hand. I look once and see her eyes are closed.

Then she stands back down on her heels and smiles at me, looks at the ground, lets go of my hand, and walks back around to the party. The first thing I do when she leaves is look around to see if anybody saw us; then I realize I am not going back to the party. I can do everything there is to do, dance, find soda in the washing machine, stand up straight, not gobble the potato chips, but I cannot walk back around that trellis and have Fenn smile at me again with his big fake face. What I do is look at my shoes, those little tassels.

I find the redwood side gate, which is six feet tall, but I can't work the old latch, so I pull and scramble up and finally place a foot on top of it to climb over. But, with one of my legs still hanging and kicking, the gate starts to swing open. I can't do anything but ride it around until it stops against the house, and I find myself looking in the bathroom window. Carol Wilkes is sitting there knee to knee with Linda, who is sitting on the tub, and they are talking like two maniacs planning an escape. Linda has her hands over both of her ears as if to hold her head together, I guess, and, though I can't hear a word they say, it is the one time in my life when I am sure that somebody is talking about me.

BAGATELLE

David Ohle

Moldenke was walking down Arden Boulevard one afternoon, in Reno. He passed the Home for Wayward Neutrodynes. One of them was perched on the stoop, licking the last of some rice from a tin pan. The neut released a sickly sweet odor and had a greasy pomade in its hair. Moldenke looked around to see if perhaps a stinkbug had been squashed underfoot. A couple of noisy sawflies were playing above its head. There was a bun of proud flesh, a pillowy lump on its upper lip. It had likely been conked there by someone wielding a billy bat. The neut said, "Say, American. You look slick. I have a deal for you. It so happens that I am rounding up bounders of your type for a little excursion that just may net us a bag of fast cash. Do you want to hear the particulars?"

Moldenke stopped long enough to give the neut a hearing, knowing they were sometimes foxy investors.

The neut said, "Is it correct to say, sir, that we have never met before, that there is no way imaginable I could know your name, that in fact, if I were able to guess it, why then you Americans would think me a mind reader and stuff sawbucks into my pocket? Is that correct?"

Moldenke said, "Probly."

The neut put aside its empty bowl and took a swig of jitney ale, passing the bottle to Moldenke. Bits of rice peppered the surface of the ale. He went ahead and had a sip, against his better judgment. When the bottle's mouth, wet with the neut's saliva, touched his lips it gave them an acidic bite.

"To show I am no piker," said the neut, "let me demonstrate my talent. May I say, first, sir, that my name is Gatlin Bang, originally from Dodge City." The neut thrust forth a hand from its sleeve. The fingers were like the feathery legs of a barnacle. Moldenke politely declined the handshake, aware of Reno's newest ordinance against public liaison with neutrodynes. "Call me Bang for short," said the neut. "Now, let me see. Your name is, uh, Muldoon. No, no. Molinski. Nah, that's not it. It's Moldenke. Yes, Moldenke. They called you Dink in normal school, am I right?"

Moldenke nodded.

"There, you see? You Americans have your names written all over you. It's a lead-pipe cinch. I can fleece them without letup, forever. Look, Dink, I want you to come along with me to Susnr tonight. They are celebrating Mummy Day up there. We can put the squeeze on the touring Americans, make plenty of bucks. We'll book seats on the *Diaxle 1010*, departing at sundown."

Moldenke backstepped a little, shaded his eyes, and looked up at Susnr, dawdling in the American sky, an uninvited visitor, a third the size of the moon. It was close enough that Moldenke could see the streetlamps of Altobello, the queen city. "I've never been up there before," he said. Susnr was pielike, presenting a broad face but a narrow profile. As it turned, one saw less and less of it, until it was but a slice.

"Well, then," said Bang. "The time is ripe. Rock 'n' Roll."

Moldenke said he would have to go home and pack his kitty bag.

"No need for that," said Bang. "The cash will flow to us like water. We will buy what we need, like the Americans do. We must leave for the depot immediately if we expect to get aboard the *Diaxle* in time for her departure."

Moldenke felt giddy, as he did every time he looked at Susnr, or came anywhere near a neutrodyne. "Okay," he said. "What's there to lose?"

Moldenke and Bang set off for the depot, which was at the foot of Arden Boulevard. On the way, Moldenke remarked how many neuts he saw sleeping in vestibules, in the gutter, everywhere that provided a refuge from pedestrian traffic. Bang said, "The ones coming down to America, they are a bunch of reprobates and layabouts, eaters of sweets, *pflum* drinkers. We have not yet learned to breed for better stock, as you Americans have."

They passed a candy shop. There was a throng of neutrodynes inside, buying licorice whips, glace nuts, nonpareils, heavenly hash, caramels, butterscotch rocks, and crystallized fruit. Bang excused itself, went into the shop and stood in line. Moldenke lolled on the sidewalk and waited. Bang came out with a bagful of marshmallows. They continued walking. "I have a sweet tooth myself," said Bang, "as did my father before me." Soon, the neut's cheeks were engorged with marshmallows. Moldenke had no taste for them, not liking the sugary sting they left in his teeth, but he ate one nevertheless, out of common courtesy.

A *pflum* vendor approached. It was a pasty stuff served in fluted paper cups, a creamy color, the consistency of tapioca. Moldenke said, "I've never tried it before." Bang suggested there was time enough to stop and sample some. Moldenke handed over a two-bit piece. He nibbled at the *pflum* as they resumed walking, feeling giddier than ever. He had to lap at it like a dog to get it out of the cup, as it was too thick to pour. It was tartly flavored, reminiscent of gooseberries.

Moldenke remembered the time, years back, when he'd been touring the Ozarks and had paid a visit to a neutrodyne settlement, which happened to be in the midst of a grand celebration. It must have been Mummy Day. There were many interesting displays, depicting aspects of neutrodyne life and lore. He paid a visit to a tented pavilion, where the work of neutrodyne anatomists was being shown, and was attracted to an exhibit of neutrodyne brains arrayed in plastocene cases, each in a different state of dissection. They looked like rather large, burst figs, the seedy contents leaking, and at the core, something that could have been mistaken for a good-sized horse bean. There was a tag pinned to the organ saying FLOCCULUS—*The flocculus has had a long history of study, often yielding contradictory evidence. The ontogenetic contributions vary greatly. Theories have been proposed to account for its modifications. Whatever its phylogenetic significance, it is known to be formed by invaginations of the head capsule* in vitro. *Then, shortly after birth, like a ship freed of moorings, the* flocculus *sails about the neutrodyne body with a will of its own. At death it is expelled from the most convenient orifice, often the anus.*

Moldenke looked up again at Susnr. It was like a jack-o'-lantern in the evening sky. He could see irrigation ditches, orderly rows of cultivated greenery, the Tektite desert, the Firecracker Sea. He could even see the crape myrtles blooming in Pilchard Park.

When they arrived at the depot, they found it a swarm of Americans waving Mummy Day banners, jostling one another, rushing to board the *Diaxle.* One could already hear the hum of its engines.

"Hey, Rock 'n' Roll," said Bang. "Not a minute too soon." They stood in the ticket line, and were fortunate enough to get the last two seats in the Sinatra Room, a loungelike accommodation with a spectacular view and a place where *pflum* was free. The ticket was twice the fare of ordinary passage, but Bang assured Moldenke it was worth every penny. Bang contributed nothing toward the price, however, saying the first earnings from the name game would take care of that.

As they were hurrying up the concourse toward the Sinatra Room,

an American boy came up behind them and cracked Bang's head
smartly with a billy bat. Bang fell. The boy ran, yelling, "Yay, I
conked a neut! I finally conked a neut!"

There was a hole in the top of Bang's head wide enough to admit a
new potato. Out of it had come the *flocculus*, steaming and rolling
onto the crowded concourse. Moldenke rescued it. It was kicked a
few times, and dirty, but hadn't been stepped on. Bang was grateful
and swallowed it like a pill, saying, "Hey, Moldenke, Rock 'n' Roll.
Nothing serious. Let's get aboard." They walked on. The palms of
Moldenke's hands where he'd held the *flocculus* were beginning
to burn and blister. Everything about these neuts seemed to be
caustic.

"That was a close call, Dink," said Bang. "You know, life can go
on without a *flocculus*, but it becomes no more than a dull picnic. On
Susnr, those born without them grow up taller and sturdier than the
rest of us. They are tireless workers and ask no wage. They are
useful and necessary, but lack the vital spark, what you Americans
call . . . uh, what do you Americans call it?"

Moldenke said, "Spirit?"

Bang said, "No, no. More like soul, mind, inner sense, heart,
genius, psychic pneuma, something like that. To tell you the truth,
we neuts just call it Rock 'n' Roll."

Moldenke said, "That's interesting."

In the Sinatra Room they were seated near an oval viewing port at
a nice table and given a pitcher of *pflum*. It was as white as milk and
thinner than the street *pflum* he'd had earlier. Then a steward came
along, taking a pinch of some powder and sprinkling it into the
pflum, which foamed and thickened.

Bang said, "*Pflum* ain't *pflum* if you don't lace it with phosphate."

"I see," said Moldenke, pouring his tumbler full.

There was a crowd of rowdy Americans at the next table. They
were singing, "Artificial respiration . . . could've saved my Clemen-
tine . . . da da da da da da da da da da da da da da da."

Pigeons roosted in the *Diaxle*'s gantry, just above the ports,
where ugly piles of their droppings collected, somewhat obscuring
the view of Susnr.

The *Diaxle*'s engines were given the juice. It lifted out of its
gantry, drifted eastward with prevailing winds, then sank into a
trough of cooler air, twirling and whipping about. An American
fainted, spilling a pitcher of *pflum*. A steward carrying a tray of
pitchers slipped, spilling further *pflum*, until the dance floor was a
soupy, foaming mess. In time, the *Diaxle* steadied itself, ascending

smoothly. The floor was quickly mopped, and a pianola duo, the Chatterjees, took to the bandstand.

"Ah, the Chatterjees," said Bang. "They are pure styling."

A steward brought out platters of knuckle and tripe, pickled in a brine sauce. Moldenke helped himself.

The Chatterjees were playing "Red River Valley."

An American at the next table leaned over and whispered in Moldenke's ear, "The name is Donne, friend, out of Reno. Let me warn you about the ordinances against buddying up with neuts. They are very stiff, especially aboard the *Diaxle*. We are captained by Knabenshue, the best flyer in the business. He's not one to tolerate any trifles. My advice is to ditch that neut at your first convenience."

Moldenke said, "This neut is a name-guesser. We have a strict business arrangement. I wouldn't really call it buddying up."

"The law is the law," said Donne.

"Tell me," said Bang to Donne, "I'll wager a fin I can guess your handle. Double or nothing. Will you enter on a bet?"

Donne dragged his chair over to Moldenke's table and put a fin under the *pflum* pitcher. "The bet is laid," he said, "I don't think it can be done."

Bang made a show of falling into a trance, moaning as though reaching into some netherworld of names for the right one, and said, "Donne. They called you Donne Gone in normal school, am I right?"

"Yumping Yesus," said Donne, "you are a genuine article."

Bang tucked the fin into its pocket.

Donne poured himself a tumbler of *pflum*. "That's quite a neut you've latched onto. You can pack in a sack of dough when you get to Susnr. I admit, I'm envious."

Moldenke sucked casually on a smoked knuckle and listened to "Red River Valley." His giddiness had subsided. He was relaxed, confident his neut was going to be a money-maker.

The *Diaxle's* captain entered the Sinatra Room, aglow in white, followed by a squadron of mates and attendants. He'd come to show himself off to these American fat cats. He mingled and chatted. The Chatterjees stopped playing long enough to salute the captain with a bit of fancy pianola work. He dipped at the waist, almost genuflected, to show his gratitude.

"What a dunce," said Bang.

"You'd better curb that talk, neut," said Donne, "before you get us all in trouble. If Knabenshue calls at our table, sew your lips. One wrong word and we could spend Mummy Day in the lockup."

Knabenshue was going from table to table in a systematic way, bussing ladies on their cheeks, gladhanding it with American men, having a toast of *pflum* at every stop.

"He'll get here eventually," said Donne.

"I'm a little nervous," said Moldenke.

"Don't worry," said Bang. "Rock 'n' Roll."

The captain was just a table away. An American was saying to him, "We feel in safe hands with you skippering, sir. Here's to a decent Mummy Day."

Donne gave Bang a last warning about keeping silent.

The captain stood at their table. He smelled of the spiciest shaving lotion. When he smiled, his moustache curled, the ends brushing the sides of his nose. It was a comical effect. Bang giggled.

Donne said, "What a ship this is, Captain. It lifts you up like a loaf. It makes you feel yeasty and expansive. We are lucky to be here."

Knabenshue said, "Is that neut traveling with either of you?"

Moldenke said, "No."

Donne said, "No."

Bang said, "Pfft, Rock 'n' Roll. I never saw them before. Do you think a self-respecting neut would travel with a pair of obvious bounders like them? No, sir. Total strangers. We so happen to have been seated at the same table."

"I see you're sharing a pitcher of *pflum*," said the captain's mate. "Isn't that rather chummy?"

Knabenshue said, "Warrant them, and take that neut out back."

Warrants were written. Bang was cuffed and taken away.

Donne said, "So much for that neut, friend. They'll jerk out its *flocculus*, make a faithful worker out of it. The neuts never learn the finer points of protocol. What poor luck."

The Chatterjees took five.

Donne returned to his original table.

Moldenke went to the gentleman's room, where he found the fixtures so ultramodern he had little idea how to use them. There were shallow tubs arranged in a circle. He guessed that one was to lie in them, to do one's business in a more or less prone position. The tubs were slanted and troughed, the troughs leading to a central collecting drum, which apparently hadn't been emptied in some time, as it was all but overflowing with a horrible sludge. Moldenke waved his arm and a carpet of golden-winged flies arose, flew in perfect unison, like a flight of cedar waxwings, and then settled on the sludge again. Moldenke had never seen that particular species before. He knew they must be getting close to Susnr.

Moldenke searched the room, in a dim light, until he found a lever marked *EMPTY DRUM*. He pulled it. He heard an electric motor being engaged. The drum spun slowly, then with increasing speed, until it was spinning so fast sludge was being flung willy-nilly over the edge, and then a port beneath opened up and the sludge was ejected into the night air. For a moment before it closed, Moldenke caught a glimpse of Susnr. They were so close he could see litter blowing in the streets of Altobello. He could see Americans getting out of jitney cabs and going into fine restaurants.

Moldenke realized there was no sanitary way, other than undressing completely, to use the tubs. The modest person he was, he was happy no one else was in the room, and thankful the light was so dim. He undressed, hung his clothes on the hooks provided, and lowered himself into one of the tubs. As soon as he did, a jet of warm, soapy water came from a spigot above his head and washed down the trough with the strength of a rushing creek. It was a wonderful feeling. He relaxed his bladder completely, perhaps for the first time in his life. His bowels moved easily. The turds rolled like walnuts down the trough and into the empty drum. He splashed some of the soapy creek onto his anus and gave it a washing. In all, Moldenke had never had a more satisfying experience at toileting. He continued to laze there awhile, almost falling asleep. The soapy water, in time, ran clear. Moldenke rinsed himself clean and got out. At the end of the room, in a stall, he found a second lever, which said *MAGI-DRY*. He depressed it. A crazy, hot tingle swam up his spine. His eardrums gurgled. There was a flash of violet light. He was dry. *Good Christ*, he was thinking, *Hats off to the engineers of* Diaxle 1010.

He began dressing.

A passenger came in, saying, "How I despise these new types of crappers. It used to be the old squat and dump, but nowadays it's a regular cleansing rite."

"You have to admire the engineering," Moldenke said.

"Soon they'll have us in diapers," said the man.

Moldenke laughed. He was feeling the effects of the *pflum*.

The man introduced himself as Bunce, out of Prarie du Chien. "I saw them carting off your neut," he said. "Knabenshue hates to be the butt of anyone's funning. I happen to be the cousin of the captain's mate. I hear the inside gossip."

As Bunce tubbed himself, Moldenke finished dressing, tying his shoes two or three times in order to linger that much longer.

Bunce said, "When you get to Susnr, be sure to remember to visit the area east of Altobello. It has been settled by the Chinese. It is a must to eat at the Palace Orienta. Prices are steep to be sure, but they fry their dragon shrimp with artistry. And also there is the French camp, west of town, where you should catch the Exposition de Chrysanthememes et Fruits. They grow melons the size of submarines. You'll see a breathing bush, whose pods are like cubes of braised lamb."

Moldenke said, "That's amazing."

"I'll tell you what," said Bunce. "It may be that with a small payment to my cousin, we can spring your neut before we land. It would be a shame, also, if you missed Mummy Day because of those nasty warrants. Maybe a sawbuck or two will persuade my cousin to speak up on your neut's behalf. A neut without a *flocculus* is like a plum without a seed, all pulp and no future."

Moldenke took two fins out of his pocket. "This is all I can afford. The tickets were expensive."

Bunce said, "It isn't much. I'll see what I can do. Saving the *flocculus* may prove tricky. Knabenshue has everyone under his thumb. You should hear my cousin's poisoned gossip."

Moldenke put the money into Bunce's trousers and went back to his table, where he found Donne drinking alone. His American friends had gotten up to dance. The Chatterjees were playing a high-strung version of "Mood Indigo." A dance instructor was leading the Americans, saying, "Shuffle . . . jump . . . toe, shuffle . . . jump, toe, flap . . . ballchange, flap . . . ballchange." The Americans bounced up and down on the turtlewood floor, shoes clicking and clacking, arms flailing, faces plastered with uncertain grins.

Donne said, "I have fond memories of my first Mummy Day on Susnr. One night I was out walking. I ran into a family of neutrodynes camping near the city limits. They were baking a small pig in a clay oven. They treated me with respect and I stuffed myself with their cooking. Afterward we smoked a weed they called yocky-dock in bamboo pipes and listened to the campfire whistle. We lay back and gazed up at America. The neutrodynes admired it, found it luscious—its verdure, its blue seas and white-capped mountains, its industrial plants and rich farms."

Moldenke felt the *Diaxle* pinwheel and then loft, as if it were a great balloon. Its hull creaked like a new rocking chair.

Donne said, "We're almost there."

A steward was making the rounds, squeezing the bulb of an atomizer, spraying a pine-scented mist into the faces of passengers.

Donne said, "They always give you a little analgesic before landing. Take as much as you can. If the docking is rough, the *pflum* can dough up in your stomach.

Moldenke did as he was told. The effect was immediately calmative. He felt tensions abandon him.

A skin of crystal ice was forming on the port windows.

The Chatterjees were playing "Green Grow the Lilacs."

Most of the Americans were sound asleep.

Donne nodded in his chair.

There was a scratching at the window, a finger digging at the ice. Moldenke leaned closer. A wider portion of the ice crust fell away. Donne sat up, alert. It was Bang, wearing a frozen mask, holding for dear life to the window-facing.

"What a rotten thing," said Donne. "They must have opened a door and booted out your neut. That Knabenshue has a mean streak."

Suddenly, like a leaf in a storm, Bang was gone.

"There goes your quick buck," said Donne. "Too bad."

*   *   *

Soon after, the *Diaxle* touched down.

"We're here," said Donne.

The *Diaxle's* engines shut down, one by one. Moldenke counted nine of them. When the last went quiet, a belch of putrid smoke blackened the Sinatra Room, seeping in from every crevice. Passengers lay on the dance floor, like a herd of crocodiles on a flat rock, gulping what fresh air they could find. Moldenke and Donne were among them, head to head, spitting up *pflum*. Even so, Donne went on with his chronicle of Susnr's wonders. "Did you know that the Susnr neutrodynes claim there are three universes? Universe one lies in the singularity's future and is dominated by ordinary matter. Universe two lies in the singularity's past and is dominated by antimatter. Universe three lies in the spacelike regions of the nanosecond world and is inhabited by charmed particles racing faster than light."

The smoke abated. Passengers were able to kneel as the cloud lifted. Moldenke's knees were as numb as slugs. He wobbled off and took his place in the line forming at the exit. Donne said he had to make a quick trip to the gentlemen's and then would meet Moldenke at the Customs counter.

The Chatterjees were playing "Trochilia," the Susnr anthem.

*   *   *

When he reached the Customs counter, Moldenke was taken into custody by a sergeant-in-charge. He was made to sit on a stool and wait several hours, then placed in a motorized van and driven to the lockup. He'd seen no sign of Donne, or Bunce either. He spent the night there, along with forty other unfortunates, sleeping on municipal beds under prickly woolen blankets. He was rousted out at five o'clock and given a breakfast of cornsop and mineral tea, then marched into the chambers of a neutrodyne magistrate by the name of Yerkimer, where he was adjudged and fined his last sawbuck. He paid the fine and was driven, in the same van, back to the *Diaxle*. As the van passed the corner of 6th and Cherry, Moldenke thought he spotted Bunce, leaning against a limestone banquette, talking things over with a neutrodyne that bore a strong resemblance to Bang.

The *Diaxle's* engines were starting up when Moldenke was put aboard. He was brought to a lower cabin, far from the Sinatra Room. It was crowded and there were no windows. The Americans were crabbing at one another. The holiday was over.

Donne came down the aisle in the clutches of a sergeant, who was kind enough to let them sit together. Donne said, "I say we make the best of it. Another year will come, another Mummy Day. It won't be the last. Next time, why don't we tour the neutrodyne farm belt. They say they've started setting out young Russian mulberries in east-west windrows. They will grow to a height of thirty-five feet and make prodigious amounts of berries, thus attracting every kind of hungry bird to feast on the grasshoppers and the army worms. The neuts can be ingenious when they want to."

The steward came down the aisle with his atomizer.

Donne said, "You know, on Susnr, a raisin dropped in a glass of fresh *pflum* will move up and down continuously, and a ball of steel will sometimes bounce higher than one made of rubber."

Moldenke took a nosefull of analgesic.

A dwarfish little neut strutted up the aisle.

Donne said, "There's one of those nasty banty neuts. I had an awful experience with one of them. This was years ago, when I was living in Altobello. It jumped into my yard from the fence. I thought, at first, it was a doll, thrown there by a neighboring kid. I went near it. Its breath had an alien stink, like rancid fat. A milky substance bubbled from its snoot. I poked it with a sharp stick. It roared up and got on my shoulder. It commanded me to go into the catbriers. 'Comb those catbriers over there until you find me a dozen bull crickets,' it said, sitting on my shoulder, its thorny legs so daintily crossed, the feet lodged in my top pocket. I spent much of the day feeding bull crickets to the banty, watching it grind the pitiful things in its ugly little craw."

The banty went by peacefully and gave them no trouble.

An American, sitting behind them, said, "Can you imagine, we'll be back in Reno by midnight? How can you possibly praise the *1010* enough?"

The steward, returning up the aisle, let Moldenke have a second breath of analgesic.

Donne said, "What can you say?"

Moldenke said, "Rock 'n' Roll."

EPIDEMIC

Ninotchka Rosca

It occurred to Lazaro Reyes, M.D., that if he could kill one child—just one child—everything would be all right again. The problem was to find *the* child. Having found him, Lazaro would know what to do: a quick glide of the scalpel across the throat, the body hung by its feet over the garden faucet drain. He was sure his hands wouldn't tremble; he would not hesitate. Such was his rage against that face of innocence: black mop of hair, brown-gold eyes, snub nose and full lips, atop a lanky body within filthy, loose clothes.

On the accursed day reality turned brittle, a series of omens had warned him. First, his pot of cattleya, those wellbred orchids, had teetered on his bedroom windowsill and, seemingly by itself, slid out the open window to smash on the driveway below. On his way to the bathroom, his feet had been snagged by his ten-year-old daughter's skateboard which, propelled by an immense kick, had zoomed down the corridor, to the stairs and into infinity. Then, his air-conditioned car, usually well-mannered, coughed, spat smoke and uttered a terrible bleat at the turn of the ignition key. It died, leaving him stranded in his own garage, for his daughters had taken the second car while the third, of course, was with his wife who was visiting her parents in the province. His own chauffeur was still on vacation, which could have explained the car's tantrum but that still left him running for the diesel public bus at nine in the morning to wedge himself into the packed humanity of offensive smells inside.

The bus had taken him to the shopping center, where he hoped to catch a cab. Despite the hour, a million people were aboard, marching in and out of shops, standing on the curb, darting forward with flailing hands and managing to lure one cab after another away from him. The summer heat and the noise made him light-headed. His collar, limp with sweat, was a comatose snake about his neck. He was certain his blood pressure was rising. A sudden pain in the area of his kidneys jolted him into turning around. But it was only a look, a stare, from a boy, age ten. "Want me to call you a cab, mister?" the boy asked. He used the proper third-person plural pronoun of the native language, signaling his immeasurable respect for the being of Lazaro Reyes, M.D.

At his nod, the boy took off, sprinting through and among the moving vehicles. Lazaro lost him in the confusion of the traffic. He thought he spotted him, playing matador with a rampaging bus, but when the kid raised his face, Lazaro saw it was the wrong child. Then another boy crossed the highway, zigzagging through black exhaust fumes, but he had a pack of cigarettes in his hand and was selling them, stick by stick, to harassed drivers of minibuses. Wrong kid. Lazaro shifted his weight from foot to foot; it was taking quite a while—fifteen, twenty minutes. Again that jolt in his kidney area. He looked over his right shoulder. Another boy of the same age, almost a twin of the first. "Want a cab, mister?" The same articulation of respect.

Lazaro nodded; the boy took off. After five minutes, he was back, leading a cab, his waving right hand laying an imaginary red carpet toward Lazaro on the curb. The doctor pulled out his wallet, untangled a peso bill and handed this to the boy, who, with a grin and a flourish, opened the passenger door. At that instant, the first boy came running, leading another cab through traffic and throng. "Sir, sir," he called out.

"Too late," Lazaro told him, just as the second cab eased itself behind the first.

The boy's face mirrored the shock of those words. It seemed to Lazaro that, in the twenty minutes the boy had been gone, he had managed to get himself even filthier. Sweat streaks ran from his temples to his jaws and the skin above his upper lip was wet and glistening.

"Oh, sir," the boy wailed. "You could've waited."

Now the second boy threw him a look of remonstrance and Lazaro quivered in anger and embarrassment. There seemed to have been a rule of conduct here, whose violation had disturbed the universe. The second boy said he would give the first a commission and to Lazaro's surprise, apologized for having stolen the first boy's customer. The elaborate procedure alerted him; he felt he was expected to make amends, perhaps to add to the remuneration given. But someone jumped into the second cab, which zoomed away while the driver of the first leaned on his horn and shouted, harsh and demanding. At that instant, a voice cried out for a cab. The second boy nudged the first, telling him to go for it.

Lazaro was already in the cab when he saw the boy streaking through the traffic. The light turned green, his cab leapt forward, its snarl masked by an even louder shriek of brakes, a thin scream and a boil of noise from the corner where he had last seen the boy. The driver stopped just long enough for a look. Lazaro saw it, too—two dirty soles, toes to the sky, on the asphalt. Beyond, two black truck tires. "Well, he certainly bought it," the driver said. "Must've been desperate." He shook his head, gave a horselaugh at his own un-called for sympathy and began the run from the shopping center to the business section of the city where Lazaro Reyes, M.D., held office.

*   *   *

His nurse-secretary had managed to keep his patients waiting. They were mostly minor cases: measles for the seven-year-old son of a friend, bronchial infection for a middle-aged woman, gout attacks for a businessman. He liked his clientele, their neatness of manner and clothes, their obedience. He spent a little more time than was warranted by their various illnesses, taking his pleasure in the handling of their bodies and in the clean scent of their flesh. Even their fevers were perfumed.

It was a ruse, of course, this lingering over minor complaints. He was putting off the Colonel, who waited outside, alone and at ease, smoking cigarettes. It was nearly lunchtime when Lazaro admitted to himself that the Colonel wouldn't leave to return another day and so he signaled his nurse-secretary to let the man in.

The Colonel was neither too tall nor too short and had a forgetta-ble face. He was somewhat stocky, having put on weight these last two years. The good life had made his chest rotund; Lazaro saw that in a few years, he would acquire the profile of the aging: barrel torso on spindly legs. The Colonel suffered this inspection calmly and then surprised Lazaro by saying that he was taking the good doctor to lunch. Today. This minute. Nervously, Lazaro glanced at his cal-endar and saw what the Colonel had seen. There were no appoint-ments listed until three o'clock.

They took the Colonel's car to a nearby Japanese restaurant. La-zaro was partial to Japanese food, believing it healthier than any other cuisine. How the Colonel had known this, Lazaro didn't ask. The Colonel decided to park right in front of the place—either because it was convenient or because his army license plates al-lowed him to park in no-parking zones. As they left the car, Lazaro felt that jolt in his kidney area again and when he looked over his shoulder, there was the boy. "Clean your car, sir?" A deep and abiding respect.

Lazaro looked at the Colonel, who nodded. The boy ran for his pail and rags and in a little while, they could see him through the misty front windows of the restaurant (humidity condensed in the air conditioning) wiping the hood of the car. The Colonel ordered sake and teriyaki for himself and told Lazaro to take the sushi since he liked the stuff. Sushi was expensive.

The Colonel said he needed a good doctor, one absolutely trustworthy. Lazaro sighed. He knew, from professional gossip, what kind of medical work military men required. Usually fixing up a girlfriend or two, at little or no cost. Lazaro had been spared for some years now but with doctors immigrating like the proverbial Capistrano swallows (where was Capistrano?), he could be grateful for that respite.

But the Colonel had other things in mind. Six of his men were in a fix (VD? thought Lazaro) and had to be bailed out as quickly, as legally as possible. They had gone on an A-and-S raid and, being flushed with success, had taken it into their heads to have a little fun, to push their luck a little further. And to cut a long story short, there was the body now and they needed a death certificate—correction, an unassailable, legal death certificate since the relatives were bitching like crazy and there wasn't time to fix *them*.

Lazaro's ears felt plugged with wax. What, he asked, was an A-and-S? The Colonel smiled. Arrest and seizure. And the body? The Colonel's lips moved very carefully, saying that the boy who bought it had frightened himself to death, his men really had no intentions of harming him. It appeared, from initial investigation, that the kid had scared himself enough to swallow his tongue and choke on it. Impossible, Lazaro said.

The flat declaration hung across them even as the steam from the food remained in the air—an ephemeral trellis. The Colonel looked at Lazaro, and Lazaro, looking into the Colonel's eyes, saw himself. He would have to see the body, he said finally and didn't know why heat rose to his cheeks. Confused, he lowered his eyes to the sushi.

The boy was waiting beside the car, his pail at his feet. Lazaro saw he had rinsed and wrung out his rags, which were now folded with care at the pail's bottom. The car was clean. The Colonel scanned it with his eyes and declared himself not satisfied; he could have asked one of his men in the motor pool for a better job for free. In the end, though, he tossed a coin to the boy and barked at him to take himself off before he was arrested for vagrancy.

The boy didn't look at the coin in his palm. He stared at the Colonel before his head swiveled toward Lazaro Reyes, M.D. The brown-gold eyes were devoid of accusation. "Sir, didn't you have any left-overs?" the boy asked. "They would've wrapped them for you. For me." Before Lazaro could answer, the Colonel barked and he found himself sliding into the front passenger seat. Lazaro, said the Colonel, could see the body now, since it was still an hour before his next appointment. Without waiting for the doctor's answer (indeed, Lazaro felt he didn't have any), the Colonel drove to the camp.

The Colonel preceded him into the morgue. Stopping by a mortuary table, he swept the covering sheet off the cadaver and stepped aside. Although an effort had been made to clean the body, an odor still clung to its lanky arms and feet. There were contusions on the chest and back, rupture and bleeding in the anal region, hematomas on the thighs and legs. The windpipe was crushed. Lazaro remarked on this to the Colonel, who replied that that meant the boy had died of asphyxiation, no doubt because of fright. Lazaro fixed his eyes on the toes; black matter rimmed the nails. After a while, he nodded. It was asphyxiation. The Colonel coughed—a delicate sound of approval—and ordered the sergeant to bring in the prepared death certificate.

At that instant, Lazaro's eyes jumped to the face. It was the boy, of course. He nerved himself to reach down and push the right eyelid up: a brown-gold pupil stared without seeing. He withdrew his hand, but the eyelid stuck and the eye went on looking into infinity. The sergeant entered and Lazaro unclipped his gold pen to sign the certificate; it was already prepared. As he scribbled his name, he asked the Colonel if the kid hadn't been too young to be . . . well, involved in a mess. The Colonel agreed but it seemed that the group in the raided house had adopted the boy from off the streets, giving him food whenever he dropped in, teaching him how to read and write as well as a host of other nonsense. He was indeed young— that was why the Colonel's men had thought him easy, that he would blab whatever odds and ends he had picked up at that den of iniquity. Unfortunately, the loyalty of the young could be so absolute, so inflexible. The Colonel sighed. After a while, he added: there were too many children. A virtual epidemic.

*   *   *

Lazaro couldn't help but admire the Colonel's perspicuity of phrase. An epidemic of children. Those brown-gold eyes, snub nose, full lips—dark calyx of misery—replicating themselves throughout the landscape. As he paced back and forth in his office, waiting for his next patient, he found his memory besieged by that face (those faces?) lurking within frames of remembered scenes. The boy sprouted from the garbage heap glimpsed by the eye's corner as Lazaro marshaled his daughters to the theater. Hordes of boys running through shopping centers, looking for customers, as he glanced at a silk shirt in the display window. The boy again fallen asleep beside his vendor's box of cigarettes as Lazaro exited from a night-club. Boys squatting on the sidewalk, backs propped on walls, their eyes crinkled against the noonday heat as Lazaro drove past in an air-conditioned car. The boy bawling, snot running through the fingers of the hand he held against his face, his keening as heartbroken as only a child's weeping could be.

An epidemic, Lazaro thought. As he worked on his next patient (tapping his chest, listening to the hiss of air in the lungs), he found himself trembling with the thought of one of those microbes (those faces) reaching full growth, the lanky body suddenly insolent with a young man's virility. The boy (no boy now but a man) would loiter in front of theater lobbies, looking over the girls who entered, including perhaps (or maybe it was a certainty) one or both of Lazaro's daughters. In such a manner would vengeance be extracted and the karmic law fulfilled. Lazaro froze, his muscles trembling as though he were being pricked by needles from head to foot.

He got rid of the patient with a few words and a prescription. He told the nurse he needed some rest and closed the door to his office. The silence was that of a mortuary. He rummaged through his equipment, testing scalpels. It seemed to him that if he could only find the first one, the original—the owner of that metastasizing face—he could do away with the problem. First, the original, he said to himself. Then, its descendants—one after another. And the world would be safe for clean, well-fed children.

As the scalpel cut through the skin of his thumb, he acknowl-edged this debt to himself: his life had been spent in the removal of disease from the pleasant-odored flesh of his patients. In its total eradication, whether by surgery, sterilization or medication. The blood that seeped out of him was rich and thick—pure, clean ichor. Indicator of health. Of well-being. Laying the scalpel down, he cleaned the wound carefully, his lip-corner jumping from the bite of the peroxide, and dressed it, his left hand clever in its manipulation of gauze and plaster. He opened his office door, showed the nurse the thumb and said it was an accident; he was upset and was going home unless there was a major case. There wasn't. As Lazaro turned off the desk lamp, his eyes fell on the scalpel, its tip tinged red. With a guilty shiver, he picked it up and slid it, its blade naked, into his shirt pocket.

His ride home (the nurse called a cab) was marked by the boy whose face (faces) appeared at every street corner. Lazaro Reyes, M.D., despite the intervening glass pane of the car window, felt the touch of those brown-gold eyes, those rather neutral, rather gentle, never-surprised eyes. Anticipation was in the air; something, something was expected to happen, was already happening. Lazaro leaned forward and told the driver to speed up.

The second car in the driveway told him his daughters were home: sweet Liza, 18, and happy Grace, 10. He paid the cab driver with relief, walked up to the front door and used his keys. When he pushed the door open, rock music wedged through and smashed against his chest—a solid haze of sound that sent the blood pounding in his temples. Still, he exhaled with gratitude at this familiarity and, entering, walked towards the stairs. That was when the floor convulsed and his feet flew up, so that he landed on his backside on the marble floor. His coccyx shriveled with the pain that rushed up his spine to his head and eyes. Through the clang of pain in his head, he saw the skateboard and with the roar of a beast, he sprang, clutched at it and hurled it at the stereo. There was a terrific sound as the record broke, the noise of its destruction coursing through the amplifiers. Then, he heard his own voice, with its incredible filth, storming towards his ten-year-old, who had rushed to turn off the stereo. He saw her bud of a mouth paralyzed open, her brown-gold eyes with their dilated pupils. A split-second image which became a little kid rushing in tears up the stairs. At that instant, Lazaro remembered the kick he had given the skateboard that morning.

Upstairs, a door slammed shut. Lazaro knew she was weeping the way she always cried: sitting on the edge of her bed, her face buried in her hands, the tears oozing between her fingers. He would kneel before her, take her hands from her face and lick those tears away, absorbing into his own body all the ache of her passage through the years. She, tickled by his tongue, would start laughing, and soon her eyes would be shining again and all her features would be restored to order.

Calmness filled Lazaro—an almost dreamy tranquility as his own sweat cooled his body. Step by step, he ascended the stairs and moved toward his ten-year-old daughter's room. He paused before reaching for the doorknob and touched his shirt pocket, feeling there the scalpel biting into the cloth. For wouldn't it be awful, awful, if upon his walking into that room, upon his prying away the hands covering the face of that figure of grief, he discovered the full extent of the boy's vengeance? What if the face beyond that barricade of fingers, the face which would blossom to meet his eyes, were the boy's?

FERGUSON'S WAGON

Barton Wilcox

E verybody who knew about it—and that was everyone in Breemsburg—told somebody else about the Ferguson place. Inquisitive
Saturday or Sunday afternoon guests might even be loaded into the
car and driven by the Fergusons just to save the explanation.

Gray Ferguson's green thumb, when it had not been counting out
change at Ferguson's Hardware, had turned the Ferguson lot into a
virtual arboretum that Gray's son, Robert Jr., would one day describe to the readers of his *Techtown Beacon* column as "aglut and
agog with beauty," before going on to catalog the midsummer sce-
nery. It was like an inventory of the unsold seed packets left over
from Ferguson's Hardware: zinnia, black-eyed Susan, verbena to-
renia, Sweet William, tithonia, stock and statice, phlox, salvia,
snapdragon, a gaudy collar of portulaca around modest petunia,
indiscriminate nemesia, lupine, love-lies-bleeding, lobelia, impa-
tiens, hollyhock and honesty, heliotrope, mums, dahlia and corn-
flower, alyssum and aster. Those were just the annuals.

Add the faithful glads, wood hyacinth, and iris towering, cycla-
men clinging, snowdrop in patches, tulip, begonia, crocus, sea lav-
ender, primrose, True Solomon's Seal, Christmas rose and red-hot
poker, mayapple, lupine, the lily—which Gray called "The Robert
Jr."—burning bush, daisy, a veritable field of poppies for general
commemoration, and a reservoir of peonies for specific graves, all
reinforced by bugbane, baby's breath, and agapanthus africanus.
Among others.

The lot was anchored by euonymus, hibiscus, pyracantha, yew,
fir, holly, crape myrtle, rose of Sharon, cedar, maple, and ash. A
plaster fountain and a few ceramic deer completed the pastoral.

So many successful high school science projects had been gleaned
from the Ferguson grounds that the Fergusons could have claimed
something dried and matted and framed in nearly a quarter of the
attics in Breemsburg. As a result, the Ferguson gardens had become
the trademark of values too often forgotten or long neglected,

such as retirement as an end in itself. This was documented in a *Breemsburg Daily News* feature quoting Gray Ferguson: "I never had a cent when I was growing up, but we always had us a nice yard." The Fergusons had framed and hung this over the mantel in the living room of the modest white bungalow, which stood two city blocks from its nearest neighbor, right on the edge of the Breemsburg city limits.

It was true that the Fergusons were luckier than many, because they had their health. Bullheaded Gray Ferguson—nicknamed for his gray crew cut or his gray work clothes, most had forgotten which—had refused prostate problems, kidney stones, bursitis, arthritis, back trouble, corns, bunions and constipation. He had suffered a heart attack, but no one had taken it seriously because everyone knew that if you got past the first one you had it made. And after almost twenty years of marriage, Gray and Ethel had a son, who was given Gray's real name, Robert, and whom no one in Breemsburg would have remembered at all if he hadn't become a celebrity.

Gray ran the hardware store every Saturday, as well as the other five days, except for the two weeks each year he drove the three of them to the Ozarks, a vacation they eventually gave up because of Robert Jr.'s exotic allergies—it turned out that Robert Jr. was allergic to Missouri—and because of his temperament.

They were quite happy when the boy was an infant. Then he had begun to want things. Gray had never known anyone to want so many things and do so little—besides making other people miserable—to get them. Gray had learned how to work during the Depression, and it distressed him that his son would grow up completely ignorant of this, despite the fact that he was told often enough that he should remember.

The boy was inundated with erector sets, chemistry sets, microscopes, footballs, basketballs, paints, cameras, etc. What he could not burn, he smashed. What he could not destroy outright, he left outdoors to rust. If something he poured down the pipes did not clog them or eat them away, then he applied it to the finish on the family station wagon with some dire result.

Gray was good at fixing things, and he looked at Robert Jr.'s products of destruction as challenges rather than annoyances. Because he enjoyed them, he felt guilty about the evenings he spent by himself in the basement, repairing toys for a boy who was to him more a poor idea for a child than an actual child.

This was eventually detected by the mother. One evening she announced from the top of the basement steps that Robert Jr. wanted his father to show him how to play football. He had been made fun of at school. Gray took his son into the backyard and showed him how to hold the ball. Then he backed up a few feet and motioned for Robert Jr. to throw it. The boy contorted his body as if throwing a twelve-pound shot instead of a football and then unwound, flipping the ball back over his head. Gray took the ball and backed up again, cocking his arm a few times in demonstration while explaining the importance of a spiral. When he finally let go of the ball, it sailed the short distance in a perfect spiral and struck Robert Jr. square in the forehead, knocking him over backwards like a milk bottle.

After some warm-up gasps, Robert Jr. finally got his lungs behind his screams, screams that could be heard in town, Gray thought. The mother appeared at the door.

"Why so rough, Gray? Why do you have to torture him?"

Robert Jr. was escorted into the living room to the bosom of sympathy provided by Ethel's bridge club. Gray stayed in the kitchen. "What happened, little man?" said one saccharine voice. Through the door, he saw his son becoming more and more abstract, looking perfectly at home among the nutcups and crystal dessert dishes. There was something disturbing and at the same time familiar about his son's face, but familiar in the way that a stranger can be familiar. Gray still had the football in his hands, and it suddenly came back to him. He saw the face of Forrest Riley, a banker who had grown up with Gray.

It had been a hot summer day and he had been making his dollar pushing the mower around the Riley's great lawn, when he had come across a football. Judging by the yellow grass beneath it, it had been left out in the weather for some time. No one was home, so he took out his pocketknife and punched a small hole in the inner tube near the stitching. Later, he showed it to old man Riley, and told him that he had hit it with the mower but that he thought he could fix it. The gentleman swore—not at Gray but at his son who was not there—and replied that if he could fix it he could have it. Since nearly everything Gray owned was something he had fixed, there was no doubt that he could.

Later, Forrest arrived with his mother at Gray's uncle's house. Weeping and breath-holding had made apples of Forrest's cheeks.

"You stole my football."

When Gray explained, Forrest's mother said, "There is a Depression on. When the Depression is over, the Rileys will be able to afford gifts for hired help."

Gray had gone to the back and had taken the ball away from his cousins and returned it to Forrest, who tucked it under his arm and did an about-face with his mother. Gray's cousins had not been able to wait to tell all of this to Gray's uncle, who then beat him for being a thief.

Every Sunday after church Gray went fishing, dragging Robert Jr., who would sulk behind his black and white Zebco Jr. rod-and-reel outfit for ten minutes, then pick it up to thrash the water, then abandon it for the more efficient method of heaving in rocks.

"Robert!" Gray would say to his son, "Sit down, you're scaring the goddamned fish away."

"I hate fishing," Robert would say.

"You don't hate it when you're catching fish, so sit down and shut up."

"I do too."

"Then why did you ask to come?"

"I didn't."

"You did too."

"I didn't either."

"You did too, goddamnit, or I wouldn't have brought you. Sit down and shut up."

"I didn't either."

It would go on this way every time. And because of the arguing, no one ever caught any fish. Not even the innocent bystanders. And Gray Ferguson hated that the fishing rights of innocent bystanders might be interfered with, especially best-liked citizens in Breemsburg.

After neither threat nor cajoling could cultivate in Robert Jr. an interest in fishing, Gray would set his son free. Whenever his son was set free, he would roam the banks of the Breemsburg reservoir like an untrained Irish setter, gathering weeds that he would lay like garlands on his father's tackle box, shrilling girlishly at every passing insect, finally pleading to go home. His father's fishing buddies would look over from where they sat on plastic lawn furniture or overturned buckets and shake their heads. They knew that some boys were just not meant to fish, but they also knew that it was the duty of the fathers to try to make them.

By the time Robert Jr. turned ten, these fishing trips had been abandoned by an unspoken agreement between father and son: one Sunday the father did not ask the son to go fishing with him; the son did not complain. The father tried the same thing the next Sunday, and it worked again. This went on for some time, until the mother noticed.

There was undefinable mutual attraction that she felt should exist between father and son, no matter what, if only because the two bodies often passed close to each other. Common blood should draw them together as the willow is drawn to the invisible spring. Once she had formed this principle—and it was a long time in its formulation—it became clear to them what she was thinking.

Ethel would catch Gray sitting at the kitchen counter probing with his index finger the evil-looking mixture of hooks and plastic insects that inhabited the tiers of his tackle box.

"Wouldn't you rather spend the day with your son?"

This was one of those things that, despite Gray's size, he had no defense for. His wife would indicate the pathetic figure on the sofa, bumping the toes of his tennis shoes together or staring at the neighbor's house through the cataracts of the aged living room window.

"Going to the creek, Robert," the father would say, then the boy's head-shaking and the father's raising of his shoulders in a didn't-I-tell-you-so shrug, which over the years had blended into a single gesture.

"You could do something *he* wants to do."

"He doesn't want to do anything."

"Every boy wants to do *something*."

"Not this one."

"Go with your father," Robert Jr.'s mother would tell him. "All the other boys go fishing with their dads."

"I don't want to be like everybody else. I hate everybody else."

It was true that the boy had seemed bored with them from birth. He never asked to spend time with his father, nor did he ever complain that his father spent too little time with him. Dark and brooding, watchful of something—no one was sure what—he seemed content to be an only child. He was made for it. He was absent from school a lot and required frequent hospital visits. He thrived on the greenish hospital light and preferred thin, colorless food.

Before the arrival of the Radio Flyer, the boy did want at least one thing in life: he wanted to go to the amusement park. And once he was old enough to discover that his father was the vehicle for getting into the amusement park, Robert Jr. occasionally formed with him a volatile bond, made and broken on the probability of whether or not they would go.

Gray hated the amusement park. It had been there from before he was Robert Jr.'s age, but the only time he had gone there as a child was with a group of children, including the wealthy Riley children (who had no doubt been forced by their father to invite him), though he hadn't a cent to spend on the rides. When he wouldn't ride, and the other children taunted him, he was inclined to pretend he was afraid rather than admit that he had no money.

To Gray, a man saving for retirement, there was something profligate about going to the amusement park more than twice a year—it was just the idea of it—even if no money was spent there. The fact was, Robert Jr. was terrified of the rides and wanted only to watch, but he wanted very badly to watch.

It was the idea of the father—once—to *make* the son ride. One of the things that Gray had pieced together about being a father was that chance could not be trusted to teach a son certain important lessons. Gray was fairly certain, for example, that his son would never properly mature unless he had been scared half to death at least a couple of times before the age of twelve. So he saw in the amusement park rides, with their cheap paint, vaguely familiar gargoyles, and thin coat of butter and gasoline, a valuable lesson. But once this lesson was halfway entered into—that is, screaming child being forced like a kicking veal calf onto a miniature train or ferris wheel—it was reaffirmed in the mind of every bystander who turned toward the commotion rising above the cacophony of the park that a child pitted against his father is stronger than his father teamed with any number of amusement park generators.

About this time the wagon arrived. Gray had meant to order a wheelbarrow for the hardware store stock, but had put down the number for a wagon by mistake. On the verge of sending it back, he had a second thought, which included his son sitting at the window, staring into his own indolent universe. It was nowhere near the boy's birthday or Christmas, and therefore it was hard to justify the expense of this Radio Flyer, even at cost.

But there was no getting around it: it was some wagon. The aroma of enamel rose from the musty box, and reminded Gray of the first factory-made boxes he had opened for Ethel's father in this very store. He had been no older than Robert Jr. was now. They were packing crates instead of cardboard boxes. In Gray's mind were Ethel's father's fingers, resting like bricks on his shoulder, and the cold pry bar, the angel hair with the cast iron nestled in it. And he had known even then what he wanted and knew that he would inherit this place and a whole world that would last forever with it, where he would be neither hungry nor alone, among the bins of seed corn and grass seed, nail kegs, spools of rope, sweeping the concrete floor with a large push broom while other children played. That was the smell that rose up from the cardboard carton containing the Radio Flyer. It said *Radio Flyer* in white streamlined letters across the slick flank of the wagon. Someone was still making something like they used to. It was some wagon. When the aroma of new enamel rose from the musty box and the rubbery paint of the wagon bed squeaked under his touch, Gray Ferguson figured that no boy could resist the brazen black and red toy. And he realized that this was what he wanted: something his son could not resist, something that would seduce him into normality.

Gray placed the assembled wagon on the concrete slab in front of the garage door and then retreated to the house. With its tongue laid back on its bed and the pinstripes trailing behind the letters on the side, the wagon fairly quivered with motion.

From the window Gray Ferguson watched the boy lug his schoolbooks down the gravel drive to the back door, as he always did, and stop in front of the wagon. The stiff corduroy stood out flat from his spindly legs, as did the starched short sleeves of purple madras from his arms. It was as though a thin, vituperative butterfly had landed.

The boy circled the wagon and on his second turn even gave it a kick, the way his father had kicked the tires of the family station wagon when it was still on the lot.

The boy dropped his books in the grass, stuck one leg into the wagon bed, and with the other dragged himself and the wagon through the thick gravel of the driveway, looking to his father like a cricket missing a leg.

Gray Ferguson ran the length of the house, stopping from window to window to follow his son. If the wagon were like everything else he had owned, Robert Jr. would drop it in favor of the living room sofa after an hour or so. But now the boy plowed the driveway with a vitality his father had never known he had in him. Gray's heart pounded as if a trophy bass hung by a lip just out of his reach; it struck him that he was a father.

When the boy hit the thin gravel near the end of the drive, he picked up speed, and Gray Ferguson realized too late that his newly rediscovered son was going too fast to stop before he ran onto the highway. He could only watch from behind the front door curtains as the wagon reached the road and his son vaulted out of it, arms thrust into the air, sending the brand-new twenty-dollar wagon straight under the wheels of a garbage truck which was making its way out of town to the Breemsburg dump.

*   *   *

"Fix it," Robert Jr. demanded.

"Not this time, goddamn you," Gray said with narrowed eyes.

Robert Jr. narrowed his eyes back at his father. "I want my wagon," he said.

"Why do you have to aggravate him?" Ethel asked.

"I never aggravated him."

"But you did. You're just like a child."

"Goddamn it, Ethel. I am not a child!" he said, getting very red in the face.

Ethel smiled. Gray thought of the twenty-dollar investment moldering away, hanging from the garage rafters, and relented.

After that the boy seemed intent on making an otherwise normal preoccupation morbid. The wagon was with him always. He took it to school every day, even though the other boys laughed at him and even beat him for it. In fact, the more he was beaten, the more he clung to the wagon and the more brazenly he paraded with it. For a year there was a series of suspensions of different boys over the abuse of Robert Ferguson Jr. He and his wagon had become a sort of institution.

That it was crippled and didn't roll quite true only increased Robert Jr.'s affection for it, and before the first year was out, Gray had to replace the wheels, which had turned to black rubber shreds. Of course, he had to order these from the Radio Flyer factory, and they cost more than the wagon itself. But the boy had given up the sofa, had for the most part stopped his whining, and had even gained some color and incipient muscle. As long as the wagon was therapeutic, the parents left the boy and his wagon alone.

Then one hot spring afternoon, Gray Ferguson looked out his shop window to see Robert Jr. and his wagon challenging a large purple Buick. The sedan was swooping over the hills into town, swallowing the road under its fat chrome beak. Robert Jr. sat bathtub-style, his spider-legs bent, knees pointed port and starboard, the tongue of the wagon pulled up to his mayfly chest. With a calculating frown, the boy pushed off at the top of the grade, which began in front of the Ferguson house and leveled off at the concrete bridge over the creek. He was directly in the center of the wrong lane.

Gray dropped his screwdriver and hammered the thin, dingy panes of the shop window with his fist and called to the boy. But the wagon stayed on course, issuing toy wagon thunder as it picked up speed. Robert Jr. had hunkered down jockey-style, the tongue of the wagon now at his nose.

As much as he remembered his terror, Gray Ferguson remembered the feeling of legs that hadn't run in a decade moving under him. By the time he reached the yard, crying out as he ran and flapping his arms at the road as if to frighten the Buick back into the hills, the wagon with his son in it had neared the bridge; the Buick had just crested the hill and rushed to meet it.

And here the memory became enormous, as if the hurtling Buick and the bug-bone chassis of a boy's wagon were particles which upon approaching each other had changed the matter of Gray Ferguson's mind, so that there existed in it many possible realities, one in which the car had swerved, several in which it hadn't.

The escape of the Radio Flyer was so close that Gray Ferguson was momentarily convinced that in some other world, the car *hadn't* swerved. Somewhere there existed a man without a son. That his son had been stuck to the grill of a Buick was nearly as real to him as the fact that Robert Jr. had beaten the car to the bridge and crossed it, reining the wagon hard to the shoulder, riding two wheels, tipping out far enough to graze the bumper with his rice-paper skull, and leaping, as a catfish might leap from Gray's own hands, back into life.

For as much as Gray could not understand it, there was a smirk of calm resolution and confidence on the boy's face, the remnants of which were only slowly fading as he twisted his wagon tongue homeward. And this look was so strange—but at the same time so beautiful—that the father let his rage fill him so that the fright fomenting in his chest would not overtake him.

"That car . . . that car . . . almost killed you," he said between the hammer blows that were landing behind his sternum.

"No he didn't," the boy answered flatly. "I was on my roller coaster." He lowered his head and swept the road with a filthy tennis shoe.

Gray Ferguson felt the anger rush into his arms, and he seized the tongue of the Radio Flyer. "Give me that goddamned wagon."

But Robert Jr. latched onto the tail end and dug his feet into the deep gravel.

The boy knew that only tears would save his wagon. He concentrated, and with his head bowed, mustered them, though they were nothing like those that came spontaneously in the face of the Kiddieland Tilt-a-Whirl.

So they stood there, the distance between them setting up like cooling lead. Over the crest of the next hill into town the big purple Buick rushed on, while on the ancient and dilapidated bridge leading out of Breemsburg, Gray Ferguson sat down hard on the bed of his son's wagon just as the hammer in his chest took two more quick blows and stopped.

They were discovered at the bottom of the hill by a garbage collector, who, returning from the Breemsburg dump, had seen the prostrate man on wheels and a skinny little boy crying, "Get off!" while trying with everything he had to push the unwanted cargo out of the wagon.

With help from her brothers, the boy's mother pried the wagon from Robert Jr.'s grip and placed it upside-down on the rafters of the garage.

*   *   *

It wasn't taken down again until Gray Ferguson added it to the compendium of forgotten gear he had laid, as it were, at the feet of his son, now twenty-five.

Robert Jr. stood by impatiently smoking Bel Airs in the door of the sweltering garage. He was loathe to look at the stuff and was here only because his mother had begged him not to make a scene before he left.

"It would be nice if you took something," she suggested. "Bear with him. I know there's nothing out there that you want, but you know he can't bear to throw anything away and it would be nice if you pretended and accepted something. One thing."

"Actually, I could use some money," he replied.

It was all stuff that had no place on the pegboard above the workbench at the back of the garage, no red silhouettes of the familiar shapes. It lay there, this stuff, awaiting miraculous resurrection the day Christ returned and all tools were made whole, or the day Gray Ferguson got around to restoring them. Gray got a certain amount of satisfaction in having beaten Jesus to the punch.

"Did I tell you that our banker—you know Forrest Riley—brought some people by to look at my flowers?" Gray asked him as he sifted through the items on the spotless garage floor.

"Yeah, you told me that one."

"This was just the other day, though."

Robert Jr. picked a piece of tobacco from the end of his tongue and looked at it.

"That's one thing I want to tell you," his father went on. "Wherever you live, take care of it. When I was a kid we never had a cent, but we always had a nice yard. Always, always, Robert . . ."

Robert Jr. was not looking at his father's junk collection but at the station wagon in which he would finally leave home after having graduated marginally from Techtown State.

The collection was ready for a Noah's ark of bygone technology: two broken typewriters, two broken desk lamps, twin semifunctional hydraulic jacks, and a pair of crutches, among other less symmetrical groups.

"You don't think you'll use any of this stuff?" asked the father.

"Not really. I don't know. Maybe," replied the son.

"What about this?"

"What is it?" Robert Jr. looked down from the top of a thin nose emitting mentholated smoke.

"It's a monkey wrench that belonged to your grandfather. They don't make them anymore."

"No."

"What about this?"

"No. Do I have to look at all this shit?"

"If your mother was out here, I'd belt you for that. Now, what about *this*."

"Wait a minute. What's that?" Robert Jr. pointed to the rafters above them, where the Radio Flyer held out its rust-covered tongue.

"You don't want that."

"Sure I do."

"What are you going to do with that in a big-city apartment?"

"I don't know. Put plants in it."

"Plants." Gray spit the word out to describe the kinds of plants that he imagined his son had in mind. "*I* need it worse than you do. To haul things in. I'll *use* it." But Robert Jr. had already pulled the step ladder off the garage wall and was setting it up underneath where the wagon hung.

"Say, I remember this. I used to spend a lot of time in this thing," he said, fingering a wheel. "Ick. There's webs all over it."

"Get down from there," said the father.

"Whose wagon is it, anyway?" the son asked. "You just don't want me to have it because it's the one thing I want." He started up, but saw that his father had gripped the sides of the ladder and had narrowed his gaze.

"You never gave a damn for that wagon," said the father. "You never took care of nothing." Robert Jr. took another step up, and to his shock, his father shook him to the ground. Gray stood over him. Robert Jr. did not move. His lip began to quiver.

"Keep the son of a bitch, then," Robert Jr. said. "Jesus Christ." There were tears in his eyes. Brushing himself off, he gave the ladder a violent kick so that it landed on top of the junk pile. "Keep it."

Gray blinked and looked at his son as if he had just recognized him. "I guess you don't want any of this stuff . . ." he said.

"What?"

"I'm gonna keep it."

"Keep it! Keep it!" the son cried, stomping to the car. "Keep it! Keep it! Keep it! Keep it!" he said, then locked himself in the back seat, lighting one Bel Air from another and throwing out the butt. "Let's go, goddamnit!" he yelled. "Mother!"

The Radio Flyer got the best red enamel that the hardware store had in stock. Gray Ferguson even traced out the "Radio Flyer" on the side, and when the red base had dried, reapplied it in white. Where the bed had rusted through, he shored it up with sheet metal and solder, then ground it smooth. The tires got tire black, the tiny hubcaps a steel wool polishing. The refinished product had the look not of a new wagon, but of a war-horse girded up, a sagging frame buckled around a stout red heart. For some time afterwards it was this wagon that was being referred to when Sunday drivers pointed out the Ferguson place and "Ferguson and his wagon."

*   *   *

Retirement established a new routine for them, but it wasn't what Ethel Ferguson had expected. When she heard the rattle of tin and hard rubber wheels, she knew that her husband had dragged his wagon from the metal shed in the backyard and was on his way up the street. At first she had found nothing especially quaint about her husband's spending much of his time puttering with a little red wagon. In the spring he hauled potted plants to the holes he burrowed around the house each season, somehow finding more room among the dense greenery; in the summer he dragged ballooning plastic bags full of lawn clippings to the curb. But now her husband had taken his wagon and begun to roam. She would see his large gray figure—still in gray work clothes and gray crew cut—moving happily up the tree-lined walk that stretched from their place to the nearest neighbor a block away.

He was not content to roam on their own three acres. There were contacts to be made, he insisted, and he would often come back with a wagonload of junk, grist for the used appliance mill he seemed to be operating out of the garage. Ethel suggested to him from time to time that he might be mistaken for the other man who dressed in work clothes and pulled a red toy wagon all over town looking for trash cans. But Gray only snorted and narrowed his eyes at her and said, "You mean my competition."

Ethel was afraid that the trash-can man had started *his* trash collecting career as a normal retiree who had one day absently walked away from his family in search of a broken toaster. But she didn't tell Gray this, for he had lost his sense of humor.

A smaller man might have been less conspicuous pulling a toy wagon, she thought. Then at other times she thought it was because the wagon was so much like everything else they owned that she couldn't stand the sight of it. It had the repainted, patched, and homey homeliness of their bungalow—in perfect repair, but with the indelible brush marks of being in perfect repair instead of being new.

One time, in a weak moment, she had confessed to Gray that she would be happy to live in an apartment, one of the new ones over in Westridge, at which suggestion he, keeping a straight face, had threatened to have her committed.

Usually, however, when the dishes were done right after their tremendous breakfasts, she forgot about it, and instead of brooding—she never brooded, because brooding, she believed, was poisonous—she would pull the head off the Saint Bernard, the ceramic one with *My Cookie Saver* painted on the little cask under its chin, and make a tray of snacks with a big glass of chocolate milk and take them out to him. If she did not know what to do with herself, she fed her husband.

*   *   *

A year or so after he left home, Robert Jr. became a reporter for the *Techtown Beacon* daily newspaper. This in itself did not arouse much interest, except in those who had thought he would never find a job. But it was soon evident that there was more to Robert Ferguson Jr. than anyone had suspected, for after a mere six months on the staff, he was given his own column. The paper was trying to "metropolitanize" its image, Robert explained in a rare letter home, and the editor preferred Robert Jr.'s sardonic treatment of local figures to the former columnist's choice of parking problems, etc.

The day came when Robert Ferguson Jr. turned from relatively harmless observations on Life in the City to scathing vignettes of small-town life. These sketches and essays dealt with growing up in "Minnowville," a thinly disguised Breemsburg.

These attacks appeared to infuse life into the sluggish *Breemsburg Daily*, which ran letters to the editor on the front page and as a result was able to sell more advertising and go up to twenty-four pages on Saturdays. It was good for the Techtown paper, too, and the editors even changed the half-century-old name of the column from "The View From the Beacon" to "Can't Go Home Again." And Robert Ferguson Jr. changed his by-line to Willy Ferguson.

In the spirit of equal time, the Techtown paper published a few Breemsburg letters in answer to the Willy Ferguson columns and then unofficially considered the issue satisfied, while the Breemsburg citizens, insulted by the rest of the state's indifference, raged on like hornets in a jar.

The Fergusons stayed home.

Gray's fishing buddies didn't say a word. They seemed to look at the whole thing as a minor irritation at worst, as if they were still watching the kid roam the banks of the reservoir, chucking rocks in to scare the fish. At least now they could fish in peace. But Gray smelled sarcasm in everything they said, and after a while he gave up fishing and stayed in the garden by himself. In the evenings he did little except stare from the living room window and wonder what a boy could see from there that would enable him to write about a whole town.

"Where does this 'Willy' stuff come from?" he wanted to know one morning. He tossed the newspaper onto the kitchen counter. Ethel Ferguson, rubbing her arms and contemplating her Sanka, shrugged. He waited, and when she said nothing he picked up the newspaper. "Who ever called him Willy? 'Willy Ferguson' sounds like a colored trash man."

"I really don't know," said Ethel. "I didn't know six months ago and goodness knows I still don't. Ask me again tomorrow or in five minutes or in five years and I probably still won't know."

"What's he got against us? What's he got against this town?"

"I don't know, Gray." She sucked her breath in like a cliff diver and braced her forearms on the counter. "I wish you'd stop reading that . . . damned thing." That said, she relaxed, smoothed the hair against the sides of her head, and looked out the kitchen window, where an assortment of bird feeders seemed to have pulled up and parked themselves in a cluster. He stabbed at the paper with his fork.

"Have you read this crap?"

"Not for three weeks," she lied.

"You meant when he wrote about *you*. It's ok when he writes about *me*, isn't it? When he started in on you it was a whole new ball game, a whole new ball of wax, wasn't it?"

"That's not true. I just get tired of arguing about it."

"I get tired, too. I get tired of busting my hump in the hardware store to send him to school so he can get a job with a newspaper and spit in my face in front of the whole world. That makes me *real* tired."

She watched him shovel in his food. "But, Gray, you don't bust your hump in the hardware store anymore."

"I said 'busted.' And you're right—it's a good thing I don't—it's a damn good thing I *am* retired. I couldn't look people in the face." He forced the paper between her elbow and her coffee cup. "Have you read this crap?"

Ethel regarded the paper warily. Between the personality test and "You and Your Pet" was the headline: "Scepter Passed in Garage Sale Guise," by Willy Ferguson, whose pale, smirking mug shot with its thin mustache was stuck underneath.

> What does your dad do when he's feeling sentimental or when he's had too many Old Milwaukees in front of the tube (two phenomena which seem strangely coincidental)? Mine cleans out the garage.
>
> The garage is a repository for all kinds of daddy memories which dads take out to throw away, but instead end up fondling and putting back right where they found them.
>
> No. That's not true. There is at least one exception. And that is when The-Son-Goes-Out-Into-The-World.
>
> The ritual begins as The Dad, rather than rubbing dung and ashes all over his face, affects a tender expression, which is supposed to disguise the fact that he's foisting useless junk upon you.
>
> As you are laden with, among other delights, a brass ten-gallon Hudson insecticide sprayer, you begin the Four Stages of Accepting the Junk of a Loved One: rejection, anger, inundation, and suffocation. In the first of these distressed states, you say flatly "no," you have no possible use for a Hudson sprayer in a third-floor walk-up. Then in spite of yourself and in the face of your father's persistence, you actually begin to think of uses for a Hudson sprayer. "Ah, hell, I guess I could make a little money on the side delousing the apartment building. . . ." Except that the sprayer has a hole in it.

It went on. But by this point, Gray Ferguson could hardly read and swallow his eggs at the same time.

He had grown heavy and red-faced in the past few years. When his mouth was full, his breathing was noisy and labored, and at every meal his wife looked at him as if he might drop dead any second.

"This is a goddamned lie."

"Why? What does it say?"

"It says I'm a senile old fart."

"Oh, honey, it does not."

"It does too. Look."

"You're just reading in between the lines."

"I'm what? Where did you get that?"

"Tonya Goering."

"That's what I thought."

"Tonya Goering reads a lot."

"I know all about Tonya Goering."

"She says all the big newspapers have somebody funny like Robert Jr. She says that everyone thinks he makes all that up, anyway."

"Funny! What's funny? You can't understand a damn word he says."

"She says he's funny."

"He hasn't written about Tonya Goering, that's all."

Ethel climbed down from the barstool and went to the cabinet to butter more toast.

"You know," said Gray, "for a writer he doesn't write very goddamned much, does he?"

"Sometimes I wish . . ." She rubbed her arms and looked at it closely, as if there were crib notes there.

"Sometimes I just wish you weren't so . . ."

He looked at her.

"What?"

"Never mind."

"Say it."

". . . hateful." She saw hate and cholesterol waiting hand in hand for him at the bottom of the basement steps. But she had remembered too late that drawing attention to his hatefulness made him more hateful.

"He's trying to get at me. I know what he wants."

"What, Gray? What does he want?"

"He wants that wagon."

He shoved the plate away and threw down his fork and stomped to the back door. She stared after him, letting him go. When she tried to imagine the future, Ethel saw it as dark and narrow and cold. She wanted to call Robert Jr. and ask him to write something nice, even if it were just a letter, but she knew that that was not the kind of thing she could do.

Then, after she had prepared the morning's cookie tray and

brought it to the back step, Gray came charging to the kitchen phone and nearly knocked her down. She saw that the door to the storage shed stood open and garden tools littered the backyard.

Gray cursed himself as he punished the dial on the phone. He should have known that the renovated wagon would prove too tempting for the neighborhood thieves. He had always disputed the existence of such thieves when company was around, displaying his unlocked work shed while extolling small-town life. But they had been there—and he should have known it—all along, like aphids, blending in with the foliage, clandestine in the dry summer, swelling yellow with greed for the better-than-new red wagon. And they had taken it.

When the two patrolmen came—one a squat veteran, the other a bucktoothed rookie with a rude haircut, both dressed in the new "urban" blue of the Breemsburg Police Department—Gray launched into a description of how he thought the burglars had pulled it off.

"I never touched nothing so you could use your fingerprint deal," said Gray, indicating the open door of the shed. He beamed with cooperation and respect. The fat cop pushed by him with a look that said he was used to getting cooperation and respect from overexcited victims.

"Now, hold on, there, Mr. Ferguson. Just what exactly did you lose?" He gave the inside of the shed an expert once-over with a giant flashlight.

Gray told him. The two cops looked at each other, then at the dew-covered lawn, where indeed there were footsteps following parallel lines along the north side of the house to the street.

"They just took a wagon? No tools? They left the lawn mower?"

Failing to see why that should make a difference, Gray described the Radio Flyer. With each detail, the officers grew less willing to share his outrage, until the squat one, deflated by his complete lack of sympathy, sighed. But Gray heard it as a chuckle, a scoffing kind of chuckle.

Suddenly it occurred to him that he had always been slightly dissatisfied with the performance of the Breemsburg police. There had been a Willy Ferguson column about "the exposed nerve common to all cops: the doughnut shop, the nap in the patrol car, free coffee, unchecked concupiscence that resulted in inequitable dispensing of traffic tickets. . . ." When he had read it, he had only understood it as something disrespectful, and he could not now remember the exact words, but he had the gist of it, and he told

them maybe if he had reported a stolen wagon full of jelly dough-
nuts they would be doing their job right now.

At this, they came to life, turned on him. The fat cop dressed him
down, arms akimbo and with the momentum peculiar to insulted
righteousness. He stood aside, then, as the rookie gave a rough
imitation. They went on in this way variously until they climbed
back into the patrol car and roared down the highway that crossed
the creek at the limit of the Ferguson's lot.

Ethel Ferguson had watched all this, debating with herself whether
to offer the policemen cookies. They had never dealt with the police
before.

The short one had punched his stubby finger into the chest containing her husband's skittish heart. Even from here, she could tell
by her husband's face that there was nothing the police of Breemsburg would do about his wagon. Breemsburg had grown too big for
police to be able to do anything about a wagon stolen from under
the nose of Gray Ferguson. Gray stood there as if the cop's big
knuckle had bruised something deep inside him. He had, after all,
called in a false alarm, and he was ashamed.

Ethel had known all along that getting rid of the wagon was too
easy a solution. She knew this by looking at Gray, who came back
into the house an old man. He kept that look for weeks. He did
things he had never done before. He didn't do things he had always
done. He began to sleep late, except on Thursday, when he got up
early, read the newspaper, and then went back to bed. When she
asked him if she should hire a neighbor boy to mow the lawn, he
was furious and said what did he look like, a cripple? But the grass
continued to grow, and the flowers—as if they had reached down to
some new source of fertility—grew to extraordinary heights. Now
the giant sunflowers turned their faces at night toward the light
from the kitchen window and looked in upon her like creatures
from an old science fiction movie.

Ethel began to look for hidden evidence that Gray had taken
up the retirement drinking those public service messages warned
about, but she found none. Finally, she knew that she would have to
find the garbage collector she had given the old Radio Flyer to and
ask him to give it back. Once she found him, though, amid the
smoldering pyres of the Breemsburg dump, he said that he had
already scrapped it. She knew he was lying. There was no scrap-
ping a wagon like that. When Ethel pulled the wagon out of the shed
it seemed to take hold of her hand. It was a great and powerful
wagon. It was a wagon that would last a lifetime.

*   *   *

Gray sat staring through a glass of cream sherry—after pork chops and rice. Ethel had dragged a large, rectangular package from under the bed and into the kitchen. He looked at it for a couple of minutes before realizing that there was something in front of him.

"What's all this?" he asked with a failing grin. "I never got you anything."

"It's for both of us," she said, rubbing her arms and pointing. "There! No! No! Other end."

After he had pried loose the staples, he peered inside and then stuck in his hand, giving his wife a quizzical look. She had known he would want to assemble it himself, so she had left the wagon just as it had come from the factory: the wheels, axles, and fasteners all wrapped in plastic and packed giblet-like into the bed. With the loosening of the staples came the aroma of fresh factory paint that she associated with childhood Christmases—her heart even sped up—then the red lip of a Radio Flyer. It was not the same wagon Robert Jr. had ridden down the asphalt hill, but no one made anything that substantial anymore.

"It's a wagon," she said, when he looked without speaking at the red tin pan in his hands.

"It sure is," he said, absently, pushing it back into the box. She saw that the lines in his red face had become cavernous and that the narrowed eyes with which he now looked up at her had grown crusty. His smile had wilted as if a blight had drifted over him.

She had violated something. She knew that. But she did not know *what*. She had said something that one should not say out loud. She had given her sixty-five-year-old man a brand new toy wagon. She took the carton from his hands.

"I guess I can put this down in the basement for now."

Gray went to the kitchen window and looked out.

"What is it?" she asked.

"These plants are dying."

She looked out, trying to see where he was looking. But there was nothing to see in the darkness.

"Maybe," she offered, "with a little trimming . . ."

"Jesus," he said, "this place is starting to look like a circus. I mean, look at those goddamned flower beds. Look at those goddamned deer, for Christ's sakes."

She wanted to put her arm around him. But there was no touching him when he was like this. He looked shrunken and wrinkled. She imagined that he was slowly disappearing. She began to cry.

"But everyone admires your green thumb," she said.

"Yeah, I could have used a little of that admiring 'bout fifty years ago."

"Forrest Riley was just by with a carload of people to show them the 'grounds.' 'Grounds,' he called them."

Gray spat in the sink.

"We're a goddamned circus."

She sat down at the kitchen counter and put her face in her hands.

"That's the nicest goddamned wagon anybody's ever given me," he said and looked over his shoulder at her. When he saw her face, he turned back to the window.

"I gotta go to the shed," he said, far away now. "He's almost got me."

*   *   *

Gray got up early the next morning and mowed the lawn. Then he went around to the shrubs and trees in the front yard, marking several with white chalk. He took a sharp-nosed shovel and began to chop through the roots of a small ash he had planted in the spring. When the tree was free of the ground, its roots confined to a globe of sticky loam, Gray lifted it out carefully and wrapped it in burlap. Then, after he had hoisted the bundle up in his arms to carry it into the backyard, he sat down with the tree in his lap and died.

*   *   *

Robert Jr. came to the funeral—as Robert Jr.—and wept loud and long. All those there—most of Breemsburg, it seemed to Ethel— were quite surprised and quite moved by this. Some of them were ashamed for the letters they had written to the editor. Others weren't. Gray's fishing buddies thought they recognized a hint of unrelated anxiety showing through the son's grief, but weren't the kind to say anything about it.

And, of course, newspapering being the unforgiving business it was, Robert Jr. did have to make a few phone calls in order to meet his deadline, so had to go back to the house shortly after shaking a few hands at the graveside. He was important now, and people understood.

After the crowd had left the cemetery, Ethel asked a favor of McKnight, the funeral director, who was, of course, glad to oblige and offered the services of the hearse. He loaded up the new red wagon, still in its box, and they drove through the streets of Breemsburg until Ethel found the intrepid dumpster patroller, who gratefully took the box but later left the unassembled wagon itself lying in the alley behind Grable's Electric like the remains of a vivisection.

A couple of days after the funeral, Ethel was leafing absently through the newspaper when she realized that it was Thursday. She looked for the "You" section, and there, in Willy Ferguson's column, she found an uncharacteristically sentimental memorial; "This Wagon Is Mine" it was called, a memorial to a father—someone's father. It was written from the point of view of a ten-year-old. It was, to Ethel, like a letter home. The one she had been waiting for. The one she felt the whole town had been waiting for.

"This wagon is mine," said the narrator. "My father gave me this wagon. And where did I take it? Far, far away from my father. Where he could never find me. Then one day I returned and found my father at the side of the road. . . ."

But no one thought the column was really about a wagon. What would have been the point of that? Many in Breemsburg—anyone at Gray's funeral—remembered the story and vouched for it. Regardless of its literal truth, though, anyone who could read knew that this was a hard-bitten young journalist's struggle with sentimentality. And that might have accounted for its popularity. No one outside of Breemsburg knew the story, but in spite of that, the column was universally clipped and it yellowed under refrigerator magnets throughout the Midwest. The column was reprinted every time Willy Ferguson went on vacation, even after he took the job that everyone said such columns had gotten him with a big Eastern newspaper. It was called a classic Willy Ferguson column.

In it, the pubescent narrator went on to describe, in Willy Ferguson's richest style, how the father—depicted throughout as the best of sports—had suffered a heart attack right in front of his son, how the stricken man had lapsed into the boy's toy wagon, which was called, incidentally, a Radio Flyer, and how the boy, small for his age and himself in poor health, had shouldered the wagon as if it were a tiny caisson, and in the tepid spring air had struggled, in innocence and with everything he had, to pull his dying father up the hill toward help and home.

CHIQUITA BANANA MUY BONITA

Will Baker

Dedos and he looked at each other only once when the couple strolled out of the ruin and then along the dusty road through the market. The camera was still in its case around her neck, while the man carried a blue nylon bag slung from his shoulder. They were talking animatedly about the great stone figures they had just seen.

The two young men stayed twenty yards back, apparently idling away the afternoon. Children they knew called out and ran along-side, grinning and teasing. Some of the market women muttered and glared, but the two men only bowed mockingly at these old crones, who brooded all day long above the dark toadstools of their voluminous skirts, surrounded by plastic buckets or sacks of coarse-ground corn, heaps of sweaters or small replicas of the gods inside the ruin.

"Holy Mother," Dedos whispered, watching the woman bend to examine a blanket. "I could camp a long time in that *quebradita*."

"Fresh tuna," Mario agreed.

The woman's blouse had pulled away from her belt, exposing a strip of skin just at the beginning of the soft ravine between her compact buttocks. She was not a bright blonde, a Hollywood, but wonderful all the same. She had the amazing small breasts of North Americans, very sharp and high. And that certain expression she had too, when she looked around and her eyes skipped over all the men in the street. Go blind, the look said to Mario. I spit on you. And I can be had any way you want.

Her man had removed his sunglasses and was arguing with a blanket seller. He was going bald and yet had a beard and very hairy white legs below his khaki shorts. The man spoke also a freakish Spanish, full of odd idioms and Mexican-radio *r*s trilled with exaggerated flamboyance. Mario no longer marveled that a man so dumbfoundingly ugly could possess such an exquisite creature. He took it as one of the conditions of life in the fabulous North.

He looked away then, for they had slipped past the couple and were approaching the corner where Rosa would be waiting with their baby. In a moment he spotted her at the food stand where her friend Consuelo fried potato cakes and made coffee over a kerosene stove. Rosa squatted on her heels, talking, her manta spread in the dirt and their daughter lying on it, singing and kicking at the sky.

The two men drifted to the cart and stood against it, looking the other way from the couple, who had replaced the blanket and now were retreating from the merchant, who reached after them, supplicating, calling as if in pain, "Good price! Pure alpaca!"

"You look like two little dogs running after that skinny bitch," Rosa said, not looking at him but teasing their daughter with a stalk of weed.

"Why not?" Dedos said and sucked in his cheeks as if he were pondering. "She already has a monkey."

Consuelo, kneading batter with her fingers, laughed out loud.

"Maybe that would be something," Rosa said. "A bald monkey between your legs." Then she glanced at Mario. "So?"

He nodded. Immediately she tossed the weed stalk aside, gathered the four corners of the manta and tied them loosely. In one motion she stood up and swung the bundled baby onto her back, ducking her head so the knotted ends nestled under her chin. When her hands were free again, she took from Consuelo two of the hot, spicy cakes wrapped in paper. Dedos and he had already pushed away from the stand and were drifting again down the street.

"Don't get your thing caught in that little bone-bag," Rosa called. "She'll pinch it off."

Just before turning the corner to the bus stop, where a crowd had already collected, Mario glanced back and saw the couple, both of them laughing and looking fondly toward his daughter, who was riding beside them on Rosa's back.

"No taxis," Dedos said and gave a sudden soft whistle of anticipation. "God likes us today." From his pocket he had taken a peaked highland cap with ragged earflaps, and now he settled it on his head. A boy in the group waiting for a bus caught sight of him and laughed, but Dedos did not respond. Mario lifted one lapel of his black jacket and with his other hand reached into the inside pocket and removed his flute, a cheap wooden one painted green with gold bands.

"Brother," he said to a man nearby, "how soon?"

"Play one tune," the man said, "it should be here."

Mario nodded, the flute already in his mouth, and blew a few soft, quick notes from an old *huayna* as he strolled slowly at the edge of the crowd. And indeed, just then people began to gather up their baskets or plastic bags or mantas stuffed with goods, for someone had spotted the bus far down the line of traffic. From the corner of his eye Mario saw the two North Americans coming down the sidewalk. They had broken away from Rosa and were looking up and down the street anxiously. He heard the man's grotesque question: *Would you do me the great favor of . . . .* Several people answered at once, some giving directions, others telling him the taxis were too far, still others urging him to take the bus which was even now approaching.

Dedos and he took seats together midway along the aisle, with empty places in front of them. On one side an old man held a live rooster trussed in a basket, only its red comb, beak and golden eye protruding; behind them, women from the market were stuffing goods under the seats and in the overhead rack, complaining loudly over one another's greed for space. Along with the exhaust and oil smells of the bus, they caught an odor of sweaty wool, coca leaves, and beer. It was the end of the day and people were weary and talkative, unwashed, and in some cases already drunk. They were all bound for the roar and murk of the great city a few kilometers distant.

"Come on now, little ones," Dedos said in Quechua. "This is just how we want it." Mario nodded, still tootling on the flute.

They came down the aisle, sidling past or gingerly stepping over bundles and boxes, frowning in their search for empty seats. Rosa was just behind them, and over her shoulder rose the child's small brown moon of a face, the little mouth agape with interest.

The camera had vanished from the woman's neck, and she now swung her arms casually, like a young boy. Behind his sunglasses the man looked alert and serious. His beard was thrust out a little and he carried the blue bag in one hand with the strap in a tight turn about his wrist. Catching his eye, Mario tilted the flute gaily and winked, while Dedos nodded and grinned like an idiot. For a moment the man hesitated, before his face closed and he looked away.

The couple took seats three rows ahead of them and Rosa paused there, saying something to them and laughing, before she moved further down the aisle where no empty places were left. She lingered there, as if uncertain. The baby reached toward Mario and cried out, but he ignored her and began another tune. Dedos yawned.

The driver called out a warning and, despite shouts of protest from those still struggling to mount the step, began to haul on the handle of the steel elbow that closed the door. There was laughter and a cheer or two as the bus lunged forward and began to jockey its way into the passing herd of motor bikes, ancient sedans, and other smoke-darkened buses.

The baby began abruptly to scream. *Too hard*, Mario thought. *Don't nip so hard*. He frowned and stopped playing the flute to watch. Standing just beside the couple, Rosa was cooing over her shoulder and bouncing on flexed knees, shifting the manta as if it were a heavy burden. In a moment the man spoke and clamped one hand on the backrest of the seat in front of him, as if to rise. Rosa shook her head and smiled shyly. The baby's eyes were squeezed shut, her face wet from tears and a worm of snot that crawled from her tiny, flat nose, but her yodels were beginning to subside into little gags.

"Come on, Caballero," Dedos hissed. "Come on, come on."

The man released the backrest to make an insistent gesture of invitation. Rosa giggled and hesitated, then shook her head again. The blonde woman had turned from staring out the window and now put a hand on the man's shoulder and spoke to him. He nodded once and heaved himself to his feet, smiling and signaling vigorously for Rosa to take his place, while the blonde also smiled and moved as if to make more room.

Rosa settled into the seat and made a great show of gratitude, arranging the bundle and wiping the baby's face with a corner of the manta. She was talking profusely in Quechua, to the amusement of passengers around them. The couple were pleased at this response, which they took as acceptance and approval of their generosity. The man made a comment, apparently joking, for the blonde woman laughed and her cheeks colored. The man slipped the blue bag over one shoulder and, gripping the luggage rack to brace himself, leaned down to offer the baby a finger.

At the next stop the driver allowed the aisle to fill jam-full with new passengers and their belongings. The air grew dense with odors and pale blue with cigarette smoke. Outside the sun touched the horizon, turning the boulevard into a long trough of shadow, but flaring like molten brass in the windows of a few taller buildings. The bound rooster was now emitting an occasional strangled crowing. The bus had picked up speed, swaying and jouncing, so those in the aisle were jostled against each other.

Mario put away his flute and nudged Dedos. They rose and shoved their way into the aisle, while a woman and young girl slid behind them immediately to take the empty seats. Through the tightly packed, leaning bodies, Mario could see Rosa's profile as she turned her head to duck under the knotted manta. For the briefest of moments her one exposed eye registered him, and then she lifted the baby, now gurgling happily, from the manta and held her in the air, laughing.

The bus was slowing, swerving toward the curb at a busy intersection. Other passengers were also getting to their feet, wrestling baskets and packages, calling out warnings and imprecations. The driver began to shout the numbers of the transfer buses as he braked to a squealing, shuddering halt. Dedos in the lead, they began to move down the aisle, shoulders and elbows working to establish position.

Rosa had interested the blonde woman in the child, and now, with a suggestive grin, pointed boldly at her womb. The woman shook her head, blushing again. Rosa exclaimed, protested, and turned to swing the baby up to the man, who shifted his bag back on his hip and crouched awkwardly to receive this spontaneous gift. Dedos, grinning his mindless grin under the ragged cap, leaned against the man as if to lever past and simultaneously bumped the bag with an elbow.

From the other side Mario caught the bag on his own hip bone while he used a forearm to take its place against the man's buttock. His free hand raked back the zipper and swift as a ferret squirmed into the bag. A telephoto lens emerged first, then vanished into one of the pockets sewn inside his jacket, and then the camera in leather case popped out and similarly disappeared. Both moves were unseen, for the bag was sandwiched between him and Dedos and, after a single glance downward, Mario's fingers worked by themselves.

He sidled around the man, who was now holding the child so that she could tangle her small fingers in his beard. *Chiquita*, he was saying, *Chiquita banana my bonita, eh?* Just behind Mario came the old man with the rooster, who apparently saw the unzipped bag for he said "Good work," loudly enough to be heard. His heart pumping hard, Mario did not turn around but kept shoving ahead roughly.

In the first step away from the bus, Dedos swept off his cap, and Mario slipped out of his jacket and folded it over one arm. Then as he walked he turned back the cuffs of his white shirt. When they were around the corner at the intersection, they angled for opposite sides of the street, moving now in the soft light of dust.

"You should see this girl," Dedos said as they separated, uttering a pretended groan of anticipation. "She works only for big money. A real Hollywood. And tonight is my night." Then he was striding away jauntily, covering ground. "See you at the old bastard's," he called over his shoulder.

Mario watched Dedos skim the cap into a trash barrel, and when he passed one on his own side of the street he likewise jettisoned the cheap flute. He felt the weight of the camera and lens against his thigh. They were new and expensive, and he would say before he even showed anything that they had something very good and would not take less than fifty thousand soles. Even so the old bastard would make another fifty. For doing nothing but advertising in the paper and serving coffee in his fashionable home, while his son laid out the cameras from last month for the tourists in search of a replacement. It was a cheat that only half went to the true artists like him and Dedos, who actually created the demand as well as supplying the product.

For a fleeting moment he regretted that he could not stick with his friend after they collected. In the old days the two of them had set aside a third of their cut just for rum and cocaine and girls. But Rosa did not permit such luxuries. A third went to her now, as an equal partner. She was saving for a bigger apartment and television. Mario admitted to himself that he was proud of Rosa, her nerve and skill. It was her idea to have the child, and in a few months working with the baby they had nearly doubled their take. Despite the little stab of longing for old times, he was sure—almost sure—that he would marry her.

She was a rare woman, was Rosa. She would be there now with the couple, probably on the curb at the next stop, apparently outraged at what had happened, indicating by halting word and gesture that they must talk to the police, be always watchful, keep their possessions close; agreeing that, yes, it was probably those two young men. The one with the old cap and the other with the flute. Green, wasn't it? But thanks be to God that would make them easy to spot. She would take the woman's hand in sympathy, delaying them as long as she could. She would lean close, and in her own tongue murmur: Skeleton, barren hole, bring us another monkey and we will skin him too.

RECOGNIZABLE AT A DISTANCE

Stephanie Bobo

When it became clear that I didn't know how to do anything to make a living, in other words when it became clear that the promise of my sensibility was not a lucrative promise, Daddy kindly sent me off to Tulane to get my M.S.W., it being agreed on all hands but my own really that social work was an appropriate field for a young woman who had insisted for many years that she was interested only in the nature of experience and what it meant to be human. I was twenty-two. My father had stopped repeating his observation that I was a "hellcat," but nobody had ever paid me for a poem. I was, after all, grown up, they said, and so for the fifth time I left my home in Hunter County, Mississippi, a home that I had treated as a sort of halfway house for some years by then, and went out into the world.

New Orleans

Although, indeed, some unfortunate romances and some unsuitable jobs had sobered me somewhat, I was nowhere near Mama's prime idea that the Plan is all right and we are just wrong. In fact, I was still thoroughly convinced that *I* was just fine and the Plan was all wrong until I got to New Orleans and began to think that there wasn't any Plan at all and everything was wrong.

No one had ever prepared me for the vengeance with which a constantly thwarted idealism can career off into a bitter cynicism. I had been wounded and depressed before, but my spirit had always knit itself back up again. I was totally unprepared for a stretch of time, and I trembled to think that it might be the stretch of my life, in which everything that I did or felt or read or saw or thought, in which, I say, everything struck at the root of me, robbed me of strong feeling, left me with dreamless nights. I tried to be good, and I did actually have a knack for working with the unfortunate and the poor, the confused and the insane, and everybody thought that I was finally doing what I was expected to do, but I was not good inside. All of my motions were the result of a sort of intellectual dry heat; a strong wind would have done me in, and even my writing stopped coming to me. I don't know what it was. I had friends, I touched people, but I was overwhelmed with this sense that I was just passing time. Three years passed.

Mine Ed

I met Ned at a party. Roy, an insipid medical student with whom I was spooning at the time, had gone to get me another bourbon and I was standing around, wearing what I then considered my inscrutable look, in a great mill of people. I saw Ned and I knew that he was the gentlest person I'd ever seen, and I knew too that he was not all there on the surface, and I knew too that this was the first thing that had aroused my interest in a long time, and I beat back the old pre–New Orleans knowledge that everything wonderful means everything horrible, and if you have some of it you have to have all of it. We watched one another awhile and I moved away from a dull med student conversation and walked toward him as though I had to walk past him for some reason, but we both knew. We stood in front of one another for a minute, amused. Ned said, I'm going to the Keys tomorrow; do you want to come?

Yes, I said, yes. Roy was rather scandalized, but people get used to whatever it is you're doing if you keep on doing it so that it's clear to them that nothing they can do can stop you from doing it. Roy broke up with me when I got back and told him I was in love with Ned. Edward was not one to commit himself to anything much, nor was I, but we moved in with one another anyway. When he got a job teaching at my old alma mater in Blufftown, Mississippi, I went with him and kissed New Orleans goodbye.

Like I Said

Ned breathed life into me, and because of him I could give it to everything I touched, and I even started writing poetry again. He was from Virginia, and, with a sort of provincial jealousy, I thought that he did not really understand ways further south. He was writing a book on that vague category of literature called Southern, and, with a primitive fear of being effaced through definition, I thought that he had probably already plugged my family into one of the vague myths with which he wrestled in his den of letters. But he left me out of it and he had the sense to recognize a thing when he saw it and not get it confused with what he thought it was before he saw it, and I knew it would be all right, that he would be kind enough not to deprive what I loved of its complexity.

But, like I said, you never can have some of it without the rest of it flailing and reeling into the party too. My father called me before we left New Orleans and said, your mama and me your mama your mama and me well we are getting a divorce, and I said Daddy I'm sorry, about time, and then I tried to be lighthearted about it but I felt betrayed inside the way I had always felt betrayed when I was cruising up the Pearl River in my little motorboat and found a nice little sandbar where I could stop and sit and think and write only to see a fat moccasin skimming his poisonous mouth along the surface of the water. I felt betrayed, I say, the way I felt when I'd had a good walk through the woods muttering to myself and deciding that the sky and the pines and the gooseberry bushes were enough after all only to find that I had poison ivy after I got home. And I was angry too because everything for once was going right for me, and now the refuge I would have had if it stopped going right was gone, and I would have to make it right all by myself. But I didn't let on about any of this; I just tried to rub it away in my secret heart. I was twenty-five. I was too old, I told myself, to feel betrayed. I felt wretched and childish and selfish.

After Mine Ed and I settled into a little two-story house on a steamy little street in Blufftown, I drove over to Hunter County to see my parents and I visited with each of them alone, my father first.

Daddy

Daddy looked forlorn and older, and I loved him then because he refused to trap his pain up in words and theories as was my wont. Not big on words, my family, not much talk except as a sort of code, like this code my father and I have when we take walks together: we name all the trees, and that is our way of saying everything to one another that we can say with certainty. So we took a long walk in the woods and Daddy named for me every tree and bush and finally when we were in the great silence of the middle of it he said, there's nothing for it, and I turned my face away from him and wept while he shifted uncomfortably from foot to foot before taking me in his arms and making me laugh by reminding me of some silly thing that happened when I was a kid.

Mama

But Mama now was a different story because we'd never paid much attention to how one another felt and the old rivalry had never been resolved and its resolution was just another item now on her list of pain. We tried to act like everything was really all right. I was standing in the kitchen with her and she was peeling an onion with a knife over the sink and she made a particularly quick and determined cut with it that went right into her thumb. She was very still for a moment clutching the onion with the wounded hand. Blood welled up from her thumb and began to slide down the side of the onion in the shape of a little Africa. Then she dropped the onion and the knife and turned the tap on and held her hand under the water and turned her face up toward me her eyes bluer and larger with the tears and choking back a sob she whispered: this can happen.

This Can Happen: Red and White

We used to keep three lovely fat white rabbits in a hutch. One day, too clever for their own good, they somehow undid the door and lolled out into the day lilies and clover. It was early spring, one of those Mississippi spring afternoons when the sun has burnt off the morning's haze, and everything is in focus, and it's still a bit cool in the shade, and everything feels green. I was standing around in the yard, looking up at the sky and breathing, and Mama went to feed the rabbits and then I heard her call my name from the edge of the yard. I went over to her and her face looked like Mary's face in those hideously colored pictures of the crucifixion that they used to show us in Sunday school. She didn't say anything. She led me down to the hutch and there on the ground were our three rabbits. The dogs had gnawed their throats and shaken the life from them then dropped them there on the new grass. Three forlorn little white bodies with great flowing crimson scarves at their necks, wasted.

We didn't say anything much to one another. We went and got a couple of shovels and buried them near where they lay. Neither of us was very strong; it took a long time. Sometimes we would stop and just look at one another. Sometimes I would stop and just stare up through new oak leaves, follow little racing jewels of sun along a branch or two. It was as if everything but the day had stopped. My mother and I were at that moment in perfect accord with one another, felt the same thing, were one woman baffled, horrified, stunned at the lack of recourse. I understood suddenly that she had always been the one who buried my accident-and-pneumonia-prone pets before I got home from school. Every failure of love and imagination, everything senseless had been crystallized into that one moment, those pitiful white bodies marred with the sloppy erasure of death, those two women making graves. We cried when we finished. When Punkin and Toulouse and Paula got home from school, we told them that the rabbits had escaped.

This Can Happen: Blood in Water

When I was about four a kid at nursery school hit me in the back of the head with the butt of a heavy metal toy gun. We had seen cowboys do this on television, but I had a lot of real blood and I threw up. So first my mother came home and then she called my father home from the hospital. He was an intern then. He bent me over the edge of the bathtub and held my head under the faucet and ran cool water on me till all the blood washed away and he could see the cut. He has the most wonderful hands in the world. When they touch things, they make everything right, and I knew I would not die. I was scared at first. I could see the bloody water going in the drain beneath my face: it was deep red, pale rose, then almost clear. The shock of the blow was gone and I was conscious only of my father holding me, the soothing rush of water, the fading blood, and I didn't feel the pain anymore because I was filled with an intense yearning for that moment to be repeated eternally. I wished then that little Johnny Took had wounded me forever so that forever my father could heal me with his love. Forever. But it was just a skin wound. No stitches. The fear went out of my parent's faces. I could not keep them at home. I went back to nursery school. Johnny's gun was confiscated.

This Can Happen

I put my arm around Mama and held her hand under the water. We busied ourselves with first aid cream and bandaids. I took her out on the porch and made her sit down. She looked relieved all of a sudden. I went back into the house and threw the onion away and washed the knife. We drank iced tea on the porch and talked about a painting she was working on. At 3:30 my two younger brothers and sister pulled up in their three separate cars from school. They looked at us as though we were guests at a dinner party who had stayed too long and had too much to drink. They trampled into the house without a word of greeting and turned on a thousand TVs, radios, stereos. This can happen, you see. You think that you're living in a place that for all its shame and spite and quirkiness has its own regional integrity, then all of a sudden it is merely America.

I Don't Suppose

I don't suppose I need tell you about Ned's English department, where several years earlier my maudlin experiments in poetry had been supported and I had been encouraged to read books, and was thus assured of never being happy with any of the jobs I could get, although I might tell you that Ned's department is more genteel, that is, more polite and repressed, than others I have seen. Political maneuvers are conducted with intense discretion and high-mindedness. Women are consistently denied tenure or driven crazy by Dr. Drive, the department head, apparently for life. Junior faculty are friendly with and wary of one another at once. Because jobs are hard to get, Dr. Drive manages to hire at least one person from one of the "better" schools a year, and these people live here as though they are exiles and make us act like caricatures of ourselves. There are a lot of cocktail parties at which people veer toward speaking honestly with one another and then excuse themselves the next day. It is commonly thought that there is much infidelity and unsavory psychic bonding beneath the courteous surface, but its nature is unknown and speculation about who is doing what to or with whom or what is never really taken seriously except among students and faculty spouses and I do not really count as either of those.

I Don't Suppose

When I got home from that first visit with my suddenly divorcing parents, Ned was kind enough not to get analytical and fictional about it, and he has been so kind as it has continued all this time now to eat at my heart in the most inexplicable way. When I look at my family I see these shifting impenetrable surfaces and I think that only someone in my family who knows the code of surfaces can understand that it says something unspeakable, horrible, that it is some face on a disease that we've all caught and pass back and forth among ourselves in caresses and blows. I am the one who wants to get analytical and fictional about it. I am the one who needs the comfort of the formula, the myth. I am the one who is lost, lost in what is going on.

Cara Victus

I have spent some time with a woman from New York who teaches Fem Lit and will not last long in the misogynous realm of Dr. Drive. We recognized one another's weaknesses immediately, spewed the highlights of our little histories at one another over a few afternoons of gin and tonics, but I could not say that Cara Victus and I are really friends. She is a lovely and frail hysterical bird, more along the lines of another warning for me, a sign of how intimate losses can make love flutter and spout and misfire in us, a sign of how the mind can transform everything it lights upon into something recognizable and dreadful, a sign that self-awareness does not mean control. At first, I wanted to fold her up in my love and calm her; but she demands too much, and I bolt at the vampire specter of demand. The fiction through which I would have to grapple to reach her is that I am a younger, culturally deprived version of herself. Tenderness and violation are her powers; she carries them in the same hand.

Something horrible will happen, something horrible will happen, poor girl, your poor daddy, something horrible just like it did to me, she said in the midst of little shrieks when I told her about my parents' divorce.

But My Family Is Not As Crazy As Some Others

I was working for a little over a year after Ned and I moved to Blufftown at a place owned by the Cupid brothers. It is a place called Youth in Turmoil (YIT) where incorrigible adolescents are sent by courts and families to stay for a few months to cool down and get socialized somewhat. I was a counselor, and this mostly meant supervising behavior modification programs for three kids at a time and supplementing those programs with leading questions, affection, and mere presence. I did best with children who played the guitar or painted or wrote, kids whose emotional problems seemed more complex and interesting to me mainly because they were capable of talking about them. Some of my co-workers liked to get the real crazies, but I never got anywhere much with crazies except for this one kid one time who liked to make spaceships out of clay and then smash them with his face: I thought he was wonderful, and he liked me too, so after a few months he stopped setting fires and biting the resident psychiatrist, and he was in pretty good shape when we shipped him out. But we usually didn't get them like that, and I requested children with minor problems.

The day came, of course, when I was assigned a child who would have been a problem for anyone. These kids often came from families and places that were foreign to my experience, but moments of intuition and close attention could undo the disadvantages of that. But this child was from a place that no one has even imagined yet. She was thirteen, fat, short, lethargic, quiet. Whether the sausage plumpness of her face or the general flatness of her character kept her from having any observable range of facial expression was something I could not decide. She responded to nothing at our first meeting. Her eyes were a brilliant blue, and they sat flat in the great fold of her face. She had the presence of a cooked, stuffed bird, or a great, impassive baby doll. She said yes ma'am, no ma'am to me; I could not get her to call me by my first name, and I could not get her to show interest in anything, could not get her to show amusement, anger, fear, confusion. She was what my friend Alex's aunt used to call another of Alex's aunts: the personification of a zero.

I saw her right after she got there and I wondered why someone had sent her there. I wondered what she, who appeared to lack all will, could have done to be sent from home at such a tender age. So after I had settled her into her room, I headed for her file and Harold Sounder's initial report. As I discovered from her file, she had exercised her will on several recent occasions by running, or trudging, away from her home, an obscure place near the coast called Erono.

Harold Sounder's Initial Report on Sensi Doloric

"Sensi Doloric is a white obese female with a remarkably flat affect. Her adjustment reaction to adolescence is complicated by her unusual sexual history, and, I might as well add, the unusual sexual history of her family. Although Mrs. Doloric, whom I met before my interview with Sensi in Hoodoo County Detention Center, is apparently concerned for the child, she has not been and is not home very much to regulate the activities of her own family and several relatives who appear to 'drop by' frequently. I say this because of several reports from social workers and courts concerning certain activities of the Doloric household that led the Doloric's neighbors to complain, the courts to intervene, and Sensi to YIT. I will now summarize the main points of those reports.

"Sensi Doloric was sexually molested by her father, her two older brothers, and a male cousin, who is now at Parchman for rape, from her third year until six months ago when the court order that finally brought her here went into effect. This abuse appears to have been recurrent although not continuous in time, as the father, the brothers, and the cousin during this time have all been in and out of various prisons, and Mrs. Doloric has on several occasions asked for and received the aid of the Law in keeping these men from her home. Mrs. Doloric is a bit reticent about these events, but a pretty clear picture of them can be gained from the reports of the physicians who have examined Sensi and the neighbors of the Dolorics who reported them. I refer you to the xeroxed reports at the back of this file. I need not point out to you that the sexual abuse to which Sensi has been subjected went far beyond exhibitionism and fondling and veered into rape, voyeurism, group sex and several other things that I, in all my years in this business, had not even heard of before this case.

"Her marks and attendance at school have been consistently poor. She has no friends that we know of. And she appears unwilling or unable to discuss what is going on.

"I suggest that we supplement her program with daily sessions with our staff psychiatrist, and I think it best that we quietly give Sensi a great deal of attention and let her recover from her hectic home life for a while until Dr. Onothat tells us how we should handle her and why the hell the legal system has sent her to a treatment center for mild social adjustment problems. Her case, indeed, is more extreme than those that we usually see, and I know already that our entire staff will wonder if what we can help her adjust to here bears even the faintest resemblance to her home environment. I know already that a great cry of outrage will go up from you all concerning the purpose, the justice, and the utility of having her here for six months and then sending her back to Mrs. Doloric's untidy household, but Sensi is, after all, here, and we must do something, and I am sure that each of you will give Sensi your best shot. —H.A.S."

I Went to See Harold

Immediately I asked that she be transferred to another counselor and told Harold, quite frankly, that I felt incompetent with such a case, but Harold told me not only that no other counselor was available but that a switch might unsettle Sensi and make her feel rejected. He called Dr. Onothat in, and after a couple of hours the two of them manipulated me into being calm about Sensi Doloric and treating her as though she were an ordinary child who had had a few arguments with her mother and smoked a little pot and got caught like most of the other residents I counseled.

Chess and Painting Were Out of the Question

I had to think of something that Sensi and I could do together for our two "one-on-one" hours each day. I tried trips to parks and zoos, but Sensi simply lumbered along beside me and stood aloof as I made a fool of myself over lions and squirrels. I tried Old Maid and Go Fish but Sensi didn't care if she won or lost. I tried jigsaw puzzles, but her marked inability to recognize and connect patterns frustrated both of us. It was difficult for me to arrange what we call "success experiences" for Sensi. Finally the two of us just sat in the dayroom together. She would not talk about school, she would not talk about the weather or clothes or the dust that settled inexorably on everything at YIT despite daily cleaning. Harold and Dr. Ono-that came up with the brilliant idea of my just being quiet and present with Sensi. Perhaps at this point steadfast, kind presence is enough and she will make the first move, they said.

Sensi and I were sitting in the dayroom together quietly. There was no one else around. I felt like going to sleep. Suddenly she said, Helen, she said, you know? I thought, at last, at last, she trusts me, she will talk about feeling fat and ugly, she will talk about resenting her mother, she will say she wants piano lessons, she will ask me to take her out for ice cream. I said, yes, Sensi, yes, go on.

She said, you know how it smells when they do it. And for the first time Sensi's eyes began to sparkle. She appeared animated, excited.

No, Sensi, I said, beaming a patient beneficence at her, I said, I do not know exactly what you are talking about, perhaps you will explain?

My Pa and my cousin Jakes she said when they you know and the house always smelled like it and I went to bed one night and my pillow been got all wet with it and Jakes and Bib that's my brother they were all laughing about it but Bib like to beat the shit out of me when I begun a'cryin'.

Then, for the first time, Sensi smiled, or rather leered, at me and I really thought that I was going to throw up. I thought that I would be very calm and say something like: please excuse me, Sensi, for just a moment; we can continue this interesting discussion when I get back. And then I would go to the bathroom and retch out the great sickness that had just welled up inside of me. But there is no physical release for the disease I'd just caught from Sensi Doloric.

*This Is What They Taught Me to Do Instead of Giving Me
a Garret and Letting Me Write Poetry*

I thought, well, she needs to cry about it a little and be comforted, but she sat there grinning before me and she wet her thin child's lips with her tongue. Sensi, I said, Sensi, I know that that must have been a terrible experience for you, but before I could continue she said, not really, it happened lotsa times. Sensi, I said, Sensi, I think this is something you should discuss with Dr. Onothat this afternoon, but I hope that in the future you will be open with me the way you have today but our one-on-one time is about up and I have to go to the recreation room to supervise games do you want to come with me there and play Monopoly or something with the others?

Not Really, She Said

I went to see Harold and I said, Harold that child has real problems that I am not prepared to deal with and I want you to give her to someone else. I can't, he said. Harold, I said, I quit. I thought, he said, you wouldn't be able to handle it when we hired you but oh no, oh no, Dr. Onothat and Sally Strew said she's bright and sensitive and knows her stuff. But you can't handle it can you Helen?

No, I Can't

After my bout with Sensi and Harold, I went home and got in bed and stared at the ceiling. When Ned got in from classes he came in and looked at me and said, what? I said, I cannot even begin and you would not even believe it if I could; I quit my job. Blind leading the blind anyway, he said, you want a drink? No, I said, I just want to die. I'll be in my study, he said, and he kissed my forehead and patted my hand and left.

I Just Lay There

One time before, after I finished college and was waiting on tables, this happened. Waiting on tables was constantly trying for me: I was efficient and polite, but that I was dutiful was somehow not enough for many customers who expected me somehow to be an obsequious part of their evening's entertainment, to be chatty, cute, and coy all at once. I found these expectations unreasonable, and I never made much money in tips.

There was new kitchen equipment and a new menu and the cooks were revenging the radical nature of the change by getting alarmingly sloppy with the food. This was a particular cause of anxiety to me because I clung, in the face of experience to the contrary, to the belief that most people really did, or really should, go to restaurants to eat.

The night was really like any other night. I was irritated, as usual, when two men persisted in calling me sugarfoot, honey bunch, little darling. I was puzzled, as usual, when I served dessert to a young couple and the woman gave a hard stare to her companion and, in a voice too loud not to be meant for me, said, but I bet she cannot even add, then stared defiantly into my face. I was filled with pity and tenderness, as usual, when a woman who had obviously been in assertiveness training firmly sent a shrimp remoulade back to the kitchen five times. And I was irked, as usual, when another woman asked me where I had gone to school and when I told her her eyes glittered with a sort of triumph and she said, hunh, and now you are here waiting on tables funny how things turn out ain't it?

Although I was rather confused by the things that my customers went out of their way to say to me, I was accustomed to them, and there was really no explanation for my suddenly bolting from the whole chore of bearing patiently their extraculinary demands when this couple came in and sat at a deuce of mine and the man, as usual, said, what do you recommend? I have never, ever, been able to lie outright, and despite my early religious training, which I abandoned perhaps too soon, I have never been able to prevaricate with any truly effective degree of promptitude. After a fatal pause during which I thought you know I really ought to say I recommend that you two go somewhere else for dinner, after a fatal pause, I say, I said, well, it depends on what you have in mind but the steak marinade and the scampi are usually good. But, he said, heaving an exasperated sigh, what do you recommend? I usually prefer the steak, I said. But, he said, arching his eyebrows and glancing at his companion before he turned to me again, as though he were patiently trying to get a child to identify correctly a number or a color, but, he said, what do you recommend? Whatever you want, I said, and fled.

I passed my four-top, four businessmen who had all ordered steaks, and they said, we do not mean to be unkind but these steaks are awful, please take them back. I apologized, took the four plates back to the kitchen, set them down, and wept. I punched out in tears. I quit.

I went home and got in the extra bed in my sister's room where I had been sleeping of late and I cried for a few hours. My father came in and I said I can't take it it's not just the work it's just living and being human, Daddy, oh, God, Daddy, do I have to keep being? There, there, he said, and he sat next to the bed holding my hand as I wept. It's not just the steaks, I said, it's me, I try not to be too sensitive, but I am. Now, now, Helen, baby-doll, he said. Oh, Daddy, Daddy, I said, it is all so ugly.

I Stayed in Bed for Three Days

Ned continued to live a normal life. He slept in the same bed with me each night as though I, too, had gone to work that day and come home tired. It was a sign of his love that he did this, that he acted as though I were in the realm of the sane by doing what I did, and it was my realization of the tenderness that he was spending on me that led me to get up on the fourth day and bathe and eat. You're all right now? he said, circling me with his arms from behind as I stood brushing my teeth. I looked at his wonderful face in the mirror. Yes, I said, yes.

My Big Brother

My brother, Geoff, who leads a normal life in Blufftown lawyering and having a family, has always been good to me and he can always make what is going on run into a channel as though the channel had been there all along as though there is a secure and predictable course for everything as though we can live with what we are. I had lunch with him in the midst of the divorce thing. Geoff, I said, brushing a tear away and taking a sip of my Bloody Mary, I do not understand it.

Well, he said, buttering a piece of bread, they are doing what they want to do and have to do, and what passes between them is something only they can know, and we will just have to get used to it.

But thirty years, I said, and Punkin and Toulouse and Paula not even out of the house yet.

Helen, you are taking this too hard. These things happen. It will be messy awhile and then everyone will be happy. I don't really understand why you are so upset about this, he said. You've been away from home for seven years now. You have a life of your own.

But they won't be there together anymore, I said.

Arguing and being miserable with one another. He smiled his ironic smile just like Daddy's.

But didn't they, I said, didn't they love each other once?

Anna Laurie

My big sister Anna Laurie is nursing her new baby and I am sitting across from her at her kitchen table. They'll be all right, she says, all of them. It's not as though we didn't expect it.

She looks down at little James nursing and I look out the window. We are quiet awhile, listening to the baby catch his breath occasionally, listening to the clock on the stove. Does it hurt, I say. No, she says, smiles.

What do you want, Anna Laurie, I say.

I want to get the hell out of here and move back to San Francisco, she says, and laughs. I drop my coffee cup on the floor and the baby begins to cry.

I Have Dreams of Visceral Threat

I dream at night that I am in a city that is one big enameled-metal building. To move around I will have to get into elevators that are like ovens. I can't take it. I can't do it. I pace around in empty white rooms until great bladders of trilling flesh begin to sprout from my back like wings and Ned wakes me up and tells me to stop grinding my teeth.

Ned

Ned is teaching an extra course so I will not have to work for a few months. I am working on a long poem. I get up in the morning and write for a few hours, whether it's coming or not. Then I bake things and do errands and then I take a nap. I work on what I have written in the morning in the afternoon. Sometimes we go out later, sometimes we make love, sometimes we play chess.

Daddy

Daddy has married for the second time and he is very much in love. He is still living on the farm in Hunter County. Mama moved to Vicksburg about a week after the onion incident. Toulouse and Paula went with her. The divorce took a year. Now Daddy is gaining weight, but he is happy. When I met his wife it was as though she had always been there.

I am glad that he is not miserable anymore, but I cannot explain the rage that welled up and then immediately subsided in me the first time I saw his new wife familiarly ruffle the graying hair at the back of his neck and beam up into his face. She is a good woman, he says. She is nice looking and there is no nonsense about her. And she is nice to me, although it is clear that she doesn't understand what it is, exactly, that I do with my typewriter or why, exactly, Ned and I continue to live "in sin."

She has four buxom, shrill-voiced daughters who click through the house in their heels sometimes when I am there. They are very normal. They talk about cars and clothes and the back-biting in the offices where they work. They look at me as though I am from another planet, and they have a cute pet name for my father. She also has five chihuahuas. And when I hug my father now, he holds me as though his embrace is all in the world that could keep me from dissolving into air.

Mama

Mama smokes too much and her voice sounds like a radio station that is really not coming in well at all. She devotes all her time to her painting now. Ned and I drive to Vicksburg to see her and Ned takes Paula and Toulouse to a disco movie. When we are alone, I tell Mama about my oven-bladder-wing dream and she frowns and purses her lips up and pounds her Benson & Hedges menthol out in a big crimson ashtray. I change the subject promptly to Monet and we have a pleasant afternoon in the only language we have in common.

We all have dinner together and Mama and Toulouse and Paula tell Ned what a hypersensitive, hot-tempered jerk I was as a child. Ned smiles at me. He has somehow included all of us in his love, and I feel a pain in my throat when I remember the few moments in which I have underestimated him. The next morning we drive back to Blufftown and I weep so violently that Ned pulls into a service station, goes into the bathroom, comes back with wet cool paper towels and bathes my face. I'm sorry, I say, sorry, ducking my head into his chest.

I Didn't Go In

At the end of summer I drive out to Hunter County. I lie to myself and say I am going to see Daddy, but I know that no one is at home. When I get to the place where I grew up, where I spent my childhood looking for adventures in the woods and scaring myself, where I spent the most memorable parts of my adolescence sitting in mimosa trees and reading Byron and staring across fields green and blasted in turn, or where I locked my door and danced frantically alone in front of the mirror to Martha Reeves and the Vandellas, where I sat under a hickory tree and wrote my first poem, a long elegy for a favorite dog, where the house had always been full of the racket of children, where my parents had nursed us through a thousand thousand sicknesses and small defeats, where my parents loved each other once, when I got to the house, I say, I started to go in but I didn't. I had a key in my pocket and I could have. But when I put my fingers on it I remembered that the last time I had spent a night there I had misplaced my key and Mama had lent me hers. It was the one I had in my pocket. I forgot to return it then, and later I had started to mail it to her until I realized that she was at another address and didn't need it anymore anyway.

Trees

I stepped into the yard and stood and all the horrendous pounding down of all the days that all of us had lived filled up the space around me; an unfathomable clutter of memories surged into all the spaces of my forgetting and I had to turn away from the house to try to start forgetting all of it again.

I watched a few cows follow a spot of sun up a hill. A huge, lone, white crane lifted up from the big pond, circled slowly once over me, then settled at the top of a pine tree very far away. I walked to the edge of the garden where there were just a few collard greens left and some late tomatoes and rows of dying cornstalks rasping in the wind. I stood there and screamed; I screamed: somebody. And as I listened to the echoes fade away I could hear those rat-dogs yipping hysterically from the house. I am here, I shouted, and the cry moaned over the pond and through the trees and never came back.

I shrugged. I started to wander around, foraging among the cedars, slipping against dry magnolia sheen, breathing the bite of dying leaves and damp under-earth. Here I have seen the dog set in her season, gritting her teeth, the calf lost and recovered on the long road, the fine young bull rolling himself into the grass beneath the apple tree, and a half acre of muscadine wracked and strangled by honeysuckle year by slow year of neglect. Things were always slipping away from all of us. I whisper a list of the names of trees to myself over and over before I get in my car to drive home. What I love here, I cannot have. I cannot even remember it clearly, and it steals my tongue but for this naming of the major terms in a language that I speak alone. In this late afternoon a sudden wind cracks the skin off this secret liturgy I am mumbling and pulls the breath from me to make things be here at all. Water oak, pin oak, pine, hickory, cottonwood, chinaberry, poplar, dogwood, holly, mulberry, apple, pear, crape myrtle, fig, redbud, wild plum, magnolia, pecan, scrub oak, sycamore, cypress, peach, willow, cedar, mimosa.

ASTRONAUTS

Wally Lamb

"N ext slide," the astronaut says. For a second the auditorium is as void and dark as space itself. Then a curve of the earth's ulcerated surface flashes on the screen and the students' silhouettes return, bathed in tones of green. This is the third hour in a row Duncan Foley has seen this picture and heard the smiling public relations astronaut, sent in the wake of the Challenger disaster to the high school where Duncan teaches. It's September; attendance at the assembly is mandatory.

A hand goes up.

"Yes?" the astronaut says.

"What did it feel like out there from so far away?"

"Well, it was exhilarating. A whole different perspective. I felt privileged to be a part of a great program."

"But was it scary?"

"I'm not sure I know what you mean."

"Could you sleep?"

The astronaut's smile, which has lasted for three periods, slackens. He squints outward; his hands are visors over his eyes. "Truthfully?" he says. "No one's ever asked me that one. I didn't sleep very well, no."

"What were you afraid of?" another voice asks. "Crashing?"

"No," the astronaut says. He has walked in front of the screen so that the earth's crust is his skin, his slacks and shirt. "It's hard to explain. Let's call it indifference. The absolute blackness of it. Life looks pretty far away from out there."

For five seconds longer than is comfortable, no one moves. Then ten seconds. "So, no," the astronaut repeats. "I didn't sleep well."

A student stands, his auditorium seat flapping up behind him, raising a welcome clatter. "How do you go to the bathroom in a space suit?"

There is laughter and applause. Relief. The astronaut grins, returning to his mission. He's had the same question in the first

121

two sessions. "I knew *some*body was going to ask me that," he says.

Scanning his juniors in the middle rows, Duncan spots James Bocheko, his worst student. Jimmy's boots are wedged up against the back of the seat in front of him, his knees gaping out of the twin rips in his jeans. There's a magazine in his lap, a wire to his ear. He's shut out the school and the astronaut's message from space. Duncan leans past two girls and taps Jimmy's shoulder.

"Let's have it," he says.

The boy looks up—a confused child being called out of a nap rather than a troublemaker. His red bangs are an awning over large, dark eyes. He remembers to scowl.

"What?"

"The Walkman. You know they're not allowed. Let's have it."

Jimmy shakes his head. Students around them are losing interest in the astronaut. Duncan snatches up the recorder.

"Hey!" Jimmy says out loud. Other teachers are watching.

"Get out," Duncan whispers.

"Get laid," the boy says. Then he unfolds himself, standing and stretching. His boots clomp a racket up the aisle. He's swaggering, smiling. "Later, Space Cadets!" he shouts to all of them just before he gives the door a slam.

On stage, the astronaut has stopped to listen. Duncan feels the blood in his face. His hand is clamped around the Walkman, the thin wire rocking back and forth in front of him.

*   *   *

Stacie Vars can't stand this bus driver. She liked the one they had last year—that real skinny woman with braids who let them smoke. Linda something—she used to play all those Willie Nelson songs on her boombox. Stacie saw Willie Nelson in a cowboy movie on Cinemax last night. It was boring. He wears braids, too, come to think of it. This new bus driver thinks her shit don't flush.

Nobody at school knows Stacie is pregnant yet, not even the kids in Fire Queens. She's not sure if they'll let her stay in the drum corps or not. She doesn't really care about marching; maybe she could hold kids' jackets and purses or something. Ever since she got pregnant, she has to go to the bathroom all the time. Which is a pain, because whenever you ask those teachers for the lav pass, it's like a personal insult or something. She couldn't believe that geeky kid who asked the astronaut today about taking a crap. God. That whole assembly was boring. Except when Jimmy got kicked out by her homeroom teacher. She's not sure if Jimmy saw her or not when he passed her. He gets mad if she speaks to him at school. He's so moody. She doesn't want to take any chances.

The bus jerks and slows. Up ahead Stacie can see the blue winking lights of an accident. The kids all run over to that side of the bus, gawking. Not her; she doesn't like to look at that kind of thing. Jimmy says there's this movie at the video store where they show you actual deaths from real life. Firing squads and people getting knifed, shit like that. He hasn't seen it yet; it's always out. "Maybe it's fake," she told him. He laughed at her and said she was a retard—that if it was fake, then you could rent it whenever you wanted to. She hates when he calls her that. She's got feelings, too. Last week Mrs. Roberge called Stacie's whole science class "brain dead." Stacie doesn't think that's right. Somebody ought to report that bitch. Those police car lights are the same color of the shaving lotion her father used to keep on top of the toilet. Ice Blue Aqua Velva. She wonders if he still uses that stuff. Not that it's important. It's just something she'd like to know.

*   *   *

Duncan is eating a cheese omelet from the frying pan, not really tasting it. He's worried what to do about Jimmy Bocheko's hatred; he wishes he didn't have all those essays to grade. Duncan replays the scene from two days ago when he'd had the class write on their strengths and weaknesses. Bocheko had done his best to disrupt the class.

"Is this going to count? What do we have to write on something so stupid for?"

"Just do it!" Duncan shouted.

The boy reddened, balled up the paper he'd just barely started, and threw it on the floor. Then he walked out.

The other students, boisterous and itchy, were suddenly still, awaiting Duncan's move.

"Okay now," he said in a shaky voice. "Let's get back to work." For the rest of the period, Duncan's eyes kept bouncing back to the paper ball on the floor. The astronaut's assembly today was *supposed* to have given them distance from that confrontation.

At the sink of his efficiency apartment, Duncan scrapes dried egg off the frying pan with his fingernails. This past week when he did the grocery shopping (he uses one of those plastic baskets now instead of a wheel-around cart), he forgot the S.O.S. Yesterday he forgot to go to a faculty meeting. He was halfway home before he remembered Mrs. Shefflot, his carpooler, whose husband was already there picking her up by the time Duncan got back to school. He knows three people his age whose parents have Alzheimer's. He wonders if it ever skips a generation—plays a double dirty trick on aging parents.

When the phone rings, Duncan tucks the receiver under his chin and continues his chores. The cord is ridiculously long; he can navigate his entire residence while tethered to the phone.

The caller is Rona, a hostess at the racquetball club Duncan joined as part of his divorce therapy. Rona is divorced, too, but twenty-three, eleven years younger than Duncan—young enough to have been his student, though she wasn't. She grew up near Chicago.

"What's worse than getting AIDS on a blind date?" Rona asks in her cheerful rasp. At the club, she is known as hot shit. Kevin, Duncan's racquetball partner, thinks she's desperate, would screw anything.

Duncan doesn't know.

She is giggling; he has missed the punch line. This is the second AIDS joke he's heard this week. Duncan waters his plant and puts a bag of garbage on the back porch while Rona complains about her boss.

". . . to get you and me over the midweek slump," she is saying. She may have just asked him out for a drink. There is a pause. Then she adds, "My treat."

Duncan has had one date with Rona. More or less at her insistence, he cooked dinner at his apartment. She arrived with two gifts: a bottle of Peachtree schnapps and a copy of *People* magazine. All evening she made jokes about his kitchen curtains being too short. Fingering through his record collection, she told him it was "real vintage." (Her favorite group is Whitesnake, plus she likes jazz.) After dinner they smoked dope, hers, and settled for James Taylor's Greatest Hits. She didn't leave until twelve-thirty, two hours after the sex. This struck Duncan as inconsiderate; it was a school night.

"I think I'd better beg off," Duncan says. "I've got essays to correct tonight." He holds them to the phone as if to prove it's the truth. Kevin is probably right about her. He's glad he used that rubber she had in her purse, embarrassing as that was.

"Oh wow," she says. "I'm being shot down for 'What I Did Over Summer Vacation.'" Duncan tells her he'll see her at the club.

Duncan's ex-wife used to love to read his students' work. She always argued there was a certain nobility amid all the grammatical errors and inarticulateness. Kids being confessional, kids struggling for truth. After they separated, Duncan kept stopping by unannounced with half-gallons of ice cream and papers he thought might interest her. Then, when she had her brother change all the locks, Duncan would sit on the front porch step like Lassie, waiting for her to relent. Once she stood at the picture window with a sheet of notebook paper pressed against the glass. *Cut this shit out*, it said in Magic Marker capitals. *Grow up!* Duncan assumes he will love her forever.

Wearing underpants, sweatshirt, and gym socks, Duncan crawls between his chilly sheets. He snaps on his clock radio and fans out the essays before him. He'll do the worst ones first. The disc jockey has free movie tickets for the first person who can tell him who sang "If You're Going to San Francisco, Be Sure to Wear Some Flowers in Your Hair."

"Scott MacKenzie," Duncan says out loud. He owns the album.

Halfway through his third paper, he looks up at the radio. The announcer has just mentioned James Bocheko.

"Bocheko, a local youth, was dead on arrival at Twin Districts Hospital after the car he was driving . . ."

When the music starts again, Duncan turns off the radio and lies perfectly still, confused by his own giddy feeling. He leans over and picks up James Bocheko's paper, which he took from the floor that afternoon and flattened with the palm of his hand. The wrinkled yellow paper is smudgy with fingerprints, the penmanship as large and deliberate as a young child's:

Strength's: I am HONEST. Not a wimp.

Weakness's: Not enouf upper body strength.

Duncan drinks bourbon from a jelly jar until the shivering stops. Then he dials his old telephone number. "Listen," he says to his ex-wife. "Can I talk to you for a minute? Something awful happened. One of my kids got killed."

At two, he awakens totally cold, knowing that's it for the night's sleep. When he rolls over, his students' papers crinkle in the folds of the quilt.

*   *   *

Stacie sits with her hands on the table, waiting for her mother to go to work.

"You ought to eat something besides this crap," her mother tells her, picking up the large box of Little Debbie cakes. She blows a cone of cigarette smoke at Stacie. "A fried egg or something."

It's the second morning since Stacie's felt like eating, but the thought of an egg puckering in a frying pan gives her a queasy feeling. She's eaten three of the cakes and torn the cellophane packaging into strips.

"Mrs. Faola's knitting a sweater and booties for the baby," she says, trying to change the subject. "Pale pink."

"Well, that'll look pretty g.d. foolish if you end up with a boy, won't it?"

"Mrs. Faola says if I wear something pink every day for a month, it will be a girl."

Her mother takes a deep drag on her cigarette and exhales. "If that wasn't so pathetic, it'd be hilarious, Stacie. Real scientific. I don't suppose you told the mystery man the good news yet."

Stacie picks at a ball of lint on the sleeve of her pink sweater. "You better get going," she says. "You'll be late for work."

"Have you?"

"What?"

"Told him yet?"

Stacie's cuticles go white against the table top. "I *told* you I was telling him when the time is right, Mommy. Get off my fucking case."

Linda snatches up her car keys and gives her daughter a long, hard stare. "Nice way for a new mother to talk," she says. Stacie stares back for as long as she can, then looks away. A ripple of nausea passes through her.

Her mother leaves without another word. Stacie watches the door's Venetian blind swing back and forth. God, she hates her mother. That woman is so intense.

If it's a girl, Stacie's decided to name her Desiree. Desiree Dawne Bocheko. Stacie's going to decorate her little room with Rainbow Brite stuff. Mrs. Faola says they sell scented wallpaper now. Scratch'n'sniff—she seen it in a magazine. Stacie might get that, too. She's not sure yet.

Everything is finally falling into place, in a way. At least she can eat again. This weekend, Stacie's going to tell him. "Jimmy," she'll say, "Guess what? I'm having your baby." She hopes they're both buzzed. She could very well be a married woman by Halloween; it could happen. God. She already feels older than the kids in Fire Queens. Maybe they'll give her a surprise baby shower. She imagines herself walking into a room filled with balloons, her hands over her face.

When the phone rings, it embarrasses her. "Oh, hi, Mrs. Faola.

No, she left about ten minutes ago. Yeah, my pink sweater and pink underpants. No, I'm going to school today."

Mrs. Faola lives in Building J. She watches for Stacie's mother's car to leave, then calls and bribes Stacie to skip school and visit. Today she has cheese popcorn. Oprah Winfrey's guests are soap stars.

"Nah, I really think I should go today," Stacie repeats. She loves to see Jimmy in the hall, even though she can't talk to him. No one's supposed to know they're semi-going out. "When *can* I tell people," she asked him once. "When you lose about half a ton," he said. She's *going* to lose weight, right after the baby. Mrs. Faola says Stacie better get used to having her feelings hurt—that that's just the way men are. Stacie would die for Jimmy. Mrs Faola had an unmarried sister that died having a baby. Stacie's seen her picture.

"Tomorrow I'm staying home," she promises Mrs. Faola. "Gym on Friday."

She guesses most people would find it weird, her friendship with Mrs. Faola, but she don't care. Last week they played slapjack and Mrs. Faola gave her a crocheting lesson. She's going to give her a home perm when Stacie gets a little farther along, too. In her mind, Stacie's got this picture of herself sitting up in a hospital bed wearing a French braid like Kayla Brady on *Days of Our Lives*. Desiree is holding onto her little finger. They're waiting for Jimmy to visit the hospital. He's bringing a teddy bear and roses for Stacie. The baby has made him wicked happy.

Mrs. Faola is right about abortion being a fancy name for murder. Stacie won't even say the word out loud. At least her mother's off her case about that.

She stands up quick and gets that queasy feeling again, but it passes. She coats her mouth with cherry lip gloss and picks up her notebook. On the cover she's drawn a marijuana leaf and surrounded it with the names of rock groups in fancy letters. She keeps forgetting to erase Bon Jovi. Jimmy says they're a real suck group, and now that she thinks about it, they aren't that good.

On her way out, she looks at the cowgirl on the Little Debbie box. She's so cute. Maybe Desiree will look something like her.

*   *   *

Unable to sleep, Duncan has dressed and walked, ending not by design at an early morning mass at the church of his childhood. In the unlit black pew he sits like a one-man audience, watching uniformed workers and old people—variations on his parents—huddled together, making their peace. They seem further away than the length of the church. In his coat pocket Duncan fingers James Bocheko's list of strengths and weaknesses. The priest is no one he knows. His hair is an elaborate silver pompadour. From the lectern he smiles like a game show host, coaxing parishioners to be ready for their moment of grace when it comes hurtling toward them. Duncan thinks of spiraling missiles, whizzing meteors. He imagines the priest naked with a blow-dryer, vainly arranging that hair. He leaves before communion.

This early, the teachers' room is quieter than Duncan is used to. He listens to the sputter of a fluorescent light, the gurgle of the coffee maker. Jimmy Bocheko stares back at him indifferently, his eyes blank and wide-set. A grammar school picture. Duncan draws the newspaper close to his face and listens to his own breathing against the paper. The boy dissolves into a series of black dots.

At 8:15, Duncan is seated at his desk, eavesdropping. His homeroom students are wide-eyed, animated.

"My brother-in-law's on the rescue squad. The dude's head was ripped right off."

". . . No, that red-haired kid in our health class last year, the one with the earring."

"Head-on collision, man. He bought it."

A girl in the front row asks Duncan if he knew a boy named Jim Bocheko.

"Yes," Duncan says. "Awful." The girl seems disappointed not to be the one breaking the news. Then she is looking at his reaction. He thinks foolishly of handing her Jimmy's list.

The restless liquor night has already settled in Duncan's stomach, behind the lids of his eyes. The P.A. hums on. "All right, quiet now," Duncan says, pointing halfheartedly toward the box on the wall.

". . . a boy whose tragic death robs us just as his life enriched us." The principal's mouth is too close to the microphone; his words explode at them. "Would you all please rise and observe a moment of silence in memory of your fellow student and friend, James Bocheko?"

Chairs scrape along the floor. The students' heads are bowed uneasily. They wait out the P.A.'s blank hum.

Duncan notices the fat girl, Stacie, the chronic absentee, still in her seat. Those around her give her quick, disapproving glances. Should he say something? Make her stand?

The girl's head begins to bob up and down, puppetlike; she is grunting rhythmically. "Gag reflex," Duncan thinks objectively.

Yellow liquid spills out of her mouth and onto the shiny desktop.

"Oh, Christ, get the wastebasket!" someone calls. "Jesus!" The vomit splatters onto the floor. Those nearby force themselves to look, then jerk their heads away. Two boys begin to laugh uncontrollably.

A gangly boy volunteers to run for the janitor, and Duncan assigns the front-row girl to walk Stacie to the nurse's office. "Come on," the girl says to her, pinching a little corner of the pink sweater, unwilling to get closer. Stacie obeys her, bland and sheep-dazed, her chin still dribbling.

Jimmy Bocheko's moment of silence has ended but nobody notices. The vomit's sweet vinegar has pervaded the classroom. Windows are thrown open to the cold. Everyone is giggling or complaining.

". . . and to the republic for which it stands, one nation under God, indivisible . . ." the P.A. announcer chants.

The first-period bell rings and they shove out loudly into the hall. Duncan listens to the random hoots and obscenities and details of the accident. "If he gives us a quiz today, I'll kill myself," a girl says.

Duncan turns a piece of chalk end over end. He wonders if the decapitation is fact or some ghoulish embellishment.

A freshman thumps into the room, skids his gym bag across the floor toward his seat. "Hey, Mr. Foley, did you know that kid that got wasted yesterday? He lives next door to my cousin," he says proudly. "Whoa, what stinks in here?"

*   *   *

Stacie keeps pushing the remote control but everything on is boring. That Willie Nelson movie is on Cinemax for the one zillionth time. She wishes she could just talk to someone like that last year's bus driver—someone who could make it clear. Only what's she supposed to do—call up every Linda in the stupid phone book? It's *weird*; he never even knew. Unless he's somewhere watching her. Like a spirit or something. Like one of those shoplifting cameras at Cumberland Farms. She lies down on the rug and covers herself with the afghan. Her stone-washed jeans are only three months old and they're already too tight. She undoes the top button and her fat flops out. She can feel it there, soft and dead against the scratchy carpet and she lets herself admit something: she didn't tell him because she was afraid to. Afraid to wreck that hospital picture she wanted. Her whole life sucks. She could care less about this stupid baby. . . .

She wakes with the sound of footsteps on the porch, then the abrupt light. She clamps her eyes shut again. Her mother's shadow is by the light switch. The rug has made marks in her cheek.

"What time is it?"

"Five after seven. Get up. I'll make supper. You should eat."

Stacie begins quietly when the macaroni and cheese is on the table. "I got something to tell you," she says. "Don't get mad."

Her mother looks disgustedly at something—a gummy strand of hair hanging down in Stacie's plate. Stacie wipes her hair with a napkin.

"There's this kid I know, Jimmy Bocheko. He got killed yesterday. In an accident."

"I know. I saw it in the paper."

"He's the one."

"The one what?"

"The father."

Stacie's mother is chewing a forkful of food and thinking hard. "Are you telling me the truth?" she says.

Stacie nods and looks away. She hates it that she's crying.

"Well, Stacie, you sure know how to pick them, don't you," her mother says. "Jesus Christ, you're just a regular genius."

Stacie slams both fists on the table, surprising herself and her mother, who jumps. "You could at least be a little nice to me," she shouts. "I puked at school today when I found out. It's practically like I'm a widow."

This makes her mother hitting mad. She is on her feet, shoving her, slapping. Stacie covers her face. "Stop it, Mommy! Stop it!"

"Widow? I'll tell you what you are. You're just a stupid girl living in a big fat dreamworld. And now you've played with fire and got yourself good and burnt, didn't you?"

"Stop it!"

"Didn't you? Answer me! Didn't you?"

*   *   *

"The jade plant looks nice over there," Duncan says. His ex-wife has rearranged the living room. It looks more angular, less comfortable without his clutter.

"It's got aphids," she says.

He remembers the presents out on his backseat. "Be right back," he says. When he returns, he hands her a small bag of the raw cashews she loves and a jazz album. His ex-wife looks at the album cover, her face forming a question. "I've been getting into jazz a little," he explains, shrugging.

Although he would have preferred the kitchen, she has set the dining room table. The meal is neutral: chicken, baked potatoes, salad.

After dinner he wipes the dishes while she washes. She's bought a wok and hung it on the kitchen wall. Duncan's eyes keep landing on it. "What's the difference between oral sex and oral hygiene?" he asks abruptly after an uncomfortable silence. It's one Rona has told him.

"Oh, Duncan, how am I supposed to know? How's your family?"

"Okay, I guess. My sister is pregnant again."

"I know," she says. "I saw your father at Stop and Shop. Did he mention it?" She hands him the gleaming broiler pan. "He was wearing a jogging suit. Gee, he looked old. He was mad at your mother. She sent him to the store for yeast and birthday candles and he couldn't find the yeast. Then there I am, the ex-daughter-in-law. He was having trouble handling eye contact."

"Did you tell him where the yeast was?"

"Yeah, then he thanked a pile of apples over my left shoulder and walked up the aisle." She turns to Duncan with a worried look. "How come he's limping?"

"Arthritis. It's weird, Ruthie. He and my mother are turning into little cartoon senior citizens. They go out to lunch every day and find fault. Last week I got stuck in a line of traffic; there's some slowpoke holding everybody up. It turns out to be my father. They're, I don't know, shrinking or something. She has a jogging suit, too. They wear them because they're warm. I can't help seeing them from a distance. It's bizarre."

Two years ago, when the specialist confirmed that his wife had indeed finally conceived, Duncan drove to his parents' house to break the news. His mother was out, his father in the back yard pruning a bush. "See what a little prayer can get you, Mr. Big Deal Atheist?" his father said, jabbing Duncan in the stomach with the butt of the clippers, harping all the way back to an argument they'd had when Duncan was still in college. When he went to hug him, Duncan drew back, resentful of his father's claiming credit for himself and his god. They'd been putting up with those fertility treatments for two years.

Duncan's ex-wife begins to munch on the cashews. "These are stale," she says. "Good. Now I won't pig out."

"I'm going out with somebody. She's divorced. Somebody from racquetball."

There is a pause. She pops more nuts into her mouth and chews. "Well," she says, "that's allowed."

"So when did you take up Chinese cooking?" he asks, pointing to the wok. He means to be nonchalant but is sounding like Perry Mason grilling a guilty woman. The wok is a damning piece of evidence.

"I'm taking one of those night courses at the community college. With a friend of mine from work."

"Male or female?"

She clangs the broiler pan back into the bottom drawer of the stove. "An androgyne, okay? A hermaphrodite. I thought you wanted to talk about this kid who got killed."

He takes Bocheko's paper out of his wallet and unfolds it for her. "Oh, Duncan," his ex-wife sighs. "Oh, shit."

"The kids were high on the death thing all day, exchanging gruesome rumors. Nobody wanted to talk about anything else. Do you think I should write them a letter or something?"

"Who?"

"His parents."

"I don't know," she says. "Do what you need to do."

On TV James Taylor is singing "Don't Let Me Be Lonely Tonight." On their honeymoon, Duncan and his ex-wife sat near James Taylor at a Chinese restaurant in Soho. Duncan and he ordered the exact same meal. Duncan is dismayed to see James Taylor so bald.

"You know my record collection?" Duncan says to his ex-wife. "Do you think it's real 'vintage'?"

"Real what?" she asks in a nasal voice. He realizes suddenly that she's been crying. But when he presses her, she refuses to say why.

*   *   *

Yellow leaves are smashed against the sidewalk. Duncan collapses his black umbrella and feels the cold drizzle on the back of his neck. An undertaker holds open the door. Duncan nods a thank-you and sees that the man is in his twenties. This has been happening more and more: people his father's age have retired, leaving in charge people younger than Duncan.

He signs a book on a lighted podium and takes a holy picture, a souvenir. On the front is a sad-eyed Jesus, his sacred heart exposed. On the back, James Bocheko's name is printed in elegant script. Duncan thinks of the boy's signature, those fat, loopy letters.

In the main room, it's that pompadour priest before the casket, leading a rosary. Duncan slips quietly past and sits in a cushioned folding chair, breathing in the aroma of carnations. Someone taps his arm and Duncan sees he has sat next to one of his students, a loudmouthed boy in James's class.

"Hi, Mr. Foley," the boy whispers hoarsely. Duncan is surprised to see him fingering rosary beads.

James Bocheko's family is in a row of high-backed chairs at a right angle to the closed casket. They look ill at ease in their roles as the designated royalty of this occasion. A younger brother pumps his leg up and down and wanders the room. An older sister rhythmically squeezes a Kleenex. Their father, a scruffy man with a bristly crew cut and a loud plaid sports jacket, looks sadly out at nothing.

Only James Bocheko's mother seems to be concentrating on the rosary. Her prayer carries over the hushed responses of the others. "Blessed art thou who art in heaven and blessed is the fruit of thy womb."

When the prayers are finished, the priest takes Mrs. Bocheko's wrists, whispers something to her. Others shuffle to the front, forming an obedient line. Duncan heads for the foyer. They will see his signature in the book. Mrs. Bocheko will remember him from the conference. "I know he's no angel," she said specifically to Duncan that afternoon, locking her face into a defense against the teachers and counselors around the table. Only now does he have the full impact of how alone she must have felt.

He sees that girl, Stacie, at the rear of the room. She is wearing a low-cut blouse and corduroy pants; her feet are hooked around the legs of the chair in front of her.

"How are you feeling?" Duncan whispers to her.

"Okay," she says, looking away.

"Were you a friend of his?"

"Kind of." She says it to her lap.

In the vestibule the undertaker is helping the priest into his raincoat. "So who's your money on for the Series this year, Father?" he asks him over his shoulder.

Stacie walks past two other girls, representatives from the student council who stare after her and smirk.

The door is opened again for Duncan. The drizzle has turned to slanted rain.

*   *   *

Stacie is lying on her bed, wondering what happened to her notebook. She hasn't been back to school in over a month, since the day she found out about Jimmy—that day she threw up. She's not going back, either, especially now that she's showing. Let the school send all the letters they want. She'll just burn them all up and flush the ashes down the toilet. She's quitting as soon as she turns sixteen anyways. What does she care?

That Mr. Foley probably has her notebook. She's pretty sure she left it in his room that morning. Of all his teachers, Jimmy hated Mr. Foley's guts the most. He was always trying to get them to write stuff, Jimmy said, stuff that wasn't any of his fucking business. What she can't figure out is why he was at Jimmy's wake—unless he was just snooping around. By now, he's probably looked through her notebook, seen the pages where she's written "Mrs. Stacie Bocheko" and "Property of Jimmy B." and the other private stuff.

Being pregnant is boring. There's nothing good on TV and nothing around to eat. She wishes she and Mrs. Faola didn't have that fight. She still wants to get that perm.

She reaches back for her pillow. Drawing it close to her face, she pokes her tongue out and gives it a shy lick. She remembers the feel of Jimmy's tongue flicking nervously all over the insides of her mouth. She remembers the part just before he finished—when he'd reach out for her like some little boy. She gives the pillow several more little cat licks. She likes doing it. It feels funny.

Then she's aware of something else funny, down there. It feels like a little butterfly bumping up against her stomach, trying to get out. It makes her laugh. She kisses the pillow and feels it again. She begins either to giggle or to cry. She can't tell which. She can't stop.

*   *   *

"Why don't you ever make us write *good* stuff?" they wanted to know.

Duncan turned from the chalkboard and faced them. "Like what?" he asked.

"Like stories and stuff. You know."

So he gave them what they wanted and on Friday every student had a story to hand in. He has read them over and over again, all weekend, but has not been able to grade them. Each of the stories ends in death; sentimentally tragic death, the death of a thousand bad television plots. Not knowing where to put the anxiety with which James Bocheko's death has left them, they have put it down on paper, locked it into decorous penmanship, self-conscious sentences they feel are works of art. How can he affix a grade?

The newspapers are full of fatal accidents. A bride has shot her husband. A girl has choked to death in a restaurant. On the hour Duncan's clock radio warns parents against maniacs, purveyors of tainted Halloween candy.

His wife is not safe. She could die in a hundred random ways: a skidding truck, faulty wiring, some guy with AIDS.

It was in a Howard Johnson's ladies' room that she first noticed she was spotting. "It's as if her body's played a joke on itself," the gynecologist explained to Duncan the next afternoon while his wife stared angrily into her hospital sheets, tapping her fist against her lip. "The amniotic sac had begun to form itself, just *as if* fertilization had occurred. But there was no evidence of an egg inside." Duncan recalls how she spent the next several weeks slamming things, how he rushed up to the attic to cry. There was no death to mourn—only the absence of life, the joke.

When he hears the knocking, he is sure it's his ex-wife, wearing her jeans and her maroon sweater, answering his need for her. But it is Rona, shivering in a belly dancer's costume. "Trick or treat," she says, holding out a tiny vial of coke. "We deliver." Inside, she lifts her coat off her shoulders and her costume jangles. She runs her chilled fingers over the stubble of Duncan's jaw.

*   *   *

The janitors have taken over the school, rigging the country-western station through the P.A. system and shouting back and forth from opposite ends of the corridor as they repair the year's damages. It's the beginning of summer vacation. Duncan sits in his classroom, surrounded by the open drawers of his desk. He's in a throwing-away mood.

What he should do is make plans—get to the beach more, visit someone far away. He should spend more time with his father, who is hurting so badly. Sick with grief: that phrase taking on new meaning. "You're not alone, I know what it's like," Duncan told him last week. The two of them were fumbling with supper preparations in Duncan's mother's kitchen, self-consciously intent on doing things the way she'd always done them. "When Ruthie got remarried this spring, it was like she died to me, too."

"Bullshit!" his father snapped. His grip tightened around a fistful of silverware. "That divorce was *your* doing, the two of you. Don't you *dare* compare your mother's death to that. Don't you *dare* say you know what it's like for me." That was six days ago. Duncan hasn't called since.

He's saved the bottom-right desk drawer for last, avoiding it as if there's something in there—a homemade bomb or a snake. But it's the confiscated Walkman, buried under piles of notices and tests. Duncan sees again James Bocheko, crouched in the dark auditorium.

Tentatively, Duncan fixes the headphones to his ears and finds the button. He's expecting screaming guitars, a taunting vocal, but it's electronic music—waves of blips and notes that may or may not mean anything. After a while the music lulls him, makes him feel removed and afloat. He closes his eyes and sees black.

The janitor makes him jump.

"What?" Duncan says. He yanks off the earphones to hear the sound that goes with the moving lips.

"I said, we're going now. We're locking up."

*   *   *

He drives to the mall for no good reason. It's becoming a pattern: tiptoeing in and out of the bright stores, making small purchases because he feels watched. At the K-Mart register, he places his light bulbs and sale shampoo before the clerk like an offering.

Exiting, he passes the revolving pretzels, the rolling hot dogs, a snack bar customer and a baby amid the empty orange tables.

"Hey!" she says. "Wait."

He moves toward them, questioning. Then he knows her.

"You're a teacher, ain't you?" She's flustered for having spoken. "I had you for homeroom this year. For a while."

Bocheko's wake. The one who vomited—Stacie something. It's her hair that's different—shorter, close-cropped.

"Hello," he says. It scares her when he sits down.

The baby has glossy cheeks and fuzzy red hair that makes Duncan smile. He pushes the infant seat away from the edge of the table.

"Did you find a notebook in your class? It's green and it's got writing on the front."

The baby's arms are flailing like a conductor's. "What did you say?"

"My notebook. I lost it in your room and I kind of still want it."

There's a large soda on the table and a cardboard french fry container brimming with cigarette butts. Behind her the unoccupied arcade games are registering small explosions. "I don't remember it. But I'll look."

"I thought maybe you were saving it or something."

Duncan shrugs. "Cute baby," he smiles. "Boy or girl?"

"Boy." She blushes, picks him up so abruptly that he begins to cry.

"How old?"

"Stop it," she tells the baby. She hooks a strand of hair behind her ear with her free hand.

"*How old* is he?"

"Almost three months. Shut up, will you? God." Her clutch is too tight. The crying has turned him red. "Could you hold him for a second?" she says.

Duncan receives the baby—tense and bucking—with a nervous laugh. "Like this?" he asks.

Stacie dunks her finger into her soda and sticks it, dripping, into his mouth. "This sometimes works," she says. The crying subsides. The baby begins to suck.

"Uh, what is it?" Duncan asks.

"Diet Pepsi. It's okay. He ain't really getting any. It's just to soothe him down." The baby's shoulders against Duncan's chest relax. "You have to trick them," she says. Then she smiles at the baby. "Don't you?" she asks him.

"What's his name?"

"Jesse," she says. "Jesse James Bocheko."

Her eyes are gray and marbled, noncommittal. He looks away from them, down. "I'm sorry," he says.

It's she who breaks the silence. "Could you do me a favor? Could you just watch him for a couple of seconds so's I can go to the ladies' room?"

He nods eagerly. "Yes," he says. "You go."

The soft spot on the baby's head indents with each breath. Duncan *sees* his own thighs against the plastic chair, his shoes on the floor, but can't *feel* them. He's weightless, connected only to this warm, small body.

"Baby . . ." he whispers. He closes his eyes and puts two fingertips to the spot, feeling both the strength and the frailty, the gap and pulse together.

THE RANGOLD CONSORTIUM

Kent Nelson

At Gardner's Labor Day Barbecue in Cos Cob, Rangold suggested, after a few gin and tonics, that we form a consortium.

"Who's we," asked Gardner, who always challenged an idea.

Rangold eyed Gardner coolly, as though to confirm complicity. "Well, Dexter and you," he said, "and me, and, of course, Wrye there." He finished by pointing at me.

"A consortium to do what?" Dexter asked.

With long deft fingers, Rangold plucked the lime from his gin and squeezed it slowly and thoroughly into his glass. He continued looking at me as if, as his attorney, I had already approved the plan. Then he looked at the other two. "Make wine," he said softly.

Gardner was a heavyset man, and in his marriage and business relationships he was accustomed to physical intimidation. With friends he sometimes became testy when the same tactics were unsuccessful. "What about this, Wrye?" he asked me.

"It's the first I've heard of it," I said.

"You can buy it cheaper," Gardner pronounced.

Rangold smiled. "Maybe you can," he said, picking up the skewer from the side of the brick barbecue where Gardner had laid a mountain of steak chunks, green peppers, tomatoes, raw cauliflower, and pineapple. "That's not the point."

"We know nothing about winemaking," Dexter put in.

Rangold ignored his bit of cynicism, and I could tell he was not about to let the matter drop. He could be quite tenacious in his own exuberant and gracious way. "I've thought about it," he said easily, "and it's natural for the four of us. Dexter can provide some of the matériel through his wife's pharmaceutical company, and Wrye has incomparable legal skills." He paused and then added, as if to counter my well-documented conservatism, "Wrye is the sort of man who would appreciate an adventure like this."

"Wait a minute," Gardner interrupted. "You're serious?"

"Do I look like a man who jests?"

"Well, I'm not so different from Wrye," Gardner said huffily. He poked the coals roughly and adjusted the air intake vent on the barbecue. "What do I contribute?"

Rangold nodded. "I didn't mean to imply you weren't so adventurous as Wrye," he said, setting up Gardner beautifully. "You supply the land."

"Land?"

"We'll convert your holdings in the Hudson Valley."

The smoothness with which Rangold offered this statement and the casual way he sipped his drink afterward gave Gardner a start. "My little bit of land?"

"I know about your land," Rangold said.

"It's a tax shelter."

"You can get the same break from a vineyard as from a farm," I said, welcoming the opportunity to play devil's advocate. I took pleasure in Gardner's discomfort.

"And Rangold?" Gardner snapped at me. "What does he do?"

Rangold smiled and brandished the skewer in his hand. His dark eyes gleamed like a child's. "It's my idea," he said. "I'm the wine taster."

Dexter laughed aloud. Per custom, he was inebriated before the food was served, and he looked at me and raised his thick, graying eyebrows. "The POWs used to make wine from raisins during the war," he said.

"Rangold was not in the war," said Gardner.

Rangold danced away, parried in the air with the skewer, then jabbed the point lightly into Dexter's green Izod shirt. "Wine is better for you than that nasty manhattan," he said. "Do you think you can prevail upon your sweet wife for a few pieces of glass? If you want, I'll speak to her."

"No, no," Dexter said, rising to the bait. He was afraid of his wife.

"Wonderful," Gardner said sarcastically. "Dexter's the hardware man, Wrye lends his legal mind, and I give up my farm. When we've given up all we have, Rangold drinks the stuff."

"It won't be 'stuff,' " Rangold said. He smiled quickly, resuming his enthusiasm. "The South is ready for wine. The Midwest, too. Many parts of the country are just awakening to civilization."

Gardner turned abruptly to me. "What do you think, Peter? You've been quiet."

I nodded and grinned. "I'm starving," I said. "When do we eat around here?"

*   *   *

At the office, during the rare lulls in my schedule, I thought about the consortium the way one contemplates a vacation in Bora Bora. Winemaking sounded exotic and alluring, but like the tropical isle, it was conjured up by a poster in a travel agency window. I was forty years old, without children, married happily to the same woman for fifteen years. Of course the consortium appealed to my romantic side, especially since Jane and I had let our own lives slip forward in the usual routine. She was busy with community projects and played tennis rather well. On the whole, I would have said she was satisfied with her life. She had wanted children, I suppose, but in the beginning the law practice took so much time I was reluctant, and then she had been caught up in a local small ensemble. For one reason and another, we had let the time pass.

And so I would have let the consortium go by, except for Rangold.

Rangold called me several times that week, and after a few minutes' discussion about investment strategy, he managed to turn the conversation to the consortium. He asked once, rather offhandedly, whether I might draw up a memorandum on Gardner's tax advantages were he to convert the farm into a vineyard. Another time he asked whether I would research the licenses we would need, the FDA requirements, the federal controls on alcohol. "We want to comply with all the laws," he said.

"Rangold," I cautioned, "even to think of this consortium requires the infusion of some cash."

"Let me worry about the cash," he said.

"I mean *big* cash."

I could almost see his smile over the telephone, the beaming grin that so often overwhelmed rational opposition. "Will you be playing tennis this weekend, Peter?" he asked, changing the subject. "I have a game, too. We'll talk."

Rangold, of course, was an enigma. Though I had known him for ten years and had been his attorney for eight, he had always been somewhat distant, even with me, his closest confidante. He had never married, but it had been quite normal to include him in our social events. He belonged to the club, and he had made us all money at one time or another with his advice on real estate, oil leases, or sleeper stocks. Aside from that, he had a sense of humor, immaculate manners, and an engaging mind. At many of our gatherings, he was the center of attention as he recited parts of a current off-Broadway show or told funny anecdotes about growing up in a small town in Oklahoma.

In his twenties and early thirties he had been a skiing enthusiast, a sailor with Bermuda race experience, and an inveterate card-player. At thirty-eight, only a few months before dreaming up the consortium, he had suffered a heart attack while playing handball over in Greenwich. Still, he had barely slowed down. He continued the same exhaustive research on undervalued companies, raced directly from work into the city for a play or a gallery opening, kept up the whirl of parties. The only discernible difference between Rangold before and Rangold after was his aloofness. He seemed to be someone trying to remember why he had come to the party.

That weekend Jane and I had a mixed doubles match with Constance and Dexter Reid on the court next to Rangold's. While Dexter chased my errant shots, I had occasion to observe Rangold closely. Despite his heart attack, he was in remarkable condition. His legs were thin and wiry, and his stomach flatter than most twenty-year-olds'. He had obviously learned tennis without the benefit of instruction, for he slapped at the ball instead of stroking it from the shoulder, but he made up for his lack of grace with a stubborn defensive game. He ran from corner to corner hitting wicked spins and throwing up a variety of baffling lobs. I shouldn't have thought the effort good for him.

"Peter, are you with us or against us?" my wife asked once. "It's your serve."

I caught the two optic yellow tennis balls she threw to me and stepped to the line to the right of center.

"Fifteen-thirty," she said. "Ad court."

I smiled sheepishly and moved over. My serve skipped to Dexter's forehand, and he returned the ball just past Jane's reach. I was left with a tentative wood shot that dribbled into the net.

"Oh, Peter," Connie Reid called across, "you could at least *try*."

When the tennis was over and I had been properly chastised for my lackadaisical play, I went and sat down on the terrace with Rangold. He had a towel around his neck and was sipping a beer, watching two ten-year-old girls rallying on the nearby court. He seemed dazed when I said hello.

"Oh, hello, Peter."

"Are you all right?" I asked.

"Six-two, six-three," he said. "That's all right against Harvey." He paused, concentrating on the white-clad form of the girl closer to us. She was tall, thin, and tanned, and had a mane of flashing blond hair tied behind her head with a blue ribbon. "You could have had a child like that," he said wistfully.

I watched the girl briefly. She was quite graceful and hit a good clean backhand, following through with her racquet toward the net. But I turned away from her. "I wanted to speak to you about the wine venture," I said.

His eyes brightened. "I was thinking of Sauvignon blanc," Rangold said. "I'm certain Gardner's farm has the right exposure. But there's research to be done." He stopped and looked at me with some uncertainty. "You don't want to back out?"

"I want more information," I said. "You know me. I need something more solid to go on."

He was relieved. He stood up suddenly and clenched the towel around his neck. "In that case, what do you say we get Dexter and Gardner and drive up to Gardner's farm?"

His urgency made it difficult to refuse. "When?"

"Now," he said. "We'll leave immediately. I thought you said you wanted more information."

Within fifteen minutes, Rangold had showered and was on the telephone to Gardner. I explained to Jane that I was making a quick business trip to the Hudson Valley and would be home by early evening.

*   *   *

Rolling hills stretched along the river, rising into bluffs and wooded knolls. The highway threaded through farmland and small towns, and Rangold grew visibly more animated, rhapsodizing about the countryside as we entered each new glade or glimpsed a new panorama. Once he nearly ran the Mercedes off the road. "Now wouldn't that be perfect for a vineyard?" he asked, pointing to a white-fenced pasture.

"I don't know what the emergency is," Gardner groused. "It takes years to make wine."

"That's precisely why we have to get started," Rangold countered, steering along the winding road. "The sooner we get growing grapes, the better."

"Why don't we just buy a winery already extant?" asked Dexter, who had had the foresight to bring a flask for the trip. "We could trade upon the name."

Rangold glared into the rearview mirror. "Have you no pride at all?"

Dexter, who suffered daily the sword of his wife's money, was terribly shaken.

"Of course he has pride," I said. "Dexter meant it would be simpler to get a cost picture if we bought an existing company. As you propose it, we don't know our contributions, and the return is suspect at best."

"Amen," said Gardner.

Rangold turned his attention to me across the front seat. "I'm surprised at you, Peter. You of all people. What about your collection of sculpture?"

"What about it?"

"What kind of return does that give?"

"No financial return, of course," I said.

"And did you buy your pieces of art because of what they cost?"

"He didn't buy them all at once," Dexter put in.

"The point is," Rangold went on, "he enjoys them. They may not be Rodins or Modiglianis, but he had collected what he finds aesthetically pleasing."

Gardner was never loathe to jump into the fray. "Peter's motives are irrelevant," he said. "You're asking each of us to invest a healthy chunk of our assets."

Rangold sighed. "No one has to put up anything if he doesn't want to," he said slowly. "I was hoping that as friends of long standing, and after what I've done for you . . ." He broke off his sentence and stared sadly out the window.

"Turn left here," Gardner said all of a sudden.

Rangold braked quickly and turned down a small dirt road which was bordered on both sides by beautifully tended apple trees.

For years Gardner had called his farm "a little plot of land that helps at tax time," and none of us had thought much about it. We were not expecting the truth that Rangold knew.

"Eighteen hundred acres," Rangold said. "I checked the county records. Of course there's some woodland, too. Gardner has a full-time manager for the horses and several other employees who live on the place."

We pulled up to the house and got out, and Rangold pointed out where we would grow grapes, where the pressing would be done, how the trucks would be loaded over by the horse barn. We were dumbfounded.

"Perfect, isn't it?" Rangold asked.

*   *   *

For nearly a month after our impromptu excursion, I did not see Rangold. I called his office several times, but his secretary said he was not available. Then he was out of town indefinitely. Dexter reported he had gone by Rangold's office personally for details so he might approach his wife about providing wine bottles, but he had been shuffled rudely to a subordinate who had never heard of the consortium. I was less concerned that Rangold was incommunicado than by another piece of uncharacteristic information I'd heard about him on the street. So I left word he should call me immediately when he got back.

When another week went by and I had still not heard from him, I drove around to Rangold's house, a modest place his parents had left him several blocks from the water. A dim glow shone from the window, but I assumed it was an automatically timed light to discourage burglars, and I nearly drove on without stopping. At the last minute, out of curiosity or premonition, I decided to make certain. I stopped and rang the bell and was surprised to hear footsteps.

Rangold answered the door. He was unshaved and his clothes were dirty and disheveled. I thought perhaps he was drunk—I had never seen him like that before—but as he motioned me inside with a wave, I could tell his eyes were as clear and penetrating as ever. He led me into the living room, which was filled to overflowing with the antique furnishings he had inherited. I sat stiffly in a swan's-neck chair.

"I understand you've been away," I said with a touch of malice.

Rangold paced a worn oriental rug. "I apologize for not returning your call," he said. "I just couldn't bring myself to it."

"I've been worried," I said, trying to take the charitable view.

He ran his hand roughly through his thinning hair and turned toward me. "You know, Peter, I envy you."

I waited for him to go on, not certain exactly what he was getting at.

"You have a reputable career, a beautiful wife, a house you're proud of . . ." He left off without direction.

"Many people have those things," I said uncomfortably. I did not think of myself as particularly astute for having arranged my life as I had.

"I know, I know," he went on. "Compared to *me* maybe you've lived less glamorously. . . ." He paused again. "I'm sorry. I've been under a great deal of strain lately."

"If I can help, I'd be glad to." I had already forgotten what I'd heard on the street.

Rangold moved to the window where he stood for a long time, staring into the dark yard. Then he whirled around and came toward me, his eyes racing past the superficialities of the room toward something deeper. "Do you mean that?" he asked.

"Yes, I do."

He paused a moment, only a few feet from me. "Why don't you and Jane have any children?"

"Why don't we?" I was shocked by the boldness of the question.

"Do you think the world is such a terrible place?"

I looked away, but I could still feel the force of Rangold's eyes on me. "We've never agreed on the subject," I said. I felt it was none of Rangold's business, but at the same time I almost wished to explain how Jane and I had reached the point of no return, how so much time had passed.

"Would you do it for me? Have a child for me?"

I held his gaze too long, calmly I thought, but I must have registered my embarrassment. Rangold was silent for a long time, walking back and forth. Then he slumped into a chair. "God, I'm sorry, Peter," he said. He lowered his head into his hands and wept.

*   *   *

Afterwards, as I drove home, I thought this behavior of Rangold's quite extraordinary, but I determined to forgive him and, above all, to keep it to myself. After all, everyone was entitled to some bouts of lunacy, especially in private and between friends.

The next morning I ran into Rangold outside the local coffee shop. He looked a thousand times better. He'd shaved and showered, and he had on a blue, three-piece suit. Whatever demon had troubled him the night before had been exorcised.

"We'll forget last night," he said. "The important thing is that you and Jane come to the Chautauqua at seven o'clock. It's my treat."

"Tonight?"

"Friday."

"Evening, I presume."

"Evening, yes," he said impatiently, as though I were making fun of his vagueness. "It will be a black-tie dinner, a great event."

I told him we'd be delighted to come, and we made small talk about sports. I was about to suggest he come up to my office to discuss the rumors I'd heard that he'd been sinking large sums of money into commodity futures—a most dangerous game—when he gave me an abrupt pat on the back. "Well, I've got to run," he said, and he was gone.

Not a half hour afterward, Gardner called. "Did you hear about Rangold?" he asked.

"Hear what?" I thought he was referring to a debacle in commodities.

"He's been in an automobile accident. A friend of Eve's just called from the hospital auxiliary."

"I spoke to him only a few minutes ago," I said.

"Apparently it's not too serious, but he's been admitted. He's still in the emergency room having tests. The guy is nuts."

I hung up and called the hospital and left a message that I would stop by to see Rangold after work. Then I called the police. I was Rangold's attorney, I told them, and wanted to learn the facts of the case.

"There's no report filed yet," the officer said. "I don't think there'll be any lawsuits, though. You lawyers sure work fast."

"We have to eat, too," I said. "What happened?"

"It was a single-car accident, so most likely he'll be charged with careless driving, unless he was drinking. Your Mr. Rangold ran right off the road and into a tree. He was lucky he wasn't hurt more seriously. He didn't have a seat belt on."

I thought about that and went early to the hospital.

Rangold was usually so flamboyantly dressed that to see him in a hospital gown was an incongruous sight. He had a small bandage on his head and several abrasions, but otherwise he seemed in good spirits—more so than he had a right to be.

"They're keeping me overnight for observation," he said.

"They should do it for safekeeping," I replied. "Did they X-ray your head?"

Rangold smiled. "We need to move forward, Peter."

"Why don't you take it easy for a few days?"

He shook his head. "No, no. You see, just yesterday, before you came over to my house, I was thinking about the sun's losing heat. Have you noticed it? That's what the scientists say. And way out in space, beyond our vision, stars are forming and breaking apart in megaton explosions." He looked at me earnestly. "It's true," he went on, "and when do you think these things happen?"

"All the time," I said, as though answering a child's riddle.

"Exactly. They're happening *now* ."

He turned away to the darkening window, and something in his gaze made me keep silent, as though I ought not disturb him in his own gray world. I waited until he turned back to me.

"Is there anything you need?" I asked. "I should get home, but I could stop off somewhere."

"A bottle of Chambertin Clos de Beze, 1961," he said, giving me his most brilliant smile.

*   *   *

The rest of the week I was busy in the office, but in the evenings I secluded myself in my den and perused the materials I'd got from the public library. I knew that before Christ wine had been a source of human nourishment, that festivals for Dionysus and Bacchus were features of early civilizations, that in myth wine was the symbol for the blood of Christ. I had drunk wine, even excellent wine. I was familiar with the names pinot noir, beaujolais, and chardonnay. But still, my ignorance was staggering. I had never truly understood the methods of wine production or the differences among types of grapes. So I studied the determinants of climate and soil, the different ways grapes could be fermented, the mixtures of additives. I examined the fashions of wine bottles and glasses, the medical opinions on the effects of wine on health; I learned about red spiders, leaf-rollers, and root fungi.

One night Dexter called. He suggested taking our wives up to the Finger Lakes district to visit the vineyards of Widmers and Konstantin Frank. "I wanted to take Connie to show her how some families operate at a profit," he said.

"Most of those places grow only the *vitus labrusca*."

"What?"

"It's the native grape noted for its foxy taste," I explained. "I'm sure Rangold will insist we try *vitus vinifera*."

"I don't care what we try," Dexter said. "Connie won't cooperate without a certain return on capital."

"Maybe we should all wait and see what happens Friday," I said. "Rangold is planning something splendid."

Dexter paused on the other end of the line. "He's been acting strangely lately," he said finally. "Do you think he has a new woman?"

The thought of a new woman had not entered my mind, but when it did, it accounted for most of my misgivings about Rangold's behavior. Some men, and Rangold was certainly one of them, could do bizarre things when they were in love.

Rangold's taste ran to exotic types not appropriate for the group at the club, and he was mindful of that. I had met several of them over the years—one on a day sail, another on a ski weekend in Vermont. Not that his women were in any way questionable in character, but by and large the neighborhood was station wagon and gabardine rather than Ferrari and frilled lingerie. At any rate, I felt better just thinking of Rangold's involvement with an ash-blond actress.

On Friday evening, Jane and I arrived at the restaurant a few minutes late. The Chautauqua was named after the progressive nineteenth-century movement intended to spread culture and the arts, and in our town it was the best of the best restaurants. We left our car with the doorman, and as we walked up the red-carpeted stairway, I saw Rangold waiting for us with an exquisite-looking woman at his side. "She explains everything," I said to Jane.

When we came into the paneled lobby, however, Rangold greeted us with a cold stare. "Where's Gardner?" he asked, looking at his watch.

Jane and I were taken aback by his tone. Rangold had never been so discourteous. I tried to smile at the woman beside him, who seemed not the least bit fazed by Rangold's rudeness. She was indeed beautiful. A trace of pink on her lips set off her dark skin and her black hair. Her dress was cut so deeply in front that Jane looked away.

"Gardner telephoned to say he'd be tardy," I said, halfway facetiously.

"*You* are tardy," Rangold retorted. "Gardner's inexcusably late."

Rangold stormed to the desk and telephoned. Within earshot of everyone, including Connie and Dexter Reid, who had joined us from the bar, Rangold upbraided Gardner and ordered him to appear. Rangold made it clear by his expression when he hung up that Gardner was on the way.

"Now," he went on cheerfully, "where were we?"

"We were on introductions," I said curtly.

"Oh, yes. This is Silvia de Santellana. I'm sorry she doesn't speak much English. She's just arrived from Chile."

Silvia was the daughter of a wealthy Chilean vintner whom Rangold had consulted. Rangold had apparently brought her up for the party as a representative of Chilean wines. She was not his special friend.

While we waited for Gardner, Rangold introduced us to other personages from the wine world—a gentleman from the Loire region of France, a rotund German from Mainz, an elderly Brazilian whose wizened face suggested a shriveled grape. When Gardner arrived in his tuxedo, out of breath and angry, Rangold was most charming. He apologized profusely, emphasizing that Gardner himself must understand the feeling of wanting everything to go right for a most important evening.

"I thought we were having dinner," Gardner said.

"Your choice of goose or lamb," Rangold said. "But first . . ."

He led us all through the main lounge and into an opulent private room. The walls were covered in red velvet, and turn-of-the-century chandeliers cast a sprinkling of diamond light over the white tablecloths. Dexter uttered an audible gasp, and even Gardner, the eternal skeptic, seemed in awe. Before us was a long table lined with hundreds of bottles of wine together with hundreds of glasses. Three waiters in white coats stood poised behind the table awaiting Rangold's signal. We were all hushed as we moved forward.

Rangold smiled, as if in conspiracy with himself. "Here," he said, "is the current state of winemaking."

He stepped forward amid a spattering of spontaneous applause and opened the first bottle himself. He poured only the bottom of his glass full, lifted the crystal rim in an exalted manner to his nose, and slid his nose across the lip. He swirled the golden liquid and examined it carefully in the light. An intensity settled into his face, as though he were seized by a fanatical vision which only he perceived.

"To Noah," he said, "who became a husbandman and planted a vineyard." He sipped the clear white wine, measured its taste upon his palate, and nodded.

*   *   *

After that evening, the consortium began to take hold. Constance Reid had apparently been won over by Rangold's performance and had agreed to retool her small manufacturing plant in East Orange, New Jersey, for the production of bottles and glasses and assorted other equipment that Rangold determined we would need. She had even offered her laboratory in Philadelphia as a convenient place to experiment with plant hybridization and rates of fermentation, but Dexter, in a bold display of independence, warned her that the consortium involved him and not her.

Gardner had caught the fever, too, and once convinced of something, he was as difficult to untrack as a runaway train. He had spoken to the Soil Conservation Service in Clermont and had already sounded out neighboring property owners about leasing additional land from them. He asked me to draw up the necessary documents for his contribution to the partnership.

"What partnership?" I asked.

"I thought you'd been working on it," Gardner said, surprised. "Aren't you the lawyer?"

"I've been waiting for instructions," I said.

"Peter, why are you forever so cautious?"

"Because of Rangold," I said.

During his mysterious absence, Rangold claimed to have visited dozens of vineyards in Europe, South America, and California in an attempt to find the best quality grape we could reasonably expect to grow on Gardner's farm. He had spent four days in Paris, too, at the *Office International de la Vigne et du Vin*, studying the world's collected literature on the subject. "As with everything else," he said, "once you step beyond the fringe, the drama becomes exceedingly complex."

He favored a *vinifera* grape, as I had expected. The one he chose was grown principally in a small area of Germany known as Unterfranken, whose wine center was Würzburg. The wine produced there, *Frankenwein*, was dry, with only the barest suggestion of sweetness, reminiscent of good chardonnays. Rangold's analysis was that the climate of the Hudson Valley mirrored almost exactly that of the *Würzburger Maintal*.

In short, after Rangold's epicurean heroics at the Chautauqua, everyone seemed ready to plunge ahead. Everyone, that is, except me. I had become more ambivalent. It did not concern me so much that the venture was dubious from a financial standpoint. After all, I had invested sums of my own in sculptures which might prove valueless. But it was one thing to choose for oneself art one likes, and quite another to become entangled in a business arrangement whose prime mover was a deranged man.

I didn't know what to tell Jane. She thought Rangold so thoroughly delightful that I hesitated alarming her about my suspicions. On the other hand, I needed her help and support if I were going to withdraw from the consortium. I knew what she would say: "Oh, Peter, why do you worry so much about what people think? Do what you believe is right."

I had not mentioned to her, either, the question Rangold had posed to me that night at his house. I had thought about it a good deal, however, the way one mulls over any new crisis. Strangely, it was Jane who broached the subject one night when we were already in bed.

"You're concerned about Rangold, aren't you?" she asked.

"Yes, why?" I rolled over toward her.

"I saw him today at the club."

"What did he say?"

"He asked whether I had conceived yet."

"Rangold asked that?"

"What have you told him, Peter?"

I sat up in bed, upset at the insinuation that I should discuss such topics with Rangold. I turned on the light and looked at her with a frown. Her darkish, graying hair was loose upon the pillow, and there were the beginnings of crow's feet at the corners of her eyes. It seemed as though I had somehow missed looking at her for years, and suddenly I felt shallow and very sad.

"Well?" she asked, as if embarrassed at being scrutinized so closely.

"I haven't told him anything."

"Where would he get such an idea then?"

I shook my head and kissed her.

*   *   *

The next evening, as I was working late in the office, Rangold called. I was angry at him, but I held off for a moment. He sounded far away, and yet at the same time, hesitant to speak too loudly.

"Where are you?" I asked.

"In Harlem."

"For God's sake, what are you doing in Harlem?"

"I've been arrested," he said. "I'm at the police station."

"Arrested for what?"

"It's a mistake, of course. Can you come down here, Peter, and get me out?"

I was not eager to go to Harlem, but I nodded to my reflection in the dark window. "Tell me where," I said.

An hour later I was at the police station, prepared with the appropriate gestures of righteous indignation, though, on the way, it had occurred to me that Rangold had not told me the charge. I assumed it would be some kind of morals rap, and was ready to argue Rangold's clean slate.

"Hold on, buster," the police sergeant said. He leaned forward, spreading his huge black hands on his desk. "You're lucky you've got a client left."

"So I've been told," I said. "Just what did he do?"

"He punched a brother in a bar," the sergeant said. "And then hit a policeman."

"That doesn't sound like Rangold," I said, lowering my voice.

"Then he runs," the sergeant went on. "Where do you think a white man can run to around here?" He stared at me coldly.

"I don't know."

When I had paid the bond and got Rangold out of lockup, he was all smiles. We left the station before my anger boiled up and over. "What in the Sam Hill are you doing in Harlem?" I asked.

"Research," he said.

"God, man, are you crazy?" I looked up and down the street but did not see his Mercedes. "How'd you get here anyway?"

"I took the subway," Rangold said calmly. "That was part of the research."

So we drove back together. Apparently he had gone into the bar for a drink, and a man had made an insulting remark about him, so Rangold had hit him. The man's friends came after Rangold, and as he backed away, someone else had grabbed him from behind. That had been the plainclothes policeman. He'd hit that man, too, and had run. "What would you have done?" Rangold asked.

"I would have stayed in Cos Cob," I said.

*   *   *

That night I dreamt about Rangold. We were in Paris together, searching among the small galleries for sculptures. I had already investigated two or three places, and Rangold was becoming impatient. I asked questions of the concierge about the sculptors and took my time examining with a magnifying glass the various pieces of art. Rangold wanted a drink. "French wines!" he kept saying. "What are we doing in this place?"

"Just be patient," I said. I circled a small marble bird whose wings were outstretched.

"We're wasting time," Rangold said. "This is France."

"Look at this bird," I told him. "It's exquisite." I was taking out my glass again, when Rangold burst across the room, tore the bird from its base, and hurled it as hard as he could to the floor.

The gallery concierge jumped up, and I shouted at Rangold, but he grabbed another piece from the window display and threw it across the room, smashing it against the wall. "French wines!" he shouted. "Goddamn it, Peter, French wines!"

I woke in a sweat at 4:45 A.M., the red digital numbers alive in the room. Outside the wind was blowing, and a branch scraped against the side of the house. I got up, careful not to wake Jane, and went into the living room. A breath of dawn was coming through the tangled trees to the east, and the events of the past days came to me in collage. Rangold, I suddenly realized, was fascinated with dying.

*   *   *

I had meant to go to him right then, but when I called, he had not answered. On my way to work I went by and found the house locked, his Mercedes gone from the garage. At eight-thirty his secretary said he had told her only that he would be out of town a few days. He had not said where he was going.

I waited anxiously.

Then one afternoon he surfaced in my office, barging past the startled receptionist and throwing open the door. "Peter," he said, "there's something I have to ask you."

"Wait a minute. . . ."

"I've driven all the way to California and back," he said. "This is important."

He sat on the edge of my desk on some files I'd been working on. He looked exhausted, as though he had been awake for several days.

"I got the D.A. in Harlem to drop the charges entirely," I said, "if you agree to make a donation to the Boys' Club."

Rangold nodded, as though whatever I said would be fine. He seemed barely able to remember the incident. In fact, he looked so tired I felt sorry for him. He'd been under such great stress for weeks, self-imposed, I knew, and yet it was clear he was troubled. For the moment, it seemed, he had even forgotten why he had come to see me.

"You see, Peter, we are all nothing," he said almost dreamily. "Nothing at all."

I smiled briefly to humor him. "Oh?"

"I have made a fortune in commodities," he said blithely. "Millions."

"Is that what you wanted to ask me about?" I was thinking of the short-term tax consequences if he had realized such a gain.

"Immaterial," he said, waving his hand. He narrowed his eyes and leaned over my desk, bracing himself on his hands. "What I wanted to ask you is . . ."

He paused, visibly shaken.

"Look," I said, "why don't you come to dinner? I was going to leave early tonight, and we'll have a drink."

Rangold shook his head. "I can't possibly. I have too much to do, too much."

"Nonsense," I said lightly. "Jane wouldn't mind, really. For a man with millions, whatever it is can wait."

He measured me with a severe gaze. "You're wrong," he said harshly. "Nothing can wait. Absolutely nothing."

"In that case, let me tell you something," I shot back, losing patience. "I'm out of the consortium."

Rangold looked at me as though struck dumb. "You can't . . ." He hesitated. "If it's money . . ."

"Damn it if I can't. No one has signed any documents. And it's not the money. I don't even know whether you intend to make any wine. So far it has all been carried off with mirrors."

I got up and went to the closet for my coat, and Rangold grasped my arm as I passed him. He was suddenly contrite. "Why don't I come to dinner? Are you sure Jane won't mind? We can talk."

I stopped off on the way home to replenish my supply of gin and Scotch, and when I arrived, Rangold was already there, talking animatedly with Jane in the kitchen. I went to hang up my coat.

"I told her I invited myself," Rangold said cheerfully.

"What to drink?" I asked.

"Nothing for me," Rangold said.

I fixed myself a stiff Scotch, and when I came into the kitchen again, Rangold wandered away. I kissed Jane and lingered a moment. "Sorry to do this to you," I said. Then I added in a whisper, "I don't think Rangold is well."

"I don't think you're well," Jane said, smiling at me. "It's no trouble. I'll just add a little water, and then I'll change my clothes to look presentable."

I went off to find Rangold, who was in the den studying my sculptures. He gazed at each one intently, yet impatiently, I thought, as though they represented to him some puzzle or challenge. He moved from a bronze horse to a bust of Balzac to the marble bird which was in my dream. "Where did you get this?" he asked, holding up bird.

"Phoenix," I said, sipping my Scotch. "It's lovely, don't you think?"

Rangold did not answer. He examined the bird in the light, then, still holding the figure, turned toward me. "What I meant to ask you, Peter, is how you have managed for so long."

"How have I managed what?"

"So *long*," Rangold went on. "How have you been able to live your life so long in this way?"

I felt my grim smile wither on my lips. "I thought you envied me," I said sarcastically. "My reputable career, my beautiful wife, my house . . ."

Rangold lifted the bird higher into the air. "Now the man who made this was alive," he said. "He may not have created the perfect figure—in fact the flaws are obvious. Yet those very flaws made it more astonishing. Do you see what I mean? Perfection would be less inspiring than imperfection." He paused, lowering the bird, but still holding it. "No risk, Peter. You're a man of no risk."

"Just because I refuse to go along with your wild schemes?"

Rangold smiled. "No," he said. "Gardner and Dexter are simpler souls than you and I, happier in their own ways, but at the same time, incapable of ideas we might entertain. We are men of dreams, Peter, but you are letting yours pass by."

I could not escape my anger. What right did Rangold have to speak to me in such a condescending manner? What kind of monster was he? And yet I felt myself shift slightly, as if a tremor deep within the ground had moved a ponderous weight in me. One action induced another so that the entire earth trembled and heaved and then resettled into a new configuration. An unaccountable brilliance seemed to flow from Rangold then, and I was reminded of the night at the hospital when he had said that stars out in space were forming and breaking apart at that very moment. I had been afraid then that I had missed something, but now I understood it perfectly. Rangold was not insane at all. He was stronger and more certain of himself than I, and he was pursuing at the very edge of his life what we all wanted to pursue but did not know how.

Rangold broke the silence. "You, of course, Peter, have other opportunities, you and Jane. But I have only the consortium, and it will take a long time. That's why I want to begin. That's why I want you in. You're my friend, Peter. We have only years, and years are not eons."

I heard Jane's footsteps in the living room, and all of a sudden, she appeared in the doorway in a bright yellow dress. Her hair was combed and fixed neatly, and her skin looked soft. A strange expression played across her face, I thought, as though she were aware of the tightness that still lingered in the room.

"Are you two solving the world's problems?" she asked.

"Yes," Rangold said. He put the bird back onto the table.

Jane smiled. "Well, dinner is ready," she said, as though that were all that mattered. She came forward and took my hand.

THE PROFESSIONAL THIEF

Alice Denham

My moment of truth, said Steadman, was when I told them how rich my family was, and I got in the fraternity. Steadman found what we photographers discover—pleasing composition. People of goodwill don't doubt great oddities if no malice is evident.

Steadman wrote he'd enjoyed my exhibit. He lived on the floor above so he dropped his card with the network logo in my box. When we talked he was so bland, I almost said no. But he had huge shimmering bluelake eyes, like Paul Newman in four-color glossy. Sincere eyes that sunlight revealed to have layer below sparkling layer of kindness, equanimity, trusting vulnerability. His eyes spoke for him. With my new lens I could capture those eyes, with late afternoon sun slicing the retinas.

Off we went on his Honda 1000 to an outdoor cafe on the towpath canal. Steadman said he was tech director on the Nightly News, so we talked shop, and I criticized the way they lit the Anchor—too harsh and solemn, meaningless closeups. Closeups only for emphasis, I tell them, said Stead, but they stress Personality. That's the problem, I said, he's a nitwit and it shows up close. We laughed together.

Light rippled on the brackish canal, in white wine glasses, and Stead's eyes above the checked tablecloth. Stead said TDs did okay but he had additional income of $4,000 a month from circuitry he designed and patented working for IBM right out of college (MS in EE from Penn). He didn't like to tell girls this, he said, because they got greedy, but from all sources, he figured he brought in $150,000 a year at age thirty. As a poor freelancer, my brow arched and arms crossed greedily. Why don't you quit and give *me* your job? I smirked. Keeps me off the street, said he. At the station they know I'm working for fun and it gives me status; they treat me better.

Stead said he was found, only days old, in a basket on a doorstep in South Africa with a tag attached saying, "My name is Grimm." His parents, who couldn't have children, were happy to have him, as they were rich, in import-export and emigrated here when he was five. That he became sterile through rheumatic fever as a child in Johannesburg, if it wasn't from working around radiation later. After IBM he worked for Surplex to support the highliving of Cherry, his rich wife whom he greatly loved, who died in a car crash. He still mourned Cherry. His family was closing their Bryn Mawr and La Jolla homes and moving to Australia, to save on taxes.

Rich, loving, sterile meaning safe. You're a walking cliché, I said, amused. What kind of basket?

Stead smiled calmly, his eyes a blue trust.

What sort of apartment did this rich young man have? I suggested we have a drink there. Oddly, an efficiency like mine only pristine, antiseptic. On the glass coffee table, a stack of photography magazines, a plastic flower, and a stack of racing magazines. I race bikes, he said. An unnoticeable sofa, and that was all, like a spy's pad that told nothing, except the person's desire to conceal every aspect of personal identity. Vodka and crackers in the icebox. I eat out, he said. The sofa pulls out, he said, and reached for me. If he was really sterile, that could help, ultimately, with a stranger. I was suspicious of everything but intrigued.

Next evening I watched Nightly News closely when, lacking ads, they ran the Crawl. Technical Director—was not Steadman. But he was there, way down, among the Cameramen. When I confronted him, he shambled shyly and said he was trying to impress me because I was a fine well-known photographer with my own exhibit, that he built himself up so I'd go out with him. Then there was my auburn hair like Cherry's, and my steely gaze, not at all like Cherry's. Pish taw, but shucks I fell for it. Even though he didn't need cash, he enjoyed humble camera work after the arduous years of high earning and overworking for Cherry. Ah, the eyes have it, Stead. He wouldn't let me photograph him.

My body curved around him, we rode bike trails through suburban woods behind great houses. I shot them so they looked like they were in dense forest. We came home, fell into each other's arms. I wanted to shoot the bike races from the racers' point of view. We made plans but he canceled at the last minute week after week. I'd see him leave the building on his bike in workman's overalls with a toolkit, also in jeans, but never a suit. He liked my darkroom; he could go through shots for hours, uh huh, uh huh, without commenting, even when asked.

One day Mother and I were walking through the lobby to her car and we bumped into Steadman and what was obviously his mother.

His sturdy-lined, brown-coated mother made my mother look patrician, a grand lady with her social chinlifted smile and offhand grace, perhaps possessed by her daughter, sporting her spring capelet. I introduced Mother and he introduced his own, who deferred to us with her head. Steadman was shaken at seeing us. I was crushed. We were all polite.

I refused to see him. He begged. It began in college, Stead confessed, when I pledged Phi Delta Theta. How could I say my father was a drug clerk when everybody else's father owned Pittsburgh? He never even owned the drugstore; Mom teaches kindergarten. So I made them rich and everybody accepted me. The more rich stories I told, the better everybody like me. That's why Cherry liked me; well, why she accepted me. Cherry liked to live high, she didn't want children, so I had a vasectomy for Cherry to keep the marriage going, while I was with Surplex. We were doing fine out there in California but her family checked Dun & Bradstreet and when they discovered my family was poor, she divorced me. His appealing eyes were piteous. Why do you think I'm sending my parents to Australia? I'm tired of the stories. It's a strain to keep them all straight.

So you're exiling your parents? I was no longer amused but dizzy. If you were doing well, Stead, what difference if your parents were poor? With your patents and your circuitry, I challenged him, and you MS/EE?

I quit college after a year, said Stead. The doctor says I'm a pathological liar.

I walked off, furious. Even that sounded like a lie.

Next time I bumped into Steadman he was with a gorgeous blonde woman and her two towhead children, his new girlfriend Cynthia, a standup comic, who wanted him to back her in a one-woman show. She looked at him lovingly; he was excited by the project. For a split second I was jealous. Wait till Cynthia finds out, I thought.

I was shooting Significant Homes for the magazine's three summer issues, from Georgetown colonials to Foxhall Road mansions to Cleveland Park Victorians, on into Chevy Chase traditional and Potomac modern and northern Virginia horsey. Steadman wanted to come along as my assistant, claiming he went on all the House & Garden tours because he was fascinated by such houses. What about your job? I don't go in till six, please, he said. I said no. How could the man expect me to trust him? Have you told Cynthia there's no money to back her? Becomingly, he blushed; it was easier to just break it off.

Steadman's fascination was such he begged to see my prints. I didn't want him in my life; I didn't want him in my apartment. Did I think he'd steal my negatives? Too busy, I said. Steadman persisted, with great softness. He'd knock. Your fan club, he'd say. My fear began to seem silly, exaggerated. He was so appreciative when I finally let him see the prints. He went over them carefully, uh huh, uh huh, examining some with a magnifying glass, wanting to know where each house was and who the rich and mighty were who resided there. You'll know when the world does, I said. No money, I said, no patents, no Surplex, and no Cherry. What did you really do before? I locked my darkroom behind us.

His blue eyes had never looked more trustworthy or compassionate.

What the hell, Stead, I know you're a liar.

Pathological, diagnosed, he said.

You're not going to impress me with guff. Why not bare your soul?

Stead twisted about in his chair like a boy wrestling with demons, petulant with guilt. Another phony show? I was in the Marines, a Communications Specialist. Electronics. What does that mean? I questioned every statement. Mostly I placed wiretaps. Where? In the home of high officials, important people. But how? They trained me to Break & Enter. Wow. I smiled, hid my shock. First, I photographed the place, made measurements, cut the window, brought replacement glass. Best was when I got in as a telephone repairman; I could place the tap right under their noses. If they had several phones, I could check out the joint. If I broke and entered, I could do more—tap the library, dining room, etc. Stead warmed to his subject, enjoying it. After the Marines I did it for the FBI, freelance. Couple of times, the cops were called. When we got back to the Station House, I showed them my credentials; they made a phone call and I was sprung.

Still smiling, I nodded encouragement. Were the taps legal? If I asked, he might clam up.

You learn lots of tricks, said Stead. You watch the house to find out daily movements and habits. I read the news and society pages daily to find out when who goes on vacation, or to Bonn, Geneva, etc. I cut glass like butter. Several times I timed it to coincide with church chimes, like a symphony. Couple of times the lady of the house caught me. By then I could bluff anybody. Hi, I'd say, about ten more minutes and your phone'll be good as new. Walked in, I'd say; I knocked, and didn't you holler, Come on in?

Whew, I said.

Once at this VIP's—you've probably photographed him—I heard the key in the door. Stead's eyes were alert, glazed. I put in the replacement glass while he unlocked the front door. I gave him the phone routine. Door was locked, he said, reaching into his briefcase. I thought he might go for a gun. I never carry a weapon. Locked it behind me, I said, for protection. Out, he said. I got.

Phew. Did he report you?

Naaah, they don't want it known, these bigshots.

You've always gotten away with it?

So far. Stead was silent. There *was* Cherry, he said. Don't *ever* take my picture, he said, and left.

Half the people in Washington highrises won't tell you what they really do. Darting through halls dressed in gray, they duck questions, look through you, won't smile even though you've seen them thirty times. Two retired CIA and FBI men wouldn't even tell me what their *fields* had been. I felt a queasy horror. Why did Steadman tell? Since he'd already blown the romance by lying, I was a handy confessor. To get away with it wasn't enough. Someone else had to know his cunning skill, validate his daring enterprise. He could hardly videotape it for the Nightly News, so he told me.

But was it true? Or was the pathological liar working me over once more? Oh my God! I'd shown my house prints to a man who robs such houses. He'd set me up. I began to shake. I panicked and phoned the precinct. How many homes did you photograph? asked the captain. Thirty, I said. Lady, he said . . .

Now that the dam had broken, I expected more confessions. Steadman didn't know I was afraid of him; Steadman didn't dream I'd caught on. I decided to film Steadman, for my own protection, for corroboration, for information. This would be a hard test of my technical ability. I set my light half-inch video recorder within the fronds of the tropical plant, aimed at the sofa. Also I got a friend who has expertise in these things to remove my onyx from the scarf pin and replace it temporarily with a tiny hidden camera. Mike in my pocket, to break and enter Steadman in my own Sting operation. Then I waited, frightened but determined.

My layout on the Foxhall Road mansions and Georgetown colonials appeared in the June issue. Stead put a note in my box: Congratulations, S. Not a wordy fellow. I invited him for a drink.

Quite an eye for detail, said Stead, settling on my sofa with the vodka rocks, facing my hidden camera. In big houses my favorite room is the library.

You were telling me about Cherry, your wife, weren't you? My darkroom was locked.

Cherry loved money, he sighed, turning to face the video as well. When Surplex found out about my phony degree, they fired me. Slowly he let his lids slide over the blue eyes and head down, looked up at me humbly, confidentially. I didn't dare tell Cherry I'd been fired. Every day I got in the Mercedes to go to work. I rode around remembering my training.

Steadman began to weave and twist again, all over the sofa, like a maniac, while my scarfpin camera and I faced him, while the video filmed him squirming like cocaine scorpions crawled his clothes. He still wouldn't look at me; his eyes rolled around and he was red, pale, and sweaty. He was good at guilt.

So I just kept doing it, said Stead. I had all this expertise and I was out of work, nothing but free time. I learned how the big boys operate. I stake out lots of houses, usually on my bike, and take shots and blow them up. Usually I do a walk-by on each house, read all the papers, take the House & Garden tours, then jump on the opportunity. Cherry dumped me anyway and I pretty much did San Diego, so I picked Washington for the lobbyists. All these guys doling out illegal money. I got a master list of who represents what special interest. Sometimes I can jimmy a door or open a window but usually I cut glass and replace it when I get in. I've been on jobs when guards walked by, didn't spot a thing. I take the money and go. I'm only interested in cash; I don't want fences to know my business. I never take a car, just my bike, in repairman clothes.

How do you find the money? Filming away for posterity. Most people don't keep cash around.

Lobbyists do. Where do you think I'd find it?

In the library, in the desk, on high shelves in books? This was dangerous fun.

Exactly. You'd be good at this. After dinner the men take their brandy to the library to talk business. It's his room, off-limits to the family.

To pass the buck? Couldn't resist that. Do their wives know?

Mostly, I doubt it. Sometimes they report the robbery as stolen jewelry, but they never mention the cash. I'm not the real thief, I'm the small-timer. When I make the papers as a jewel thief, I get a laugh because I never touch anything but green. His eyes looked startlingly innocent.

Cherry, what happened to her? Get the whole story. Stop trembling.

She married a rich guy and got back in her family's good graces. Stead's eyes turned infinitely mournful. You like the Eyes? he asked proudly.

The camera's lapping them up right now, I thought.

My friend the phony priest taught me how. He used to cash checks for a living. He never got turned down. We practiced together—soulful eyes. His became soulful. Trustworthy eyes. Innocent, well-meaning, good-guy eyes. Calm, friendly, confiding eyes. Steadman showed me each one with subtle differences. Shy, modest, humble eyes. Eager-to-please eyes.

Wearing the humble and eager eyes, he said, I don't want you to think I'm a thief. When I reach my goal of $300,000 I'm going to quit, dye my hair blond, disappear into California and hang out on the beach.

Where's the money now? I asked suspiciously.

In safe deposits around the country. I'm close—a couple more jobs'll do me.

Steadman expressed gratitude, said he felt much better now he'd finally told someone who didn't faint with shock. The professional thief from upstairs declared me his friend.

Then he said calm as ice, I'll take the camera. I knew you were photographing me. I'll take it out and give you the setting back.

Instinctively I shoved it into my blouse.

You want me to rip it off your neck? Steadman snatched the scarfpin camera and turned at the door. I wouldn't do you any good, he said. I'm diagnosed as a paranoid schizophrenic with pathological tendencies; it's on my record. I'm a masterful liar. A violent psychopath.

Then, only once, I saw his real eyes.

Not long after, a Foxhall Road mansion I photographed for the magazine was robbed. Jewelry worth two million was reported stolen. No sign of false entry. The glamorous widow who lived there had hidden under the bed when she saw him on the stairs. He'd dragged her out, tied her up and raped her. She was lucky to be alive, she said. There were large photos and drawings of the jewelry in the papers. I gave the cops my videotape and watched it with the widow. It was Steadman, she said.

He was long gone. He must've washed the walls; the cops got no clues, no prints from his apartment. At the Nightly News, Steadman still worked as a cameraman. But he wasn't the man I knew, or the widow had suffered. The cops questioned everybody at the network, high to low, and nobody recognized him. I gave the cops all his tales, including South Africa and the tag Grimm on the basket with the found baby. Penn, the Marines, San Diego, Cherry. IBM, Surplex, the FBI. Bike racing. His poor mother, from some town in Pennsylvania. What did he introduce her as? My mother.

Not likely that Steadman, sic, would be hanging out as a dyed blond on a beach in California, having handed me that destiny. There were only two true things I knew about him. He drove a Honda, also gone, and he had lived on the floor above me. He was straight about one thing. He was a masterful liar.

POETIC DEVICES

Jim Hall

My language is a great two-headed fish that lives only in one pond in a remote mountain region. No other two-headed fish exist, and the greatest experts say that my two-headed language has no relatives in the whole world. This fish is Basque.

But it didn't take me long to understand that if I wanted to be the richest man I could be, I would have to leave behind my language. I would have to learn to speak in American.

I moved to Vermont.

This is in the country of America where everybody owns something expensive. Usually they own a very fast car. This is necessary because in America it is said, "Time is money." I came to Vermont, America, because I wished to become rich. It was an impractical wish. For everyone in that country wants the same thing. Two hundred and twenty million wishes, and all exactly the same. The air is packed with this wish.

But I believed my wish would happen, for I was using an approach that appeared most unusual. I wanted to become rich by writing poems in this language.

I had learned that there was only one rich poet in America. He lived in California. This is the reason I chose Vermont. In a country so big, I was certain that there was room for at least two rich poets. This appeared reasonable.

The other reason I lived in Vermont was that it was the home of Robert Frost, who said, "Free verse is like playing tennis with the net down." I believe Mr. Robert Frost became a rich man because of ideas like this. All verse should cost something, like a tennis ball.

This is also the part of America where another rich poet once lived. The most famous and wise and rich Mr. R. W. Emerson. He said, "I think nothing is of any value in books, excepting the transcendental and extraordinary." I agree with this sentence too.

One more sentence I agree with is: "The death of a beautiful woman is, unquestionably, the most poetical topic in the world—

164

and equally is it beyond doubt that the lips best suited for such a topic are those of a bereaved lover." This was said by a man named Allan Poe who never became very rich, but it was only because he died in a gutter before people got to know how great he was. If Mr. Allan Poe had not died in this gutter, he would be a rich poet now.

I found a beautiful woman who was also extraordinary. And she was also a user of the form of meditation named transcendental. This is a word very hard for me to pronounce. Her name was Fay Trigger. This sounded like a beautiful name to me, and I used it in several of my poems.

Fay Trigger worked in a bar in the town I picked to grow rich in. The bar's name was Snowdrop. This is poetical too. Here is Fay, and how she talked:

"One more night in this jerkwater hole and I'll puke. If I didn't have such a damn good disposition, I'd cut the throat of the next bastard that walked in here drunk looking for a warm fanny to pinch."

Some of her words were so extraordinary they were not in my dictionary.

She was beautiful too. Her hair was blonde and sometimes when she woke in the morning and I turned on the fluorescent light above the bed, I could see a rainbow of green and blue shining through her hair.

I bought her many things to show her I loved her.

Much of the money Grandmother gave me, I spent on the beautiful jewelry and perfumes she was used to wearing. She also liked beer and chocolate.

I was happy. For when I came to Vermont, I knew nobody, and could speak only a few lines from poems I had memorized, and some other words that would buy food for me. And then all at once I had a lover, with blonde hair. The next morning after Fay Trigger and I fell into our love, I wrote my first poem in America.

Everywhere I read it I was successful, money was thrown to me. It seemed to be a wonderful country for poets. People who wanted to be rich themselves still knew when they saw a man with a good idea, and they helped him become rich by this extraordinary custom of money throwing.

Sometimes the poor ones threw pieces of their food. I knew for sure I was not playing with the net down.

Fay Trigger wanted to blow this hole. By this she meant she wanted us to travel so I could grow richer by reading my poems in bars across the country of America.

Without once forgetting the wise words I had memorized in my bedroom in the Basque country, I set off with Fay Trigger. When we sat down on the bus, and it began to move, Fay Trigger said this:

"I got more baggage than I bargained for on this one. It's like being responsible for a retarded gerbil."

This is a simile. It is a very poetic device. Fay Trigger, whose blonde hair was now red for our travels, had learned this simile idea from my poems.

We stopped in the largest city in America and bought a hot breakfast where the buses arrive. I looked into a newspaper, while Fay Trigger talked to an American policeman. She was a friendly woman. She said this:

"Creeps and worms. I'm too softhearted and the creeps and worms see it right off and then what do you know, I'm a mother hen all of a sudden."

Very poetic. I couldn't help myself. I listened while I pretended to look at the heaviest newspaper ever made. This is an hyperbole. It is one of my best devices. I use it to put humor in a poem. If I think someone is beautiful, like Fay Trigger, I will say, "Her voice outsung the choir." This means it is easy to hear Fay Trigger even if there are a hundred people talking at once, like at the bus station.

In my newspaper I saw an advertisement for a poetry reading. The richest poet in America was to read his poems that night! He had come on a bus all the way from California to do this to me. This news made me lose my hunger. I had hoped that this poet from California would be content to stay home. But I then knew that, like me, he must have been given so much money from his neighbors that he had to go away. Heavy fish swam in my stomach.

The policeman who had listened to Fay Trigger asked me a question. I did not hear him at first. Then I heard him,

"You deaf?" he asked me.

I felt very sad about this rich poet coming to New York City. Now I would have to go to another town, because he would take all the money for poetry from this town. Then I thought, no, I will stay here, and not run away like a nanny goat. I will let them choose between my poetry and the richest poet in America's.

Again the policeman asked me something.

"Let's see some ID."

I said, "No, I can't see any right now. I must write a new poem about this sadness."

"I want to see some identification," he said to me. He sounded unhappy.

"You'll have to see it alone, sir," is what I answered. He seemed to be a very lonely man. He needed a friend like Fay Trigger. Fay Trigger? Fay Trigger! She had gone.

I stood up and picked up my satchel full of socks and poems. This is zeugma. It is rare and difficult. It is only the second zeugma I have ever written. My first one was, "Fay Trigger threw her shadow and empty beer can out the front door."

Fay Trigger had vanished. There were people everywhere in that big room hurrying, slouching, spying, sleeping, but none of them were Fay Trigger. The big fish swimming in my belly took a deep dive.

The lonely policeman said to me this:

"The lady had a bus to catch."

This sounded like a poetry device to me. It reminded me of what is called a euphemism.

"A bus to catch," is all I could say. But I knew this meant not a bus, but it meant Fay Trigger had died out of my life. The fish in my bowels swam quickly up into my heart and then my neck. Allan Poe, the poor poet, had experienced something similar.

The policeman used these words on me next:

"O.K. there creep, let's move on."

With my satchel by my side I walked with this policeman out into the dreary clouded day. This device is called objective correlative. It means the sun felt just the way I did.

"The square garden is in what place?" I asked this policeman.

He pointed with his big stick.

Oh, the feelings that poured through me as I walked toward the famous square garden. The feelings were too many to feel at once. The big fish was now many minnows. This is called alliteration. It is easy to do. I sometimes have done it without even meaning to. Each minnow was feeding on the new buds of my heart. These buds had grown just to hold the love I had felt for Fay Trigger.

I sat down on the sidewalk before a store selling books for adults and wrote a poem. It came to me so fast that I had not any time to use paper. I wrote it on my hand. It was for Fay Trigger, and it was the greatest poem in the western world. This is another hyperbole.

When I had finished, I had to hurry to reach the square garden in time for the richest poet in America. I stood in a line of people. It was a cold night and many of these people were wearing fur coats. And for pants, blue jeans. This seemed paradoxical to me.

I made small changes in the poem on my hand. I crossed out many adjectives. I put in some synesthesia. This is a device that I like. If you felt great sadness for, let us say losing Fay Trigger, you might say, "the cold empty odor of mink fur filled the dusk." This is too complicated for me to explain. But I understand it, anyway.

When I gave money to the man in the window, he gave me a ticket. I counted the money of my grandmother. It took me only a few seconds to do this. When I first came to America it would take me almost five minutes to count my money. This is progress.

There were thousands of people inside the square garden. All of them whispering like a congregation before Holy Communion. I sat behind two young women who had long blonde hair. Their hair fell over the backs of their seats and lay on my leg. This picture made me remember Fay Trigger, and the night I met her, and how her blonde hair lay open like a dancer's fan down the back of her blue coat. I wanted to touch the hair that lay on my knee, but the small fish bubbling in my heart kept me from moving.

Fay Trigger had said this when I told her about my love for her sunlight hair:

"I never met a black-haired man yet didn't want to jump on a blonde. And next week if I want me a blonde boyfriend, I just get out the black dye bottle."

Fay Trigger. I read the poem on my hand quietly to myself. The fat girl in a raincoat beside me looked at me and said, "You sure you got the right seat?" She made me remember Fay Trigger. Fish tickled in my throat. They swam behind my eyes fluttering as they went.

Just then all the lights blacked out and the curtains rolled open and there, in a spot of light, stood the richest poet in America. He stood behind a table much like the table where Fay Trigger and I ate our bean sandwiches. He wore blue jeans and a coat and a shirt for sweating, and a tie around his neck. His beard was gray. Behind him there was a white refrigerator. And in his hand was a bad headache. This is a device I don't use much because it is too hard to pronounce. It is called metonymy. I meant to say that in his hands was a very large jug of wine.

This confused me until I remembered what the rich R. W. Emerson said: "Bards love wine, mead, narcotics, coffee, tea, opium, the fumes of sandalwood and tobacco or whatever species of animal exhilaration." R. W. Emerson would have loved Fay Trigger. They also would have agreed on things because she was transcendental. This means that she enjoyed sitting in a chair with her eyes closed and trying to stay awake.

The richest poet in America took a long drink from his bottle and everyone applauded except me. The blonde hair on my knee flipped up and down. And the fat girl in the raincoat was the last person to stop her clapping. She wore a wide grin. I asked her what this meant, this wine drinking.

"It means he's drunk out of his gourd," is what she said to me, without looking away from the richest poet.

Then the poet walked over to the refrigerator and opened the door of it. The refrigerator was full of beer cans. It was not clear to me if he preferred wine or this beer.

Once again the audience around me clapped. The fat girl in the raincoat stomped her feet repeatedly and continued to clap after everyone had stopped.

The poet took out a beer can and ripped the opener off like he was tearing the head off a bluebird. This is another simile. For the third time the audience applauded. There were those who whistled. The fat girl was among them.

No poems had been read yet, but still the audience had clapped very hard, and if they had not given already their money to the man outside, they would have no doubt thrown their money to the stage.

Then he began to talk and what he said was not poetry. Here is some of it:

"This beats the living crud out of working for a living. It used to be I'd lie around in a damn pus-infested hotel and pull the shades down and get plastered and feel sorry for myself. Gawd, now I stay in the Hilton, have a boy bring me some Jamaican rum and get plastered and count my money. I mean, I don't understand this almighty country."

Once more there was cheering and applause. The richest poet in America was having trouble standing up. He had one hand on the table where his wine bottle was and this hand was continuing to slip. The wine bottle on the table fell onto its side and rolled off the table. It smashed on the stage floor.

The clapping for this was very loud. People began to talk to each other. The fat girl in the raincoat said, "Shhhhhhh."

He said more then:

"I mean nobody gives three hoots in hell about poetry. I don't think they ever did. I remember when I was in school, before they discovered I was a damn pervert and had my ass removed, there was a teacher went on and on about this poem and that poem. Saying it was beautiful cause it was full of this message or that message. I mean, if you want messages hang around the telegraph office, is what I say."

The fat girl loved this remark, and to prove it she whistled and stomped her feet at once. The two blonde girls in front of me decided there were other things they had to do, and they left.

The richest poet in America threw his beer can at the audience and went to the refrigerator for another one. He came back and sat on the edge of his table and said this:

"I mean, I don't have diddly squat to say to the world. What can I tell a Hindu or a Muslim or a Republican." Many people laughed now. I felt sad for the richest poet in America. He was trying very hard to remember a poem so he could begin. But he had been given some bad wine. This is what he said next:

"I'm just a wino and a stupid jerk from Pasadena who sleeps under the freeway and has whores for sweethearts. What can I tell old Miss Crampedy britches about anything? I ain't in the hills and dales and china teacup business." At this moment, the richest poet in America fell off the table. He lay kicking his legs like a beetle on its back. He tried to stand up but the great strong hand of wine pressed him down. This is personification.

The fat girl beside me laughed hard at this, then she stood up in her seat and looked very serious. Two men came onto the stage and helped the richest poet to stand up. The large room swayed as he was helped to the side. This is a device known as transferred epithet. The room didn't sway; it was the richest poet who swayed. But because he was swaying the large room seemed to be under his influence and swayed as well. Knowing about such matters can help you see how powerful poets are, even when they are very drunk.

This was a perfect moment to make myself known to New York City by reading my poem about Fay Trigger. The fat girl was still standing on her chair. She said this to me as I moved past her seat to the aisle:

"That man has more charisma than a roomful of presidents, even when he has the DTs." Then she said this, "Hey, toad, you forgot your bag."

This was true. But I could no longer reach my seat, for at that moment the poetry audience began to flow toward the exit doors. I was pushed backwards by several old women. One of them asked me this:

"Did you ever?"

The fat girl in the raincoat was calling to me from somewhere in the crowd. She had lifted up my suitcase filled with socks and poems and was shouting at people to let her get through.

The old woman who had spoken to me before spoke again when

the fat girl arrived, shoving people with my suitcase. She said, "I never."

The fat girl dropped my suitcase on the marble floor and said this to me:

"What you got in this thing, dead chickens?"

"Poems," I told her.

"Yeah, right," is what she replied. She took out a cigarette and lit it. Something about this reminded me of Fay Trigger.

"I am a poet. And now that I find the richest poet in America is very ill with alcoholism, it appears I will be needed."

She coughed smoke and said, "Riiiiight." We watched the people pouring out of the auditorium.

"I shall take the richest poet in America job, since now it seems to be open."

She dropped her cigarette and ground it into the marble floor and stared at my eyes in a manner that Fay Trigger often used just before she was about to say, "And a pig was ice skating to the Blue Danube, too." This device is new to me.

The fat girl in the raincoat said this:

"Everybody in this damn building is a poet. This town is lousy with poets. There're more poets here than sand at Coney Island, and you think you're going to score big. What gives you that idea?"

What she said to me was news. Bad news. I said to her:

"You are using hyperboles, please tell me, or some device new to me."

"Wow," is what she said. "Wow, what a royal goof."

I felt a great whale wallow inside my chest. This is a pun. Something hot happened to my eyes.

"Everyone here is a poet?" I asked her.

"Everydamnbody in the United States of America is either a poet or trying to be."

This seemed to include Fay Trigger. I wondered if Fay Trigger had been, perhaps, loving me so she could learn the secrets of poetry from me. The whale sprouted a funnel of water.

"And you without even speaking English better than a beaner with his shirt still wet . . . What a goof!"

It rose up out of the deep blue water of my soul and thundered its tail against the surface of my ocean.

I spit on the back of my hand and rubbed the words there, making them a blue smear.

The fat girl in the raincoat spun around quickly and pulled a man out of the crowd. He looked very shocked. He wore a tuxedo.

"Can you give a reading of your poems tonight?"

"What time?" he asked her. She pushed him back into the crowd.

"See what I mean? You could yank anyone out and they'd say the same."

Across the marble floor I carried my suitcase of socks and worthless poems. The fat girl followed me to the door of revolutions and stood in my way and said this:

"Even the muggers, friend. Even the rapists, even the damn hookers are staying up late writing poems. You don't have a prayer. Listen, I know, I teach seven-year-olds to write the stuff. And mongoloids. I mean mongoloids, for Christsakes.

"I mean, it's an insult to me and to all of us, especially to him tonight, to say you can come walking out of nowhere and become a hotshot. No way, José. I mean, that man has worked his ass off to be up there tonight. He's the real thing. The real king. There aren't twelve people in the United States of America that understand every single nuance of what he says. He's the deepest, friend. The very deepest."

I replied to her in words she could not pronounce.

And she regarded me with far-off eyes like I was on the deck of a departing ship. I felt myself pull free from the great country of America where she stood surrounded by the swarming poets. I felt myself cut out into the marble sea, into the fog of my own impoverished language.

Into a language where the important things are the simple things to say. You say them plainly and in a way that causes no one to be unsure, and no one to need an explanation. You can turn to an old woman with whiskers on her chin who is selecting peppers from the vegetable bin, and you can say to her, "These tomatoes and peppers smell tasty." And she will understand you. And you, you will be rich.

UNDER THE SWAYING CURTAIN

Robert Thompson

But the small children, under the swaying
curtain,
Speak in low voices as you do on a dark
night.
                    —*"The Orphans' Gifts," Rimbaud*

1

—Kill me, man, you shitting?

Whistler leaves his desk and sits near Chan Lai Washington. It is late in an August afternoon, and both of the boys are being kept after their eighth-grade summer school class because of a prank, but now the prospect of big business temporarily cuts through the humid tedium.

—Hey Whistler, I want to hang out with you guys. I didn't mean to tell on you.

Chan Lai smiles in the simple, full way that sometimes makes Whistler want to punch him, but thirty or forty pills, of all sorts, for nothing but letting Chan Lai tag along now and then . . . this is great, good luck.

—And just where you gonna get 'em?

—Green keeps the ones he finds in the lockers. He keeps 'em in a couple places, and I can take some from each.

—Goddamn, says Whistler, and Chan Lai breathes easier. Chan Lai has not actually told on Whistler, but he laughed when the nun asked who had stolen Melba Newell's shoe. When she questioned him, Chan Lai admitted to passing the shoe along, and then, seeing other hands raised, Whistler admitted stealing the shoe for a joke. Melba Newell is the victim of many jokes of this type because she has big breasts, and because she has big breasts the nuns usually act as if Melba caused it all. But Mother Julia's justice is as unpredictable as a fly in November, and after pointing out the brief yet eternal rewards for honesty, she assigns three math-check problems apiece

173

to Whistler and Chan Lai: to Whistler for stealing the shoe and to Chan Lai for thinking it funny. But Chan Lai does not think the situation is funny at all once he discovers that Whistler is implicated. Though he does not turn his head to check, Chan Lai can feel Whistler's cold, black eyes boring into the back of his head for the rest of the class.

—Dig it, man. You just have it this Friday eve and we party. But you don't raise your hand on me again, right? That shit ain't worth shit, man, what the fuck shit you doing?

—You got it, Whistler, says Chan Lai, the angles of his face scrambling. They be there, don't worry.

2

Chan Lai had not planned to tell anyone, much less share with anyone Father Green's stash of pills, but the incident of Melba Newell's shoe has its plus side for him. Over the last several months he has hoped to find some way to be included with Whistler and his gang of seven or eight others; his fantasies no longer engage him as once they did. The epics which once launched him into sleep, which he had faithfully built detail by detail, appear to him now as examples of what other, much younger children believe. He had been The Man In The White Suit, who wore white shoes and socks and pants and coat and everything, except his underwear was black, and who smoked a brand of South African tobacco which left only white ashes. But eventually this hero proved too cloying to be even false; the victories came before Chan Lai had time to think of another struggle, and this death-by-success is the fate of other fantasies Chan Lai abandons at puberty. His *One Note Symphony*, featuring thousands of musicians making a single sound for hours, was followed briefly by a *Two Note Symphony*, but then the series is dropped. The invisible camera, which during his early grades could activate on a mental command so that his teachers could see him doing his homework, now seems as useful and interesting as the schoolwork, which is not interesting at all. And though not so long ago he held long, remorseful conversations with God, often now he falls asleep without a single prayer. He still believes in God, but he sees Him less as the creator of his soul than as a landlord there of the inner-city, absentee variety.

Chan Lai neglects to tell Father Green about this change in God's status; they rarely talk about religion except when Chan Lai puts it into one of his stories. On the Thursday night before the party, he steals the pills from the shoeboxes in the closet while the priest says his breviary in the church. When the priest returns to the room, he goes to the bed where Chan Lai is sprawled on his stomach, writing in a looseleaf tablet. He squeezes the boy's neck, and then commences a backrub.

—Still at it, hmm?

—Wait'll you read this, Father.

—Melrak again?

—Well, it is, but things are different now. There's sex.

—For heaven's sake don't show it to Mother Julia.

—Think I'm crazy? It's not about us anyway.

Father Green stands up, closes his eyes, and wipes his brow with a bandanna, then goes to adjust the electric fan so it rotates. The August humidity is terrific.

—I'll let you read it tomorrow, says Chan Lai. Saturday for sure.

—Hell's bells, Charly. Put on pajamas. I've told you before about wearing something when I'm not in the room. Use your fucking brains.

Chan Lai stops writing and looks over at the priest who is lighting a cigarette now. The boy smiles; he's rarely heard the priest use that kind of language.

—Underwear is all I brought over.

—Well, put them on. It's simply ordinary common manners, he says, closing the door to the bathroom adjoining his bedroom.

Chan Lai gestures to the closed door with his middle finger, and he says, I can sleep on the cot if you want.

But with his underwear on he returns to the priest's double bed, thinking, *Leave him to Voosh.* Voosh is one of the last of Chan Lai's working fantasies. Its function is to make a white sound of images, after which nothing need be remembered. Voosh is what the ear would hear if able to stare at the sun. And though, as with all his other fantasies, Voosh has grown tamer with use, even as simply a word Voosh functions as a means to forget. The wasted things of the world are its identity. Spewing coffee grounds and cigarette butts with every breath, its lungs made of doughnut holes and turtles' eggs, Voosh trundles into mind center heaving pyramid pulleys, shitting eggshells and ticket stubs, blowing tonsils out its nose, burping banana skins. And Chan Lai is writing and has forgotten their argument when the priest comes out of the bathroom in his silk pajamas.

Father Green sets the clock on the dresser for his six o'clock mass in the morning, turns on the television and then sits on the bed and removes his slippers. He removes and winds his wristwatch, puts his dentures into the waterless glass; he winds his head clockwise around his neck and then counterclockwise, and lies down.

—Jesus, what a day.

Chan Lai closes his notebook.

—Finished it perfect, man.

—Good for you, Charly.

—You gonna finish the backrub?

—And what backrub is that, did I write a check?

—The one you started when you come in.

—Well, not with that T-shirt on, says Father Green.

3

Under the vat where the stomach-tube formula is stored, the two lovers in Chan Lai's latest Melrak story meet for sex. The earth's weather is an always scorching summer, and the stomach-tube formula must be kept cool, so the vat is in an underground bunker. It is the coolest place for miles. The character Chan Lai likes most is the Blue Mutant, a creature who can disappear and hover on ceilings at will. Outside, he would float endlessly up into space, but inside the bunker the Blue Mutant is perfectly safe on the ceiling when the lovers enter. The man is black and has a badge designating him as the chief mixer of the formula; the woman is yellow and badged as the chief distributor of the food. Both wear little more than rags, but they are *proud* rags. The man tells the woman that God will bless the vat of stomach formula if they have sex on the little mattress under the vat. She believes him. Chan Lai is uncertain, but he sends the Blue Mutant across the ceiling to watch them, and their intercourse is the rest of the story. At the end God does bless the vat, appearing over it briefly as a ball of fire. And this is new. Across Melrak's rubbled terrain God usually acts through occasionally running faucets or the birth of an undeformed child. Chan Lai is not surprised when Father Green says, I think it's one of your best, Charly.

—I think you're right. I tried to work in the feeling I get when you do it to me, says Chan Lai, raising up on his elbows. It's probably just like that with women, wouldn't you think?

—Is that what you told them at the party tonight?

—Huh?

—Is that what you told them at the party?

—Didn't tell anybody anything at the party.

Father Green knows better than to think Chan Lai would talk about him, but then, if he truly knew better . . . the truth is that it is Father Green who wishes not to talk. He has noted the boy's reluctance to talk about his evening out; he hopes to shut down the conversation by asking Chan Lai about it. And it works. Chan Lai gets out the deck of cards, but the boy plays stupidly and the priest has to work at losing. This is not the usual problem, but he can tell the boy has had drugs of some sort. And what is usual anymore? Father Green asks himself. Though the priest is determined to avoid repeating his lie to Chan Lai, he is often suspicious that this is what the boy is trying to get out of him whenever they talk alone. He is certain it is only a matter of time before their relationship appears in one of the boy's stories. There's no sin in the loss of semen so long as it's swallowed by a priest. Ah yes, that was it. Sharing a lie can be as rich as sharing a truth, at least in the beginning, but Father Green has known for more than a week now that a way out must be found. And does the boy know it is a lie? Could it be he really doesn't know? Father Green isn't sure, nor can he bring himself to ask. He knows that increasingly his thoughts break into both accusatory and alibi-filled speeches by scowling and weeping lawyers before a jury where he sits in the defendant's chair with a long straw in his mouth that ends in his pants. His great hope is that his last days won't be spent in a mental institution.

*   *   *

—Gin, says Chan Lai, dropping his hand.

He falls back on the pillows. The priest collects the cards and puts them away. Chan Lai rolls onto his stomach. The bed seems to be both sinking and spinning. If he were to ask himself, did he believe or not believe what Father Green had said about his sperm, his answer would be neither. That was something one could haggle over if the last judgment got boring. What he is thinking of, in fragments, is the evening he's just been through. Feeling the old man's glazed and slightly scratchy palms work up his spine, he remembers walking down the alley into the sun with Whistler and Colby and the others, and resting in the wicker laundry basket staring up at the basement chutes, and the girl on her back trying to vomit, and from there at last the jumble which means Voosh has arrived.

—That feels good, says Chan Lai, half into the pillow.

Father Green is at a bad angle.

—Well it's damn near over, says the priest. My back feels like splitting in two.

—Gyp, says Chan Lai.

*   *   *

Early in the morning he wakes and he is not breathing. It is one of the strangest of all ways to wake. Your eyes open, and still it does not hit you what is wrong. And then you breathe and remember you stopped and the stopping woke you. Father Green no longer watches television, but he is not yet snoring. Chan Lai sits up, lights a cigarette, and blows smoke rings into the blue haze of the sound- less television set. He waits for Voosh. Voosh doesn't come. He takes out the small, rectangular mirror, holds it diagonal to his temple and pretends he is filming the room. This is a new habit of his, and he likes it. The mirror has certain advantages over imagina- tion: it is neutral, precise, manipulable. But it is embarrassing when used in public. After they met in the schoolyard, Chan Lai, bringing up the rear, took the mirror from his shirt pocket and looked into it at the seven of them sloping into the crimson sunset, until he noticed that Malt was looking back at him in disbelief.

—Hey man, that Charly been hitting the shit ahead of time.

Two or three manage to turn their heads before Chan Lai can return mirror to pocket, and Colby came over to him to ask, What you do with that thing?

—It's an eye test, said Chan Lai, taking the mirror out again. You try and beat your eyes to the mirror.

—You somethin' else, Washington, and he laughed a kind of shout that stopped dead in the air after one note. Just tell me you got some downers, man.

—I got it must be eight different kinds. I gave 'em all to Whistler.

—And off Green no shit?

—Yeah, but I can't say, you know?

—Sure enough, dig it.

Colby moved away and Chan Lai was relieved. Without con- sciously mapping it out, his strategy for the night was to be left alone as much as possible, for he felt his position as pill supplier as a vulnerability: he could not be sure if any of them meant what they said to him tonight. Let them find him after a week or two simply a part of them from habit, like a new pair of glasses.

Chan Lai didn't know the names of any of the pills, but at the party he asked Whistler to give him one that would be *fast and out.* Old Lady Grady, whose apartment it was, took a few of the pills from Whistler and retired to her kitchen to drink beer and play cards with two neighbors. Five girls sat in a close circle in the living room.

—Only two of 'em got a steady, Colby told him.

The boys kept a looser circle on the other side of the living room until after the wine arrived. Chan Lai sat in a corner and watched; the process seemed to be that the girl danced with the boy whose pill she accepted, but one girl took them from several boys. The music was loud and disco, and the August heat and the sweat of the dancing and the perfume of the girls filled the room. Chan Lai puffed on a passing joint that tasted like exhaust from a bus, and the red and blue lamps, the curious patches on the carpet . . . and he leaves the party and sits on a corner of the ashpit in the backyard to breathe fresh air. He hears a police siren close by and he goes down to the apartment building basement and lies down in a brimming wicker laundry basket. The world is too big upstairs.

Too big outside. But he likes that he can hear the music of the party, of several parties, coming down through the laundry chutes. There are six chutes; all of the larger sounds in the apartments above filter down to the basement, and in the dim light of the solitary bulb Chan Lai falls asleep. He dreams that he lives here, among the chutes, free to float up to this apartment for lunch, the other one for television, still another one for bed. And he remembers his dream perfectly even after the strange, whirring sounds of sheets coming down a chute wakens him with a start. He looks about, lonely for the feeling of the dream, suddenly frightened by the basement. Inside the apartment, the spell is all there again, only more intensely now. Three couples lie on the floor alongside one wall of the living room, grappling in ways that make it impossible for Chan Lai to keep his eyes either off or on them, and the dancers keep the music loud and fast, so the room fills with pockets of lust and frenzy. He feels almost desperate to take out his mirror, and two other thoughts hover: this party is something like what Melrak has maybe once a month, and maybe I got born from some party like this. He goes to the kitchen for more wine, and he is back in the living room a minute when the girl stops dancing, drops to the floor, twitching on her back as though someone under the rug is punching her. She seems to be making noises, but they aren't heard until the stereo is turned off, and someone screams for Grady.

—She's dead, says Grady. She's dead. Now just what in the sweet Jesus am I gonna do now?

And along with a rush of others, Chan Lai runs out the back door.

Now he shakes the shoulder of the priest, who, yes, Chan Lai can tell, has been asleep.

—Can't be time yet, says Father Green, fumbling for his watch.

—Hey Father, I'm sorry, but listen, I got to confess.

*   *   *

—But you didn't tell anyone where you got them?, Father Green asks again. He has heard the boy's confession, and has explained that before Chan Lai could be guilty of murder he would have had to intend her death, that Chan Lai had not directly given her even a single pill, and besides, one didn't know for sure what the girl died of, or even actually if she is dead, and besides . . . until Chan Lai says, Okay, okay. As for the theft, well, there was no need for restitution in a case like this. Father Green paced the room and said that in fact he found a kind of symmetry at play here, for he'd gotten the pills from the students. But the priest is unable to calm himself even after going through his rationales twice. Chain-smoking in bed, massaging the boy's neck, he asks again, You didn't tell anyone you got the pills from me?

—I just said I knew where I could cop 'em.

—Oh, let's try to sleep. But we need a foster home for you Charly, yes, we really do. I'm going to talk to Mr. Hinneman.

Chan Lai rolls over to see the priest's expression.

—A home?

—Well, a foster home. Much nicer than here. Something to consider, don't you think?

—I dreamt a kind of home tonight, he says, and he tells the priest about his dream in the laundry basket.

—I expect you'd get stuck in those chutes, but that's a nice dream, Charly. You go back to sleep with it.

—But it's that simple, Father? You could swing that?

—We'll see. I think so, but we'll see.

The priest rolls over in bed to his customary position, sandwiching his head between the pillows. Is it that simple, the priest wonders; events seemed to be going either fairly well or straight to hell.

So maybe I get to get out of here, thinks Chan Lai, half-asleep.

4

Father Green searches both St. Louis daily newspapers for the next two days, but finds no news article about the girl. He looks at the obituaries also, but Chan Lai does not know the girl's name, or will not tell him. But two girls of fourteen and one girl of twelve have died. No police came by to question him, but a detective has interviewed some students. He flushes down the toilet the rest of the pills from his shoeboxes; he has thought of them as insurance of an easy suicide. He has rarely thought of killing himself; on the other hand he thinks it only practical to possess comfortable means.

After seven flushes no more pills return to the bowl; that instant he regrets having flushed them. *Now, when there may be a use!* he thinks. And the same ambivalence overcomes him with the foster home procedures. Having cornered the gaunt, potbellied social worker on his Monday rounds, Father Green asked Jim Hinneman if a foster home could be found quickly. Hinneman laughed when the priest told him it was for Chan Lai Washington.

—Has he been raising shit lately? I thought it was supposed to be his adjustment here was the best deal, like all around.

—Yes, I thought so . . . or so I thought. But now I don't know, but I think I do. Maybe we've been selfish about keeping him here, as an influence, because he has made such a good adjustment. But I think he ought to know something else, because he is pretty bright.

—Case load for homes is pretty long, Father, said Hinneman, leaving the priest feeling dubious about a quick placement.

Chan Lai's two weeks of serving six o'clock mass are over, and when the boy searches him out to ask about the foster home, Father Green only says, It's in the works. And it is in the works. Three days after they spoke, Hinneman calls to say he has found a foster home— his own. Being privy to the inner workings of the welfare apparatus, he says the transfer can be managed in less than two weeks, providing the boy is willing. The next day when they meet in a rectory visiting room to make a plan, in spite of himself and all his conscious purposes, Father Green bridles at Hinneman's satisfaction with the proceedings. When the social worker talks about adoption before having spent more than two days with the boy, the priest can hold himself back no longer and suggests that it might be better if they wait until a black foster home is found . . . you know, with the emphasis on cultural roots these days . . . his voice trailing off as the smile grows on Hinneman's white face.

—That was the clincher, Father. You see, my wife is black, our kids will be mulattoes when we have some. I mean, they won't be mixed like Charly, but he'd be in the spirit so to speak.

—He prefers his given name, Chan Lai.

—That so? Say, can you think of anything else?

—Not sure I get you.

—I mean, can you think of special things, little things, that he likes, habits. I mean, preferences or something?

—Oh he's just a boy, says Father Green. As his understanding of Hinneman's question dawns, he is aware that in fact he can tell Hinneman nothing about the boy's likes and dislikes. He exercises phlegm for a moment.

—You know, he says then, television . . . girls are coming on now I should think.

Hinneman leaves. Father Green looks down at the long ash of the extinguished cigarette between his fingers.

—His thighs look white in the moonlight.

*   *   *

At least there's a different bishop now, thinks Father Green as he waits in the hallway outside Mother Julia's office.

The bishop had extended his hand to let the young priest kiss his ring, to let him know the interview was over. In all the thirty-six years Father John Green had served as priest, this had been the only run-in he'd had with the church hierarchy, so far. But this single thing had stamped him early in his career as *questionable material* in the archdiocesan file.

Before St. Gregory's orphanage had been secularized to receive federal monies, there had been a tiny chapel on the second floor, and he was assigned to say Saturday morning mass there at eight o'clock for the children from known Catholic families. It depressed him deeply. Usually more than half of the six to twelve children who were prodded into attending slept through most of the mass. He got the idea to put a circle of cellophane tape, sticky side out, inside the cuff of his cassock. At the consecration, he stuck the tape onto the back of the large, white host. When he raised the host in the air, gently he pressed the other side of the tape onto the lower rim of the marble crucifix above the tabernacle, and let the host stay there by itself while he genuflected. It looked very much as if the host were suspended in midair, and the children who weren't sleeping were often impressed. He felt that whatever imparted faith was at least poetic truth, no doubt somewhat as Saint Nicholas got started. But the nun who came in late one Saturday morning was also impressed, or shocked, for she fainted. The bishop was impressed not at all, but then, Father Green had just confessed to the mechanics of the miracle. Standing and leaning over the huge desk, the bishop said, This will be our secret, Father, unless—and he paused here to flash his teeth—unless it ever happens again. And in that case, Father, in that case we would have to share all the details with your psychiatrist.

The miracle does not recur. Father Green grows old at St. Gregory's and grows large. *A walking shut-in, if you ask me.* Years ago, that was what his brother called him, his brother Harry, who was already a Monsignor when he approached John and offered to engage in ecclesiastic politics to secure John a more promising position. I'm just doing this for Mom, said Harry. But Father Green is neither ambitious nor bitter. He has no skinny man inside who wants out; he has several skinny men inside, all of whom want to stay in, or at least not go out any farther than a touch of the hand.

—Ahh, but you're early, Father, forgive me.

—Good morning, Mother.

—But you should have knocked! Come in. Say you haven't been waiting long, have a seat. I'm in the middle of going through the same pre-school panic, right on schedule. It's chaos!

He follows her into the absolutely orderly office, relieved, certain she has not asked to see him to talk about the pills, the dead girl, the boy. She sits in one of the two chairs away from her little desk, and he sits in the other.

—Mother, your chaos is the most measured of anyone I know. You damn well ought to run the country.

She blushes and her lips clamp into a smile. This happens every time he succeeds in working a *damn* or *hell* into his conversation with her. Already he feels the mixture of depression and anxiety that he associates with being near her.

—But, uhh, you wanted to see me Sister Clair said?

—Yes, Father. It's about Charly Washington. You know, I taught Charly this last summer session. We get on. But I was thinking, you and he are closer. I mean he has a high regard for you, more than Sister Clair, say. So I was thinking, wouldn't it be better, for the boy's sake, doing it on the right foot you might say?

—Not sure I catch your drift, Mother.

—Well, if you were to see him off. When Mr. Hinneman comes to get him. Charly Washington. Tomorrow. Eleven o'clock, I think.

—Yes, yes, I see, that's considerate of you. But I'm going to be at the school. Sister Clair has offered to go with the boy. I've spoken with her.

—But Father, she says and then lightly sighs. We sisters are used to doing this inventory. It's boring, but we get the whole thing done in a morning. And I think you and Charly have a special . . . it's such a . . . landmark day for him, leaving us and . . .

He gets out of the chair, walks across the room, and leans on the mantel over the bricked-up fireplace.

—It's my relationship with the boy that leads me to ask this one, I think, pitifully small favor, Mother. If you think it's not appropriate for Sister Clair, perhaps you could do it. Charly likes you a good deal. I'm ah . . . miserable seeing him go.

Unexpectedly a feeling of peace comes over him, and the slight pressure on his shoulder from her hand feels wonderful, feels perfectly right, feels warm; for a moment he wonders where he is.

—Surely, Father, I'll do as you say. Forgive me.

—Nonsense, he says. Very kind of you, Mother.

5

There are four beds in Chan Lai's room, which he shares with Fred and Jerry, who have already said goodbye and are playing corkball in the schoolyard. He expects to have the room alone, but Jaime Travelier is stretched out on his stomach in the fourth bed, tracing pictures from a comic book.

—You here?

—Hey Charly Chan. Just checked in. Smoke some dope?

—Better not, Jaime. Mother's coming pretty soon.

—She wrote you personally, huh?

—No Jaime, guess what's happening. I'm leaving, gonna go to a foster home, leaving this hole behind.

For a moment Jaime stares at Chan Lai's face to see if this is a put-on, then he returns to the comic book.

—I get your bed then. Not gonna be long here myself.

Chan Lai suspects this is true; Jaime comes only when his alcoholic parents have to be dried out. Most of the children in the orphanage have known parents or a parent. Most of the parents come back to take their children. Most of them come to take their children back many times. A family is the usual, easy, natural way of happenstance. Didn't the world of things break down into families? Of course. He must bring families into Melrak. Why should they waste their radioactive lives away as a sect? Why not as families, with something in common besides survival? He'd get busy on that when settled into his new room, or in his cell. There are important things I can do no matter what happens, he thinks. He tells himself that it makes no difference if a cop comes before Hinneman. A detective has already been asking questions. One of the boys at the party has never returned home, and Peter Schuski's parents called in the police. Chan Lai worried more about the girl and asked Whistler about her. Whistler grabbed Chan Lai's arm at the bicep, squeezing, glaring, saying, Don't know about her, Chinaboy. Do you?

—Know about what? I don't know, okay?

So the girl is gone, Peter Schuski is gone. They are swallowed by some Voosh-like thing operating in the real world to swallow people up. Or the girl and Peter Schuski have eaten whole the thing that spews everything out, and together they're fucking and laughing at the shit spewing over all us left behind. Yeah, you never know, that may be the luckiest day in her life, thinks Chan Lai. Some nights he prays to her, and unlike God, she is always there. But he remains unsure of which person she is sending to get him.

—You want these planes? he says, picking up his favorite, the red Messerschmitt.

—Keep your shit, man, says Jaime, looking up. You may be back, you know? Like tomorrow.

—Just what makes you happy, says Chan Lai, going to the window. The suitcase Hinneman gave him is packed, as are the three large paper bags. There are still notebooks and pennants and scrapbooks to take . . . the Hinnemans said he could bring everything— they had a room he could live in alone. When he gets there he will close the door to it, and they will knock again to say dinner is ready. Not one door within the Hinneman's apartment has a lock on it except for the bathroom, just the opposite of the orphanage. And they have a laundry chute.

From the window Chan Lai sees Hinneman's car pull into the schoolyard lot. He hears the clacking of beads down the hallway. Jaime puts his comic under the pillow and sits up. Mother Julia pauses at the doorway.

—Good morning, boys. Jaime, are you settled in?

—Yes, Mother.

—We've been offering up our rosaries for Lucinda. We pray for her every mass. Will you tell your parents that, Jaime?

—Yes, Mother.

At the window where Chan Lai still stands she says, I think that's Mr. Hinneman's car, isn't his car blue? Oh, Jim . . . Jim?

While Mother Julia yells out the window, Chan Lai gathers his bags onto his bed.

—Chinaboy, you going to live with Hinneman the soshy worker?, asks Jaime.

—Looks like it. Who's Lucinda?

—My sis.

—So what happened?

—She OD'd, he says, running a finger across his throat.

—Mr. Hinneman will wait for us down there. Are we ready, Charly?

—Yes, Mother.

—Well, take this. It's a copy of your birth certificate. It's an important document, so keep it where you'll always remember. And this is your diploma. This is the last year we give diplomas for each grade, so don't lose it or we'll probably not be able to give you another. Do you understand?

—Yes, Mother.

—All these bags are yours?

—Yes, Mother.

—Well, Charly, do you know we're going to miss you?

But he says nothing, though she indicates it is his turn.

—You're going to be very happy, I think. You know I think sometimes if only I had your years what I would do and it makes me nearly dizzy.

But he has determined to say nothing.

—Jaime, can you be a gentleman and help us carry some of these bags to the car? And I'll take the suitcase. Oh, thank you, Jaime.

He follows behind her and Jaime. At the car, though he knows he should say goodbye, he cannot speak. Chan Lai studies the ornament on the hood of the car until Hinneman puts the baggage away and opens the car door. Chan Lai sits down. He stares straight ahead. Before his eyes a puff of tissue paper appears and Hinneman says, Here.

CASH CROP

Connie Willis

O h, Haze," Sombra said. "Aren't you excited about tomorrow? Our new dresses and the school all decorated with flowers?"

"Yes," I said, trying to see down the hill to the peach tree. Francie always waited by the peach tree after school, triumphant that she had made it home before the downer. But this morning Mother had come to take her home, and I could not see any figure standing beside the stunted tree.

"I can hardly wait to see the flowers!" Sombra said. "Mamita says they always bring yellow roses. And red carnations. Do you know what carnations look like, Haze?"

I shook my head. The only flowers I had ever seen were my mother's greentent geraniums.

Earlier today the district nurse had talked to Mother for a long time. I had heard the words "scarlet fever" and "northern," and the nurse's face had become flushed and angry as she spoke. "Flowers!" she had said angrily. "They buy us off with flowers and antibiotics when they should be sending us a centrifuge so we can make our own antibiotics. They take our grain and give us flowers!" And Mother had hurried Francie home.

"Just think," Sombra said, looking up at the dusty haze, "right now the *Magassar*'s orbiting. Floating up there in space with its hold full of flowers." She was shivering, hugging her arms across her chest. We had ridden the dustdowner home, clinging to the narrow seat under the sprinklers, and both of us were wet from the spray.

Dirty downers, my father called them. "They buy us off with the downers when they could be doing climate control, when they could be eliminating the strep altogether." All I seemed to be able to think of today were angry words against the government. There shouldn't be, with graduation coming. The government had sent a special ship just for the occasion of our first graduating class. They had already sent fabric for graduation clothes with the last grain ship, and although Sombra's romantic notions about the ship floating overhead with its hold full of flowers were not quite right and the *Magassar* was instead already filling its massive hold with compressed grain and alcohol from the orbiting silos, when it did land tomorrow there would be gifts and special foods from the earth, fresh fruits and chocolate, and Sombra's flowers. Yet all I heard were angry words.

Father had threatened to dismantle the dustdowner that circled our stead daily and build a cannon out of it. "Then when the government men tell me they're doing all they can about the strep, I can tell them what I think." The government's argument was that the strep outbreaks were being caused by the dust, so they sent the automated sprinklers crawling up and down the adobe-hard roads between the steads, wasting Haven's already scarce water, the heavy wheels stirring up dust that the sprinklers didn't even touch. The quarantine and sterilization regulations the first steaders set up did more to keep the strep under control than the downers ever would.

The steaders made their own use of them, hitching supplies and messages on the back to send them between the steads. During quarantines the district nurse sent antibiotics that way and sometimes a coffin. And all the kids caught them on the way to and from school, if they could time it, arriving home damp and disheveled to face angry mothers, who told them they would get a chill and catch the strep, who forced the government-supplied Schultz-Charlton strips into their mouths and wrapped them in blankets. I had seen Mamita Turillo do it to Sombra and Mother to Francie. Not to me. I was never chilled. The breeze on my wet shirt and jeans today was cool, but not cold.

"Oh, you're never cold," Sombra said now, her teeth chattering. "It isn't fair."

Even in winter I slept under a thin blanket and forgot my coat at school. Even in Haven's sudden, intense summer that was nearly here, my dust-colored cheeks didn't flush like Sombra's red ones. Sweat didn't curl my dust-colored hair as it did her black hair. Sombra looked like a greentent flower, her body tall and narrow, her cheeks and hair bright splashes of color. I only came to Sombra's shoulder, and I looked more like the flowers Mother tried to plant outside the greentent—dusty and pinched, they never bloomed.

I was not the only one. A few of the first-generation steaders, like Old Man Phelps, were short and hardy, and more and more of the new hands Mamita boarded fresh off the emigration ships looked like me. I looked out across our stead and Sombra's, with the bare hard road and low mud fence dividing the pale sweeps of winter wheat and the pinkish-brown haze in the sky above them. Maybe the emigration people had decided to send people as colorless and dusty as Haven itself in the hope the strep would overlook them.

I could see Father's peach tree at the corner of our stead, where Sombra would turn to go another quarter mile to her house, but no Francie. Only one thing would have made Mother come and get her: somebody sick here in the western.

"Sombra," I said, "do you know of anybody sick in this district?"

"Yes," she said, unconcerned. "Old Man Phelps. I heard the district nurse tell your mother."

"Scarlet fever?" I said blankly, but it could not be anything else. It was always scarlet fever. Stray streptococci brought by the first steaders had taken to Haven's dry, dusty climate like cherrybrights to a tree. It was always there, waiting for a shortage of antibiotics. There had been a heart-stopping outbreak in northern three weeks ago, seventeen reported, mostly children, and a local had been slapped on the district by the district nurse. It shouldn't have spread to western. What was worse, Mr. Phelps brought us within two of a planetwide quarantine. Mr. Phelps, one of the oldtimers who never got the strep, down with scarlet fever.

"The district nurse told your mother there was nothing to worry about. Mr. Phelps lives alone, and she said she could stop an outbreak with the antibiotics the *Magassar*'s bringing.

"If the *Magassar* lands," I said. A faint scratchiness of fear was beginning behind my throat. Two more reported cases and the *Magassar* would go back to earth without even landing. There would be no graduation.

Sombra said, "Mamita says there's no reason for them to quarantine us without antibiotics. She says they could drop the antibiotics from orbit. Do you think that's true?"

The scratchiness became almost an ache. "No, of course not. If they could, they would. They wouldn't leave us without any antibiotics if there was any way to get them to us." But I was remembering something from a long time ago, when little Willie died. Mother telling me to get out of the house, out of her sight, and Father saying, "Don't take it out on Haze. It's the government that's left us to the wolves. Blame them. Blame me—I brought you here, knowing what they were doing. But not Haze. She can't help being what she is." The ache was worse. I swallowed hard, and when it didn't go away, I pressed the flat of my hand against the hollow space between my collarbones and swallowed again. This time it went away.

"Of course not," I said again, feeling much better. "Don't worry about Mr. Phelps. He won't stop our graduation. There's got to be an incubation period, and by the time it's up, the *Magassar* will already be on the ground. The local's probably already got it stopped."

We were nearly down the long hill to the corner, and I didn't want to leave her thinking about a possible quarantine. I said, "Mother finished our dresses last night. Are you going to come over to try it on?" Sombra's flushed cheeks darkened. "To make sure about the hem," I said hesitantly. "To see how we're going to look tomorrow."

Sombra shook her dark head. "I'm sure it'll be all right," she said uncomfortably. "Mamita has a lot of chores for me today. With the *Magassar* coming in tomorrow. She's taking the new hands to board again, and so she said she wanted me to bring in everything ripe from the greentent for the supper tomorrow night. I wish Mamita had made our dresses," she finished unhappily.

"It's all right," I said. "I'll bring it over tomorrow morning. We'll get dressed together."

It had been a mistake to mention the dresses, and a worse one to have had Mother make them for us. I had been to Sombra's house countless times, with Mamita bright and cheerful as a cherrybright, feeding us vegetables from the greentent and asking us about school, reaching up on tiptoe to pull Sombra's curls away from her face and, no taller than me, hugging me goodbye when I left. When Sombra came home with me, Mother was rigid and erect as one of the tallgrasses that shaded our porch. She had not spoken a dozen words to her during all the fittings. We should have had Mamita make the dresses.

Yesterday Sombra had tried on her dress timidly. I had not seen it so nearly finished before, with the red ribbons pinned where they would be threaded through the bodice. "Oh, Sombra, you look so beautiful!" I had blurted out, "Oh, Mama, it's the loveliest dress I've ever seen."

Mother had turned on me with a look that made Sombra gasp. "I will not allow you to call me that," she had said, and slammed the door behind her. Sombra had shimmied out of the dress and into her jeans so fast she nearly tore the thin white cotton.

"It's because of the babies," I had said helplessly. "She had seven babies that died between Francie and me. Little Willie lived to be three. I remember when he died. It was a planetwide and there wasn't anything to give him and he laid upstairs in the big bed crying, 'Mama! Mama!' for five days."

Sombra had her shirt buttoned and her books scooped up. "She lets Francie call her Mama," she said, her cheeks flaming with anger.

"That's different," I had said.

"How is it different? Mamita lost nine babies to the strep. Nine."

"But she has you and the twins left. And all Mother has is Francie."

"And you. She has you." I had not known how to explain to her that Francie, with her blue eyes and yellow hair, made her think of San Francisco, of earth. Francie and the geraniums she tended so carefully in the hot, damp air of the greentent. And when she looked at me, what did she think? She had found me that day after Willie died, hiding in the greentent, and had switched me. What was she thinking then? And what did she think this morning when the district nurse told her Mr. Phelps had scarlet fever and we were within two of a planetwide? The scratchiness had returned, this time as a dull ache. I knotted my hand into a fist and pushed against it, but it did no good. I wondered if I'd better take a strip when I got home.

"You're worried about them imposing a quarantine, aren't you?" Sombra said. We were nearly down the hill, and I had not said anything the whole way.

"I was wondering if they'll have pink carnations tomorrow," I said. "I was wondering if they'll give us some to wear in our hair?"

"Of course. Mamita said so. You'll have red roses. You'll be so pretty." The long walk down the dusty hill had dried us off. She looked hot now, the sweat on her forehead curling her dark hair. "Let's sit down a minute, all right?" She sank down on the low mudbrick fence and fanned herself with her books. "It's so hot today."

I looked over her head at the peach tree. It was no taller than me and folded in on itself so that it barely gave any shade at all. Its leaves were narrow and so pale a green the dust made them look the same color as the wheat. There were little pinkish-white specks between the leaves. I squinted at them.

"Don't you think it's hot?" Sombra said.

This was the only one of Father's trees that had lived past the ponics tanks. It had lasted five years now, though it had never borne fruit. And now there were the pale specks all over it, which could be moths or sorrel ants. The ache pressed dully against the hard bone of my sternum, bending me forward under it. I put the edge of my fist against the pain, pressing hard into the bone, willing myself to straighten. Mother was always telling me to stand up straight, to try to look at least as tall as I could, not like some hunched dwarf, and I would straighten automatically, my whole body responding. I willed myself to hear her voice now. My shoulder blades pulled back, stretching the ache with it till it had pulled out to nothing. I stood still, breathing hard.

"I can't sit down," I said breathlessly. "I have to go right home."

"But it's so hot! Do I feel hot to you?" She pulled me onto the wall with her and pressed her cheek against mine. It was burning against my chilled face.

"A little," I said. I must take a strip when I get home. And tell Father about the tree.

"You're not getting sick, are you?" she said. "You can't get sick, Haze, not for graduation. You go right home and go to bed, all right? I don't want you sending us under a planetwide."

"I will," I promised her, climbing over the fence and into the field for a closer look at the tree. The specks were larger than I had thought, almost the size of. . .

"Oh, Sombra," I shouted after her delightedly, "we won't go under a planetwide, and I'm not getting sick either. I've had a good omen. There'll be flowers for graduation."

"How do you know?" she shouted back.

"I thought the tree had something wrong with it," I said. "But it doesn't. It's in bloom!"

She grinned in happy surprise. "You mean blossoms?" She was over the low fence in an easy step and peering eagerly at the tiny tight blossoms. "Oh, they're just starting to come out, aren't they? Oh, Haze, think how pretty they'll be!"

A red cherrybright whizzed through the air over our heads and lighted unafraid on the top of the tree, shaking the branch in our faces. The folded blossoms bowed and dipped.

"The pink blossoms are for my ribbons," Sombra said happily, "and the cherrybright's for your red ribbons!" She put her arm around my waist. It felt warm through my thin shirt. "And you know what they mean?"

"That we'll be beautiful tomorrow! That nothing can possibly go wrong because we're going to graduate!"

"Oh, Haze," she said, hugging me, "I can hardly wait." She ran back to the road. "Bring my dress over first thing in the morning and we'll get ready together. Everything's going to be perfect," she shouted to me. "The day is full of omens."

*   *   *

No one was in the house but Francie, sitting at the kitchen table, dawdling over her lessons with a strip in her mouth.

"Papa's in the greentent. With Mama," she said, taking the strip out of her mouth so she could talk. It was the bright red of a negative reading. Active strep blanched the strips like a person going white from fear. "Are you scared?" she said.

"Of what?"

"Mama says two more and they'll call a planetwide. There won't be any graduation."

"There will so, Francie. There hasn't been a planetwide in ages."

"How do you know?"

"I just know," I said, thinking of the peach tree and what Father would say when he saw it was in bloom. He would think it was a good omen, too. I smiled at Francie and went out to find Father.

He stood in the door of the greentent, blocking it with his bulk. Mother stood across the ponics tanks from him, holding onto one of the metal supports. Through the thick plastic, she looked as if she were drowning. Her hand clutched the strut so hard I thought she would pull the whole tent down.

"It's what they want," Father said. "It ties us to them. We'll be doing just what they want."

"I don't care," she said.

"It will take away every chance of a cash crop. You know that, don't you?"

"Mr. Phelps died this morning. There have been seventeen cases in northern."

"The *Magassar* will be landing tomorrow. We don't have to . . ."

"No," she said, and looked steadily at him. "You owe it to me."

His hand on the doorframe tightened until I could see the veins stand out on his hands.

"The peach tree's in bloom," I blurted, and they both turned to look at me, Father with blank drowned eyes, Mother with a look like triumph. "It's a good sign, don't you think?" I said into the silence. "An omen. It means the *Magassar* will land tomorrow and everything will be all right. . . . Anyway, it has to have some kind of incubation period, doesn't it? People can't just catch it in one day."

"It's a new strain," Mother said. She had let go of the strut and was pushing dirt around the base of a geranium. "The district nurse said it appears to have a very short incubation period."

"She doesn't know that," I said earnestly. "How could she know that for sure?"

She looked up, but at father, not at me. "Mr. Phelps had taken a strip that morning. It was negative. You would not have expected Mr. Phelps to get it at all, let alone so quickly. Maybe others you wouldn't expect will get it, too."

The call box, attached to the plastic feederlines above the ponics tanks, barked suddenly. The sharp, short signal that called the district nurse. The signal that meant our district. Mother looked at me. "What did I tell you?" she said.

My father let go of the doorframe, and took a step toward her. "Move your geraniums to ponics," he said. "I need the plaindirt to plant more corn in." He turned and walked away.

I helped Mother move the geraniums into the tanks, my body tensed for the alerting bark of the box, but it did not ring again. After supper we stayed in the kitchen, and when we went up to bed, Father carried the little box with him, trailing its wires like ribbons, but the box did not sound again. Oh, yes, the day was full of omens.

*   *   *

The pale pink haze was gone in the morning, replaced with the clear chill to the sky that meant night frost. I took Father down to the tree before breakfast to look at the peach blossoms. They dropped like scraps of paper at his feet when he put out his hand to a branch. "The frost got them," he said, as if he didn't even mind.

"Not all of them," I said. Some of them, crumpled and tight, like little knots against the cold, still clung to the branches. "The frost didn't get all of them," I said. "It's supposed to be warm today. I knew it would be warm for graduation." He was looking past me, past the tree. I turned to look. A cherrybright fluttered on Sombra's fence. Our good omen.

"No!" Father said sharply, and then more gently as I turned back to him in surprise. "The frost didn't get them all. Some of them are still alive." He took my arm and steered me back to the house, keeping himself between the tree and me, as if the frozen blossoms were my disappointment and I could not bear to see them.

At the greentent I stopped. "I have to take Sombra her dress," I said, barely able to keep the excitement of the day out of my voice. "We have to get ready for graduation." He did not let go of my arm, but his hand seemed to go suddenly lifeless. I patted his cold hand and ran into the house to get Sombra's dress and down the steps past him with it over my arm, fluttering pink ribbons as I ran. He still stood there, as if he had finally seen the frozen blossoms and could not hide his grief.

*   *   *

It was not a cherrybright. It was a quarantine sticker, tied to one of the distance markers. I stood for a moment by the peach tree looking at it as my father had done, the dress as heavy on my arm as my hand had been on his. "No!" I said, as sharply as he had and took off running.

I could not even let myself think what breaking quarantine meant. "I don't care," I told myself, catching my breath at the last corner of the fence. "It's graduation," I would tell Mamita. "The *Magassar* will be landing with all those flowers. We have to be there."

Mamita would look reluctant, thinking of the consequences.

"One of the hands has it, doesn't he? The new ones always get it. But this is our *graduation!* You can't let him spoil it. Think of all the flowers," I would say. "Sombra has to see them. She'll die if she doesn't see them. Give her a strip. Give us both one. We won't get it."

I climbed over the fence, careful of the dress. Even folded double, it almost dragged on the ground. The gate would be locked. I cut through the field at a dead run and came up to the house the back way, past the greentent. The door stood open, but I could not see anyone through the plastic. Sombra must have hurried through her chores to get ready and left the door open. Mamita would kill her. I could not stop to shut it now, because someone might see me and turn me in. I had to get to Mamita and convince her first.

I knocked at the back door, leaning against the scratchy stalk of a tallgrass, too breathless for a moment to say any of the things I had planned to say. Then Mamita opened the door, and I knew I would never say any of them.

I could hear a baby crying in the house. Mamita passed her hand over her chest, pressing as if there were a pain there. Then she put her hand up to her forehead. There were brilliant scarlet creases on the inside of her elbows. "Why, Haze, what are you doing here?" she said.

"I brought Sombra's dress," I said.

A sudden, hitting anger flared out of her black eyes, and I stumbled back, raking my arm against the tallgrass. It came to me much later that she must have thought I brought the dress for Sombra's laying out, that she had felt the same anger as Mother did when she saw me standing and still healthy while the babies died, one after the other. I did not think of that then. All I could think was that it was not one of the hands, that it was Sombra who was sick.

"For graduation," I said, holding the dress out insistently. If I could make her take it, then it would not be true.

"Thank you, Haze," she said, but she didn't take it. "Her father's already gone," she said. "Sombra's . . ." And in that breath of a second, I thought she was going to say that she was dead already, too, and I could not, would not let her say that.

"The *Magassar* will be landing this morning. I could go over there for you. I could catch a downer. I'd be back in no time. The *Magassar*'s bringing a whole load of antibiotics. I heard the district nurse say so."

"He died before the district nurse could get here. He wouldn't let me call until we found Sombra in the greentent. He didn't want to spoil her graduation."

"But the *Magassar* . . ."

She put her hand on my shoulder. "Sombra was the twentieth," she said.

I still could not take in what she was saying. "There was only one call. That makes nineteen." One call. Sombra and her father. One call.

"You should go home and take a strip, dear," she said. "You'll have been exposed." She put her hand to my cheek, and it burned like a brand. "Tell your mother thank you for the dress," she said, and shut the door in my face.

*   *   *

When Francie found me, I was sitting under the peach tree with Sombra's dress across my lap like a blanket. The last of the blossoms fell on the dress, already dead and dying like the flowers aboard the *Magassar*.

"Papa says for you to come up to the house," Francie said. Mama had curled her hair with sugar water for graduation. The curls were stiff against her pink cheeks.

"There isn't any graduation," I said.

"I know *that*," she said disdainfully. "Mamma's been making me take strips all morning long. She thinks I'm going to get it."

"No," I said, my cheeks burning from the brand of Sombra's cheek, Mamita's hand. The pain pressed against my sternum and would not go away. "I'm going to get it."

"I *told* Mama I didn't even sit near her. And how you never let me walk home with you two, how you always ride the downer. She sent for me as soon as she found out about Mr. Phelps, and Sombra wasn't even sick then. But she wouldn't listen. Anyway, you never get sick. She probably won't even make you take a strip. And Sombra wasn't sick yesterday, was she? So you probably weren't exposed either. Mama says the incubation period is really short." She remembered why she had been sent. "Papa says you're supposed to come *now*." She flounced off.

I stood up, still careful of the white dress, and followed Francie through the field of scratchy wheat. They don't know about my breaking quarantine, I thought in amazement. I wondered why Father had sent for me. Perhaps he knew and wanted to talk to me before he turned me in. "What does he want?" I said.

"I don't know. He said I was supposed to come and get you before the downer came. There's been one already, with a coffin. For Mr. Turillo."

I stopped and looked back toward the road. The downer rattled past the peach tree, spraying water over the scattered blossoms, wetting the coffin it pulled behind it. Sombra's coffin. He had at least tried to spare me that. And now I would have to try to spare him my dying, as much as I could.

*   *   *

I imposed my own quarantine, sneaking a strip as soon as I got back to the house. I had been afraid that Mother would make me take one, but she didn't, although Francie was already sitting at the kitchen table when I came in, protesting the bright red strip Mother held in her hand. I held the strip I had stolen behind my back until I could get out to the greentent. I took it there, huddled under the ponics tank in case it took a long time. It blanched white as soon as the paper was in my mouth. I did not need the strip to tell me I was getting sick. Sombra's cheek, her mother's hand, burned on my face like a brand.

No one reported me. I did not doubt that Mamita, much as she loved me, would have turned me in. This was more than a planet-wide. It was a local, too. The *Magassar* had already broken its orbit and was heading for home. We were on our own, and the only way to stop it was to keep the quarantine from being broken. Which meant Mamita had the fever, too, that maybe all the people on the Turillo stead were dead or sick with it and no one to help them.

I tried to stay out of everyone's way, especially Francie's. I talked with my head averted and asked to do the wash and the dishes so I could sterilize my own things. I picked a fight with Francie and called her a tagalong, so that she avoided me as carefully as I did her. Mother paid no attention to me. She had eyes only for Francie.

*   *   *

Three weeks after Sombra died, Father said at supper, "The local's off at Turillos'. Mamita's over it. The district nurse cleared her this afternoon."

"The twins?" Mother said.

He shook his head. "Both of them died. But none of the hands came down with it. Six months here and not one of them has had so much as a white strip."

"It was an unusual strain," Mother said. "It doesn't prove anything. They could all die tomorrow."

"I doubt it," he said. "The incubation period was very short, as you said. But none of the hands got it." He put a subtle emphasis on the word *none*.

"Yet," Mother said. "I'm sure Haven isn't through coming up with new strains. We're still without antibiotics." The fear I had expected was not in her voice.

"They intercepted the *Magassar* halfway home and told them we'd had no new cases in a week. They're holding where they are for a week, and then if there are no other reporteds, they'll come back." He smiled at me. "I'm full of good news today, Haze. The peaches didn't freeze after all. We're getting some fruit starting."

He turned and looked at Mother, and said in the same cheerful tone, "You'll have to move the geraniums out of the ponics."

Mother put her hand up to her cheek as if he had hit her. "I talked to Mamita," he said. "She said she'll buy all the corn we can give her. Cash crop."

"Can I move the flowers back to plaindirt?" she asked.

"No," Father said. "I'll need to put the corn wherever I can."

She looked at him across the table as if he were her enemy, and he looked just as steadily back. It was as if a bargain had been struck between them, and the price she was paying was her precious flowers. I wondered what price Father had paid.

"If the peaches aren't frozen, they could be our cash crop, Father," I said urgently. "They'll ripen almost as fast as the corn and you know how hungry everyone will be for real fruit."

"No," Father said. His eyes never left her face. "We need the cash from the corn. To pay for something. Don't we?"

"Yes," she said, and pushed her chair back from the table. "You have your cash crop and I have mine."

"I want to put the corn in tomorrow," he shouted after her. "Pull your geraniums out this afternoon." Francie was staring at him wide-eyed. "Come on, Haze," he said more quietly, "I'll show you the peaches."

*   *   *

They did not even look like fruit. But they were there, hard little swellings like pebbles where the tight blossoms had been. "You see," he said, "we'll have our cash crop yet."

The quarantine sticker was gone from Sombra's fence. My strip had been white again this morning, and the ache that never quite left me was deeper, into my lungs now.

"First-generation colonies don't have cash crops," Father said. "They're too busy hanging on, too busy trying to stay alive. They're abjectly grateful for what the government gives them—greentents, antibiotics, anything. Second-generation aren't so grateful. The wheat's doing well and they start noticing that the government's help isn't all that helpful. Third-generation colonies aren't grateful at all. They have cash crops and they can buy what they need from earth, not beg for it. Fourth-generation stop growing wheat altogether and start manufacturing what they need and to hell with earth."

"We're fourth-generation," I said, not understanding.

Father had carried down a bucket of lime-sulphur and water and a wad of cloth rags to paint the peaches with. He dipped a rag in the bucket and pulled it out dripping. "No, Haze," he said. "We're first-generation, and if the government has its way, we'll be first-generation forever. The strep keeps us down, keeps us fighting for our lives. We can't develop light industry. We can't even keep our children alive long enough to graduate them from high school. We've been here nearly seventy years, Haze, and this is our first graduation."

"They could drop the antibiotics without landing, couldn't they?" I said. Little Willie upstairs in the big bed crying for Mama. "They could wipe it out altogether if they wanted to." Father was bending over the sulphur-smelling bucket, dipping the rag in the liquid. "Why aren't you doing something about it?"

I expected him to say there was nothing they could do, that it was impossible to manufacture antibiotics without filters and centrifuges and reagents, which the government would never ship us. I expected him to say that the only manufactured goods they shipped were those guaranteed not to be vandalized for parts and that the main virtue of the dustdowners as far as the government saw it was that they could not be turned into equipment for making antibiotics. But he wiped industriously at a peach and said, "We will be second-generation yet, Haze," he said. "We'll have our cash crops, and the government won't be able to stop us. They're shipping us the one thing we need right now, and they don't even know it."

I knelt by the bucket, dipping the worn cloth in the sulphur-smelling liquid.

"When I first tried to grow peaches, Haze, I used ordinary peach seeds from back home. I started them in the ponics tanks and some of them lived long enough to bloom and I crossed them with others that had survived. Do you remember that, Haze? When the green-tent was full of peach trees?"

I shook my head, still kneeling by the bucket. I could not even imagine it. Now there was no room for anything, not even mother's geraniums.

"I bred for what I thought they needed—a thick skin to stand the sorrel ants and a short trunk to stand the wind, but I couldn't do any genetic engineering. There isn't any equipment. I could only cross the ones that did well, the ones that lived long enough to bloom. I knew what I was breeding for, but not what I would get. I never thought it would be so . . . stunted and turned in upon itself. . . ."

He was not looking at the tree. He was looking at me. The rag he held was dripping whitish water on the toe of his shoe. "We have people working in emigration, some of them colonists, some of them not, looking at the gene prints and deciding on the emigration permits. We all thought your mother . . . her genetic prints were almost exactly like Mr. Phelps's, and he'd never had the strep. I've only had it twice in all these years. If it was a few points off, still it would be close enough, we thought. You cannot do the same things to people that you do to peach trees. Because it matters when they die.

"All I have left is this one pale and stunted tree," he said, and squeezed out the rag on the ground and began painting the fruit again. "And you."

*   *   *

The next day we trenched the tree, filling the narrow moat with dried mud and straw to keep the sorrel ants away. Father did not say anything more, and I could not tell anything from his face.

The day after that I had a negative strip, and I looked at it a long time, thinking about how I was never hot, never cold, how I had never had strep as a child. But Mr. Phelps had died of scarlet fever.

Mr. Phelps, who looked like me and never felt the cold. And Mother's gene prints were almost like Mr. Phelps's.

I ran down to the tree, almost tripping in the tangle of ripening wheat. Father was standing by the tree, examining one of the peaches. It was no larger that I could see, but it had lost a little of its greenish cast.

"Do you think we should put a moth net on?" he said. "It's a little early for moths."

"Father," I said, "I don't think anything we do will help or hurt it. I think it's all in the seed."

He smiled, and his smile told me what I had been afraid to see before. "So I've been told," he said.

"I'm immune to the strep, aren't I?"

"Her prints were almost exactly those of Mr. Phelps. I only had the strep twice. We thought it would be close enough, and after you were born, we were sure it would." He looked through me, as he had done on that day when he saw the sticker on Sombra's fence. "I have done the best I can for her. I have tried to remember that it was not her fault, that I brought her here to this, that it is my fault for thinking of her as I thought of my peach trees. I have let her turn Francie into a greentent flower that cannot possibly survive. I have let her treat you like a stepchild because I knew you could survive no matter what she did to you. I have let her . . ." He stopped and passed his hand over his chest. "There is a cache of blackmarket penicillin in the greentent for Francie. It took the cash crop to do it. It will save her once." He looked away from me toward Turillos'. "I think it's time to send you to Mamita's. She's got all the hands to do for. She'll need you."

He sent me back to the house to pack my things. The day was very hot. Halfway across the field I put my hand up to my forehead, and I could feel the damp sweat curling my hair. It will be cooler under the peach tree, I thought, and started back toward the tree. But halfway there the haze seemed to thicken almost to clouds with a fine pink tint, and the temperature to drop. It will be warmer in the greentent, I thought, shivering. I turned back the way I had come.

I hit one of the supports in the greentent when I fell. Francie will see that it's down, I thought, Francie will find me. I tried to pull myself up by the edge of the ponics tanks, but I had cut my hand when I fell and it bled into the tanks.

Mother found me. Francie had seen the greentent sagging heavily on one side and run to the house to tell her. Mother stood over me for a long time, as if she could not think what to do.

"What's wrong with her?" Francie asked from the doorway.

"Did you touch her?" Mother said.

"No, Mama."

"Are you sure?"

"Yes, Mama," she said, her bright blue eyes full of tears. "Shouldn't I go get Papa?"

And at last she knelt beside me and put her cool hand on my hot cheek. "She has the scarlet fever," she said to Francie. "Go into the house."

*   *   *

They put me in the big bed in the front bedroom because of Francie. I tried to keep the covers on, but it was so hot that I kicked them off without meaning to, and then I shivered so that they had to bring more blankets off Francie's bed.

"How is she?" Father said.

"No better," Mother said. "Her fever still hasn't broken." Her voice was less afraid than it had been in the greentent. I wondered if the planetwide had been lifted.

"I called the district nurse."

"Why?" Mother said, still in that quiet voice. "She doesn't have anything to give her. The *Magassar* won't come back again."

"There's the penicillin." I wondered if they looked as they had looked that day in the greentent, each clutching the frame of the bed as they had held onto the supports in the greentent.

Mother put her hand to my cheek. It felt cool. "No," she said quietly.

"She'll die without it," he said. I could hardly hear his voice.

"There isn't any penicillin," Mother said, and her voice was as still as her hand on my cheek. "I gave it to Francie."

*   *   *

Something worried at the edge of my mind. I tried to get a hold on it, but my teeth were chattering so badly I could not. The pain in my chest burned like a flame. I thought if I could press with my hand against it, the pain would lessen, but my hand felt muffled, and when I tried to look at it, it was as white as a positive strip.

Mamita had told me to take a strip when I got home. I did and it was white. But that could not be right, because the incubation period was very short, and I had not gotten sick for nearly a month. But I already had it, I thought. That day Sombra had asked if I was getting sick and there had been that pain behind my sternum that nearly doubled me over by the tree, I had already been getting sick.

I was edging closer to the worrisome thing, but it was so cold. I never felt the cold. Or the heat. Sombra had leaned forward to me on the wall and said, "Don't I feel hot?" and the pain had almost doubled me over. She was already getting sick, but so was I. I had been getting sick that day, and I had gotten over it.

I pulled my hand free of the blankets, and that started me shivering again. The hand was still white and clumsily heavy. I put it over the hollow space between my collarbones and pressed and pressed, my whole body straightening, tautening with the pain until it stretched to nothing.

Then I got up and put on my graduation dress, fumbling over the buttons with my bandaged hand, a little weak from the fever, but better, better.

*   *   *

Father was standing by the peach tree, throwing the peaches at the road. They bounced when they hit the hard mud and rolled against Turillos' fence.

"Oh, Papa," I said, "don't do that."

He did not seem to hear me. The dustdowner was kicking up its little trail of dust far down the road. He picked a hard peach off the tree, covered it with his big fist in a grip that should have smashed it, and pitched it at the distant downer.

"Papa," I said again. He whirled violently as if he would throw the peach at me. I stepped back in surprise.

"She killed you," he said, "to save her precious Francie. She let you die up there crying out her name. Putting her hand on your cheek and tucking you in. She murdered you!" He flung the peach down violently. It rolled to my feet. "Murderer!" He turned to wrench another peach off the tree.

I put up my hand in protest. "Papa, don't! Not your cash crop!"

He dropped his hands and stared limply at the dustdowner rattling down the road toward us. It was pulling a coffin behind it. My coffin. "You were my cash crop," he said quietly.

I remembered Mamita's face when she thought I'd brought the dress for Sombra's laying out. I looked down at my white shroudlike dress and my hand wrapped in the white bandage. "Oh, Papa," I said, finally understanding. "I didn't die. I got better."

"She gave the penicillin to Francie," he said. "While you were still in the greentent. Before she even let Francie come to get me.

Your hand was bleeding. She gave her the penicillin before she even bandaged your hand."

"It doesn't matter," I said. "I didn't need the medicine. I got over the scarlet fever myself."

It was finally coming to him, bit by bit, like it had come to me in the big bed. "You were supposed to be immune," he said. "But you got it anyway. You were supposed to be immune."

"I'm not immune, Papa, but I can get over the strep myself. I've been doing it all along, all my life." I picked up the peach at my feet and handed it to him. He looked at it numbly.

"We were breeding for immunity," he said.

"I know, Papa. You knew what you were breeding for, but you didn't know what you'd get." I wanted to put my arms around him. "Haven will always be coming up with new strains. It would be impossible to be immune to all of them."

He took a knife out of his pocket, slowly, as if he were still asleep. He cut into the peach in his hand, sawing through the thick, dusty skin to the sudden softness underneath. He bit into it, and I watched his face anxiously.

"Is it all right, Papa?" I said. "Is it sweet?"

"Sweet beyond hope," he said, and put his arms around me, holding me close. "Oh, my sweet Haze, we bred to fight the strep, and look, look what we got!"

He held me by the shoulders and looked down at me. "I want you to go to Mamita's. You can't help here. But the hands all have gene prints like yours." His eyes were full of tears. "You are my cash crop after all."

"Now run," he said and walked away from me, back through the field toward the house. I stood for a minute, watching him, unable to call to him, to shout after him how much I loved them all. I climbed over the fence and stood in the road, looking at the litter of unhurt peaches. The downer was finishing its determined circuit at the top of the hill. If I hurried I could ride my own coffin to Mamita's and not even get my graduation dress wet. It seemed to me suddenly the most joyous chance in the world—to ride my own coffin, triumphant in my white dress with its fluttering red ribbons.

I stopped to catch my breath at the top of the hill and looked back at the peach tree. Francie was standing by it, with her hand raised almost in a question. Mama had done her hair in sugar curls for some occasion, and they did not move in the dusty wind that fluttered the red ribbons on my dress. She seemed as still as the brown haze that surrounded her, hugging her thin arms against her chest. I was too far away to see her shivering. Perhaps I would not have known what it meant if I had: I was not bred to read omens.

"I'll bring you some penicillin," I shouted, though she would have no idea of what I was saying. I shouted past her to Papa, who was too far away already to hear me. "I'll bring you some if I have to walk all the way to the *Magassar*."

"Don't worry!" I shouted. "They'll lift the planetwide. I know it." The dustdowner rattled past me, drowning out my words, and I ran to pull myself up onto the splintery edge of the coffin. "Don't worry, Francie!" I shouted again, putting my bandaged hand up to my mouth and holding on tight with the other. "We're all going to live forever!"

LIEBERMAN'S FATHER

François Camoin

Lieberman had his eyes on his chicken salad and so at first didn't see the woman. She stopped short at his table and stood, swaying a little this way and that, looking like a person who has just bumped into something and is wondering if she's hurt herself. To the people at the next table it was clear that what she'd bumped into was Lieberman.

"Excuse me," she said.

Lieberman looked up. He saw a thin woman who looked athletic, like a jogger, well-preserved. He thought she might be fifty years old, might be sixty.

"Hello, Martin."

"Do I know you?" Lieberman said.

"No," she told him. She pulled out a chair and sat down across the table from him. "A little water? You don't mind? It's a shock."

Lieberman poured for her. "What's a shock?"

"Well," she said. "This isn't going to be easy for you."

Lieberman laid down his fork. "What isn't?"

She emptied her glass and set it back on the table. "That's better." She sat back and looked and looked Lieberman in the eye. Her face was attractive, he thought. Serious.

"I'm your father," she said.

Lieberman looked around. If anybody had heard the woman they didn't make a sign. No heads turned.

"Did I understand you?" Lieberman said.

"I'm your real father," the woman said.

"I have a father. He's sixty-eight years old and lives in New Jersey. He's a retired carpenter."

"I know," she said. "A religious man. He never had much time for his family." She coughed. "Would you mind if I had a little more water?" She drank it slowly, looking over the rim of the glass at Lieberman.

"You followed me in here," he said.

206

"To tell the truth, yes. Don't get mad. This is the first time I've seen you up close like this in fifteen years. This California weather doesn't agree with me. Not enough humidity—a person could dry out like a dead leaf if he doesn't drink water all the time." She studied Lieberman. "You don't look bad. A little heavy, maybe. But you have a good tan, good muscle tone. I can see you take care of yourself."

"What's it all about?" Lieberman said. "What do you want from me?"

"Forty-six years old. And you have your own discount store already: eighteen departments, though I understand cameras aren't doing so well. But at your age that's something. You should be proud."

"I have a partner," Lieberman said.

"Segal? I've seen Segal. Don't worry, I didn't tell him who I am—I don't want to cause you embarrassment. Segal's a money man; it's your ideas that make the place go, am I right?"

Lieberman felt himself blush. "Maybe."

"You've done all right. Two daughters, Ruth at UCLA and Laura married to a psychologist. And you have a beautiful wife, even if she is a *shickse*."

"She converted," Lieberman said.

The woman shrugged. "To Reformed. What kind of a Jew is that? Might as well be a Unitarian."

"Excuse me," Lieberman said, "but what business is this of yours? Why am I discussing my family with somebody who followed me into a restaurant?"

"They're my family too," the woman said.

"Enough is enough," Lieberman said. He signaled to the waitress for his check.

"Don't believe me—it's still God's truth. I'm your real father, Martin."

He left money on the table and walked away. When he was outside he looked back through the plate-glass window. She was still at his table. She poured herself another glass of water, looked up, waved at Lieberman.

*   *   *

Sheila Lieberman liked to eat dinner out on the patio under the trees, where she could look out over the Valley. "What's the sense of living in California if you can't eat outside?" she said when Lieberman complained about the heat and the smog.

"Maybe it was Segal," she said. "He has a peculiar idea of a joke sometimes. He could have hired this woman to do it so he could see your face tomorrow morning."

Lieberman shook his head. "Segal's idea of a joke is a rubber fly under my napkin at lunch. He wouldn't spend that kind of money for a laugh."

"Then it was a crazy person."

"What else?"

"I don't know. Maybe you ought to call your father and ask him."

"Ask him what?" Lieberman said. "If he's really my father? He's sixty-eight years old; he's doing what he always wanted to do all his life; he locks himself up with his books all day and he's happy as a clam. I'm going to ask him now, after forty-six years, if he's really my father? Long-distance?"

A gust of wind brought down a shower of dry brown needles, and Lieberman covered his plate with his hands. He looked up into the white pine and saw that the disease was spreading. On his last visit the tree surgeon had folded Lieberman's check into his pocket without thanks and shrugged. "We'll give it a little time. See how it responds. But I think you'll have to cut it down."

"It's dying," Sheila said, following Lieberman's look.

"We'll see." He began to eat slowly. "What would I tell him?" he said. "My father and I haven't talked in twenty years except to say hello and how are you once a month on the telephone. He doesn't want to talk to me."

"You love him," Sheila said.

"He doesn't know what love is," Lieberman said.

The next day he looked closely at Segal to see if the other man was playing a joke after all. They shared one big office at the store, with desks that faced each other on opposite sides of the room. They also shared Miss Lash, a graduate of the Bryman School who could type like a machine gun and take dictation faster than the partners could talk. Lieberman suspected that Segal was taking her out at night, but in the office she treated them both with the same impersonal courtesy.

"I talked to my father on the phone yesterday." Lieberman said.

Segal looked up from the invoices and order blanks scattered on his desk. "He's still in New Jersey?" Lieberman saw nothing out of the ordinary in his face. "You ought to tell him to come settle out here—it's healthier. Lots of nice places down by Laguna Beach; he could be with people his own age."

"You know how it is," Lieberman said. "He doesn't want to take a chance. What if he didn't like it?"

The store stayed open every night until ten o'clock, but unless it was inventory time or there was trouble with one of the departments, Lieberman was gone by six. Home was a slow twenty-minute drive along Ventura Boulevard; it gave him time to put the store out of his mind and become a family man again. Lieberman didn't want to be like his father, who had come home five days a week, put away his carpenter's tools and disappeared into the little room he'd added to the back of the house, where he kept his books. On Saturdays he'd been gone all day, of course, and on Sundays it was the books again. Lieberman wanted a different kind of life. Also he felt that Sheila needed him. Now that both the girls were gone from the house she had become moody: sometimes sad, sometimes frantically gay. Sometimes she sat close to Lieberman on the couch, not satisfied unless some part of herself was touching him; other nights she disappeared into her sewing room and watched her twelve-inch TV until Lieberman gave up and went to bed.

This night she chose the television and Lieberman lay in the bedroom for a long time, staring up into the dark, only half in control of the thoughts that flew through his head. When he finally fell asleep, it was to dream of the woman who said she was his father. In the dreams she lived in the old family house in New Jersey and she kept calling Lieberman long-distance in California. "Come home, Martin. It's healthier out here; you could be with your own kind of people."

A week went by and Lieberman stopped expecting to see the woman again. Los Angeles is full of crazy people—what's one more? He thought about Segal and Miss Lash: were they going out nights together? What could he do about it? Then he came out of the store a few minutes late, opened the front door of his Buick and found the woman sitting in the passenger seat reading a paperback novel, waiting for him. She bent down the corner of a page to mark her place.

"Did you call your father and ask him?" she said.

"I call him every month," Lieberman said. "What should I ask?"

"Your mother was nineteen years old when she married him," the woman said. Seeing her close up in the light from the parking-lot lamps, Lieberman realized she must have been quite handsome when she was young. Her voice was a strong contralto; like her face it had character.

"Look," he said, "I don't know who you really are. . . ."

"Your father was away all day long; sometimes when he was working a job out of town he didn't get home until after dark. Your mother was lonely—it was her first time away from her family. What happened was the most natural thing in the world. She shouldn't be blamed."

"My mother died fifteen years ago," Lieberman said harshly.

"I was at the funeral. I don't suppose you remember."

"No," Lieberman said. He unlocked the ignition and started the motor. "I've had a long day; I want to go home."

"I was the same age as your mother," the woman said. "I was in college studying mathematics."

"At Princeton?" Lieberman said sarcastically.

"Columbia. I was home for the summer."

Lieberman pushed impatiently at the accelerator; the car roared and rocked slightly without moving forward. The transmission was still in park.

"I was in my last year already," the woman said. "I started college at sixteen."

"A genius," Lieberman said.

"I told you," the woman said. "You're a success because you come from good stock. Not that some of it isn't due to your own efforts, naturally."

"Enough!" Lieberman shouted.

"Go on, get angry; it'll do you good."

"How could anybody believe this?"

"Let it out. Yell if you want to."

"Get out of my car," Lieberman said. He reached across her and opened the far door; when she was outside he yanked the door shut. She stood there while he drove away. When he looked in the mirror she hadn't moved.

He drove slowly along Ventura Boulevard, past Coldwater and Woodman, not hearing the music on the radio. On the corner of Van Nuys there was a bar and he slowed down, but as he was turning into the parking lot he thought he saw Segal with his arm around Miss Lash going in the front door; he drove on.

"You're late," Sheila said. The television was off; she was listening to a record.

Lieberman let himself sink slowly into a chair. "She was there again," he said. "I don't want to talk about it."

"So don't talk about it. She's a crazy person—tell her to leave you alone."

"I did."

"She won't."

"I know," Lieberman said.

"I had a call from Laura today."

"Good. How is she?"

"Not good."

"What did she say?"

"Nothing. We just chatted. But I could tell by her voice."

"She didn't tell you anything?"

"No."

"Well then we'll have to wait until she does. I never did want her to marry David Shupack," Lieberman said. "Even if he is a psychologist. He doesn't have feelings."

"Everybody has feelings," Sheila said.

Lieberman shrugged. "As long as she loves him."

The record ended and Sheila got up to turn it over. "I looked at the tree again today," she said. "It's getting worse."

"Maybe it needs more water."

"It's already like a swamp around the roots."

"Maybe we're watering it too much," Lieberman said. "Call the man tomorrow and have him come over and take a look."

"Every time he comes it's twenty dollars and all he has is bad news."

"I love that tree," Lieberman said. "I don't have time to plant another one and wait ten years for it to grow to where we can enjoy it. Call. What's twenty dollars?"

He pressed his face against the window; in the patio floodlights the pine looked healthy, but Lieberman knew his wife and the tree surgeon were right—it was dying.

"I'll cut it down myself," he said.

The next morning he went to the hardware department of the store and picked out a chain saw and two coils of nylon rope. He set them by his desk and Segal looked at him curiously but he didn't explain. Did Miss Lash look tired under the makeup? He couldn't be sure. Segal had bags under his eyes, but Segal always had bags under his eyes. Was it any of his business? He put it out of his mind and made plans to straighten out the camera department.

At noon he rolled his chair back and stretched. Segal was dictating a letter; Miss Lash was keeping up without effort.

"Lunch?" Lieberman said.

Segal shook his head. "I'm not really hungry. You go ahead; maybe I'll send out for a sandwich later."

The delicatessen on Sepulveda was full of real-estate salesmen talking loudly and Lieberman stopped in the doorway, undecided. Sometimes David Shupack took time from his mental-health clinic to eat here, but Lieberman didn't see him anywhere. What could he have said to his son-in-law anyhow? What's the trouble between you and Laura? I know there's trouble because Sheila heard it in her voice the last time she called? The waitress was coming his way with a sheaf of menus but he waved her away and went back out to his car. Maybe he'd have a sandwich with Segal.

But when he got back the office door was locked. He tried his key; the cylinder turned and the bolt slid back but the door didn't give. Lieberman put his ear to the wooden panel and heard scurrying inside, and low urgent voices. Segal and Miss Lash. He turned and walked out; as he passed the perfume counter the girls giggled.

Sheila was surprised to see him. "You never come home for lunch on Wednesday. Is something wrong at the store? You want to eat?"

"Fix me anything," Lieberman said. "Chicken salad, an egg, anything."

He ate without hunger, to fill his stomach. Sheila perched on a kitchen stool and watched him. "Can you believe it?" Lieberman said. He pushed the plate to one side. "Right in the office during lunch time. The door wouldn't open, thank God. I think he had the good sense to put a chair under the knob otherwise I would have walked right in on them."

"It's the time of life," Sheila said. "A man his age—you could almost expect it."

"What age?" Lieberman said. "Segal's forty-six. My age. A year older than you."

"I looked out the window this morning," Sheila said, "and I think I saw that woman. The one who's been following you."

Lieberman's heart gave a jump. "Are you sure?"

"How could I be sure? I've never seen her before. But there was a woman hanging around across the street looking at this house. She looked like a nice person. Not crazy."

"What did you do?"

"I couldn't decide. What if it was just someone out for a walk? So finally I went out to talk to her, but she was gone."

"She'll be back," Lieberman said. "If she comes to the door, don't answer. I don't want you to get mixed up in this if she's crazy."

"If?" Sheila said.

"You know what I mean. Maybe I'll call David tonight and ask him what he thinks."

"He's a marriage counselor. What would he know about crazy women?"

"A psychologist is a psychologist. He went to seven years of school; they must have taught him something besides marriage problems."

"Don't talk to him about Laura."

"All right," Lieberman promised.

"And don't be too hard on Segal. It might happen to you someday."

"Not with the secretary."

"Don't be so sure," Sheila told him. "People get desperate."

*   *   *

When Lieberman opened the office door, he saw that Miss Lash was gone.

"I gave her the afternoon off," Segal said.

"How long have we been partners?" Lieberman said.

"I don't know. Eight years?"

"Nine."

"Are you going to give me a lecture on not fooling around with the help? Don't you think I know already?"

Lieberman searched for words. "In the office?" he said. "With everybody out there? They knew what you were doing. It isn't civilized."

Segal hung his head. "All of a sudden she was so beautiful. Little tits like oranges. I could see them under her blouse. It made me crazy. You were supposed to be gone to lunch."

"At least thank God for the chair under the doorknob," Lieberman said.

"That was her idea. I couldn't think—I was like a madman. She likes me, Lieberman. We have good times together. We even talk."

The great pleasure in his eyes made Lieberman feel defeated. "We can't keep her," he said.

"You're right," Segal said. "I'll find her another job."

"All right." He got up and slapped Segal on the back, awkwardly. "All the same," he said, "you're being a damn fool."

"I know," Segal said. He added, almost to himself, "But it's so fine."

*   *   *

When Lieberman talked to his son-in-law on the telephone he was never quite certain that he wasn't actually talking to somebody else. David Shupack had a completely neutral voice. Lieberman explained about the woman.

"Does this make sense to you, David?" he asked.

"Cases like this aren't exactly run of the mill," David said. "But they're not unheard of."

"She knows everything about me," Lieberman said.

"People who are crazy in one way often function well in other ways. Knowing all about you helps her convince herself of her fantasy, so she does some research. It's all part of the pattern."

"I thought you psychologists never used that word *crazy*."

"Maladjusted, neurotic—what's a word? She's not in touch."

"This is your opinion? She's nuts?"

"Without meeting her myself I can't tell for sure, naturally."

"What else could it be?"

"The world is a crazy place," David said. "Who knows, really?" There was something odd happening to his voice.

"How's Laura?" Lieberman said. Sheila hissed a warning; he waved it away. "How's my little girl?" he said.

A strange sound came back to Lieberman through the telephone. "What's that?" he said. "Are you there, David?" The sound stopped and Lieberman realized that his son-in-law had been crying. "David?"

The neutral voice, when it came back, had an odd dignity that Lieberman didn't remember having heard in it before. "Martin, I think she's seeing another man. I don't want to talk about it."

"The whole fucking world is falling apart," Lieberman said to his wife when he hung up the phone.

"You never swear," she said.

"I wouldn't be surprised if she *is* seeing somebody else," he said.

"David wouldn't be the first husband who's imagining things. Who really knows?"

"He's a cold fish," Lieberman said. "Who could blame her?"

"I'm going to watch a little TV," Sheila said. "Don't wait up for me."

"Good night," Lieberman said.

*   *   *

He began to look for the crazy woman and caught himself feeling disappointed because he didn't see her. She didn't come to the house again, and she didn't come to the store. She's crazy of course, Lieberman told himself, but that doesn't mean she might not have some good advice for me. People who are crazy in one way often function very well in other ways. If she was going to disappear like that why did she come into my life at all? Once he thought he saw her going down the aisle between calculators and infant wear, but when he tapped her on the shoulder she turned out to be just another old woman with an unpleasant face. A California face.

He called his father in New Jersey, but from the first hello Lieberman could tell that the old man didn't want to talk to him about anything that mattered.

"Were you in the middle of something important?" he said.

"What's important?" Lieberman could see his father, three thousand miles away, shrugging his shoulders.

"I didn't want to interrupt anything, that's all. Do you want me to call you back later?"

"No, no. Talk. How are you? How's the family?"

"Fine," Lieberman said bitterly.

"You don't sound good."

Lieberman had intended to be calm, but his good intentions evaporated. "It's everything," he said. "Sheila's going through some crazy thing, watching television every night until three in the morning; Laura's having trouble in her marriage; my partner's running around with a twenty-year-old girl and says he can talk to her. Talk!"

"Stop," his father said.

"What?"

"Martin, I'm old. I'm sorry you're having trouble in your life, but to tell the truth I don't want to hear about it. Don't tell me details."

"My tree's dying," Lieberman said.

"What tree? What's that about a tree? Are you crazy?"

"It's dying," Lieberman said. He hung up.

He sat with his head in his hands. From the sewing room he could hear the sound of a television quiz show.

The telephone rang. "Hello," Lieberman said.

"You hung up on your father?"

"I'm sorry," Lieberman said.

"It's nothing personal," his father said. "For more than sixty years now I've had troubles of my own, and now I want to be done with it. I have a right to a little peace. Call me any time, but don't tell me everything. Just in general."

"In general, I'm going crazy," Lieberman said.

"Everything'll work out in time," his father said. "Try not to get worked up so much. Sheila's a good girl—I always liked her."

"So why didn't you come to the wedding?" Lieberman said.

"That's all past. Why bring it up now after twenty years?"

"Just once," Lieberman said, "couldn't you tell me you made a mistake, you're sorry?"

"What good would that do?"

"I don't know," Lieberman said. "I'd like to hear it, that's all."

"Forget it," his father said. "That's my advice. Don't be so concerned with wrongs done to you. Past is past. Call me again when you feel better. In the meantime take care of yourself."

*   *   *

In the morning Lieberman stepped out in his robe to pick up the *L.A. Times* and saw the woman standing at the corner, half-hidden behind a flowering bush. He waved the folded newspaper. "Hey!" he called out. "Wait."

He thought she smiled at him, but he was too far away to be certain. "Wait!" he shouted. But she was already gone.

"You should be glad she didn't insist on talking to you again," Sheila told him. "Maybe this means she's giving up her craziness and she's going to leave you alone."

"There was something very nice about her," Lieberman said. "I could tell she was a warm person even if she was crazy."

*   *   *

The rest of the story? You know it already. You know Lieberman: he's like you and me. How else could it happen? Tell me the truth.

Lieberman stands at the bottom of the tree with the saw throbbing in his hand, preparing himself for the first cut. "Are you sure you know what you're doing?" Sheila says.

"First the front notch, then the back cut," Lieberman recites. He's been reading a book from the public library. "It has to fall right there." The psychiatrist next door, Eisenberg, drawn by the sound of the saw, has come out of his house and is hovering near his new brick barbecue pit, gauging the length of Lieberman's tree, calculating angles in his head. He looks worried.

Yesterday Segal's wife called Lieberman at home and cried about Miss Lash; later, while Sheila was watching a rerun of "Outer Limits," Laura called and explained to Lieberman that it was all right for her to be seeing another man. "I don't really think I've ever been in love before," she told her father.

Lieberman makes the first cut; Eisenberg watches him. The sawdust flies; chips make a little pile on the grass. Nobody has noticed the woman who appears at the bottom of the garden, silent. She comes closer. Lieberman stands back; the wood in the notch he has made is yellow-white, looks healthy, oozes clear sap. He wonders if he's doing the right thing. He turns to go to the other side of the tree and for the first time he sees her. "Hello," he says. He begins the back cut; he leans into the saw, watches the chain bite, the bark fly; he concentrates on his task, aware that behind him Sheila and the woman have come together and are talking easily, as if they'd known each other for years.

He told Segal's wife to be patient—it was a matter of age and Segal would come back if she gave him some room for his foolishness now. But as he talked he was remembering the glad light in his partner's eye when he looked at Miss Lash, and Lieberman felt he was telling a lie. Segal's wife doesn't have tits like oranges. The saw's motor slows and barks in a deeper tone as Lieberman cuts deeper into the trunk. Eisenberg is holding a hand over his mouth. His eyes look a little crazy.

Lieberman steps back; everything is ready to happen. He gives the tree a little push. It cracks loudly, begins to lean forward; the ropes hold, guide the slow fall. Lieberman turns to the women. "No problem," he says. "Just like in the book."

The rope on the left side breaks. The backlash catches Lieberman above the eyes like a long bullwhip; it stuns him. The tree slips to one side, away from Eisenberg and his barbecue; it catches the corner of Lieberman's house. Cedar shakes make a fountain against the blue sky, roof-timbers snap. The bathroom window falls out in one piece to lie on the grass, a long branch reaches out and topples Lieberman's chimney, another backhands the television antenna off the roof. Lieberman moans; a drop of blood falls down his nose; the forgotten chain saw chug-chugs quietly in his left hand. Eisenberg stares. Suddenly the psychiatrist laughs, a loud quacking laugh. He looks around guiltily, clamps the hand tight over his lips and runs inside his house.

Later, in the living room, the woman covers the long cut on Lieberman's forehead with surgical tape from the medicine cabinet. He sits on the couch, holding a cup of coffee, thinking *Who can tell about life?* over and over, the same words singing through his head like a stuck record. *Who can tell?*

"Laura wants to come home and live for a while," Sheila says. "David's leaving her."

"Let her go and live with the other one," Lieberman says.

"She can't, Martin. He's married."

"That's just fine," Lieberman says. "That's wonderful."

The woman strokes his forehead. "Your other girl's so very different," she says. "Gets straight A's in school and you don't have to worry about her at all. That's how you were when you were her age—nobody had to worry about you."

The smell of sawdust and sap comes through the hole in the roof. Also the sound of Eisenberg laughing again. The woman holds Lieberman's hand. "How could it be your fault? You gave her everything. You're a terrific father. Some kids just don't work out. But you did; I'm very proud of you."

I need, Lieberman thinks. *I want. I need.* What's truth compared to that?

Daddy. Lieberman practices it under his breath, no more than a thought the first time. The cut on his forehead throbs with the beat of his heart. Eisenberg laughs again, an ugly duck sound. I loved that tree, Lieberman thinks. The woman touches his cheek. *Daddy*, Lieberman whispers, holding her hand tight, making up his mind.

SECOND HANDS (1970)

Kevin McIlvoy

I think the worst coward can ignore fear even when it sweeps over and over you like the second hand of a clock. I'm a platoon leader and pretty much the worst coward in my outfit, so on a mine-sweep operation I'll try to think of something that I can picture whole and concentrate on completely. If it's something stupid like a horny fantasy or a basketball game or a two-pound boring book I've read, that's okay too as long as it will stretch itself out in me, block the twitch of that second hand so I don't mess up.

That's how it is that lots of times I imagine my sister Peg keeping me company on sweeps. We're just a year apart in age so you could say we grew up soldiers in arms. I'm lucky how I can be on my third month in-country but, thanks to Peg, not actually be "here" as much as I'm in New Mexico. If it's 1300 hours here in An Loc, right now in Las Almas, New Mexico, it's one day earlier and four o'clock in the afternoon.

*   *   *

"You don't understand," my dad said, "about radio. And you don't know about loyalty either."

"I wish he'd give it a good blow," Peg said.

We were talking about Arthur Godfrey's nose and the lifetime supply of congestion which filtered his voice.

"But he wouldn't sound the same," Mom said.

"It'd be a shame," said Dad, "Nobody'd listen to him."

I really couldn't stand Arthur Godfrey. It's no credit to me how much energy I could put into hating somebody who played ukelele, sang with a full nose, and called people "Bub." But, man, I hated him and Hope and Welk and Benny and Gleason and that whole gang of the radio-era living dead.

"Mr. Godfrey cares about people," Mom said. "You can tell he does."

This all happened one afternoon in '69 on the last Friday in

219

November, the culmination of Hawaiian Week Bargain Days at the Albertson's Grocery in my neighborhood. Peg and I had a cart with bad wheel alignment. Mom and Dad's cart had the same problem.

Grocery shopping as a family was not something we regularly did. But I was leaving soon for Basic and my older brother Anthony was due home from Nam in three weeks, so Mom was feeling sentimental, remembering back when Anthony and Peg and I used to go with her, me in the cart seat, Anthony pushing, and Peg riding underneath.

Peg had talked me into going with her and Mom. Then the three of us had ganged up on Dad, who agreed to go with us on the condition that we'd buy real food, lots of it, and not the pinchfuls of crap that were his usual high-blood-pressure curse.

We didn't have a list or anything. The way I thought of it, our job was to move real slowly close behind Mom and Dad's cart and look for something like what they were looking for but which they might have missed. To keep Mom happy we would have to buy some milk and cheeses and a few nongrocery items, though the real challenge was to discover the carcinogenic, high-cholesterol, sugar-laced stuff that would be so good it could actually kill my dad and might at least do hidden damage to the rest of us.

Peg said that Dad liked root beer—we should get him some A & W. He overheard us and said we should get Hires, it was better. We put four big bottles in the cart, and when Mom looked over her shoulder to see if I bought the right kind, I held them up to show her they were non-diet. She pretended to frown at me, pushed her wobbling cart forward.

My mother is beautiful. But here in-country I have some problems picturing her as being more complete than my wallet photo of her. She doesn't always wear her hair that way, whipped up into a firm, sticky, Lady Bird wave. Still, that's all I can see. Dark, penciled Kodak-gray eyebrows; Kodak-black eyelashes and eyes. Grim grin. And I can't see her hands. Sometimes I'll try to remember her hands and her arms and legs where they ought to be somewhere on either end of her photo. Useless.

Peg looks a lot like my mom in some ways. So when I'm trying to think of things about my mom, I'll think of Peg's Mom-type smile, which is, at its best, a compromise between her emotions. You can't see her teeth when she smiles. And Peg has light blond down along her chin that you can make out in a certain light and which I think Mom has also.

While Mom bought some eggs and yogurts and things, Peg and I leaned into the tall, closed refrigerators next to all that. Dad whispered, "Careful!" covering Mom's eyes when we pulled out some Budweisers.

"John," Mom said, "you don't have to act so goofy. We're in public, don't you know."

Peg did a pitch-perfect mimic: "Really, John! You're embarrassing us, don't you know."

We were enjoying ourselves, Mom included. I'm not a deep guy—I don't think of myself like that, but this was near to the time I was going to leave everyone, so I was constantly looking for the story in the lines on my own palms. I wondered about why we couldn't always be as happy as we were on that Albertson's expedition.

The next two aisles were *Housewares, School, Misc. Supplies,* and *Hygiene, Health, Paper Goods.* We looked at the shelves, at all the extension cords and tube socks and boxes of Empire pencils, Elmer's glue, and the half-dozen different brands of toilet-bowl cleaner, the roach motels, the roach sprays, the roach and pest bombs. Mom sailed us past the douches and tampons, the other hygiene stuff, the contraceptive jellies. Mom was what people would call "prudish," though we wouldn't razz her about that because it was ingrained in her. The way we thought about her was that she was "refined," a word plenty different than "prudish."

My dad had his hands right next to hers on the cart. His nails were ugly and knuckles uglier. For twenty years he's been building cinder-block walls for Oscar Rado & Sons, Co., and he has his job tattooed onto him. His skin on his arms and neck and face is pitted; if you look close, you see the grit trapped under it even at his forehead and around his mouth. His blond-turning-gray hair is Brylcreemed; he finger-combs it straight back. You try to find something in him that relents and you almost can't. Except, he has a big, hard gut that goes about to the center of his chest over which he wears silly-looking white Mexican wedding shirts. And, here's another thing: as if to punish him for his unique style, Mom has made all his white socks washing-machine pink. I can see that. I can look right through my own fear at that. When we turned the corner of that aisle, a nine- or ten-foot cardboard Koa-Koa Sauce palm tree with motorized limbs swayed before us in a pretend tropical breeze. Mom said, "That's nice. They didn't have that last year."

Ice Cream & Novelties, Breakfast Entrees was the widest aisle in the store, with a long freezer box running up the middle, shelves over it and shelves across from it on either side.

We decided to split up, Peg and I taking *Ice Cream & Novelties* and

Mom and Dad *Breakfast Entrees*. I asked Peg if we should get the frozen brownies, the blintzes, or the Pralines 'n Cream ice cream. She put all three in our cart. "Mom," she said across the freezer, "I'm going to pitch in some money for these things." Peg was working for the *Sun-Bulletin*, had her own apartment but never much money, so it was a nice thing for her to offer.

Mom said, "Well," and looked at our cart, "if you're going to be silly you might as well pay for it."

"What'd you get?" Dad asked.

I held up the ice cream.

"Wow," he said. Like a little boy would say it. Beautiful. You have to know that we just never much saw that side of him. Like a boy in knee pants and suspenders.

Peg touched my hand and nodded at him. "Yeah," I said, but didn't say, "Peg, I love you for being so great." In my family you left that unspoken. Of course, you could find ways to show it: Eskimo Sandwiches, Top Whip, Mrs. Hibble's Peach Custard.

At the end of the freezer aisle, on a display all her own, was Little Debbie. Dad stood next to her, gazed down where shelves of Little Debbie cakes and brownies and rolls were arranged over her cardboard skirt. I genuflected before her to choose Dunk 'Em Sticks, which would have been his choice exactly. I knew that even in Aisle 5 (A—*Mexican & Macaroni*; B—*Salad Dr. & Pickles*) you could find ways to show how you felt: Vienna Sausage W. B-B-Q Sauce and Vlasic Hot Pepper Rings and Teeny Weenies.

My mother was getting into the fun. She was going to go along now, do this for Peg and—probably—especially for me. But I had a suspicion that at home she would hide or throw away every junky, wonderful gift.

I directed us to the back of the store, where *Quality Meats* were in a freezer box stretching to almost the whole width of the Albertson's. The butchers were working, so you could see them behind their sliding windows, spinning the hooked carcasses like dance partners, sawing away at the ribs, chopping at the stumps of limbs, and wrist-flicking the parts onto white formica tables. Each of their butchering knives was more perfectly suited to its purpose than any weapon ever tempered for war.

We bought pork ribs because they were one of the mortalest sins of all for Dad's diet. Peg went to the palm tree, returning with two jars of Koa-Koa Sauce. "Hot Style or Medium?" she asked.

"Medium," Dad said, "and Hot Style."

I have separate photos of Mom and Dad. They took a twenty-fifth anniversary picture but neither liked it; the separate ones satisfied them better. They have twin beds, his with a shamrock-green corduroy bedspread, hers with a kind of churchy comforter that has blossoming camellias on it. On the weekends when they take naps, he sleeps on her bed, she sleeps on his. If it's Sunday, 1100 hours here, then in New Mexico it's Saturday, 2 P.M.: my parent's nap time.

We did two passes of the meat freezer. It impressed me how the rows of tongues and feet and brains merited their own small but carefully crepe-decorated section in the freezer box—a place of honor, as if the butchers wanted to acknowledge the grace of these body parts, separate them from rumps, flanks, shoulders.

In the next three aisles we bought Cheez-Its, Cardinal Potato Chips, Oreos, and Windmills. Mom also bought coffee, grapefruit juice, saltines. *Candy & Nuts* and *Baby Supplies* were on the same side of Aisle 2. Dad picked out some malted milk balls and red hots. Peg and I followed after, tossing some Butterfingers and Circus Peanuts in our cart.

Mom pointed out the cost of diapers to Peg. "Six dollars a box," she said, and when Peg ignored her, she added, "Babies get more expensive all the time, don't you know." Peg was engaged to A. J. Berdam and, by Mom's reckoning, Peg should see that marriage and diapers went hand-in-glove. But Mom wouldn't say that. Her sense of propriety made her say "purkie" instead of "fart." The evening news body counts and the black-and-white footage were "deplorable," don't you know.

I'm wrong, I know I'm wrong about this whole way of thinking, but just because I can't shoot my anger straight doesn't mean I don't have to shoot. We'll be on a sweep like this through a grove of trees where the aboveground roots can confuse you and, even after defoliation, the damn shadows stream everywhere. I'll get a mental picture of Mom and Dad and Arthur Godfrey and Gleason and Hope and the gang turning off the radio to watch the TV. Before long, Hope makes a crack about some beauty queen whose "body (wink, wink) counts." Gleason jabs his arm out for an uppercut at a gook and shrieks, "One of these days—right in the kisser!" Welk asks if they can bring on the bubbles. And Godfrey, his poor beat-up nose dimming, says, "Deplorable, eh, Bub?"

If it's 1300 hours here, then in New Mexico Mom and Dad are waking up from their naps. My dad's hair looks like he dreamed in trenches; the pillow-sunk side of his face is older than the other. My mom puts in her bridge, which she calls her "partial." I'll bet she looks different without her molars and eyeteeth, but I've never seen her without them, not once.

On Aisle 1A Mom bought bananas, celery, and carrots, none of which were compatible with the Fritos, Bacon Puffs, and shoestring potatoes we bought on Aisle 1B.

The bakery was in that same part of the store. Dad chose a pecan pie, still hot, from the pie rack.

"Enough is enough," said Mom, making him put it back. He gave her a chin-out, frowning look. She stuck her tongue out at him— propriety right out the window. We all laughed. We made fun of her; I wish that wasn't true, but we did—we poked fun at her.

Then, after everything was rung up, Dad had the bag boy bring him the pie. It must have been hot on the bottom and hotter on the edges because Dad shifted it in his hands, rushing us to the car. By now it was five-thirty in the evening.

Driving through the neighborhood, I slowed down to have a long look at everything. Mrs. Rado's new backyard wall was higher, her windows barred since the burglary a month before. Across the street from her house, the oldest Armenterez boy was raking leaves; he was a weight lifter, making his body molten, cooling it down, all the sheaths of muscle angrily glowing, becoming larger and larger by the day. We figured him—the whole neighborhood figured him— as the kid who burglarized Mrs. Rado, and we knew how it satisfied him to see her changing her home, frightened of her own home because of him, just him.

"She can't move," said Dad. "She can't afford to sell."

Mom said, "It's so sick."

The car got quiet. When we parked in my parents' driveway we could hear both the high school and university bands practicing for the branch campus Homecoming on the next weekend. We took the sacks in our arms, listening to the boomcashinking and bleating. The brass sounded purer than it had on other, warmer winters. Maybe the chilled metal of the saxes and cornets made crisper notes, or maybe in the cold the players' lungs were less overeager, their tongues more agile on the reeds and mouthpieces.

We took the bags around the house to the back door because Mom didn't like us tramping the living room carpet. On my second trip, the jar of Hot Pepper Rings bumped out of my bag and shattered everywhere on the ground. I started to clean it up, but Dad asked Peg and me to put groceries away, said he and Mom would be the cleanup crew. It was a mess, I said, and since I made it I ought to clean it up. But Mom said it was their job. They took an empty coffee can out with them and got started.

Looking at them through the kitchen window, Peg said, "Today was fun, don't you think?"

"Can you believe Mom?" I said.

Peg stuck her tongue out and did her imitation: "Enough is enough."

We had at least six bags to unload. "Peg," I said, "you think we made too much over him?"

"They're both—you know—they're scared, Ben." I felt she was saying that she understood how scared I was too. She handed me the Bacon Puffs. "Want some?" she asked. We opened the bag and chomped on some. We drank root beer, decided Dad was wrong, that A & W was better than Hires; we talked about our brother Anthony, how he would be out of Nam in a few weeks and come back to make them feel okay. No one was better at that.

I asked Peg about Mrs. Rado: whether or not the old woman would be able to keep up the business with Mr. Rado dead now and the sons gone; whether she thought Dad's job with Rado & Sons was in trouble. We both knew Dad was planning to retire early. So I don't know why I asked Peg all that, except—hell, I don't know why I asked.

Peg said, "She'll have to back out or have it all blow up in her face."

"Goddamn," I said.

It didn't surprise us how long Mom and Dad were taking to clean things up outside. We stopped unloading bags in order to watch them. They were on their hands and knees, picking up the slivers of glass, putting them in the coffee can between them. Their shoulders and hips were close, so sometimes they touched, but they never bumped. Though they might both reach for the same piece of glass, they instantly knew who would take it. In about the same way, I knew my sister Peg's fakes and feints and she knew mine too, the way good soldiers have to know these things. I always really did believe we could read each other's thoughts.

This is what I think; this is what I know Peg thought: Mom and Dad would search out every shard and sliver. In the morning, they would get down on all fours together in order to painstakingly check the same place, because Anthony and Peg and I once ran barefoot through their yard and because they believed what might have hurt us once could again.

AUNT MOON'S YOUNG MAN

Linda Hogan

That autumn when the young man came, there was a deep blue sky. On their way to the fair, the wagons creaked into town. One buckboard, driven by cloudy white horses, carried a grunting pig inside its wooden slats. Another had cages of chickens. In the heat, the chickens did not flap their wings. They sounded tired and old, and their shoulders drooped like old men.

There was tension in the air. Those people who still believed in omens would turn to go home, I thought, white chicken feathers caught on the wire cages they brought, reminding us all that the cotton was poor that year and that very little of it would line the big trailers outside the gins.

A storm was brewing over the plains and beneath its clouds, a few people from the city drove dusty black motorcars through town, angling around the statue of General Pickens on Main Street. They refrained from honking at the wagons and the white, pink-eyed horses. The cars contained no animal life, just neatly folded stacks of quilts, jellies, and tomato relish, large yellow gourds, and pumpkins that looked like the round faces of children through half-closed windows.

"The biting flies aren't swarming today," my mother said. She had her hair done up in rollers. It was almost dry. She was leaning against the window frame, looking at the ink-blue trees outside. I could see Bess Evening's house through the glass, appearing to sit like a small, hand-built model upon my mother's shoulder. My mother was a dreamer, standing at the window with her green dress curved over her hip.

Her dress was hemmed slightly shorter on one side than on the other. I decided not to mention it. The way she leaned, with her abdomen tilted out, was her natural way of standing. She still had good legs, despite the spidery blue veins she said came from carrying the weight of us kids inside her for nine months each. She also blamed us for her few gray hairs.

She mumbled something about "the silence before the storm," as I joined her at the window.

She must have been looking at the young man for a long time, pretending to watch the sky. He was standing by the bushes and the cockscombs. There was a flour sack on the ground beside him. I thought at first it might be filled with something he brought for the fair, but the way his hat sat on it and a pair of black boots stood beside it, I could tell it held his clothing, and that he was passing through Pickens on his way to or from some city.

"It's mighty quiet for the first day of fair," my mother said. She sounded far away. Her eyes were on the young stranger. She unrolled a curler and checked a strand of hair.

We talked about the weather and the sky, but we both watched the young man. In the deep blue sky his white shirt stood out like a light. The low hills were fire-gold and leaden.

One of my mother's hands was limp against her thigh. The other moved down from the rollers and touched the green cloth at her chest, playing with a flaw in the fabric.

"Maybe it was the tornado," I said, about the stillness in the air. The tornado had passed through a few days ago, touching down here and there. It exploded my cousin's house trailer, but it left his motorcycle standing beside it, untouched. "Tornadoes have no sense of value," my mother had said. "They are always taking away the saints and leaving behind the devils."

The young man stood in that semislumped, half-straight manner of fullbloods. Our blood was mixed like Heinz 57, and I always thought of purebloods as better than us. While my mother eyed his plain moccasins, she patted her rolled hair as if to put it in order. I was counting the small brown flowers in the blistered wallpaper, the way I counted ceiling tiles in the new school and counted each step when I walked.

I pictured Aunt Moon inside her house up on my mother's shoulder. I imagined her dark face above the yellow oilcloth, her hands reflecting the yellow as they separated dried plants. She would rise slowly, as I'd seen her do, take a good long time to brush out her hair and braid it once again. She would pet her dog, Mister, with long slow strokes while she prepared herself for the fair.

My mother moved aside, leaving the house suspended in the middle of the window where it rested on a mound of land. My mother followed my gaze. She always wanted to know what I was thinking or doing. "I wonder," she said, "why in tarnation Bess's father built that house up there? It gets all the heat and wind."

I stuck up for Aunt Moon. "She can see everything from there, the whole town and everything."

"Sure, and everything can see her. A wonder she doesn't have ghosts."

I wondered what she meant by that, everything seeing Aunt Moon. I guessed by her lazy voice that she meant nothing. There was no cutting edge to her words.

"And don't call her Aunt Moon." My mother was reading my mind again, one of her many tricks. "I know what you're thinking," she would say when I thought I looked expressionless. "You are thinking about finding Mrs. Mark's ring and holding it for a reward."

I would look horrified and tell her that she wasn't even lukewarm, but the truth was that I'd been thinking exactly those thoughts. I resented my mother for guessing my innermost secrets. She was like God, everywhere at once knowing everything. I tried to concentrate on something innocent. I thought about pickles. I was safe, she didn't say a word about dills or sweets.

Bess, Aunt Moon, wasn't really my aunt. She was a woman who lived alone and had befriended me. I liked Aunt Moon and the way she moved, slowly, taking up as much space as she wanted and doing it with ease. She had wide lips and straight eyelashes.

Aunt Moon dried medicine herbs in the manner of her parents. She knew about plants, both the helpful ones and the ones that were poisonous in all but the smallest doses. And she knew how to cut wood and how to read the planets. She told me why I was stubborn. It had to do with my being born in May. I believed her because my father was born a few days after me, and he was stubborn as all get out, even compared to me.

Aunt Moon was special. She had life in her. The rest of the women in town were cold in the eye and fretted over their husbands. I didn't want to be like them. They condemned the men for drinking and gambling, but even after the loudest quarrels, ones we'd overhear, they never failed to cook for their men. They'd cook platters of lard-fried chicken, bowls of mashed potatoes, and pitchers of creamy flour gravy.

Bess called those meals, "Sure death by murder."

Our town was full of large and nervous women with red spots on their thin-skinned necks, and we had single women who lived with brothers and sisters or took care of an elderly parent. Bess had comments on all of these: "They have eaten their anger and grown large," she would say. And there were the sullen ones who took care of men broken by the war, women who were hurt by the men's stories of death and glory but never told them to get on with living, like I would have done.

Bessie's own brother, J. D., had gone to the war and returned with softened, weepy eyes. He lived at the veterans hospital and he did office work there on his good days. I met him once and knew by the sweetness of his eyes that he had never killed anyone, but something about him reminded me of the lonely old shacks out on cotton-farming land. His eyes were broken windows.

"Where do you think that young man is headed?" my mother asked.

Something in her voice was wistful and lonely. I looked at her face, looked out the window at the dark man, and looked back at my mother again. I had never thought about her from inside the skin. She was the mind reader in the family, but suddenly I knew how she did it. The inner workings of the mind were clear in her face, like words in a book. I could even feel her thoughts in the pit of my stomach. I was feeling embarrassed at what my mother was thinking when the stranger crossed the street. In front of him an open truck full of prisoners passed by. They wore large white shirts and pants like immigrants from Mexico. I began to count the flowers in the wallpaper again, and the truck full of prisoners passed by, and when it was gone, the young man had also vanished into thin air.

Besides the young man, another thing I remember about the fair that year was the man in the bathroom. On the first day of the fair, the prisoners were bending over like great white sails, their black and brown hands stuffing trash in their canvas bags. Around them the children washed and brushed their cows and raked fresh straw about their pigs. My friend Elaine and I escaped the dust-laden air and went into the women's public toilets where we shared a stolen cigarette. We heard someone open the door, and we fanned the smoke. Elaine stood on the toilet seat so her sisters wouldn't recognize her shoes. Then it was silent, so we opened the stall and stepped out. At first the round dark man, standing by the door, looked like a woman, but then I noticed the day's growth of beard at his jawline. He wore a blue work shirt and a little straw hat. He leaned against the wall, his hand moving inside his pants. I grabbed Elaine, who was putting lipstick on her cheeks like rouge, and pulled her outside the door, the tube of red lipstick in her hand.

Outside we nearly collapsed by a trash can, laughing. "Did you see that? It was a man! A man! In the women's bathroom." She smacked me on the back.

We knew nothing of men's hands inside their pants, so we began to follow him like store detectives, but as we rounded a corner behind his shadow, I saw Aunt Moon walking away from the pigeon cages. She was moving slowly with her cane, through the path's sawdust, feathers, and sand.

"Aunt Moon, there was a man in the bathroom," I said, and then remembered the chickens I wanted to tell her about. Elaine ran off. I didn't know if she was still following the man or not, but I'd lost interest when I saw Aunt Moon.

"Did you see those chickens that lay the green eggs?" I asked Aunt Moon.

She wagged her head no, so I grabbed her free elbow and guided her past the pigeons with curly feathers and the turkeys with red wattles, right up to the chickens.

"They came all the way from South America. They sell for five dollars, can you imagine?" Five dollars was a lot for chickens when we were still recovering from the Great Depression, men were still talking about what they'd done with the CCC, and children still got summer complaint and had to be carried around crippled for months.

She peered into the cage. The eggs were smooth and resting in the straw. "I'll be," was all she said.

I studied her face for a clue as to why she was so quiet, thinking she was mad or something. I wanted to read her thoughts as easily as I'd read my mother's. In the strange light of the sky, her eyes slanted a bit more than usual. I watched her carefully. I looked at the downward curve of her nose and saw the young man reflected in her eyes. I turned around.

On the other side of the cage that held the chickens from Araucania was the man my mother had watched. Bess pretended to be looking at the little Jersey cattle in the distance, but I could tell she was seeing that man. He had a calm look on his face and his dark chest was smooth as oil where his shirt was opened. His eyes were large and black. They were fixed on Bess like he was a hypnotist or something magnetic that tried to pull Bess Evening toward it, even though her body stepped back. She did step back, I remember that, but even so, everything in her went forward, right up to him.

I didn't know if it was just me or if his presence charged the air, but suddenly the oxygen was gone. It was like the fire at Fisher Hardware when all the air was drawn into the flame. Even the chickens clucked softly, as if suffocating, and the cattle were more silent in the straw. The pulse of everything changed.

I don't know what would have happened if the rooster hadn't crowed just then, but he did, and everything returned to normal. The rooster strutted and we turned to watch him.

Bessie started walking away and I went with her. We walked past the men and boys who were shooting craps in a cleared circle. One of them rubbed the dice between his hands as we were leaving, his eyes closed, his body's tight muscles willing a winning throw. He called me Lady Luck as we walked by. He said, "There goes Lady Luck," and he tossed the dice.

At dinner that evening we could hear the dance band tuning up in the makeshift beer garden, playing a few practice songs to the empty tables with their red cloths. They played the Tennessee Waltz. For a while, my mother sang along with it. She had brushed her hair one hundred strokes, and now she was talking and regretting talking all at the same time. "He was such a handsome man," she said. My father wiped his face with a handkerchief and rested his elbows on the table. He chewed and looked at nothing in particular. "For the longest time he stood there by the juniper bushes."

My father drank some coffee and picked up the newspaper. Mother cleared the table, one dish at a time and not in stacks like usual. "His clothes were neat. He must not have come from very far away." She moved the salt shaker from the end of the table to the center, then back again.

"I'll wash," I volunteered.

Mother said, "Bless you," and touched herself absently, near the waist as if to remove an apron. "I'll go get ready for the dance," she said.

My father turned a page of the paper.

The truth was, mother was already fixed up for the dance. Her hair looked soft and beautiful. She had slipped into her new dress early in the day, "to break it in," she said. She wore silk hose and she was barefoot and likely to get a runner. I would have warned her, but it seemed out of place, my warning. Her face was softer than usual, her lips painted to look full, and her eyebrows were much darker than usual.

"Do you reckon that young man came here for the rodeo?" she hollered in from the living room, where she powdered her nose. Normally she made up in front of the bathroom mirror, but the cabinet had been slammed and broken mysteriously one night during an argument so we had all taken to grooming ourselves in the small framed mirror in the living room.

I could not put my finger on it, but all the women at the dance that night were looking at the young man. It wasn't exactly that he was handsome. There was something else. He was alive in his whole body, while the other men walked with great effort and stiffness, even those who did little work and were still young. Their male bodies had no language of their own in the way that his did. The women themselves seemed confused and lonely in the presence of the young man, and they were ridiculous in their behavior, laughing too loud, blushing like schoolgirls, or casting him a flirting eye. Even the older women were brighter than usual. Mrs. Tubby, whose face was usually as grim as the statue of General Pickens, the Cherokee hater, played with her necklace until her neck had red lines from the chain. Mrs. Tens twisted a strand of her hair over and over. Her sister tripped over a chair because she'd forgotten to watch where she was going.

The men, sneaking drinks from bottles in paper bags, did not notice any of the fuss.

Maybe it was his hands. His hands were strong and dark.

I stayed late, even after wives pulled their husbands away from their ball game talk and insisted they dance.

My mother and father were dancing. My mother smiled up into my father's face as he turned her this way and that. Her uneven skirt swirled a little around her legs. She had a run in her nylons, as I predicted. My father, who was called Peso by the townspeople, wore his old clothes. He had his usual look about him, and I noticed that faraway, unfocused gaze on the other men too. They were either distant or they were present but rowdy, embarrassing the women around them with the loud talk of male things: work and hunting, fights, this or that pretty girl.

The dancers whirled around the floor, some tapping their feet, some shuffling, the women in new dresses and dark hair all curled up like in movie magazines, the men with new leather boots and crew cuts. My dad's rear stuck out in back, the way he danced. His hand clutched my mother's waist.

That night, Bessie arrived late. She was wearing a white dress with a full, gathered skirt. The print was faded and I could just make out the little blue stars on the cloth. She carried a yellow shawl over her arm. Her long hair was braided as usual, in the manner of the older Chickasaw women, like a wreath on her head. She was different from the others, with her bright shawls. Sometimes she wore a heavy shell necklace or a collection of bracelets on her arm. They jangled when she talked with me, waving her hands to make a point. Like the time she told me that the soul is a small woman inside the eye who leaves at night to wander new places.

No one had ever known her to dance before, but that night the young man and Aunt Moon danced together among the artificial geraniums and plastic carnations. They held each other gently like two breakable vases. They didn't look at each other or smile the way the other dancers did; that's how I knew they liked each other. His large dark hand was on the small of her back. Her hand rested tenderly on his shoulder. The other dancers moved away and there was empty space all around them.

My father went out into the dark to smoke and to play a hand or two of poker. My mother went to sit with some of the other women, all of them pulling their damp hair away from their necks and letting it fall back again, or furtively putting on lipstick, fanning themselves, and sipping their beers.

"He puts me in the mind of a man I once knew," said Mrs. Tubby.

"Look at them," said Mrs. Tens. "Don't you think he's young enough to be her son?"

With my elbows on my knees and my chin in my hands, I watched Aunt Moon step and square when my mother loomed up like a shadow over the bleachers where I sat.

"Young lady," she said in a scolding voice. "You were supposed to go home and put the children to bed."

I looked from her stern face to my sister Susan, who was like a chubby angel sleeping beside me. Peso Junior had run off to the gambling game where he was pushing another little boy around. My mother followed my gaze and looked at Junior. She put her hands on her hips and said, "Boys!"

My sister Roberta, who was twelve, had stayed close to the women all night, listening to their talk about the fullblood who had come to town for a rodeo or something and who danced so far away from Bessie that they didn't look friendly at all except for the fact that the music had stopped and they were still waltzing.

*   *   *

Margaret Tubby won the prize money that year for the biggest pumpkin. It was 87 inches in circumference and weighed 190 pounds and had to be carried on a stretcher by the volunteer firemen. Mrs. Tubby was the town's chief social justice. She sat most days on the bench outside the grocery store. Sitting there like a full-chested hawk on a fence, she held court. She had watched Bess

Evening for years with her sharp gold eyes. "This is the year I saw it coming," she told my mother, as if she'd just been dying for Bess to go wrong. It showed up in the way Bess walked, she said, that the woman was coming to a no good end just like the rest of her family had done.

"When do you think she had time to grow that pumpkin?" Mother asked as we escaped Margaret Tubby's court on our way to the store. I knew what she meant, that Mrs. Tubby did more time with gossip than with her garden.

Margaret was even more pious than usual at that time of year, when the green-tent revival followed on the heels of the fair, when the pink-faced men in white shirts arrived and, really, every single one of them was a preacher. Still, Margaret Tubby kept her prize money to herself and didn't give a tithe to any church.

With Bess Evening carrying on with a stranger young enough to be her son, Mrs. Tubby succeeded in turning the church women against her once and for all. When Bessie walked down the busy street, one of the oldest dances of women took place, for women in those days turned against each other easily, never thinking they might have other enemies. When Bess appeared, the women stepped away. They vanished from the very face of the earth that was named Comanche Street. They disappeared into the Oklahoma redstone shops like swallows swooping into their small clay nests. The women would look at the new bolts of red cloth in Terwilligers with feigned interest, although they would never have worn red, even to a dog fight. They'd purchase another box of face powder in the five and dime, or drink cherry phosphates at the pharmacy without so much as tasting the flavor.

But Bessie was unruffled. She walked on in the empty mirage of heat, the sound of her cane blending in with horse hooves and the rhythmic pumping of oil wells out east.

At the store my mother bought cornmeal, molasses, and milk. I bought penny candy for my younger sisters and for Peso Junior with the money I earned by helping Aunt Moon with her remedies. When we passed Margaret Tubby on the way out, my mother nodded at her, but said to me, "That pumpkin grew fat on gossip. I'll bet she fed it with nothing but all-night rumors." I thought about the twenty-five dollar prize money and decided to grow pumpkins next year.

My mother said, "Now don't you get any ideas about growing pumpkins, young lady. We don't have room enough. They'd crowd out the cucumbers and tomatoes."

My mother and father won a prize that year, too. For dancing. They won a horse lamp for the living room. "We didn't even know it was a contest," my mother said, free from the sin of competition. Her face was rosy with pleasure and pride. She had the life snapping out of her like hot grease, though sometimes I saw that life turn to a slow and restless longing, like when she daydreamed out the window where the young man had stood that day.

Passing Margaret's post and giving up on growing a two-hundred-pound pumpkin, I remembered all the things good Indian women were not supposed to do. We were not to look into the faces of men. Or laugh too loud. We were not supposed to learn too much from books because that kind of knowledge was a burden to the soul. Not only that, it always took us away from our loved ones. I was jealous of the white girls, who laughed as loud as they wanted and never had rules. Also, my mother wanted me to go to college no matter what anyone else said or thought. She said I was too smart to stay home and live a life like hers, even if the other people thought book learning would ruin my life.

Aunt Moon, with her second sight and heavy breasts, managed to break all the rules. She threw back her head and laughed out loud, showing off the worn edges of her teeth. She didn't go to church. She did a man's work, caring for animals and chopping her own wood. The gossiping women said it was a wonder Bessie Evening was healthy at all and didn't have female problems, meaning with her body, I figured.

The small woman inside her eye was full and lonely at the same time.

Bess made tonics, remedies, and cures. The church women, even those who gossiped, slipped over to buy Bessie's potions at night and in secret. They'd never admit they swallowed the "snake medicine," as they called it. They'd say to Bess, "What have you got to put the life back in a man? My sister has that trouble, you know." Or they'd say, "I have a friend who needs a cure for the sadness." They bought remedies for fever and for coughing fits, for sore muscles and for sleepless nights.

Aunt Moon had learned the cures from her parents, who were said to have visited their own sins upon their children, both of whom were born out of wedlock from the love of an old Chickasaw man and a young woman from one of those tribes up north. Maybe a Navajo or something, the people thought.

But Aunt Moon had numerous talents and I respected them. She could pull cotton, pull watermelons, and pull babies with equal grace. She even delivered those scrub cattle, bred with Holsteins too big for them, caesarian. In addition to that, she told me the ways of the world and not just about the zodiac or fortune cards. "The United States is in love with death," she would say. "They sleep with it better than with lovers. They celebrate it on holidays, the Fourth of July, even in spring when they praise the loss of a good man's body."

She would tend her garden while I'd ask questions. "What do you think about heaven?" I wanted to know. She'd look up and then get back to pulling the weeds. "You and I both would just grump around up there with all those righteous people. Women like us weren't meant to live on golden streets. We're Indians," she'd say as she cleared out the space around a bean plant. "We're like these beans. We grew up from mud." And then she'd tell me how the people emerged right along with the crawdads from the muddy female swamps of the land. "And what is gold anyway? Just something else that comes from mud. Look at the conquistadors." She pulled a squash by accident. "And look at the sad women of this town, old already and all because of gold." She poked a hole in the ground and replanted the roots of the squash. "Their men make money, but not love. They give the women gold rings, gold-rimmed glasses, gold teeth, but their skin dries up for lack of love. Their hearts are little withered raisins." I was embarrassed by the mention of making love, but I listened to her words.

*   *   *

This is how I came to call Bessie Evening by the name of Aunt Moon: She'd been teaching me that animals and all life should be greeted properly as our kinfolk. "Good day, Uncle," I learned to say to the longhorn as I passed by on the road. "Good morning, cousins, is there something you need?" I'd say to the sparrows. And one night when the moon was passing over Bessie's house, I said, "Hello, Aunt Moon. I see you are full of silver again tonight." It was so much like Bess Evening, I began to think, that I named her after the moon. She was sometimes full and happy, sometimes small and weak. I began saying it right to her ears, "Auntie Moon, do you need some help today?"

She seemed both older and younger than thirty-nine to me. For one thing, she walked with a cane. She had developed some secret ailment after her young daughter died. My mother said she needed the cane because she had no mortal human to hold her up in life, like the rest of us did.

But the other thing was that she was full of mystery and she laughed right out loud, like a gypsy, my mother said, pointing out Bessie's blue-painted walls, bright clothes and necklaces, and all the things she kept hanging from her ceiling. She decorated outside her house, too, with bits of blue glass hanging from the trees and little polished quartz crystals that reflected rainbows across the dry hills.

Aunt Moon had solid feet, a light step, and a face that clouded over with emotion and despair one moment and brightened up like light the next. She'd beam and say to me, "Sassafras will turn your hair red," and throw back her head to laugh, knowing full well that I would rinse my dull hair with sassafras that very night, ruining my mother's pans.

I sat in Aunt Moon's kitchen while she brewed herbals in white enamel pans on the wood stove. The insides of the pans were black from sassafras and burdock and other plants she picked. The kitchen smelled rich and earthy. Some days it was hard to breathe from the combination of wood-stove heat and pollen from the plants, but she kept at it and her medicine for cramps was popular with the women in town.

Aunt Moon made me proud of my womanhood, giving me bags of herbs and an old eagle feather that had been doctored by her father back when people used to pray instead of going to church. "The body divines everything," she told me, and sometimes when I was with her, I knew the older Indian world was still here. I'd feel it in my skin and hear the night sounds speak to me, hear the voice of water telling stories about people who lived before, and the deep songs coming out from the hills.

One day I found Aunt Moon sitting at her table in front of a plate of untouched toast and wild plum jam. She was weeping. I was young and didn't know what to say, but she told me more than I could ever understand. "Ever since my daughter died," she told me, "my body aches to touch her. All the mourning has gone into my bones." Her long hair was loose that day, and it fell down her back like a waterfall, almost to the floor.

After that I had excuses on the days I saw her hair loose. "I'm putting up new wallpaper today," I'd say, or "I have to help Mom can peaches," which was the truth.

"Sure," she said and I saw the tinge of sorrow around her eyes even though she smiled and nodded at me.

Canning the peaches, I asked my mother what it was that happened to Aunt Moon's daughter.

"First of all," my mother set me straight, "her name is Bess, not

Aunt Moon." Then she'd tell the story of Willow Evening. "That pretty child was the light of that woman's eye," my mother said. "It was all so fast. She was playing one minute and the next she was gone. She was hanging onto that wooden planter and pulled it right down onto her little chest."

My mother touched her chest. "I saw Bessie lift it like it weighed less than a pound, did I already tell you that part?"

All I saw that day was Aunt Moon holding Willow's thin body. The little girl's face was already gone to ashes, and Aunt Moon blew gently on her daughter's skin, even though she was dead, as if she could breathe the life back into her one more time. She blew on her skin the way I later knew that women blow sweat from lover's faces, cooling them. But I knew nothing of any kind of passion then.

The planter remained on the dry, grassy mound of Aunt Moon's yard, and even though she had lifted it, no one else, not even my father, could move it. It was still full of earth and dead geraniums like a monument to the child.

"That girl was all she had," my mother said through the steam of boiling water. "Hand me the ladle, will you?"

The peaches were suspended in sweet juice in their clear jars. I thought of our lives, so short, the skin so soft around us that we could be gone any second from our living; I thought I saw Willow's golden-brown face suspended behind glass in one of the jars.

*   *   *

The men first noticed the stranger, Isaac, when he cleaned them out in the poker game that night at the fair. My father, who had been drinking, handed over the money he'd saved for the new bathroom mirror and took a drunken swing at the young man, missing him by a foot and falling on his bad knee. Mr. Tubby told his wife he lost all he'd saved for the barber shop business, even though everyone in town knew he drank it up long before the week of the fair. Mr. Tens lost his Mexican silver ring. It showed up later on Aunt Moon's hand.

Losing to one another was one thing. Losing to Isaac Cade meant the dark young man was a card sharp and an outlaw. Even the women who had watched the stranger all that night were sure he was full of demons.

The next time I saw Aunt Moon it was the fallow season of autumn, but she seemed new and fresh as spring. Her skin had new light. Gathering plants, she smiled at me. Her cane moved aside the long dry grasses to reveal what grew underneath. Mullein was still growing, and holly.

I sat at the table while Aunt Moon ground yellow ochre in a mortar. Isaac came in from fixing the roof. He touched her arm so softly I wasn't sure she felt it. I had never seen a man touch a woman that way.

He said, "Hello," to me and he said, "You know those fairgrounds? That's where the three tribes used to hold sings." He drummed on the table, looking at me, and sang one of the songs. I said I recognized it; a song I sometimes dreamed I heard from the hill.

A red handprint appeared on his face like one of those birthmarks that only show up in the heat or under the strain of work or feeling.

"How'd you know about the fairgrounds?" I asked him.

"My father was from here." He sat still, as if thinking himself into another time. He stared out the window at the distances that were in between the blue curtains.

I went back to Aunt Moon's the next day. Isaac wasn't there, so Aunt Moon and I tied sage in bundles with twine. I asked her about love.

"It comes up from the ground just like corn," she said. She pulled a knot tighter with her teeth.

Later, when I left, I was still thinking about love. Outside, where Bess had been planting, black beetles were digging themselves under the turned soil, and red ants had grown wings and were starting to fly.

When I returned home, my mother was sitting outside the house on a chair. She pointed at Bess Evening's house. "With that man there," she said, "I think it best you don't go over to Bessie's house any more."

I started to protest, but she interrupted. "There are no *and*s, *if*s, or *but*s about it."

I knew it was my father who made the decision. My mother had probably argued my point and lost to him again, and lost some of her life as well. She was slowed down to a slumberous pace. Later that night as I stood by my window looking toward Aunt Moon's house, I heard my mother say, "God damn them all and this whole damned town."

"There now," my father said. "There now."

*   *   *

"She's as dark and stained as those old black pans she uses," Margaret Tubby said about Bess Evening one day. She had come to pick up a cake from mother for the church bake sale. I was angered by her words. I gave her one of those "looks could kill" faces, but I said nothing. We all looked out the window at Aunt Moon. She was standing near Isaac, looking at a tree. It leapt into my mind suddenly, like lightning, that Mrs. Tubby knew about the blackened pans. That would mean she had bought cures from Aunt Moon. I was smug about this discovery.

Across the way, Aunt Moon stood with her hand outstretched, palm up. It was filled with roots or leaves. She was probably teaching Isaac about the remedies. I knew Isaac would teach her things also, older things, like squirrel sickness and porcupine disease that I'd heard about from grandparents.

Listening to Mrs. Tubby, I began to understand why, right after the fair, Aunt Moon had told me I would have to fight hard to keep my life in this town. Mrs. Tubby said, "Living out of wedlock! Just like her parents." She went on, "History repeats itself."

I wanted to tell Mrs. Tubby a thing or two myself. "History, my eye," I wanted to say. "You're just jealous about the young man." But Margaret Tubby was still angry that her husband had lost his money to the stranger, and also because she probably still felt bad about playing with her necklace like a young girl that night at the fair. My mother said nothing, just covered the big caramel cake and handed it over to Mrs. Tubby. My mother looked like she was tired of fools and that included me. She looked like the woman inside her eyes had just wandered off.

I began to see the women in Pickens as ghosts. I'd see them in the library looking at the stereopticons, and in the ice cream parlor. The more full Aunt Moon grew, the more drawn and pinched they became.

The church women echoed Margaret. "She's as stained as her pans," they'd say, and they began buying their medicines at the pharmacy. It didn't matter that their coughs returned and that their children developed more fevers. It didn't matter that some of them could not get pregnant when they wanted to or that Mrs. Tens grew thin and pale and bent. They wouldn't dream of lowering themselves to buy Bessie's medicines.

*   *   *

My mother ran hot water into the tub and emptied one of her packages of bubble powder in it. "Take a bath," she told me. "It will steady your nerves."

I was still crying, standing at the window, looking out at Aunt Moon's house through the rain.

The heavy air had been broken by an electrical storm earlier that day. In a sudden crash, the leaves flew off their trees, the sky exploded with lightning and thunder rumbled the earth. People went to their doors to watch. It scared me. The clouds turned green and it began to hail and clatter.

That was when Aunt Moon's old dog, Mister, ran off, went running like crazy through the town. Some of the older men saw him on the street. They thought he was hurt and dying because of the way he ran and twitched. He butted right into a tree and men thought maybe he had rabies or something. They meant to put him out of his pain. One of them took aim with a gun and shot him, and when the storm died down and the streets misted over, everything returned to heavy stillness and old Mister was lying on the edge of the Smiths' lawn. I picked him up and carried his heavy body up to Aunt Moon's porch. I covered him with sage, like she would have done.

Bess and Isaac had gone over to Alexander that day to sell remedies. They missed the rain, and when they returned they were happy about bringing home bags of beans, ground corn, and flour.

I guess it was my mother who told Aunt Moon about her dog.

That evening I heard her wailing. I could hear her from my window, and I looked out and saw her with her hair all down around her shoulders like a black shawl. Isaac smoothed back her hair and held her. I guessed that all the mourning was back in her bones again, even for her little girl, Willow.

That night my mother sat by my bed. "Sometimes the world is a sad place," she said and kissed my hot forehead. I began to cry again.

"Well, she still has the burro," my mother said, neglecting to mention Isaac.

I began to worry about the burro and to look after it. I went over to Aunt Moon's against my mother's wishes, and took carrots and sugar to the gray burro. I scratched his big ears.

By this time most of the younger and healthier men had signed up to go to Korea and fight for their country. Most of the residents of Pickens were mixed-blood Indians and they were even more patriotic than white men. I guess they wanted to prove that they were good Americans. My father left and we saw him off at the depot. I admit I missed him saying to me, "The trouble with you is you think too much." Old Peso, always telling people what their problems were. Margaret Tubby's lazy son had enlisted because, as his mother had said, "It would make a man of him," and when he was killed in action, the townspeople resented Isaac, Bess Evening's young man, even more since he did not have his heart set on fighting the war.

* * *

Aunt Moon was pregnant the next year when the fair came around again, and she was just beginning to show. Margaret Tubby had remarked that Bess was visiting all those family sins on another poor child.

This time I was older. I fixed Mrs. Tubby in my eyes and I said, "Miss Tubby, you are just like history, always repeating yourself."

She pulled her head back into her neck like a turtle. My mother said, "Hush, Sis. Get inside the house." She put her hands on her hips. "I'll deal with you later." She almost added, "Just wait till your father gets home."

Later, I felt bad, talking that way to Margaret Tubby so soon after she lost her son.

Shortly after the fair, we heard that the young man inside Aunt Moon's eye was gone. A week passed and he didn't return. I watched her house from the window and I knew, if anyone stood behind me, the little house was resting up on my shoulder.

Mother took a nap and I grabbed the biscuits off the table and snuck out.

"I didn't hear you come in," Aunt Moon said to me.

"I didn't knock," I told her. "My mom just fell asleep. I thought it'd wake her up."

Aunt Moon's hair was down. Her hands were on her lap. A breeze came in the window. She must not have been sleeping and her eyes looked tired. I gave her the biscuits I had taken off the table. I lied and told her my mother sent them over. We ate one.

Shortly after Isaac was gone, Bess Evening again became the focus of the town's women. Mrs. Tubby said, "Bessie would give you the shirt off her back. She never deserved a no good man who would treat her like dirt and then run off." Mrs. Tubby went over to Bess Evening's and bought enough cramp remedy from the pregnant woman to last her and her daughters for the next two years.

Mrs. Tens lost her pallor. She went to Bessie's with a basket of jellies and fruits, hoping in secret that Bess would return Mr. Tens's Mexican silver ring now that the young man was gone.

The women were going to stick by her, you could see it in their squared shoulders. They no longer hid their purchases of herbs. They forgot how they'd looked at Isaac's black eyes and lively body with longing that night of the dance. If they'd had dowsing rods, the split willow branches would have flown up to the sky, so much had they twisted around the truth of things and even their own natures. Isaac was the worst of men. Their husbands, who were absent, were saints who loved them. Every morning when my mother said her prayers and forgot she'd damned the town and everybody in it, I heard her ask for peace for Bessie Evening, but she never joined in with the other women who seemed happy over Bessie's tragedy.

Isaac was doubly condemned in his absence. Mrs. Tubby said, "What kind of fool goes off to leave a woman who knows about tea leaves and cures for diseases of the body and mind alike? I'll tell you what kind, a card shark, that's what."

Someone corrected her. "Card sharp, dearie, not shark."

Who goes off and leaves a woman whose trees are hung with charming stones, relics, and broken glass, a woman who hangs sage and herbs to dry on her walls and whose front porch is full of fresh-cut wood? Those women, how they wanted to comfort her, but Bess Evening would only go to the door, leave them standing outside on the steps, and hand their herbs to them through the screen.

My cousins from Denver came for the fair. I was going to leave with them and get a job in the city for a year or so, then go on to school. My mother insisted she could handle the little ones alone now that they were bigger, and that I ought to go. It was best I made some money and learned what I could, she said.

"Are you sure?" I asked, while my mother washed her hair in the kitchen sink.

"I'm sure as the night's going to fall." She sounded lighthearted, but her hands stopped moving and rested on her head until the soap lather began to disappear. "Besides, your dad will probably be home any day now."

I said, "Okay then, I'll go. I'll write you all the time." I was all full of emotion, but I didn't cry.

"Don't make promises you can't keep," my mother said, wrapping a towel around her head.

I went to the dance that night with my cousins and out in the trees I let Jim Tens kiss me and promised him that I would be back. "I'll wait for you," he said. "And keep away from those city boys."

I meant it when I said, "I will."

He walked me home, holding my hand. My cousins were still at the dance. Mom would complain about their late city hours. Once she even told us that city people eat supper as late as eight o'clock. We didn't believe her.

After Jim kissed me at the door, I watched him walk down the street. I was surprised that I didn't feel sad.

I decided to go to see Aunt Moon one last time. I was leaving at six in the morning and was already packed and I had taken one of each herb sample I'd learned from Aunt Moon, just in case I ever needed them.

I scratched the burro's gray face at the lot and walked up toward the house. The window was gold and filled with lamplight. I heard an owl hooting in the distance and stopped to listen.

I glanced in the window and stopped in my tracks. The young man, Isaac, was there. He was speaking close to Bessie's face. He put his finger under her chin and lifted her face up to his. He was looking at her with soft eyes, and I could tell there were many men and women living inside their eyes that moment. He held her cane across the back of her hips. With it, he pulled her close to him and held her tight, his hands on the cane pressing her body against his. And he kissed her. Her hair was down around her back and shoulders, and she put her arms around his neck. I turned to go. I felt dishonest and guilty for looking in at them. I began to run.

I ran into the bathroom and bent over the sink to wash my face. I wiped Jim Tens's cold kiss from my lips. I glanced up to look at myself in the mirror, but my face was nothing, just shelves of medicine bottles and aspirin. I had forgotten the mirror was broken.

From the bathroom door I heard my mother saying her prayers, fervently, and louder than usual. She said, "Bless Sis's Aunt Moon and bless Isaac, who got arrested for trading illegal medicine for corn, and forgive him for escaping from jail."

She said this so loud, I thought she was talking to me. Maybe she was. Now how did she read my mind again? It made me smile, and I guessed I was reading hers.

All that next morning, driving through the deep blue sky, I thought how all the women had gold teeth and hearts like withered raisins. I hoped Jim Tens would marry one of the Tubby girls. I didn't know if I'd ever go home or not. I had Aunt Moon's herbs in my bag, and the eagle feather wrapped safe in a scarf. And I had a small, beautiful woman in my eye.

A SERIOUS TALK

Raymond Carver

Vera's car was there, no others, and Burt gave thanks for that. He pulled into the drive and stopped beside the pie he'd dropped last night. It was still there, the aluminum pan upside down, a halo of pumpkin filling on the pavement. It was Friday, almost noon, the day after Christmas.

He'd come on Christmas day to visit his wife and children. Vera had warned him beforehand. She'd told him the score. She'd said he had to be out before six o'clock when her friend and *his* children were coming for dinner. They had sat in the living room and solemnly opened the presents Burt had brought over. Other packages wrapped in shiny paper and secured with ribbons and bows lay stuffed under the tree waiting for after six o'clock. He watched the children, Terri and Jack, open their gifts. He waited while Vera's fingers carefully undid the ribbon and tape on her present. She unwrapped the paper. She opened the box and took out the cashmere sweater.

"It's nice," she said. "Thank you, Burt."

"Try it on," Terri said to her mother.

"Put it on, Mom," Jack said. "All *right*, Dad," Jack said.

Burt looked at his son, grateful for this show of support. He could ask Jack to ride his bicycle over some morning during these holidays and they'd go out for breakfast.

She did try it on. She went into the bedroom and came out running her hands up and down the front of the sweater. "It's nice," she said.

"It looks great on you," Burt said and felt a welling in his chest.

He opened his gifts: from Vera a certificate for twenty dollars at Sondheim's men's store; a matching comb and brush set from Terri; three pairs of socks and a ballpoint pen from Jack.

*   *   *

He and Vera drank rum and coke. Terri looked at her mother and got up and began to set the dining room table. Jack went to his room.

Burt liked it where he was—in front of the fireplace, a glass in his hand, the smell of turkey in the air.

Vera went into the kitchen. Burt leaned back on the sofa.

Christmas carols came to him from the radio in Vera's room. From time to time Terri walked into the dining room with something for the table. Burt watched as she placed linen napkins in the wine glasses. A slender vase with a single red rose appeared. Then Vera and Terri began talking in low voices in the kitchen.

He finished his drink. A small wax and sawdust log burned on the grate, giving off colored flames. A carton of seven more sat ready on the hearth. He got up from the sofa and put them all in the fireplace. He watched until they flamed. Then he finished his drink and made for the patio door. On the way, he saw the pies lined up on the sideboard. He stacked them in his arms, all five, one for every ten times she had ever betrayed him. He got out of the house with the pies. But in the driveway, in the dark, he'd dropped one as he fumbled with the car door.

*   *   *

He walked around the broken pie and headed for the patio door. The front door was permanently closed since that night his key had broken off inside the lock. It was an overcast day, the air damp and sharp.

There was a wreath made out of pine cones on the patio door. He rapped on the glass. Vera looked out at him and frowned. She was in her bathrobe. She opened the door a little.

"Vera, I want to apologize for last night," he said. "I'm sorry I did what I did. I want to apologize to the kids, too."

"They're not here," she said. "Terri is off with her boyfriend and Jack is playing football."

She stood in the doorway and he stood on the patio next to the philodendron plant. He pulled at some lint on his coat sleeve.

"I can't take any more after last night," she said. "You tried to burn the house down last night."

"I did not."

"You did. Everybody here was a witness. You ought to see the fireplace. You almost caught the wall on fire."

"Can I come in for a minute and talk about it?" he said.

She looked at him. She pulled the robe together at her throat and moved back inside.

"Come in," she said. "But I have to go somewhere in an hour."

He looked around. The tree blinked on and off. There was a pile of tissue papers and empty boxes at the end of the sofa. A turkey carcass filled a platter in the center of the dining room table. The bones were picked clean and the leathery remains sat upright in a bed of parsley as if in a kind of horrible nest. The napkins were soiled and had been dropped here and there on the table. Some of the dishes were stacked, and the cups and wine glasses had been moved to one end of the table as if someone had started to clean up but thought better of it. It was true—the fireplace had black smoke stains reaching up the bricks toward the mantel. A mound of ash filled the fireplace, along with an empty Shasta cola can.

"Come out to the kitchen," Vera said. "I'll make some coffee. But I have to leave pretty soon."

"What time did your friend leave last night?"

"If you're going to start that, you can go right now."

"Okay, okay," he said.

He pulled a chair out and sat down at the kitchen table in front of the big ashtray. He closed his eyes and opened them. He moved the curtain aside and looked out at the backyard. He saw a bicycle without a front wheel resting on its handlebars and seat. He saw weeds growing along the redwood fence.

She ran water into a saucepan. "Do you remember Thanksgiving?" she said. "I said then that was the last holiday you'd ever ruin for us. Eating bacon and eggs instead of turkey at ten o'clock at night. People can't live like that, Burt."

"I know it. I said I'm sorry, Vera. I mean it."

"Sorry isn't good enough any more."

The pilot light was out again. She was at the stove trying to light the gas burner under the pan of water.

"Don't burn yourself," he said. "Don't catch yourself on fire."

She didn't answer. She lit the ring.

He could imagine her robe catching fire and him jumping up from the table, throwing her down onto the floor and rolling her over and over into the living room where he would cover her with his body. Or should he run to the bedroom first for a blanket to throw over her?

"Vera?"

She looked at him.

"Do you have anything to drink around the house? Any of that rum left? I could use a drink this morning. Take the chill off."

"There's some vodka in the freezer, and there is rum around here somewhere."

"When did you start keeping vodka in the freezer?"

"Don't ask."

"Okay, I won't."

He took the vodka from the freezer, looked for a glass, then poured some into a cup he found on the counter.

"Are you just going to drink it like that, out of a cup? Jesus, Burt. What'd you want to talk about, anyway? I told you I have someplace to go. I have a flute lesson at one o'clock. What is it you want, Burt?"

"Are you still taking flute?"

"I just said so. What is it? Tell me what's on your mind, and then I have to get ready."

"I just wanted to say I was sorry about last night."

She didn't answer.

"I think you're right about this vodka," he said. "If you have any juice, I'll mix this with some juice."

She opened the refrigerator and moved things around. "There's cranapple juice, that's all."

"That's fine," he said. He got up and poured cranapple juice into his cup, added more vodka, and stirred the drink with his finger.

"I have to go to the bathroom," she said. "Just a minute."

He drank the cup of cranapple juice and vodka and felt better. He lit a cigarette and tossed the match into the big ashtray. The bottom of the ashtray was covered with cigarette stubs and a layer of ash. He recognized Vera's brand, but there were some unfiltered cigarettes as well, another brand—lavender-colored stubs heavy with lipstick. He got up and dumped the mess into the sack under the sink. The ashtray was a heavy piece of blue stoneware with raised edges they'd bought from a bearded potter on the mall in Santa Cruz. It was as big as a plate and maybe that's what it had been intended for, a plate or a serving dish. But they'd used it as an ashtray. He put it back on the table and ground out his cigarette in it.

The water on the stove began to bubble just as the phone rang. She opened the bathroom door and called to him through the living room: "Answer that! I'm about to get into the shower."

The kitchen phone was on the counter in a corner behind the roasting pan. It kept ringing. He moved the roasting pan and picked up the receiver cautiously.

"Is Charlie there?" a flat, toneless voice asked him.

"No," he said. "You must have the wrong number. You have the wrong number."

"Okay," the voice said.

But while he was seeing to the coffee, the phone rang again. He answered.

"Charlie?"

"You have the wrong number," Burt said. "Look here, you'd better check your numbers again. Look at your prefix."

This time he left the receiver off the hook.

*   *   *

Vera came back into the kitchen wearing jeans and a white sweater and brushing her hair. He added instant coffee to the cups of hot water, stirred the coffee, and then floated vodka onto his. He carried the cups over to the table.

She picked up the receiver, listened, and said, "What's this about? Who was on the phone?"

"Nobody," he said. "It was a wrong number. Who smokes lavender-colored cigarettes?"

"Terri. Who else would smoke such things?"

"I didn't know she was smoking these days," he said. "I haven't seen her smoking."

"Well, she is."

She sat across the table from him and drank her coffee. They smoked and used the ashtray. There were things he wanted to say, words of devotion and regret, consoling things, things like that.

"Terri also steals my dope and smokes that too," Vera said. "If you really want to know what goes on around here."

"God almighty. She smokes dope?"

Vera nodded.

"I didn't come over here to hear that."

"What did you come over here for, then? You didn't get all the pie last night?"

He recalled stacking pie on the floorboards of the car before driving away. Then he'd forgotten all about it. The pies were still in the car.

"Vera," he said. "It's Christmas, that's why I came."

"Christmas is over, thank God. Christmas has come and gone," she said. "I don't look forward to holidays any more. I'll never look forward to another holiday as long as I live."

"What about me?" he said. "I don't look forward to holidays either, believe me."

*   *   *

The phone rang again, and Burt was the first to pick it up.

"It's someone wanting Charlie," he said.

"What?"

"Charlie," he said.

Vera took the phone. She kept her back to Burt as she talked. Then she turned to him and said, "I'll take this call in the bedroom. Would you please hang up after I've picked it up in there? I can tell, so hang up when I say."

He took the receiver. She left the kitchen. He held the receiver to his ear and listened. But he couldn't hear anything at first. Then someone, a man, cleared his throat at the other end of the line. He heard Vera pick up the other phone and call to him: "Okay, you can hang it up now, Burt! I have it! Burt?"

He replaced the receiver in its cradle and stood looking at it. He opened the silverware drawer and pushed things around inside. He tried another drawer. He looked in the sink. Then he went into the dining room and found the carving knife on the platter. He held it under hot water until the grease broke. He wiped the blade dry on his sleeve. He moved to the phone, doubled the cord in his hand, and sawed through without any trouble at all. He examined the ends of the cord. Then he shoved the phone back into its corner near the canisters.

Vera came in and said, "The phone went dead while I was talking. Did you do something to the phone, Burt?" She looked at the phone and then picked it up from the counter.

"Son of a bitch!" she said. "Well, that does it. Out, out, out, where you belong." She was shaking the phone at him. "That's it, Burt. I'm going to get a restraining order, that's what I'm going to get. Get out before I call the police." The phone made a *ding* as she banged it down on the counter. "I'll go next door and call them if you don't leave now."

He had picked up the ashtray and was stepping back from the table. He held the ashtray by its edge. He was poised as if he were going to hurl it, like a discus.

"Please," she said. "Leave now. Burt, that's our ashtray. Please. Go now."

He left through the patio door after telling her goodbye. He wasn't certain, but he thought he'd proved something. He hoped he'd made it clear that he still loved her. But they hadn't talked. They'd have to have a serious talk soon. There were matters that needed sorting out, important things that had to be discussed. They'd talk again. Maybe after these holidays were over and things were back to normal.

He walked around the pie in the driveway and got into his car. He started the car and put it into reverse. It was hard managing until he put the ashtray down.

TALES FROM ALLEYWAYS

Naguib Mahfouz

Translated by Soad Sobhi, Essam Fatouh, and James Kenneson

1

Behind a barred basement window a child's small face.
To any likely passerby he cries, "Hey, Uncle, please . . ."
The passerby stops. "What do you want?"
"Out. I want out."
"What stops you?"
"The locked door."
"No one is with you?"
"No one."
"Where is your mother?"
"She locked the door and left."
"Where is your father?"
"He left a long time ago."
The passerby interprets the situation in one way or another. Then smiles and goes on his way.
The child's face, small behind the bars. Looking out with longing at the street, at people.

2

Every mosque seems to have a man who wanders around outside with a censer, wafting smoke over people for a pittance. In our alley, it was Am Sukry, a poor man with a big family jammed into one room. His youngest child was named Abdu. Since he was the last grape in the bunch, his father decided to have him go to the mosque school, where he excelled from the first day. The sheikh of the school advised Am Sukry to send Abdu on to primary school.

Am Sukry hesitated for some time, unable to decide whether to apprentice Abdu to a tradesman or set him on the long road of book learning. The decision was difficult, for a pupil would have to be a parasite on his father for many years while an apprentice could help out with daily pay. However, Am Sukry at last chose schooling, and

252

Abdu's high grades soon dispelled his worry and fluffed his wings with pride. When Abdu graduated from primary school, his father beamed and said, "Now I have a son who's a government employee."

Yes, but Abdu insisted on going to high school—never mind that he had to go in a raggedy suit, patched shoes, and a greasy tarboosh. Because of his excellence and his ability to talk about politics, he walked with his head held high. Then he won admission to the engineering college on a full scholarship. And then got chosen to go to study in England. From that day on, Am Sukry's name changed to Abu el-Muhandis, Father of the Engineer, and he became famous throughout the district. His son's intelligence became a proverb. In his youth, Am Sukry had dreamed of joining the protection gang, even of being the boss, or, at the very least, of winning an important fight, but time brings changes and marvels.

* * *

Abdu comes to occupy a very high post in the ministry, and thanks to him we get electric lights in our alley.

3

There's a worker in our saddlery named Ashur id-Denf, about forty, married, and the father of ten children. His outstanding characteristics are immense strength, tough looks, and wretched poverty. He works from dawn till midnight and is always tired and hungry. He strangles with distress if he happens to catch sight of well-to-do people in the coffeehouse or if the aroma of roasting meat happens to reach his nostrils. He envies the donkey at the mill in the saddlery as much as he envies the perfumer or the lumberyard owner.

One day he remarks to the imam of our mosque, "Allah creates wealth but forgets my children."

This infuriates the imam, who shouts back at him, "Our prophet Mohammed, God bless him and grant him salvation, spent several nights with a big stone bound against his stomach in order to appease his hunger, so get out of here, God damn you!"

Around midnight Ashur id-Denf is on his way home from the saddlery, plowing through the darkness, when he hears a soft whispering voice. "Hey, Am Ashur!"

He stops and turns his face toward a closed ground floor window of the house belonging to Sitt Fadeela, the lucky widow who is going to inherit the *waqf* of the Shananeery family. "Who's calling?" he asks.

"I want you to do something for me. Come in," says the voice.

The place is so dark that the stuffed crocodile over the door is visible only as a vague outline. He passes through the door and moves toward the sitting room by following a ray of light glimmering from a peephole in the door. He sees Sitt Fadeela sitting cross-legged on a Turkish sofa and stands there in front of her, exuding the crude, penetrating odor of his sweat. In his eyes, she is a lush cow, provocative and appetizing—but she's also a serious and modest lady, so his insides churn with contradictory feelings. The woman says, "I need oil and cake."

She says it with simplemindedness, a feigned stupidity which betrays an innocent cunning. Her scarlet face confesses for her, and he sees in her drooping eyelids the miracle of consent and submission. But it's not the submission which first occurred to him, not at all, for she's still quite untouchable, completely in control of herself, a prudent schemer. By the time he leaves her, he knows she wants him legally!

For a long time he simply can't believe it and thinks he has fallen into a dream, but he does marry the rich widow and thus starts being mentioned in our alley as a great exception to the rule, a rarity, a great example. Without protest, he lets the marriage contract include a clause allowing her to divorce him and he leaves, as stipulated, his job in the saddlery. Then, in a new suit, in a new skin, and in a halo of wealth, he presents himself to people. Sitt Fadeela wanted him to keep his first wife, so he does, and since she and her children are provided with a generous monthly allowance, they bless the marriage from the bottom of their hearts. And so Ashur lives out his old dream and feels happy and satisfied.

*   *   *

Sitt Fadeela turns out to be a woman not only beautiful but perfect as well, and she loves him, takes good care of him, and makes him a new man. She's gracious, well-bred, and faithful, but she won't give up even one little piece of his life.

From the first minute, Ashur feels she is intent on total possession of both his surface and his core, self and shadow, even his thoughts and dreams. Whether in the garden or the guest room, it's between her hands that he lives, and even when he spends an hour in the coffeehouse he spots her shadow looking in at him through the windowpane. Still, in spite of all this, he continues basking in love, comfort, and satiety.

*   *   *

Once Ashur grows accustomed to good things, once the miracles of plenty are clothed in habit, boredom creeps into his soul. He develops a craving to be alone and hence wanders around aimlessly by himself, perhaps stopping to joke with a friend or commit some innocent folly, but he still has a feeling of being watched, subjugated, hunted. It's true that he lacks nothing, but he's a prisoner. Silk chains, replacements for his old iron ones, draw tighter around his throat and boredom floods his soul.

He finds time long, he finds time heavy, he finds time an enemy. One day he says to her, "Open me a shop."

"What for? You have everything you could possibly want."

"Every man works, even the beggars," he complains.

He's convinced she's afraid that if he starts working he'll be able to do without her, even become financially independent, but all he wants is a chance to be free of her fixed stare.

*   *   *

Ashur id-Denf goes back to his old way of rebellion and complaint. His tongue repeats slogans about grievances and injustice and their consequences.

His anger boils over and he decides to do what he wants, so winds of dissent sweep away the calm of the happy house.

*   *   *

Finally, his anger goes too far and he slaps her right cheek. She kicks him out of heaven and he leaves defiantly. . . .

*   *   *

He faces many problems after his expulsion, making a living only with difficulty; he's forced to get involved in some dubious business and gets beaten up at the police station one day.

Then the lady feels sorry for him and proposes a peaceful settlement under her old terms, but he refuses adamantly several times and goes his own dangerous and trouble-strewn way.

Thus he becomes a rarity of an extraordinary kind in our alley.

4

I'm on my way to the arch when the flour merchant's door opens and his three daughters come out. Light beams from them, dazzling sight and soul. Their hair is light, their eyes blue, and their unveiled faces glow with pure beauty. A horse cart is waiting for them, but I stand between it and the girls, nailed to the spot. They notice my captivation, and the one in the middle, who is plumpest and has the fullest lips, says, "What's with this guy, blocking our way?"

I still don't budge, so she exclaims mischievously, "Hey, you, wake up!"

Overwhelmed by the flood of life in all its obscurity, I reply, "My nightingale, *khoon deli khord wakuli hasel kared.*"

They burst into laughter, and the oldest girl says, "He must be a dervish."

The middle one adds, "He must be crazy."

I fling myself into the dark archway and stagger around until I reach the light of the *takiya* square.

My head buzzes and my heart whispers in the ecstasy of buds before blooming.

Their ravishing portraits hang deep in my deepest gallery.

Seeds of love planted too early to grow.

5

Our alley has gone through a period which might be called the Age of Zenab.

Her father peddles fruit, her mother eggs. Zenab is the last grape in a cluster loaded with males. She is beautiful to the point of extravagance, and in her beauty lies her story.

When she was a baby, she was passed from hand to hand like a toy, and the first hints of beauty gleamed forth in her childhood. In early youth she became a paragon of brilliance and splendor.

Her father, Zedan, commands his wife to seclude the girl inside the house at all times.

Her mother agrees this is a good idea—but grudgingly, since she would much rather see Zenab go out and earn her own living, if only that were possible.

So many suitors turn themselves into fawning dogs for her that the family is embarrassed. Her mother says, "Well, it's simple justice that her destiny be formed by her beauty."

So, for that reason, her mother refuses the hand of her sister's son, a mere horse cart driver, thus breaking family ties and causing quarrels between the two sisters which the whole alley—the spiteful, the curious, and the condemnatory—watches.

Two men propose to her at almost the same moment, Hassan and Khaleel, apprentices, respectively, of the tarboosh maker and the butcher. They get into a ferocious fistfight from which each emerges with permanent injuries.

Immediately after this, the schoolteacher, Farag Idduri, asks for

her hand. Since he is a respectable gentleman, a government official, and in comparison to someone of Zenab's background the
dream of dreams, the mother announces, "This is the man we favor
for her hand."

But Ali the waterpot peddler blocks the teacher's path one day
and whispers in his ear, "If you truly love life, stay away from
Zenab."

The teacher asks protection of a husky relative who is used to
threats and fights and who beats up the waterpot peddler. But Ali
carries his grudge quietly until one day he ambushes Farag Effendi
and puts one of his eyes out!

So for the sake of peace, all the decent folk in the alley give up
their proposals, and no one is left in the arena but gangsters and
tough guys.

The infuriated mother screams, "What rotten luck!"

Gangsters and bullies tangle with each other, drubbings continue, and threats pile up while the Zedan family maintains total
neutrality out of fear of reprisals. In spite of all their trials and
tribulations, they still get jinxed by people who say they are very
lucky! One day Zedan finally says to a few of his friends, "Lucky?!
We've been annihilated by a curse called beauty!"

The battle rages on, injuries increase, and Zenab and her family
become an embodied curse which causes hatred, envy, resentment,
and the craving for revenge.

Zedan never has a chance to breathe in peace and fears that one
of these perfidious ruffians will act treacherously with Zenab herself, ruining her forever. . . .

One morning we can't find the slightest trace of the Zedan family.
Despondency and sorrow descend. I suffer from a frustration no
one notices. I ask myself sadly, "Is it impossible for beauty to thrive
in our alley?"

6

Bergowi is dedicated to his work in the falafel shop.

Kefrowi happens by one day and asks for a drink of water. A
humorous whim seizes Bergowi, and he points to the donkey
trough. "There's a trough. Have a drink."

Some of the customers chuckle, making Kefrowi angry. "You're
an uncouth coward!" he shouts.

Bergowi gets mad too and yells, "To hell with you and all your
ancestors!"

They fire insults at each other, and a group of watchers of all ages gathers. The imam of the mosque tries to calm things down, but when no one pays any attention to him, he stalks away in a huff.

The battle heats up. Kefrowi grabs a brick and throws it at the shop. When it breaks the big gas lamp hanging from the ceiling, Bergowi loses control of himself, snatches up the falafel pan, and beats Kefrowi over the head with it till he's dead.

Relatives of Bergowi and Kefrowi converge on the scene and a bloody battle ensues. Bricks, clubs, and knives are wielded. Several men are killed and the rest end up in jail.

For a long time I never see anything but women dressed in black in the houses of both Bergowi and Kefrowi. This makes me feel sorry, of course, and I say what should be said on such occasions.

But a number of people in our alley honor the memory of this destructive rage and recite tales of the bloody battle with a pride utterly disdainful of jails and hangings.

7

A guest says to my mother, "Nazzlah—may Allah forgive her!"

My mother says she hasn't heard the latest about her yet, so the guest goes on. "She chased a certain young fellow until he fell for her and had to marry her. He took such good care of her that she was the happiest woman in the whole district—but now look at her, the whore, she's left him because his illness has got him down."

My mother questions her further about the situation, so the woman continues. "He lies there, prostrate in bed, alone, spitting blood and coughing till his lungs burst, wishing for death. When I visit him, he says, 'Look, Aunt, what Nazzlah has done.' I comfort him and try to cheer him up, but all the time my heart is breaking. . . ."

And I imagine the sick man, the blood, and the whorish woman.

Some time later, the guest comes to see my mother again, saying, "Will wonders never cease? Only a few months have passed since Hassan died and now the brazen hussy has made his brother Khaled fall for her and marry her."

My mother shouts, "Nazzlah?!"

"Who else would do such a thing? May Allah wreak His vengeance on you, oh Nazzlah, daughter of Amuna."

And I conjure up visions of the dead man, the lover, and the whore.

Time passes. I am studying in my room when I hear my mother greeting a guest. "Welcome, Sitt Nazzlah."

Very interested, I ask myself, "Could this be the whore?"

I sneak into the dark hallway and peek into the living room. I see a woman between forty and fifty, full-bodied, beautifully shaped, and elegantly dressed. I have to admit that she is a provocative woman, worthy of falling in love with. I have recently heard the news that her second husband, Khaled, also died—after giving her a son—and that she has left their apartment opposite the archway to move into a small place near us. I realize that my mother couldn't have been greeting her sincerely, so, after she leaves, I say, "She is a wicked woman."

But my mother says prudently, "Allah alone knows what's inside the heart."

"You sympathize with her even though you don't welcome her?"

"I've heard a lot, but what I see is a weak woman with a son and no husband and no money."

Whenever I get a chance, I watch her from the window. I recall the two dead men, Hassan and Khaled, but I don't care. I feel I'm about to begin an adventure more dangerous than any I have been through before. But this story never gets off the ground. . . .

One morning an echoing scream convulses our alley.

Word spreads that a neighbor threw lye in Nazzlah's face and accused her of trying to steal her husband.

Nazzlah loses her charm forever.

She is forced to take a job in the public bathhouse of the neighborhood.

A deep sorrow fills me for a long time, and I repeat what my mother said: "Allah alone knows what's inside the heart."

8

Hasham Zayid and I sit near each other on the same bench.

Though he is tall, husky, and muscular, he is also shy, kind, and well behaved. Because his mother is a rich merchant who not only owns houses in Birma Street but is also the partner of the biggest spice merchant in the neighborhood, we regard Hasham with admiration and envy. Ibrahim Tawfeek's jokes sneak up on him from behind, and Hasham is unable to stifle his laughter. Since the teacher sees him instead of the real culprit, he is the one who gets to take the punishment—a slap, a punch, a kick—and he takes it with the submissiveness of a polite student.

Hasham fails and has to leave school, but when his mother dies, he becomes in an instant one of the most influential people in the alley. Our paths separate. Once in a while I see him sitting in a carriage or, in native dress, enthroned in a halo of sycophants. His character becomes weird, so I avoid even shaking hands with him. He begins to swagger, put on airs, and exploit his power aggressively, imposing his will on people. How could a shy, kind boy have changed into this ferocious monster? I ponder and wonder in vain. . . .

Not a day of his life passes without a fight, for he considers wallops quicker than words and prefers clubs to fists. He takes over the square, and we all avoid him like the plague.

Had he lived during the gangster period, he would have been a *futuwa*, a leader; as it is, he is nothing but a pest to both police and alley. He spends a lot of time in the local jail but gets out by bribing the officers and the sheikh of the alley.

Although he's always surrounded by a court, he doesn't have a single friend. In spite of his wealth, he never marries, nor is he known to care about women.

His attitude toward his mother's memory is puzzling and thought-provoking, for sometimes he recalls her with deep sorrow, praying for mercy on her soul, but at other times he criticizes her with bitter sarcasm, saying things like, "She was niggardly and greedy, she neglected herself to the point of being dirty, and she treated the servants with insane severity. . . ."

One day he goes too far in attacking her and then—suddenly— breaks into tears, forgetting himself completely. When he becomes aware of his weak behavior, he laughs, but later heaps anger on everyone who witnessed his tears, holding a grudge against them. . . .

And Hasham Zayid vanishes from the alley and from his house.

He is missing so long that he begins to dissolve into dark oblivion.

You hear people say he has emigrated and you hear people whisper that he has been murdered and his body hidden.

THE BOYS FROM THIS SCHOOL

Kathy Miller

He is one of the boys from this school, so he wears a green military uniform and has a shaved head. He is a freshman and his name is James. He stands at the door of Kelly's office to talk to her after class. As she looks up at him, she runs her hand through her short blond hair; she always wonders if her students think she looks attractive or merely curious in the flight jacket, trousers, and jump boots she wears because she would rather look like them than like the few older female faculty in their skirts and pumps. The students watch her in her office as if she were a changing display, waiting to see what she will do next.

James, in his first essay, wrote about the time his father made him shoot the entire litter of the family cat, pop, pop, pop. Now he is writing an essay about the training of Nazi SS troops. In the beginning they are each given a puppy. For several months the puppies are their only friends. At the end of the training, they shoot their puppies. Then they are SS men. James is a sensitive and intelligent student. He gets A's on everything he writes. Kelly prides herself on her objectivity, even though, in some cases, she wonders if it is morally right.

James is at least six-two, with pale blond hair and light blue eyes, a thick, dreamy nose and mouth, and acne on his pale skin. Forty years ago he could have been a young Nazi instead of a young ROTC cadet. He wishes he would have been a Nazi. He would have made an excellent Nazi. He would rather kill people than cats, this blue-eyed boy, this perfect gentleman of death, who salutes and says ma'am and keeps a knife neatly under his bed and a homemade bomb with half the explosive power of a stick of TNT in his drawer between his underwear and his socks. It occurs to Kelly that he enjoys making bombs the way she enjoys making chocolate chip cookies for her class. He enjoys blowing things up the way she enjoys keeping things alive—plants, animals, students. Perhaps this is why they get along.

He is looking forward to summer vacation, he says. He just got a letter from his friend in Long Island who is studying to be a minister. They will rappel down his friend's three-story mansion, test out new explosives underneath expensive cars, pursue drug dealers with the intent of scoring not drugs but a kill, and in general, fight the good war. It is the only war there is for him to fight. Kelly smiles into his eyes and notices that the conversation becomes less exciting whenever they veer from the topic of destruction, so they veer from it less and less until he has to go.

Next she writes a letter for a junior who is going on trial the following week for assaulting, with his friends, three students from another college—two guys and a girl. He is guilty of the crime; that is not in dispute. What will be argued is the seriousness of its nature: Was it a felony or not that he broke several ribs in his wild swings and removed a tooth from the front of the face of the girl? Kelly writes that in class the student is well behaved and cooperative, and that at their class party he assisted her in throwing two drunker, meaner students out.

This is not a reform school that Kelly works at. It is a military college, where good boys go bad. Kelly works here hoping to change something but knows she probably will not. She works here because she is young and inexperienced and couldn't find another job. She works here because she finds the students interesting and knows the school will go on whether she works there or not. When the students ask her why she came, she tells them she is on a cross-cultural exchange from her California way of life. What Kelly has learned in this exchange is what she always suspected—that men go to war and to colleges like this, not because they have to, but because they enjoy the camaraderie and the sense of purpose it gives to their lives.

Kelly is glad it is Friday. Tonight she will go home and do what she always does on Friday nights. She will grade essays. There is no time during the week. There are too many interruptions. She feels the students need her; they give a sense of purpose to her life. On Friday nights no one needs her, so while her students go out she grades essays at home alone. She has promised her students they can come over and have a party on Saturday night, so on Saturday afternoon she will do the laundry and the dishes and clean the cat box. Her students want to make chocolate chip cookies and drink beer and play cards. They enjoy doing these things, and watching them Kelly is usually both bored and amazed. She would like some adult companionship at these parties, but she doesn't know any adults willing to come watch her students play cards. She doesn't know many adults willing to do anything.

After she types the letter, she answers a memo from the department head and outlines the presentation she will make on Sunday evening to the Board of Trustees. It is a great honor for a first-year teacher such as herself to be able to speak to the board. Normally the board listens to no one. But she has been hired to direct the freshman composition program and will make a speech about writing across the curriculum. Since it involves the entire university, the board will listen to her. Her department head, who is fifteen years older and who has never spoken to the board, will accompany her, mainly so he will appear to be in charge of everything she does. Kelly looks at her watch, then goes in to teach her fourth and last section of freshman composition for the day.

The one student in the room wants to know what they are going to do in class. "I'm going to be brilliant," she says, "and you are going to be inspired."

When class starts they discuss the novel that James has based his Nazi report on. Kelly finds it interesting that these students—who are willing to shave their heads and wear the same green suit for four years—have a passionate hatred of Communists. "The Kill a Commie for Lunch Bunch" she calls them to their faces. When she asks them what should be done about the South American crisis they shout, "Nuke 'em till they glow!"

She also prides herself on having an open classroom, though wishing she could offer them more direction in their exploration of politics and life, but she has so many vague and contradictory feelings—such as that the Bible is sexist, along with almost everything that has been written before or since—and she hates to tell that to her composition and literature class of twenty-four outspokenly Catholic and Protestant young men. She is afraid they will start shouting at her as they so often do.

Today as they discuss the role of women in the Third Reich, Tim, a smiling, wide-eyed cadet, shouts out, "Keep 'em barefoot and pregnant!"

Kelly asks him to repeat that.

"You got to keep women barefoot and pregnant," he says.

He is still smiling so Kelly smiles back. "That takes a lot of nerve to say in this class," she says.

"I don't care. You got to. Barefoot and pregnant," he says.

Kelly keeps smiling. She doesn't know how else to win this one. Since coming here Kelly thinks often, "Nobody told me there would be days like these."

"You're trying to teach us to be Communists," someone in the front row says when class is over.

"If I don't, who will?" she replies.

It is five o'clock and there is one student left in her office. His name is Scott and he has dark circles under his eyes. He shows Kelly where his roommate has scratched him. His roommate is petitioning to get his room changed. Scott's roommate is his best and only friend. Scott wonders, "Do you ever think of killing yourself, Professor Lockhart?"

"Yes," Kelly answers, then smiles at him. For once she is glad that she, on occasion, has considered suicide. It seems that for once it might do someone some good. Scott wants to drop a class. He is flunking and is afraid his father will beat him. Scott is always afraid his father will beat him. This is because his father always does.

She asks Scott how old he is. He is twenty-one. She doesn't believe him. He says okay, he's not twenty-one. She tells him he is old enough not to let his father beat him. He says it is not as simple as that. She knows that it isn't. She says he is old enough to leave school and be on his own. He says it is not as simple as that. She asks why not. He tells her that he is on parole. Scott, with his butch haircut and doe-soft eyes and perfectly developed *latissimus dorsi* muscles, tells her that three years ago he murdered someone, in a fit of rage. And then he tells her that he is having trouble in school because he can't hold his pen right. His hand has been broken in so many places that he can't move it fast enough to keep up.

And then her student Scott, with his doe-soft eyes and perfectly developed *latissimus dorsi* muscles, stands up and takes off his shirt, showing her a scar that runs from the inside of his elbow to his wrist. Then he puts his shirt back on and tries to distract her by asking if he would get an A if he took her class. He is not really her student yet, only her advisee. She advises him to see the school therapist. Scott doesn't want to see a therapist because he doesn't want to make baskets or play with dough. She says they only do that in group homes. Her student Scott has to go back to lacrosse practice. She says the exercise will do him good.

"What exercise?" he says. It is only the beginning of the season and they are having a test on the rules and he has to write with his goddamn hand.

Kelly wants to hold each one of her students and tell them it will be okay. She wants to stroke their backs where their commanding officers have stuffed snow down their shirts and made them stand at attention until it has melted, and to stroke their shaved heads where the officers have thumped them with the stones of their large class rings. She wants them not to go to bed alone at night as she does, overcome with desire for comfort. She wants to take away all of their pain and all of her own. That is the power she wants over them. Standing in front of them at the chalkboard she wants to make love to the whole class, spread herself over them and protect them from rejection and harm. But she is only an average-sized woman in a green uniform who can do very little to help them besides give them cookies and easy grades and mildly interesting parties.

*   *   *

Because it is April and there is still snow on the ground, the theme of the party is a luau. Kelly tacks a girl posing in her bikini for suntan oil on her door to mark it. She is always surprised by how cute her students look in their civilian clothes. One has a bandanna tied around what is left of his hair, making it look wild and punk. Others wear silver-lensed sunglasses and smoke cigarettes. The cigarettes tremble in their hands as they pass them to each other. They open bottles of beer and start juggling canisters of flour and sugar for the cookies. Kelly sets everything out as fast as she can, then goes into the living room to play tapes. She wants to be everything for them except their mothers. They are here to escape their mothers.

Kelly wants the students to know who she is. She wants someone here at this school to know who she is. She spreads out her collection of magazines—a travel book on California, a European *Vogue*, *Pumping Iron II*, and a copy of *Young Miss*, which she gets to make up for her missing adolescence. The feature article is "Date Rape." This is the article her students pass around to read. It is the article she read, too. Someone says it is interesting. Then the only 4.0 freshman in the university pronounces that it is a bunch of crap. The students stop reading the magazine and begin making fun of the women in *Pumping Iron II*.

The party begins to drag. The cookies aren't finished yet, the boy who is supposed to bring the keg hasn't come, and they are all sitting quietly in their chairs, reading. What do you expect from an English teacher's party, Kelly thinks. Then she looks up at the door and smiles as two students from last semester, Lenny and Don, walk in with a big, geeky-looking guy and six-packs lined up under their arms. They ask Kelly why are people reading, for christsake, at a party?

The evening begins to move faster. Kelly takes Don and two other students to the store for more beer. With the money left over Don buys a package of "Loving Hands" gloves. "Fully lined," he says, ripping open the bag before they have paid for them. "Complete protection." The woman at the counter does not smile as he dangles the bright yellow tips in her direction. He pulls them on, stretching the cuffs and waving his fingers at himself. "Flexible, long-lasting," he says.

A loving hands party, Kelly thinks.

When they get back James, the young Nazi, is spread across Kelly's bed. Unfortunately, he has not yet been trained in drinking. Kelly sits down beside him. She strokes his back. The other students come into the room. They begin going through her things. They like her dresses, they say, pulling them out one by one. Kelly pulls out a mini-dress and a pair of bloomer pants. She tells Don and Lenny to go try them on. They take them and disappear. Their friend, the geek, turns out to be a football player. He puts his arm around Kelly. He thinks she will sleep with him, with anybody, because he has seen her kiss James. He tells her, in a drunken slur, "I could be an English teacher."

"Why do you think that?" Kelly asks. Right now she is thinking no one on earth is qualified to be an English teacher, especially herself.

"All you have to do to be an English teacher is to be horny," he says.

Kelly laughs. "Want an earring?" she says, handing him a large rhinestone one.

"Yeah, I guess," he says, taking it and putting it on.

Kelly pushes him out of the bedroom and closes the door. She kisses her student James for a while. "Don't you feel weird?" she says.

"Yeah," he says.

"I do too," she says, smiling and kissing him again. She strokes his back and his shaved head. "How do you know I love having my back rubbed," he says. She doesn't want to tell him that everyone loves to have their backs rubbed. She wants him to believe he is special, because right now he is special, no matter how many times they have both done this before.

She hears the students outside her door. She pushes back the sleeping bag on her bed and tells them it is okay to come in. She wants them to know she and James still have their clothes on. She wants them to know she is all right. Lenny and Don appear. They are wearing her clothes. Don, in particular, looks smashing in her red dress, red necklace, and black bandanna. She loves how he is color-coordinated. The blue in her bloomers matches the blue in Lenny's jacket, too. She hugs them. They smile at her and James. Maybe she is all right. Maybe everything will be fine in the morning and she will still be their English teacher. They walk out and close the door behind them.

When it comes time, she tells her student James that she doesn't want to be lovers with him. She tells him she wants a boyfriend and not a one-night stand. She has never told anyone this before. He tells her okay and smiles. Kelly looks at him. How can it be this young Nazi, her student, nineteen years old, who is smiling and saying okay, she doesn't have to do anything with him, something not even her boyfriends have ever said. Who raised him not to argue with her or throw her aside? How does he live with the complications of what he believes? It is daylight before they go to sleep, and they still have not made love. For the first time in a long time Kelly is happy.

When she wakes up she can't keep her hands off James and soon he has a hard-on. Maybe it would be okay to make love now, she thinks, now that they have spent the night together. But James jumps out of bed and stands almost on his toes in the corner of the room, his hands clenched at his sides. Kelly moans a little. She is usually the one to panic and get out of bed. Then she looks at how perfectly beautiful he is. You would never know, in his ill-fitting uniform, that his slim, muscular legs rise into his flat, white groin, where now his penis rises red and hard, below his long, flat stomach. And then his chest begins to develop, the two curved squares of his breasts rising up, branching out into the bulging wings of his shoulders and upper arms. Before she can ask why he has left, he comes back to bed.

She can't not make love to him now, Kelly thinks, and then he says into her ear, "No. No, you're not going to have a one-night stand this time." How does she tell this killer of cats and maker of bombs that for the first time in a long time she feels human and loved? She holds him and strokes his back and doesn't realize until later that thank-you was all she had to say, he would have understood.

After James leaves, Kelly finds her red dress folded on the living room chair. When she finishes cleaning the house she realizes that her bloomers and the rhinestone earrings are gone. Lenny and the geek must have worn them back to the dorm. In the afternoon she takes a nap, then irons her only good blouse and skirt, reviews her presentation, and takes a shower, glad not to be sticky with come. She checks the map the department head has given her and drives herself to the restaurant where she will be the only woman at the meeting of the board composed mainly of alumni.

*   *   *

He is also one of the boys from this school, only now instead of wearing a green uniform, he can afford custom-made Italian suits in any color he wants. He is a trustee and his name is Frank. At forty-five he is the president of the country's largest advertising firm and a feather in the university's cap, a bad boy made good. He is large, at least six-four, with dark, thinning hair, a tan, and the remnants of rowdy charm. Kelly recognizes him from the school's catalog. He is talking to her department head. They are both belting back Scotch. Kelly hopes she looks invisible in her cream suit. The department head introduces her. Kelly shakes Frank's hand.

"Can I get you a drink," he says.

"No thank you, sir," she says. She is embarrassed because she doesn't consider herself old enough to drink, but Frank doesn't mind, he is still smiling and shaking her hand. She is surprised when he wants to know where she is from. Her department head is surprised to hear where she has been.

The other board members arrive and Kelly circulates. She wishes she were at her party again, eating cookies and reading magazines. She wonders where everyone wishes they were. Frank smiles at her a lot. She goes to stand near him. It makes her feel secure. Everyone is standing near Frank. He is so large and magnetic, like a friendly Irish setter, that he makes everyone feel secure. During dinner he keeps smiling at Kelly, but then she feels less secure.

After dinner she escapes to the restroom. On her way back she meets Frank. He is smiling and waiting for her. He tells her they could go drinking or to his room. Kelly laughs and hits his arm. The oldest trustee, who is about ninety-six, plods by. He lifts his hand towards them. Kelly and Frank salute back. Kelly wants to die.

"Come here, let's talk," Frank says. He takes Kelly's hand and goes to a more secluded hallway. Kelly likes to talk. She likes to talk and kiss and hold hands. Frank puts his tongue in her mouth and her hand on his crotch. He has a hard-on. She squirms away.

"Okay, let's get back," he says.

"What?" she asks.

He straightens himself up and they go back.

To give her presentation Kelly stands at her table, facing the board. Her department head is by her side, but she doesn't bother to look at him. Mainly she looks at Frank. She is surprised by how easy everything is. Everyone seems human to her now. The old man they passed in the hallway smiles at her. They laugh at her jokes. When it is over everyone claps.

Frank asks her to stay for a drink. She says she can't. She kisses him on the cheek.

"Good night, Blockhart," he says.

She looks up. "Only my friends call me that."

"I am your friend. I feel like I've known you a long time."

He watches her slip in the new snow in her high heels. She smiles at him and waves good night. When she gets home she puts on her sweat clothes and begins grading. The phone rings, and before she picks it up she knows it is Frank. He is used to getting his way. He wants her to come back. She wants him to talk. She asks him why interesting, intelligent men are not interested in interesting, intelligent women. He tells her he would be if he didn't have a wife.

"Oh," she says.

He has a hard-on, he says.

"I think," she says, "that going to this school frees all of you from the last of your ability to love."

"That's probably about right," he says. "Now could you come over?"

Kelly asks him about his wife. He loses his hard-on telling her. She feels like she should do something for him. He asks her to describe what she would do if she were there. She describes what she would do if her student James were there. Frank breathes heavily into the phone while he masturbates. Then he tells her that he has come all over his martini underwear. There are white spots next to the olives in all of the glasses. He tells her he needs a towel. She keeps him talking for a few minutes, then says good night and hangs up. She goes to her room to sleep in the sleeping bag still spread out on her twin bed the way she and James left it that morning. She wonders if James will ever come back or if Frank will ever call again, and then she forces herself to go to sleep, because tomorrow will be Monday and the boys at her school will expect her to be prepared.

CROONER'S PARTY

Michael O'Hanlon

It's late in the day, time to start thinking about where to hole up for the night. Kris Kringle Three Two does the thinking. He has Kris Kringle Three Three send out long coded messages which detail night instructions for Abominate and the Blueswords units. Buddha or Deadly Tracker Three square things away for Crooner.

At the junction where Route Kant intersects a smaller stream, there are three Regional Forces-Popular Forces outposts. The junction is a ragged T, one outpost at the top of the T, the other two facing each other across the stream which is the leg, Route Kant. The Crooner elements are going to move away from the water, trying to seal the area behind where Langley got hit today. The riverboats need bank security if they're going to beach for the night, so they'll stay inside the Ruff-Puff outposts. Some Blueswords units will patrol all night up one arm of the T, as far as Whiskey Three One, to assist in sealing the AO.

Kris Kringle Three Two gave a briefing about the Ruff-Puffs once, when the river force was new in-country. Gentlemen, the Regional Forces-Popular Forces are organized under the concept of a local militia. They generally have their families living with them inside their outposts, which are usually constructed of mud and logs. They have their own fields near the outposts, which they cultivate for their subsistence. Their purpose is to project a GVN presence into areas where regular ARVN units do not normally operate, and to provide security for the indigenous population living in their areas. The Regional Forces-Popular Forces operate almost exclusively within the areas where they live. An analogy may be made between Viet Cong local force units and Regional Forces-Popular Forces on the one hand, and Viet Cong Main Force units and regular ARVN units on the other hand.

Abominate attended the briefing. He said later That was horseshit.

Seeing who's still alive in Ruff-Puff outposts is about the biggest

270

post-Tet job, once the cities are saved. The Ruff-Puff outposts are all over the Delta, looking often like Old West forts, flying mustard-colored flags with red strips. They're not garrisoned by many men. Who knows? Ten? Fifty? The outposts are always on the riverbank. The women and children maybe count as garrison, maybe not. Depends on who's supposed to hear the figures.

They're dead ducks, any given night, and they know it. Any night Charlie wants to bring enough power to bear on one outpost, it's gone. The outposts never move. Charlie's had mortar-aiming stakes set in the same place for years. Any given night. The only real hope of the outposts is to hold on for a while and count on the wires. The wires are the only real hope. Concertina wire circles round and round each outpost, making a direct assault impossible unless a path is blown clear. There are stories of VC volunteers wrapped in explosives throwing themselves on the wire. The other wire that gives these outposts hope is the radio antenna. That's your only real hope, Ruff-Puff. Hold on to the riverbank by your fingertips until arty, or gunships can get there. If you can hang on until daylight, and you've got a little pull, maybe you can get an airstrike. Don't count on anything, Ruff-Puff. If Charlie can get it together to hit four or five outposts in the same night, there may not be enough help to go around.

That's what's happened with Tet. Demoralized, decimated, beaten, the VC still seem to have enough guys to overrun the major cities, at least for a few hours or days. The weird thing is, Charlie's got enough guys to do in a lot of Ruff-Puffs too. All the help is needed to save the cities. Charlie's tried to have his cake and eat it too. He wants to hold some major cities, and he wants to burn down Ruff-Puff outposts. Somehow, he's done a good job. Piles of ashes, torn-up barbed wire, burned logs. That's what a lot of the Ruff-Puff outposts look like. Piles on the riverbank. No people around. The people are who knows where, living on the Route Four ferry maybe.

Part of post-Tet is steaming down small streams to see which Ruff-Puff outposts are still in business. Almost no one is answering the radio, so a firsthand look is the only way to be sure.

The three outposts around the T-junction of Route Kant are okay, and they're secure for the night. Nobody's gonna fuck with 'em with all this firepower here as overnight guests. Blueswords Mike One, Blueswords Mike Two and all.

The outposts are mud and logs. The families live inside and work small fields outside the posts by day. No one's going outside at night. These places button up tight in the dark. If the next outpost over is getting overrun, these guys are going to say God help the poor fuckers—but they're not going out to help. Who's to blame them anymore? They have to stay here a lot of nights, and you have to get some sleep sometime, right Ruff-Puff? There's no getting short for them, no freedom bird back to the Big PX. Besides, Charlie owns the dark. You know that Ruff-Puff, and we know that. And he doesn't like anybody messing with his dark.

The Blueswords units pull in for the night, using all three outposts for bank security. Later on, Abominate Three will designate the units to get underway for the night. Now is a quiet time, a blue hour, turning dusk and before dark.

By is sitting on the bank with a couple of Vietnamese from the outpost. He seems to be enjoying himself, talking a lot to his two companions. You can never tell with By. They've found something in the stream that all three men seem excited about as they stoke up a small fire on the bank. Not a fish. Perhaps a snail. Whatever it is wiggles its agony as they place it over the fire. The movement has barely ceased or hasn't yet when they take it from the fire and begin dividing the meal three ways.

Jesus Fucking H. Christ. Did you see that?

Snipe and some of the other crew members of Blueswords Mike One watch in horrified fascination. The Trigger Fingers heard about some Vietnamese up in Eye Corps who ate some live poison spiders that the NVA had left as booby traps, hanging down in the dark in a tunnel complex. They swear it. They talked to advisers in a bar in Da Nang who were with the Vietnamese when they did it. No shit. They captured them VC spiders. They had handfuls of 'em, running away up their arms and everything. They just crammed them in their mouths. We had a beer with the guys who seen it.

Boats tells them to shut up. Boats is already afraid of the coming night. The meal is almost over. By and the two men from the outpost relax in seeming contentment by the fire. They talk, until Boats waves By back aboard. There's no reason for calling him back, it just makes Boats uncomfortable the longer By sits over there.

Boats doesn't understand. He's sitting on the canopy above the coxswain flat, talking to Celery Salt One. I don't know how these people can live this way, sir. I remember that briefing about how they shit in the river, and put garbage in the river, and take their drinking water out of the same river. I know they try to use the tides to help that, taking the shit out and bringing good water in. But Jesus. They all got worms. Somebody said they only live to be like thirty-seven. That's younger than I am. I just don't see what's the use. God I hope my kids never have to live in such a way. I hope they never even see such a thing. But I guess that's why I'm out here, so they never have to.

How are the kids doing, Boats?

Okay, sir, I guess. This Tet thing's really screwed up the mail. I don't know. The wife says the older one's wanting to grow his hair long, and says some of the kids at school are using drugs. He won't go out for any sports. I don't know. I wish.

Boats lets his wish trail away. It's the wish of the boat, except for 40 Mike Mike Loader, and maybe By. The wish to be in centerfield, Memorial Park, where the ancient lights are no good, every fly to center an adventure and a terror in the dark. The wish of the steering wheel in the way, the tumbling haste into the back seat in half unzipped clothes, and wet fingers. The wish of a fresh radio beat, on the grass with a blanket. The wish of being high on a ridgeline, above timberline, almost at dark. The guide book says Get down before dark, and the wind is up and cold. Still, there's a wish to stay. The wish is all over the boat. You can feel it hanging there, at this particular hour, before dark. At no other hour, just now. Even the Trigger Fingers feel it. They shut up. The darkness comes. The wish lifts. The only wish left is not to be designated one of the units underway for the night.

Celery Salt One this is Abominate Three. Message to follow. Break. Take Blueswords Mike One, Blueswords Tango Five, Tango One, and Tango Three. Conduct Weimar between Whiskey One Niner and Whiskey Three Three. Over.

Okay, Boats. That means us.

Yes, sir. Boats is trying to finish off a can of fruit cocktail before the boat gets underway. The fruit cocktail tastes all the same in the dark. The cherries have their roundness, which distinguishes them to the tongue from the pear and peach cubes. Good stuff. Boats flings the empty can in the river. There are three cans of fruit cocktail in each C-ration case. Three cans out of twelve meals, and fruit cocktail never comes with Ham and Motherfuckers. There's still talk about By's meal.

In the morning, the pressure is worse. There are footprints all through Crooner's and Langley's night positions, some as close as four or five feet away. Whoever was in there last night, Tay Do or whoever, just picked up and walked away, right by the Delta Dogs who were supposed to seal the area. To top it off, they hit some Chemist Sair Snips units which were interdicting Route Hegel. Buddha's furious, and Kris Kringle himself is pretty pissed. Bulky

Baton is under pressure to get supplies into the AO, especially to Chemist who shot up a lot of ammo yesterday.

The Blueswords units which have been on night blockade return to the Ruff-Puff outposts at first light. Crooner has moved inland away from the streams, so there isn't much for the Blueswords units to do except spend the day at Ruff-Puff outposts. You can bring a radio up on Chemist, or Langley, or Crooner circuits, and listen to the contact, or you can shut them off and enjoy the sun. One circuit has to be maintained in case Kris Kringle Three Two comes up with instructions, and the Blueswords boat common has to be maintained. Otherwise, there is nothing to do.

When there is nothing to take over, Boats takes over. He has Trigger Fingers hauling up buckets of brown water and swabbing decks. Green decks don't need swabbing as often as the gray ones in the real Navy, but Boats doesn't know what else to do, so he keeps his crew doing things that used to be the right things to do.

Everybody tries to get some sleep. Gunner and 40 Mike Mike Loader both sleep inside the 40 mount because it is shady, but there isn't much air stirring in there. The walls of the mount heat up. No one knows how they stand it. Below the coxswain flat in the engine space and the little crew's compartment, it is unbearable. Everybody tries to get sleep in the shade available, moving around the 40 mount and around the coxswain flat and 20 and 50 mounts.

Boats has Red maintain the radio watch. The situation is too tight to let a Trigger Finger handle the radio watch. With Crooner and Langley and Chemist all having contact, Kris Kringle Three Two will be up on the horn sooner or later.

It is a lazy afternoon. Lazy, but good. The kids from the Ruff-Puff outpost sell us some ice, so we can ice down the chocolate milk. The day is hot, no breeze, but the cold chocolate milk makes all the difference. The milk's not bad warm, a little too sweet that way.

About 1600 Hotel, Kris Kringle Three Three has traffic from Kris Kringle Three Two for Abominate. Red says it is a long message, Groups Five Four. Boats starts getting on edge right away, but hell, blow it off. Let Abominate make Abominate Three break the message and soon enough he'll let us know what's going on. Until then, blow it off. No one's had a good night's sleep since well before Tet, and tonight we'll be underway again, so blow it off. Boats can never learn that, and it costs him.

Abominate Three calls an officer's meeting on the fantail of Blueswords Charlie One, the command boat. Not a big meeting. Abominate, Abominate Three, Celery Salt, and Celery Salt One. They are the only officers at the meeting, and the only Blueswords officers. The meeting is wonderful news for Abominate Three. It means he has the message broken and has Abominate off his back on that score, plus he is going to have some company aboard besides Abominate. Abominate Three is a very sensitive man, and he suffers a lot having to ride the same boat with Abominate all the time.

The meeting takes place on the fantail of Blueswords Charlie One, right above the engines which are still running. You can never shut them down and let the currents and the tide do what they want with the Blueswords units.

Kind of a shock. That's what the meeting is. Even Abominate shows it a little bit. He is keeping his mouth shut, letting Abominate Three explain Kris Kringle Three Two's message. That is such a blessing. Abominate cleaned out a whole bunker complex once with his breath, near the Mouse Ears.

The meeting is fun, all like a big game. The game is to guess how many of Chemist's Sair Snips units are on the bottom of the Can Tho River, Route Goethe. Celery Salt is senior, so he gets first guess. He guesses zero, and Abominate Three says he is wrong, so he loses. Then it is Celery Salt One's turn. He guesses zero, too, because these boats are especially designed for in-fighting on these rivers and if there's one thing they can do it's stay afloat. Not one has ever been sunk and not one ever will be unless Charlie can get something heavy this far south that he's never gotten down here before. These boats were designed especially for the Mekong Delta, and they can take anything the Delta can dish out.

Abominate Three says all guesses received so far are wrong. The atmosphere seems like even Abominate has had a guess and was wrong, and has fallen silent. Abominate Three says Two. The correct answer is Two. Two Sair Snips Alfas are now on the bottom of the Can Tho River.

That is a different game, guessing about Alfa boats. They are nowhere near as tough as Mikes and Tangos. But still, no Alfa has ever been sunk before, either. Are you sure, Abominate Three? How the fuck can they have two Alfas sunk?

Okay. Here's what happened. Last night most of Chemist had blockade stations along Route Goethe to try to seal the AO. Buddha and Kris Kringle think the Tay Do Battalion and elements of the 303rd Main Force are trying to exfiltrate the AO by crossing the Can Tho River and are trying to reach Base Area 478 southeast of the river.

Exfiltrate? Do you mean they're not trying to move toward the city anymore?

That's the way it looks. Buddha and Kris Kringle think we've preempted the attack on the city. Now, they want the AO sealed, and both these Main Force battalions destroyed. That would pretty well end the capability of the VC in the southern Delta.

You got all that out of a Groups Five Four message?

Here's what happened. Chemist was trying to seal the AO on that side last night while we were blockading this side. One of his Sair Snips Alfas took a recoilless hit right at the water line. It was a lucky shot, but it sunk the boat. The crew got off okay. Today, Chemist had a couple of units guarding the site where the Alfa went down, so sappers couldn't booby trap the wreckage before salvage gets there, or couldn't get at the weapons or radar or radios. Another Sair Snips Alfa was beached along Route Goethe, when another Alfa came steaming by too fast close in-board. The wake washed over the fantail of the beached Alfa, and it sank in about ten seconds. All the crew got off, except one guy who was taking a nap in the forward compartment and got caught.

Abominate Three pauses. The only sounds in the pause are the engines, and some Ruff-Puff kids playing over on the bank. Holding a fantail meeting always smells like diesel fuel.

All right. That's the situation. Now here's what we've got for tonight. Kris Kringle Three Two wants us to be able to cover as much ground as possible. This is a big chance to destroy the two best Main Force battalions down here. Chemist is going to move closer to the city, and also move units up Route Gottsched, in case there's any exfiltration in that direction. He's already stretched pretty thin, because of casualties yesterday and the day before, and what happened with the two Alfas today. Kris Kringle Three Two is arranging for Sair Snips to rotate with Bacardi Tango, but it won't happen for a couple of days.

What we've got to do is take over Chemist's section of the Can Tho River, and also maintain units in this area to seal this side of the AO. Now, Celery Salt One, you take four Tangos and Blueswords Mike One to the stretch between Whiskey Two Two and Whiskey Niner on Route Goethe. That's where the sunken wrecks are. Set up the four Tangos on blocking station, and use Blueswords Mike One for security on the two wrecks. Kris Kringle Three Two's trying to get clearance for you to take some Ruff-Puffs from here for bank security.

Celery Salt, you take Blueswords Mike Two and four Tangos and set up blocking stations on Route Goethe and Route Cassirer between Whiskey Three Eight and Whiskey Five. Abominate and I will stay in this area with the remaining units. Be prepared to get underway by 1900 Hotel. Any questions?

You said we might get some Ruff-Puffs for some bank security?

Right. Crooner doesn't have anybody to spare. We're trying to get the Ruff-Puffs from these three outposts. We have to get clearance from 18 Able Lakes; he's at district headquarters down here. If you get the Ruff-Puffs, load them on your Tangos and use them as you see fit for bank security at the two wrecks. Any more questions?

Ruff-Puffs. Ruff-Puffs for bank security. Can you believe that? That's exactly what everybody aboard Blueswords Mike One says. They believe the sinkings easier than they believe the Ruff-Puffs. Ruff-Puffs? For bank security? Can you believe that? Boats isn't the only one scared. Snipe says if we got a thousand Ruff-Puffs, that would be enough security against one Main Force VC. Not one Main Force Battalion, but one Main Force guy.

Gunner is the steady hand. He says at least we can string the Ruff-Puffs along both banks opposite the wrecks, and give infiltrators something to think about, maybe make them trigger an ambush prematurely. Some bank security's better than none. The boats are like rubber ducks in a bathtub on their own at night.

Celery Salt One this is Abominate Three. Reference, uhh, Romeo-Poppa personnel, uhh, Affirmative. Uhh. Be prepared conduct Germany my location, uhh, time, I shackle Lima Zula Delta Whiskey unshackle Over.

Abominate Three, Celery Salt One. Uhh. Roger. Understand affirmative Romeo-Poppa personnel. Over.

Boats, you hear that? We got the Ruff-Puffs for tonight. We got to pick 'em up over by Abominate at 1845 Hotel.

Embarkation time arrives. All four troop carriers show up at the pickup point, the Ruff-Puff outpost at the top of the stream junction. The Ruff-Puffs are going to suffer terrible casualties if all four troop carriers are used. They're going to die of loneliness if they're spread out over four boats. There are only eighteen Ruff-Puffs, some barefoot, some wearing sandals, some wearing tennis shoes, baseball caps, handkerchiefs on their heads, bareheaded, shorts, undershirts. Jesus Fucking H. Christ. Look at them weapons.

What a raggedy-ass bunch of motherfuckers. Look at them weapons. The Ruff-Puffs have the leftovers from the first Vietnamese-Chinese War, twenty-one hundred years ago. They do have a couple of grenades, but Jesus. They might as well throw cans of Ham and Limas if we get hit.

Abominate Three this is Celery Salt One. We have, uhh, I shackle

Delta Charlie unshackle Romeo-Poppas aboard. Uhh, their six-gun seems to be a little, uhh, bent. Uhh, interrogative more Romeo-Poppas and uhh, bigger six-guns. Over.

Celery Salt One this is Abominate Three. Roger your interrogative. Break. Negative. Bigger six-guns and more Romeo-Poppas are staying here.

Celery Salt One this is Abominate. If you don't think your Ruff-Puffs have got enough guns, then chop some cranks off that cock-sucking crew and give 'em to the Ruff-Puffs. Now get underway. Out.

The Trigger Finger in the port 50 mount shakes his head in marvel at Abominate. He was standin' up forward near Charlie One's 40 mount. I could see him from here. But he still heard what was goin' on. That old fucker's got ears in the back of his head. He don't miss nothin'.

The Ruff-Puffs don't want to go out on a night like this. There aren't rag-tag local yokels running around the woods these days. It's the Tay Do and the 303rd. The Ruff-Puffs don't have enough radios or don't speak enough English to know what's going on around here, but they know enough from their years of holding onto their little T-junction of the streams to know they don't want any part of whatever it is.

This is a chance for them to see the big time, get out and see the world, the Can Tho River, Route Goethe. The eighteen Ruff-Puffs squat on their heels in the well deck of Blueswords Tango Three. They don't even look up over the armor plate.

What do you think, Boats? How should we use 'em?

I don't know, sir. Whatever you think is best.

It would be nice to ask Gunner what he thinks, but he's already settled into the 40 mount; General Quarters are set.

Okay, Boats. Let's get this together. What was the name of that guy we're supposed to contact for gunship or artillery support?

Uhh, Witty Roach Oscar, sir.

According to Abominate Three, the story on Witty Roach Oscar is that he's a round-eye advisor who's been at a Ruff-Puff outpost on the Can Tho River for a long time. Since Bunker Breaker is tied up with Crooner and Langley tonight, Witty Roach Oscar is the man to talk to to get help fast.

Okay, Boats, we're gonna have kind of a lonesome picnic out here tonight, so we have to keep close track of where we are so if we get hit we can get arty or chopper support.

The two sunken Alfa boats are actually about six hundred meters apart on Route Goethe. The thing to do seems to be to have nine Ruff-Puffs on the bank at each location. There aren't enough for Ruff-Puffs on both banks of the Can Tho River, so which bank is the bigger threat? Probably the north, since that's the side of the river the Tay Do and 303rd are supposed to be on.

Boats, where's By? Get him up here so we can explain to him what to tell the Ruff-Puffs.

After a lot of pointing at the chart and numbers shown by flashing fingers, By seems to understand what's called for. He boards Blueswords Tango Three to tell the Ruff-Puffs. In a few minutes, he's back. With more chart pointing and fingers, By gets the idea across that all eighteen Ruff-Puffs are going together to one spot, on the south bank. North Bank Number Ten. Beaucoup VC. The Ruff-Puff decision is irrevocable. By says that in his own way. There's no time to argue. It's almost dark and time to get set up. The eighteen Ruff-Puffs set up together on the south bank, the four troop carriers steam on downriver with instructions to set up their blocking stations and break radio silence only if absolutely necessary. No sense in reminding the Tay Do that we're here, since they already know. The Ruff-Puffs have a Prick 25 radio with them on the bank. If for some God-forsaken reason they're needed, By will have to get on their frequency. The best hope for the Ruff-Puffs seems to be that they don't fire on us in the dark.

Okay, Red. Sing about Five Five. The way we'll do this is to steam between the two wrecks all night. Boats, you got to help me keep track of where we are. This isn't a bunch of raggedy-ass local yokels we got here. If we get hit, you call Witty Roach Oscar, I'll call the four Tangos downriver. What they may try to do is get in close to our Ruff-Puffs, or in close to one of the Ruff-Puff outposts to get us to shoot up the Ruff-Puffs, so we got to be real careful on that.

Boats, you got to help on this one. We have to be sure of our exact location if we do get hit, so we can get some help on top of it real fast. We have to know exactly where we are.

All Witty Roach Oscar's got to go on is where the two wrecks are, and where our Whiskey checkpoints are. We've got to watch for any little thing that he can go on if we get hit.

One last thing, Boats. Absolutely no exposed topside personnel. You get that word out good. Okay, Red. Let's get it going.

The night begins slowly. Red has a small transistor radio in the coxswain flat, tuned low to Armed Forces Vietnam Radio Network. The news comes on the hours, with a beeping mark. Although the radio is tuned very low, everyone in the coxswain flat can hear it. The coxswain flat's dark, except for the faint red glow of the radios tuned to the operational frequencies. The radio lights are hidden from the banks.

Boats, if you see Gunner's pipe anywhere outside that mount, you tell him to get back inside or I'll have his ass. I want that 40 ready all the time tonight, and I don't want any lights.

Nine minutes downriver, Blueswords Mike One loops around a sunken wreck, steams nine minutes back, turn. Sir, Gunner says we made each run in exactly nine minutes. He told me on the weapons circuit.

Okay, Boats.

There's no pride in regularity. The Tay Do'll pick that up quick as shit. Red, next run, we'll turn around a little short of the wreck, after that, a little long. Every run different. I'll tell you when.

Steam seven minutes, turn. Loop long around the upriver wreck. Eleven minutes. Good. Red, turn her to the right this time. Left next time. Port and starboard. Boats, keep track of our location. We both got to do it. That small Ruff-Puff outpost there. Mark. Eight hundred meters. Nine minutes. Turn left.

2300 Hotel news. Fuck. Is it only eleven o'clock? Red, toss me up a can of chocolate milk, will you?

Thanks. Turn.

Witty Roach Oscar is the night's entertainment. He sounds tough, dry, good. He sounds thirty-seven years old. He's been on this river a long time. When we told him we call it Route Goethe he sort of dry-laughed over the radio. He can't pronounce it either. He's up on his circuit a lot. He says they're in the same schoolhouse they were in last night. He calls in choppers and we can see them pouring red lines at the ground upstream, maybe around Whiskey Eight.

Witty Roach Oscar says that the Ruff-Puff outpost that got over-run at Tet is under attack. He calls for chopper support. Oscar says they're in the lumber mill, where they were night before last.

Shit. Red, call him and ask where the lumber mill is. Witty Roach Oscar says it's downstream, opposite our Whiskey Two Two. The choppers pass over, down there and receive ground fire. We watch the intersecting red lines fight it out.

Shit. The Tay Do's got Tyree. He speaks English. After all this time he's got to be tuned into this same circuit as Witty Roach Oscar. They can go anywhere they damn well please. That's the lesson of the Can Tho River. Witty Roach Oscar knows that. That's what's so fucking funny about him. He's all business coordinating arty and gunships, but he thinks it's funny. You can hear that in his voice.

Up and down. Turn left, Red. Left, damnit. Turn right. Seven hundred meters up, nine hundred back. Mark, mark our position. Listen for the news. On the hour. Lot of time till morning, Boats. Concentrate now. 0100 News. What were those scores, Red? Turn it up just a touch, huh?

Eight hundred yards, turn when we get to that lumber mill, Red. Come back, turn this one short. No patterns. Boats, hand me a cigarette, will you? Your family want to stay on the farm in Ohio, Boats?

Snipe's brewed up some coffee down in the engine space. The cups are old C-ration cans unwashed for years. Snipe coffee. There's no time for bullshit. Got to keep track. There's light from that spirit house, Boats. That's real close to that Ruff-Puff outpost. Mark that real good.

Port turn.

This is AFVN Radio with the 0300 Hotel News. For R and R the weather in Kuala Lumpur is hot and humid, Hong Kong clear and cool, Sydney hot and humid, Tokyo overcast, and in beautiful Hawaii sunny and warm.

Where you going on R and R, Boats?

Hawaii, sir. Gonna meet the old lady there.

Kids comin'?

No, sir. They're stayin' on the farm with my folks. Just me and the wife.

Up and down. Smoke a cigarette. Drink some chocolate milk. Eat a can of Ham and Limas. No. Don't. Talk to Red. His freckles hold his face into a gaze ahead at the black water. The sunken wrecks are marked by small buoys, very hard to pick up in the dark. Red, cut her back; Sing Five Zero for the next run.

0400 News. Heavy fighting in the Central Highlands. This is fucking ridiculous. This guy Mister Tyree just sits over on the bank and listens to this same radio station. Turn to the left. Six hundred yards. Starboard turn. He just sits out there, jacks us around all night, then lowers the boom.

Cold on the river. Turn right, turn left. Are we going upstream or downstream? Now concentrate, goddamnit. Concentrate good. If you let Boats and Red know you're not sure if we're going upstream or downstream, then we're all fucked. So concentrate. Now. Now. There's the lumber mill. Downstream side. How you doin', Red?

Fine, sir.

Dangle us, jerk us around, Mister Victor Charles Tyree. Give it to us just before it gets light. Damn your fucking ass to hell Mister Motherfucker Three Tyree.

Snipe's brewed more coffee. Witty Roach Oscar has been quiet a long time. The 0500 Hotel News. Now coffee and 0500 and you got no fucking excuse for not hanging on until light. Now hang on.

Goddamn Tyree just do it.

0600 Good morning Vietnam this is AFVN Radio Network with the news. Now here's Sergeant Lenny Decker with a few hints on preparing C-ration Ham and Eggs for breakfast.

You hear that, Mister Motherfucker Three Tyree? You understand that? Breakfast time. It's getting light. We outlasted you.

It's light. Cigarette butts and empty milk cans are all over the deck in the coxswain flat. Turn left and ease into the bank, Red, where those Ruff-Puffs are. Boats, get By up here. Blueswords Tango Four, Three, Seven, and Niner this is Celery Salt One. Return my location vicinity Whiskey One One. I say again, Return my location vicinity Whiskey One One. Break. Tango Four. Over.

Celery Salt One Blueswords Tango Four. Roger. Out.

Red rams the bank way too hard. He smiles sheepishly, tired. He's too good a coxswain to ram banks. Boats kind of looks, but he's too tired to yell. Gunner comes out of the 40 mount and stretches his stumpy body. His pipe will be next.

The Ruff-Puffs come rumpled and sleepy-eyed out of a nearby hootch, where it looks like they spent the night in the hootch's bunker, inside partly below ground level. At least somebody had sense enough to get in out of the cold last night. One of the Trigger Fingers, the 20 Mike Mike gunner, points at the Ruff-Puffs. Yeh, they'd have been a fuck of a lot of help if we needed 'em last night.

Boats, call Abominate Three and tell him we're okay.

Celery Salt One climbs out from between the 50 mounts, sees a crowd of people stretching on the fantail, pissing in the river, breaking open a new case of C-rations.

A half hour to have some breakfast, and a ten-minute sit in the sun, which is just coming up. Three Oh minutes. Be nice, wouldn't it, Red.

Celery Salt One this is Abominate Three. I have traffic from Kris Kringle Three Two. Groups Four Three. Are you prepared to copy?

HECTOR COMPOSES A CIRCULAR LETTER TO HIS FRIENDS TO ANNOUNCE HIS SURVIVAL OF AN EARTHQUAKE, 7.8 ON THE RICHTER SCALE

David Zane Mairowitz

Mexico City. 23 September, 1985
Dear David,
Knowing that a letter from me has slightly more chance of reaching you across the world than one sent to me here (my local post office is a heap of stone), I'm preempting your questions and (I trust) your concern by making the following announcement: I AM ALIVE. THE CITY IS NOT DESTROYED. I thought at first to write to each of my friends separately but I've decided now to photocopy this brief note and send it out as a circular. (At the same time I would ask you to make copies and pass them on to any mutual friends you might think of.) I can't tell when I'll have a moment to write at length, but I'm sure you'll understand it might not be for some time. The most urgent thing is that you don't worry about me and above all not try to phone. The central communications office went down in the first quake. For the moment, just take my word for it: I'M ALIVE and not lying under the rubble of my apartment block as you may imagine.
Muchos abrazos,

Hector

P.S. Some of you may have expected news of Beatrice. The fact is I can't provide any. That is to say, she is not dead, or so it would seem. I have been on her trail since the first moment the fat gourmet worms I was eating disappeared from my plate, since the cinema across from the restaurant where I was to see the reissue of *Singin' in the Rain* an hour later budged a meter to the left then one to the right before severing itself in two from the marquee, down the center aisle, exposing Gene Kelly and Debbie Reynolds to those of us sitting, too sick to be astonished, in the restaurant. What I am saying is that not only was the left side of the street spared while the right collapsed in on itself, but also that the stone edifice of the cinema appeared to have cracked while the plasterboard projection box and flyweight movie screen stood functioning, albeit robbed of sound. And we—those of us who had been sitting along the plate glass restaurant window, which bowed but stood like the rest of our side of the street, scarcely believing yet in the tremor—watched the film.

It was in what-must-have-been-a-scarce-second that Beatrice appeared to me, as I had last seen her years before, backing out of our cemetery rendezvous, machete in hand to make sure I did not follow her, leaving for me on a gravestone the court injunction preventing me from entering her premises in future. I imagined, with Gene Kelly now swooning and ripped along the perfect axis of his dancer's body in this tiny aftershock some perhaps fifty seconds later, that everything in our lives was cleft open to miraculous spontaneity, now, that catastrophe would make bitter sisters charitable, calm the distraught and reunite fractious enemies as the bombing raids of popular wars were cracked up to have done.

And so I went for her, not altogether from fear of finding her dead, but rather to see if she lay perhaps prostrate under brick and if, the choice being between suffocation and my pulling her free, she would proffer a helpless hand or retreat forever into the dark stone. In any case, in that moment of divided earth nothing could be taken for absolute, not even her hatred for me, that perfect dynamo which could in its heyday set forest fires at long distance and turn windmills on the airless caverns of the moon.

I staggered out into the street. The riot squads were already overreacting, bayonetting bystanders away from the central area, but it was gratuitous. We were becalmed in the murderous city, docile as never before, because I'm sure that we somehow always expected this, knew at every moment of our life and dreams that it would come to us haphazard and equally deserved. And in the first blindings of tear gas I made my way to the Century Hotel where I knew I could at least count on the offer of a tearful bourbon, if not a room for the night.

Whether or not he recognized me, his eyes scattering aimlessly in shock from the spectators to the first corpses being dragged out and deposited on the street, I did nothing to gain the attention of the hotel manager. Surely my designs had called for reinforced steel girders on the Japanese model to resist shocks like today's, and if these were not approved or passed under the table because of the cost it was not my fault. Still, I could not discount that the hotelkeeper, in his rage, might blame me for the smoldering rubble of his building, the only one to suffer damage on this street. Only the neon "Hotel Century" sign, hanging like a tooth from its root, still flashed amidst the shattered concrete fast turning to powder. In what must have been the seventh or eighth floor, now bluntly pinned to what might have been the third or fourth, a couple lay caressed in the clamping hotel walls. The ceiling seemed to have snapped to "his" back as he pressed "her" beneath him; three of their arms hung through the bedstead which now perched free of its supporting wall precariously out into the summer night. The executive suite where Beatrice insisted we spend our first night simply because I had built it (and where I had to use my influence with the manager to eject the honeymooners next door to provide adjoining accommodation for her police shadow) with its lackluster interior decor now sat across the street on top of another building. The mock-colonial archway of the roof terrace and the adjoining ceramic swimming pool were swept out into the eucalyptus-lined square behind the hotel from which we first heard the machine gun fire, incessant, as I tried to push into her for the first time only to find her slipping free, creating her own space and corner into which she would receive me only when she herself had determined the angle and counterpressure of skin, and peered through the blinds, to see the rioting students being massacred under cover of night.

With all hope of transport gone, I would have to walk north across the devastation, a journey of perhaps two or three hours which would get me there in the middle of the night, an arrival which, assuming Beatrice was not sandwiched between floor and roof-beam, was to play chess with scorpions for pawns. For whatever else might have danced in a spirit like hers—the far nights of rum and mescaline-soaked Gauloises—her body also deigned, through some involuntary self-hypnosis, to accept, from time to time, sleep. That owls did not hoot or cocks dare crow during such times was not a miracle of nature, but a sure decree of her totalitarian hand.

*   *   *

My office was on the route. I could doze there the several hours before daylight and then choose afresh whether to go forward or not. The building was intact, save for a fissure across its face and, with all my private files and city-financed plans for demolishing the shanty towns and building new slums in their place locked inside, I was suddenly relieved I had not built it myself. The lights worked.

Despite the blackouts this section of the city had been spared. I sat down at my video display terminal and thought to write my survival letter, to send it off somehow swiftly (perhaps amongst the airline hostesses I had known and pressed between arrivals and departures in neon-glaring airport hotels, who could post the thing to London, Amsterdam, or Copenhagen). Yet, as I threw the switch to illuminate the screen, I knew the earthquake had struck here too in the seclusion of my workplace. The machine was no longer silent, but somehow distantly coughing. I typed my message, exactly as you find it above, and called for a print-out, but the machine simply fused, choked, switched itself off, and, scarcely audibly, "wept."

There was nothing for it but to press into service my old portable Remington which stood on my desk next to the blueprints for some death-trap high-rise flats which would now surely (or perhaps not so) never be built. In the typewriter was a paper which read:

PLANETARY POTENTIALS:
In 1985, the big planetary lineup already began which goes until the year 2000: the planets are coming into a smaller segment of the sky. The magnetism in that area (say some prophecies) could pull the earth off her axis—earthquakes could be one of the more gentle results. . . .

Without hesitation I checked the three locks on the office door. Children had often tampered here in hopes of stealing my ballpoint pens, and each time I had replaced the outmoded model with the most sophisticated in American anticrime devices. I knew that now the night patrols were already out in force, gangs of thugs dressed as Red Cross workers pushing through roadblocks in stolen ambulances to lighten jewelers' windows and banks in the city center knowing that, for once, the police were not lurking in the area, springing illegal road traps for born-yesterday motorists who would in turn be forced to paper upturned palms, but striking useful paths through gaping mobs so that anonymous corpses could be flung into makeshift mortuary wagons. Yet I was sure these had not struck here. Nothing out of place, no lock sprung. The window had not been smashed open, nor its iron bars sawn off. No, this section of town was unharmed, at least this building. Nothing could have indicated that Beatrice had been here, perhaps just steps before me, and left her mark. There was no mistaking her on the paper, not merely the threat ("earthquakes could be one of the more gentle results"), assuming, as she would, personal responsibility for natural catastrophe, but also the typewriting which, by its sure pressure to cut holes in high-quality paper, provided evidence solemn as a signature.

Allowing myself forty-five seconds of despair, I considered my immediate itinerary: write my circular letter, find the airline hostesses who would surely be grounded now and waiting for escape flights, find and strangle Beatrice, look for something to drink which would not cloud my clarity nor give me malaria nor involve archaeological exploration, lock my office door and place tiny upright matches against it to see if they were still standing the next time I returned to base.

You, all of you there on safe ground, you just can't know what it was like for us on the night of the first quake. We didn't act out of self-concern or even instinct for survival, didn't think of loved ones, nor even about the totally obvious chance of a second tremor, avoiding at all costs the inside of buildings, for most of the city went back to sleep that night in their death-traps; no, we thought on that first night of all the projects we never finished, as if we now had suddenly only a strategically limited time to do so, say, eighteen hours or less.

*   *   *

On the southern corner of the northern zone, on the street where I had played crucifixion football, where I hid out for days after stealing my first Mercedes hubcaps and where, behind the street's only tree, I tested the stretch-tights of a babyfat teenager from Ohio, half the roofs were blown off. I was moving further and further (as I now know) from the epicenter of the quake and you might simply turn a corner to find nothing dislodged, yet here the houses stood while the roofs caved in, whether from hasty construction or from a peculiar tilt to the fault line no one could be sure. Many had been replaced with plastic but not my mother's, which had come down like a children's slide to the pavement, blocking access to the front door. The only way in was up and over, and it was not the modest climb which checked my immediate entry but the hard-edged piano battering the night from within. For years my mother had sat out her infirmity in front of that upright, slaughtering the only piece of sheet music she owned, *Selections from "Showboat,"* and that she could now, in this hour of mass death, muster a riff of honky-tonk, set me to pondering whether this newest affront of Beatrice's did not peppermint-brush the hangman's smiling teeth.

Look, I said, climbing you while my aging mother sleeps in the next partition of these paper-thin walls fills me with dread.

"I'm your mother now."

Still, Beatrice, I won't terrify that woman next wall by letting you reach the pitch of your ecstasy, knowing how you rage and bang, how you shout things that would scar her for the rest of her few years when you sit on me.

"I'll play the piano instead."

Not now, Beatrice, it's the middle of the night, but you shackled her only at your peril, why did we have to come here anyway just to satisfy her whim of running all the stops in my biography, and now the first strains of a Chopin mazurka, heavy with footwork and ferociously chorded, won the day, or rather, night, so that my wheelchaired mother, who had never known me to bring home a lover, much less a celebrity urban terrorist in semi-hiding, in wondering if this was a selection from "Showboat" left out of her sheet music, was surely suppressing a natural rage only in the staggering aura of this Afro-winged beauty at the clavier. No, Mamacita, no this is Beatrice banging up new walls in our house, it's *the* Beatrice, bank-robbing daughter of the President of the Bank of Mexico whose glamour photo you can recognize in any post office, whom the police have official orders to shoot on sight but don't dare because she is her father's favorite and her father regularly entertains Henry Kissinger and his concubines, the very same Beatrice who has decided she will hang out with us for a time, will-us, nil-us, and that means we'll be famous on the street what with the Federales, those you see in the Chevrolet out there wearing Chicago White Sox baseball caps, watching the house and drowning out the Chopin with their break-dance transistors.

I climbed up the slope of the fallen-in roof and peered into the black hole of the house. I must have been somewhere above the tiny alcove-kitchen for I could smell the pork fat and cornmeal of recent ritual. Here I didn't dare light a match, my mother being in the habit of leaving the gas open, although, with the roof gone, the fumes would have risen up to heaven, if any.

Sliding down the inner wall I found my feet and made for the central room from which the piano assault beckoned. The room was artificially dark, but the hesitant tracks of moonlight picked out the silver paint shining in the hair of the plaster Virgin or Guadeloupe in her adobe wall-niche, the flickering ready razor of the male figure crouched by the piano, the glass cases housing actual photographs of several saints, my drunken dead father, Susan Hayward and, by some mistake, D. D. Eisenhower. What do you want here anyway?

"I'm looting the place."

A hasty match showed a man, more a boy, scared, hanging on the piano but surely not playing it.

"There are other houses to loot, Señor. I found this one first."

"This is my mother's house, creep."

"You are going to rob your mother?"

This delightful chat might have carried us to daylight, might have taken a turn for tequila, my mother always had a cold breakfast in case someone ever turned up who of course never did, but for the piano which persisted without mercy in playing itself, starved of all and any human consort.

"What are you stealing?"

"The piano. But as soon as I touched it, it started to shake and play."

I knew my mother could not have installed a piano roll, knew equally only one person in the entire Federal District of Mexico whose piano playing could continue long after the thunder-caress of her fingers had passed over the instrument like the Angel of Death. In any case, you could not get the piano out the front door which is barricaded. You'd have to lift it up over the walls.

"You going to help me?"

"No. Not my mother's piano. Steal something else."

"You got an idea?"

There is in some cupboard a silver spoon from babyhood, a collection of Gringo baseball cards is worth a peso or two, don't touch her bed linen, she'd never survive that, I've always hated that fucking Virgin of Guadeloupe but who'd buy that except a fucking Gringo. I bought her a transistor radio some years ago she never listens to.

*　　*　　*

Exploding bottles of propane lit my way across the night, showing me I was on course toward the dreadful slums of the north, on whose outskirts we have lived in relative splendor because Beatrice needed to rise from her comfort each day and witness the world as it is in its bitter holes. Never giving a penny of her father's millions to begging slum Indians (except the Mayans, for whom she had a weakness), she would nonetheless buy the cheapest rags in the open markets and dress down amongst them to do her shopping, pretending to be poor until once she failed to efface her silver nail varnish and had to run her knuckles through a potato scraper weeks after.

This was all in the era she had organized the kidnapping of her father to finance the urban-guerrilla five-week plan of her ex-lover (into whose bold indentation on our marriage bed I slumped more than once), another Zapata-look-alike spoiled middle-class brat who robbed drive-in banks behind the wheels of a Porsche and distributed the profits to the local Friends of Heroin Society. (But some of you surely know that story, for she would have asked for translations of the literary ransom note for the foreign press.) In any case it all came to nothing (as you no doubt know) because, on the eve of the attempt, she discovered, for the first time, that nature, whom she had kicked and bullied for years, who served (along with me) as fawning handmaiden, had deceived her. Never one to accept into herself any device or medicament which might make a clockwork of her body or control the fatal delivery of egg and blood, she had connived, after her own fashion and in the teeth of life's sadistic grinning bookmakers, to outwit the call of the species. This was at first a categorical denial of all penetration which, soon enough, did not provide any proper degree of risk for her spirit and gave way to a thousand quick-breath withdrawals orchestrated and impeccably timed by her inner clock. And then, after she had swallowed her pride to share quarters with me (as opposed to hit-and-run contractions in the back of her car, in back alleys, in the sea), she recorded her waking temperature every morning to catch her hours of fertility for a brief abstinence, and even at the front of absolute certainty she had exercised to develop a means of clamping fast the walls of her woman's self at the ultimate, damming and forcing the invading flood back down the canal of regret.

Yet despite the angry swoon she played out at the sudden hardening of her breasts and the first nasty rush of sickness, I knew (without daring to say) that such misfortune could never have taken Beatrice unawares, no, not Beatrice who must have felt the earthquake some minutes before the rest of us, as wild deer do; thus, contrary to the public face she put on the outrage against her body, she must have, from some deep reserve of peculiar normality, wanted it.

And I recall this now, walking through the crowded shanty towns in flames, hysterical fire fighters seeking water sources which lay buried under mortar and corpse, because in my sudden quest for Beatrice I would have to face the gloom of seeing my children for the first time in years.

Outside the district of burning shacks where the wealthy villas suddenly opened out along the eucalyptus-lined boulevards the corpses were no longer thrown in heaps but evenly spread and covered with cloth to keep off the flies, often with the name of the dead written in pink chalk on the pavement between his or her legs. And as the second killer tremor delivered itself in the first light, a 7.3 Richter this time, I heard again the words of my master builder: earthquakes don't kill people; buildings which fall on them do. For as I watched the wounded being carried into the hospital complex I'd built on the edge of the barrios to serve the rich and poor alike in my (or rather in Beatrice's) idealism, the entire works went down. Buildings that half hung in space after the first crack went to pieces now in the aftershock. But the only new catastrophe in the area seemed my hospital, the powdery bones of which stared out at me across the gates with hundreds, perhaps thousands, trapped inside. Sirens ripped the slow waking line of morning, and panic, which had not surfaced the night before, now forced the dawn to march double-time, swallowing the flat horizon against its slow nature. A hospital orderly grabbed my shoulders while rushing by, and shouted for me to join the digging team, every hand was needed. And, to be sure, this was my rubble and death-house to scrape free bare-knuckled. But I had come a far progress from the gourmet worms to these outskirts of Beatrice, sleep was calling, the expression on my face and my mood turning murderous.

"The comrades in the Pancho Villa Faction are teaching me how to make remote-control explosives."

What for this time?

"To blast down all the ugly cheap buildings you put up."

*   *   *

On her street it was not merely Beatrice's Volkswagen Beetle which had survived the second quake. Other cars were overturned, their chassis severed, cherished Oldsmobiles from the American '50s had smashed their tail fins through brick walls, some smoldered and, in others, the tremor had set engines running only to sputter dead forever. But all the district's Volkswagens stood unharmed in place or, around the corner where another water main had burst and made a river of the dusty street, several Beetles floated by, sooner or later coming to rest on the dry shores of other neighborhoods.

It was of course not possible for Beatrice to have gone anywhere without her car, not even down the street to retrieve the children's football from a neighbor's garden. These were not just wheels, but the wings of her absolute mobility; she had even trained as a mechanic so she could repair it herself at a moment's notice, and she might be seen under it any time of day or year, her child-full belly protruding through the designer overalls, her high-heels perched up on the pavement.

But she was not there. I had an old key, but she had changed the lock a dozen times to bar an entry I'd never intended. Anyway, the door was open to the touch. Inside, breakfast was finished, the filthy plates remained in place as always, the stereo, the television, the cassette recorder were all playing to the full, as was Beatrice's way whether *a casa* or no. In my daughter's room there was a bra thrown hastily on the unmade bed. Ah. I'd been that long away, and suddenly, in my lower back, I felt a twinge of discordant muscle to remind me of days and nights bent over my architect's blueprints which had done me permanent injury. Picking up the bra (still in pain) I could not resist examining the size on the label, at which I dropped into a (still painful) longing I could not dare allow continue for more than a scattering of seconds before noticing, to my crusty relief and the triumph of my chromosomes in her, that it was Mick Jagger on my daughter's wall, not Michael Jackson.

The little dresses in the boy's room were surely Beatrice's smart-work. An American softball was all I could find to distinguish him, no handguns, of course, no weapons for children to fit the ideology of his pistol-packin' mama, o.k., I agree, somebody has to disarm in these bullet-riddled times and why not the young boys to give example to the old boys, but were the dresses and pastel scarves his idea or Beatrice's? And did he play baseball in these frills with the T-shirted half-naked boys of the barrio and, if so, and he was assigned to pitch, how shall he raise his knee to follow through on the down foot in throwing the perfect curveball if he must avoid tangling his leg in undersilk? Yes, I know, there was to be no compulsion to perpetuate the lies of the social race; we were, after all, not the inheritors of dead-weight but pioneers of the unthinkable, cha-cha-cha, I know all that, Beatrice, but will he, this boy-thing, one day twist from his caressing do-anything chains and hate his mother for punishing him with freedom?

I'm too weary to think of an answer, and besides, I have made my way to Beatrice's bedroom where, as always on coming home (it doesn't matter how many years have passed), I rush to examine the tracks left by her latest lover. This room seemed the only part of the house affected by the earthquake, ashtrays with still-smoldering tip-ends, sheets ripped at the lower end by indiscreet toenails, the half-filled glass of Southern Comfort now comforting drowning horseflies, underwear hanging from the slats of venetian blinds, the evidence of two head-imprints on the pillows, strands of red hair (hers) and blond (not), two coffee cups, one on either side, both lipstick marked (I see. So.), and I could think only of poor Socorro the first time I engaged her, and Beatrice walking in on her, kneeling on the wooden parquet waxing in between the cracks, asking what's this, this is Socorro, Beatrice, I've hired her to clean and cook and look after the children—do you think I will stand for having a cleaning-slave in my house?—no, Beatrice, I knew in advance you would not tolerate it, knew you had lived the disgrace of it in your father's mansions, had your boots freshly shined and ready miraculously outside your door every morning before school, knew it would be the ultimate humiliation for your just-discovered notion that poor people should not be exploited and that you'd rather live in your filth than give this honest old woman a good-paying job which she desperately needs, look at her going pale there on the floor knowing you are going to fire her we'd better speak English, but we have no time to learn each other, Beatrice, the children steal our hours, the housework our souls, all this must sound terribly mundane for a part-time urban terrorist, I know, but we must be free, both of us, to be ourselves.

"Nobody buys or sells my freedom!"

No, this is true. Or even gives it to you gift-like. You get it in dreams or in armed hold-ups, in any case, Beatrice, you are the snatcher of it, but your snatching-wrists are lately burdened with these two small beings . . .

"Three."

Yes, in any case, three, how will you manage your Tantra Yoga classes, your commissioned statue of Zapata for the district square (which, I don't dare tell you, they will never accept in the nude), the dishwashing, get the children to school without this gift of Socorro I'm making you, all the while trying not to hear the word "three," can you really have said that?

In the house I found no trace of this third child. Through intermediaries I discovered it was a girl, and I'm sure some of you know more about it than I do, although, as we all know, Beatrice never writes or answers letters, at best sends a costly telegram. Perhaps you know where she sleeps, where her clothes are, her chamber pot, she must drop somewhere in this asylum-inspired design of Beatrice's housekeeping.

Only the plaster reproduction of Chalchiuhtlicue, water goddess of Teotihuacan, which Beatrice had carved herself, now standing on its flat head in the middle of her sitting room, kept me from turning back and starting south for the city, Beatrice-less, my journey at an end. I have to tell you that Beatrice was in the habit of turning statues and objets d'art upside down in order to create instant ashtrays when she had misplaced, or could not be bothered to empty, her own. Still, there was no trace of dust on this unfortunate up-turned queen's base; what's more, you didn't need a measure to see that she had been placed deliberately symmetrically dead center in the room.

Quickly I turned on her taps; water. This was no invocation to repair burst pipes. No, the tough precision of the thing spoke of less transitory fear. I could imagine Beatrice one day explaining that the statue had dislodged from its pedestal, rolled to the midpoint of the room and stood on its head to announce its divine displeasure. But I knew that this indelicate position of the goddess was the fruit of black rumor, and I was already reading Beatrice's mind in this (as I was then and ever expected to do).

When it finally came to me it was on the frontier of a sleep I had avoided for more than a day's passing. It "woke" me ruthlessly, and I knew I had to get to her somehow, where she had fled into the eye of the rumor, those many kilometers away, with the city at a stand-still.

Were it not for our years of falling in each other's turns of mood, the thousand daily guessings of meaning, backs turned in the con-jugal bed, even before the words could form on the other's lips, I would never have found her car keys. But I knew where they were surely to be found, that is to say, somewhere buried under some-thing, flung down in a return from the previous night's excesses, kicked or tripped over and perhaps lodged in soiled laundry, who knows. I might now have walked back to my blueprints, begun rebuilding the city for inflated fees, and been well shot (to choose a phrase) of Beatrice. But my foot went immediately to its rough work, kicking aside first the undergarments, the empty milk con-tainers, the Patti Smith LPs free of their sleeves as usual, the *I Ching* bent face open to the following judgment:

> The powerful prince will be honored with horses in great quantity.
> During one day he shall be three times welcomed.

Then, at last, with reluctant fingers in the cactus plants, the stack of unopened letters from the year gone by, the bowl of rotting mangoes. In the pockets of her jeans on the laundry mountain were cigarette butts squashed out by fingers, a five-hundred dollar (US) bill, a spent tube of lipstick, and equally, in her handbag—amidst the collapsed Mars bars, expired passports, the pornographic snapshots of herself, a can of self-protection tear gas—but no keys. Only when I bent to wash my failing face in the sink did I notice them hanging from her toothbrush.

As I pulled away from the house the Volkswagen choked and sputtered, refusing to receive the placement of its gears, the accelerator pressing back at my foot. As most of you who visited us know, no one but Beatrice was ever allowed to occupy the driver's seat and, after all these years, the car simply could not accept the touch of alien limbs in control. Yet sensing what it wanted, I slammed the gears nastily into one another, drove with one foot on the gas, the other on the brake, blaring the horn even with no other vehicles passing, the radio switched on to overkill, headlamps alight in the glare of day, sunroof rolled open, so it could imagine itself powered by its proper mistress and carry me out of the panic-stricken city. It was equally a matter of smashing all speed limits, even without other motorists to rush up just behind and overtake, driving on the pavement if necessary or into oncoming traffic to maintain my (that is, her) pace. I expected any moment to be stopped, since all private cars were prohibited, but mine had become, in a sense, an emergency vehicle, carrying my ruins out of the devastation to this last rendezvous, and to make certain of it I held a white handkerchief out of the window as I left the city unprevented. In the glove compartment was, as always, her Colt .45.

And a cassette tape which, when pressed into service, gave out what was clearly Beatrice's self-recorded breathing exercises and full-bellied screams in the penultimate "transition" phase of the birth of our third child. These wails and the midwives' coo along the length of the Mexico-Laredo Highway filled me with terror, not of what was to come, but of the imperfect past.

*   *   *

The Pyramids of Teotihuacan were still standing. The two earthquakes had surely struck here, opening up roadside caverns for us to fall into, but the ancient sites, built not only to defy nature but to swaddle it, laughed at my own pretension to map out dynamic space and fill it with arbitrary ugliness. Running along the Avenue of the Dead I cast an eye at each of the temples but knew in advance that Beatrice, having assured herself after panic that "her" pyramids had survived, would not choose ground level for a rendezvous which must take place, knowing I would surely follow her here.

I know that most of you have seen the film she was allowed to

make (over the dead bodies of the official anthropologists who were
no match for Papa's influence in the government and who, anyway,
were either paid to shut up or farmed out to curate minor ruins in the
provinces) of herself dancing naked on the Pyramid of the Moon (and
for which Papa used the Kissinger hot-line to bribe an Academy
Award nomination), because you need to remember the film to set up
the frame and shot (not again!) of what was to come next. Try to recall
the scene in which the ancient priests (a Mariachi band hired to play
the ancient flutes and ritual tambourines), flanked by the National
Guard reserves (whose demanded price for protecting Beatrice and
film crew from being stoned by outraged archaeology students was
to appear in the film as well as gross 1% of the box office, if any) climb
the long steps of the Pyramid of the Sun behind the Sun-God arriving at last, after an endless unedited sequence, at the summit only to
discover that the Moon-Goddess has tricked them and dances instead across the street (if you like) on the Pyramid of the Moon. Now
fires are lit and smoke signals sent to and fro across the impossible
black ether-void which separates sun and moon. At the moment of its
zenith, with the sun setting exactly symmetrically in front of its
pyramid (as the ancient architects had planned it), just as both God
and Goddess are about to hurl themselves into their respective sacred
fires and re-emerge as the sun and moon of the solar system proper—
the moon less brilliant because the other male-dominated gods have
thrown a rabbit in her face (don't ask me)—there is suddenly and
inexplicably a long close-up of Beatrice's belly. That she was already
swelling with our third child would be evident to anyone who knew
her, but why she had chosen this method to announce it to her friends
and fans the world over I cannot tell.

Yes I can.

Look, Beatrice, look at us, builders of the future city on the pyra-
midal model (me), sculptors of the new clay gods in our own image
(you, naturally), robbed of our dreams by these howling sleepless
brat-nights, tortured titans who bought an ironing board and took
out insurance policies. So that when she let the camera focus on her
belly it was her way of telling the world and me, wherever I by that
time was (in fact sitting in mortified disguise in my local cinema
where the distributor had been greased a small fortune to show it as
a short subject to a captive audience waiting—and howling—for the
Clint Eastwood feature), that she intended to have this baby (and
any number of others) despite my insistence that she take her father's
private jet and fly to London to put a full stop to the first paragraph
of this new biography running short in her woman's insides.

And as I climbed the long steps to the top of the Sun I began composing my circular letter in my head, to show I'd survived the earthquake along the Cocos tectonic plate, 7.8 on the Richter scale, its shock waves coming at 40 km per second, knowing you would expect this news of me, furious with myself for having nothing to write with and thinking to ask Beatrice, at the top, if she could find it in her heart to lend me her glow-in-the-dark felt tip pen which writes simultaneously in rainbow colors and which, when fondled, gives off the scent of raspberries.

This German tourist quietly eating his lunch at the top of the pyramid was surely not Beatrice and, sitting down to get my breath, I knew I could not. I rolled myself into a tight knot, choking from the altitude and my weariness, thinking of the last Tarot Beatrice insisted on reading for me even as she meticulously cleaned and loaded the six chambers of her pistol. The Death card never even bothered to turn up. No, in the center line was the Empress—on the axis of past-future and reality-dream, flanked everywhere by numbered swords, with the Fool and the Tower-Struck-By-Lightning in the dark row of things to come. It's clear from the cards (had she fixed them?) that I have to kill you, she said, apologizing, I have to do it, if not now, then later on.

"Every time I throw my shadow up on a wall, I find you standing on it."

If so, Beatrice, it's because, from the first, I've always wanted to be just behind you so as to put whatever you might need swiftly in your hand, but I know that, just as you expected this of me long ago when we were agents of each other's desire, now I've become watchman of your tower and I know, this being the end of us, surely, I know that what you need is to run all the red lights on the Paseo without me pressing my heels on the windscreen in panic of my tiny life, know that even now as you load your gun and I am reminding you that there is school tomorrow and a gunshot will surely wake the children, even now my instinct to survive (as opposed to yours, to live, die if need be and come back for a second or third joyride) is suggesting to you that you put your contact lenses in, you could not live with the indignity of missing your target and, as you fumble in your impossible handbag—stuffed with your collection of shoelaces of ex-lovers—I'm gone.

Here on the Pyramid of the Sun this shot should at long last have found me. For there, across the Plaza of the Moon, on the other Pyramid, knelt what seemed to me (I could not be sure because the afternoon sun was caught between us) a sniper, a woman, taking aim at me. If this was or was not the shadow-work of the afternoon on the face of the Moon, I advised the sunbathing German to descend out of sight, then made my own slow path down the long steps and into the desperate valley, heading for the smaller Pyramid, not merely to ask Beatrice to take me back but to rendezvous at last—the shadows changing and snarling again now high above me—with the gold-inlaid bullet of her dark chamber.

THE SECRET FEATHER

Robb Forman Dew

On that Saturday afternoon before the ice and while the exterminator was still roaming around her house, Jane phoned Diana Tunbridge to tell her that she was coming over, after all. They arranged to meet halfway across the meadow so that they could walk back together to Diana's where Jane would spend the night. By the time she had collected her things and packed her backpack, she was overtaken once again by that familiar dolefulness that assailed her whenever she deserted her mother and father. It worried her to leave them to their own devices even when she was angry at them. They were still sitting quietly in the living room when she came downstairs, and she stopped in the doorway to say goodbye, but both Avery and Claudia were abstracted, and her mother was a little irritable.

"All right, then, Janie. You are going?" Claudia raised her hand in a listless dismissal. "We'll see you tomorrow. Have a nice time." This was not a wish for Jane, or encouragement. It was what her mother said by rote while her mind was working on something else entirely, and as always when Jane stepped outside her doorway, she was swept through and through with a peculiar kind of loneliness. She suffered a paring away and sparseness at the very core of herself that left her unhappily disburdened.

She set out through the meadow, and as she wound down the path through the grass she saw Diana already waiting under the cluster of trees where they always met. Without considering it, Jane slowed her approach to allow some substance of the day to fill her a little. Besides, this was not just any piece of land between two houses; she had invented this terrain at age eight when her parents had bought four acres from the Tunbridge's and built their house. The steep path between her house and the Tunbridge's was of her own making, and it wound narrowly through the high grass. Diana was sitting beneath the Four Trees—four great pin oaks that formed a hollow square. Summer before last she and Diana had buried a cache of candles and matches and a flashlight there in two layers of Zip-Loc bags and a larger plastic bag enclosing those and fastened with a twist-tie.

They had marked the turnoff to the Troubled Rocks with a handful of assorted stones that they had arranged to look as if those various pebbles had merely rolled into place there along the main path. Only the girls could detect that separate trail so subtly marked through the head-high weeds, and they could find their way along it to a large boulder and some other good-sized rocks that lay in an inexplicable clearing. Jane had gone there alone, now and then, willing herself to sit among those stones even when the low-moving clouds threw her into deep shadow beyond which she could see the sunshine. At a moment like that she would press herself flat back against the boulder under the terrifying weight of that dark beam, but sometimes such an abrupt and selective darkening of the day opened out before her an abyss of desolation so extreme that she lost any faith in her surroundings. Otherwise, on most days, she was sure that that large boulder brimmed with serenity and that she could draw some of it into herself merely by her own proximity to it.

"I don't think we should call them the '*Troubled* Rocks,'" Diana had said when Jane first led her to them. They had spent arduous days debating these points, naming their landmarks. "I think it would be better to call them the 'Rocks of Trouble.' Because we can come here if *we're* in trouble, or if we're depressed or something. I mean, the *rocks* can't be troubled, Jane. What about the 'Comfort Rocks?'"

Jane had disliked the meter. "No, Diana. That just doesn't have the right sound." And she had drawn her straight, pale eyebrows together in an unchallengeable expression. Privately she invested those few stones with an ability to suffer and to solace. Pummeled as they were, mute and exposed, tossed into this space by some ancient force—Jane *believed* in them. When Jane gave herself over to this landscape she extended the connection between reality and sentiment. Each facet of this world that she had named had personal significance, and she would move through the meadow in a state of exquisite melancholy that was a permutation of nostalgia. Here was order. Here was control. Here was peace, and here was she; she was known.

Farther on across the meadow was the Secret Feather River, which was a drainage ditch that, over the years, had cut deep, grassy banks down the hill. Two miles away water streamed off the carefully laid planes of the golf course, running off the greens and fairways into unobtrusively placed red clay pipes, through which it was channeled into a cement tunnel and carried along underground, until it poured out into this culvert at the top of the hill and flowed beautifully clear all the way to the Lunsbury Sand and Gravel Works and into the Missouri River. When Jane and Diana had first discovered this stream, it, too, had been hard to name. Jane had first said to Diana that it was the "River of Paradise," but that had been met with such condescension on Diana's part—she had not even acknowledged it as a serious notion—that for a while it had been the "Blue Feather River." Diana had suggested that one day when she had found a jay's feathers strewn mysteriously along the bank. It was a good name, but Jane was always chagrined to give any amount of control to her best friend.

"If we just call it the 'Secret Feather,'" she said, "then no one would even have any idea that it's a river or anything. It would be a code, you see?"

"Why 'Secret?'" Diana had said, and Jane had taken that chance to use impatience to get her way.

"Because, Diana, it's *our* secret that it's a river!" And that had been all right.

Along the banks of the Secret Feather, Jane and Diana were sometimes early settlers. They stored provisions in the high coves, and Jane took charge because she had read *Little House on the Prairie* and the other Wilder books, too. She assured Diana that the television show was simplistic and revoltingly sentimental.

"It's really just awful," she said. "My father calls it 'Little Shack.'" She instructed Diana in ways of gathering wood for winter and berries and nuts. Of course, when winter came the land died; the grass was flattened under the weight of snow, and Jane and Diana traveled to each others' houses in the front seats of their parents' cars, driving the three miles around.

But on that Saturday in late fall, before the ice storm, when Jane had entered her own territory and spotted Diana waiting in the meadow, a slight expansion of herself took place. When she saw her friend sitting patiently under the Four Trees waiting for her, she began to have weight in the world, and will, and determination of a sort. There remained a persistent sullenness within her, but by the time she reached Diana, Jane had begun to get a picture of her own self in her mind. She was so much a part of what her parents were as a couple that when she was within her own house it was almost as if she were entirely erased, although this concept only manifested itself as a feeling she had; it was not a clear thought. But now there ran a picture in her head of herself walking down the hill while Diana waited. In this picture all the future, all the moments which she could see falling one upon another like a line of dominoes, all of it was dependent just upon her own actions, on what she would do next. She was filled for one instant with an enormous sense of power and importance in the scheme of things. She continued to walk toward Diana, but she moved now with more intention, and Diana saw her and got up to meet her.

They made an interesting twosome. Separately neither one of them was particularly remarkable. They were young girls of an indeterminate age. But when they were side by side Jane looked quite awkward and bony, and Diana looked like a miniature adult. All of the parents in Lunsbury with children in this age group said to each other that Diana would be a beauty, and she was such a nice girl, too, and smart. But when Jane and Diana were together it was instinctively to Jane that people addressed a collective question: "What can I do for you girls?" "What flavor ice cream cone do you two want?"

It was Jane with her stern, slender face and sensibly cut hair that people became attuned to, as people do with a constant, subliminal sensoring. But it was an unreasonable attention Jane attracted. Who could tell about her? Her school work was erratic, but her teachers admired her. Her clothes weren't always coordinated; her tongue was unreliably sharp; her honesty was questionable. She was a puzzle to the parents of children in her orbit, because she *was* stellar. She was a puzzle and perhaps a threat, but grudgingly they, too, admired her. And those baffled grownups courted her on behalf of their daughters and even coveted her approval for themselves, as much as they thought about such things.

Diana brushed grass and debris from the legs of her jeans and walked along beside Jane, attending her in the way any two children can be observed as leader and devotee. They had known each other since kindergarten, and they knew each other's moods. Diana recognized at once, on that Saturday afternoon, that Jane had about her a bleakness that might transform itself at any moment into mild contempt for Diana, herself, or any of Diana's plans. To the west the sky lowered toward them, gray and gloomy. Diana wanted Jane to cheer up; she wanted the sleepover to be fun; she wanted to engage her friend's interest.

"Did you see what happened in Math Lab yesterday?" Diana said, leaning around as they walked to observe Jane's face. She chattered on, knowing not to wait for a reply. "God! It was Chris

Barraclough. Didn't you see what he did? I couldn't believe it. I had on my plaid wraparound skirt. You know. That ties in back. He was already sitting down at the back of the room when I came in, and when I went by his desk he took hold of one end of the tie-ends!" She paused but got no reaction from Jane. "And then he keeps saying, 'Diana, you're in my way. Come on, Diana, I can't see. What're you standing around for? Aren't you going to sit down?'" She had imitated Chris Barraclough's sing-song mockery. Now her voice dropped back into its regular scale. "He really did! What do you think that means?"

Jane only glanced at Diana with a quick frown of disparagement.

"Well, Jane! I couldn't move or my skirt would have come untied and just fallen off. I mean, it was only tied in a plain bow. And I couldn't do anything, because you know how Mrs. Dehaven is. Oh, my God. I was so mad."

Jane still didn't say anything, and they walked a little farther before Diana tried again. "Have you finished *The Secret Garden* for Great Books? We have to have a report on it by Monday."

"*The Secret Garbage*," Jane said.

"I know," said Diana. "Well, are you reading *The Summer Birds* instead? I started it, but it was really strange."

"*The Secret Garbage* and *The Summer Turds*." Jane said. "Christ!"

"Oh, come *on*, Jane!" Diana was finally irritated. Jane could be so tiresome. "Maggie said that *The Secret Garden* was her favorite book when she was growing up."

Jane's attention was completely engaged for a moment. She so much admired the familiarity of the Tunbridge family, in which the parents were not "Mom" and "Dad" but Maggie and Vince, their real names. By an unasked for and special dispensation, she, too, as Diana's closest friend, had been urged to address them by their first names, and she did this often and with gusto, especially if she were with them in public. It seemed to her that such an unexpected intimacy conferred upon her a superior status.

Diana was in front of Jane on the path now, where it narrowed on the steepest part of the hill, and they continued down the slope without any more conversation, each one mulling over one thing or another. When they drew abreast, though, Jane was more animated.

"Your hair looks good like that," she said to Diana in the cautious way she gave compliments. Diana's mother had carefully braided her daughter's hair in a single, thick, brown rope that intertwined luxuriously from the crown of her head to the middle of her back.

Green grosgrain ribbons were woven through it to match Diana's green sweater.

"It's a French braid. I really wanted to try it, but it takes hours. I'll never be able to wear it to school like this." But Diana wasn't at all worried about that, really, because at the moment she was just glad that Jane had cheered up.

They went on to talk about their teachers and their friends and their enemies. To a great extent it was school that shaped their lives and how they spent them, and that was what they were discussing, not frivolously. As their conversation wound out, they became more intense, bending their heads close together, chins down in contemplation. The subtleties and complications of the days at school were endless and delicate.

And, in any case, here were two children who watched the news with attention every night, who knew all the nations of the world and their capitals and their forms of government. Those two girls were beginning to fall in and out of love on a minor scale; they took computer science every other day; they did posters supporting a nuclear freeze for their art project; they were on the verge of having reproductive ability. It might be that they said any number of things that had been said time and time before. They might have a conversation that would bore any thoughtful adult, but what in the world could they have talked about that would not be important?

In their grammar school, rumors were always circulating that Lunsbury was targeted for a first hit by the Soviet Union in the event of nuclear war. In fact, when all the children gathered in the classrooms together or crowded each other in the lunch lines, they took special relish in reminding each other of that very fact in loud voices. It was now and then passed among them as a trophy, a source of some excited civic pride. At night, in their own homes, each child sometimes brooded about the possibility of the vaporization of his or her own parents, siblings, and pets. Each year a few children experienced an early crisis of the awareness of mortality, but they received out-patient treatment at the University Mental Health Facility, and they mostly weathered it as well as anyone does.

There was no doubt about the fact that being blown to dust was not a good way to die, but in the lunchroom over their tacos they weighed it against the desirability of perishing slowly from radiation poisoning or cancer, or even being hit by a car as a student from their school had been two years ago. "Oh, my God!" they said. "He was just a vegetable for two months before he finally died." And it came down to the fact that it was only death they were considering, and one way or another it was a subject they were bound to consider eventually. The possibility of annihilation didn't ever, for more than an instant, lessen the immediate concerns of those sophisticated children.

And it was never the thought of death that bothered Jane. She spent her energies battling a peculiar hollowness that often rendered before her a setting devoid of depth. Today she finally caught refractions of herself from her friend, Diana, from the tensile grass, from the old oaks too thick to bend but rolling their heads like pinwheels in a crazy spinning of leaves and branches.

And under the old trees, so buffeted by a low turbulence that their tops seemed to be turning on a fixed stem—under the trees as Diana and Jane walked through the meadow in Lunsbury, Missouri, those two girls were as much a part of the destiny of the earth as the nuclear power plant which lay fifteen miles away in Fairhill, or the ICBM missile base seventy miles away in Sheldon. There they were, two girls who might have remarkable lives or might not, might be happy or might not. They were just two eleven-year-old girls walking across a meadow who might do anything at all.

*   *   *

At the Tunbridge's that afternoon Jane could not settle down to anything. She was giddy with the effort of trying to appease the odd sense of yearning that had come over her as soon as she caught sight of the broad brick hull of the Tunbridge house when she and Diana had curved across the meadow. There it sat on the bluff with its wooden appendages of porches, garages, and gabled extra rooms that had been added over the years to meet the family's needs or to comply with various architectural upheavals. Maggie said that the main house was essentially a "center hall Georgian," but Vince had laughed and said that it was "just a basic 'dog run.' The hounds run in the front door and out the back."

To Jane, the house bespoke continuity. The Missouri River, which the house had originally overlooked, could still be seen from the upstairs windows, but it had receded and trains passed at intervals below the bluff on tracks that had carried the first train from St. Louis to St. Joe, tracks which the house predated by fifty years. Vince's family had built this house, and he had filled Jane and Diana with tales of all its terrifying history and secret places when they were little girls. Jane could never enter the building without wanting to reacquaint herself with every room, its every mystery. But finally the two girls settled down with Vince in his study, where he was watching a football game with Diana's brother, Mark, who was five years older than Diana.

The Tunbridge family was divided by appearance into two factions that didn't seem to be related. Mark, and Diana's nineteen-year-old sister, Celeste, were their mother's children, with her amiable lankiness, light hair, and wide-boned friendly faces. Vince was shorter than his wife, but he was also perfectly proportioned so that he seemed better made, more carefully put together. His eyes were blue, like Maggie's, but otherwise he was dark and intense, and Diana, who was so much younger than her siblings and so resembled her father, was like an afterthought that only he had had. But while Diana's energy was precociously controlled and meted out with care, that same trait in Vince always made Jane anxious when she was in his company. His restraint, his discretion, was tense and palpable. In spite of herself, she was never comfortable with her friend's father, although he flirted with her and singled her out in any group. Just now when the girls settled in front of the television, he turned his attention to Jane immediately.

"The ladies are going to join us, Mark," he said. "Now what can I get for you two? Janie? A Scotch? Join me with a beer? What'll it be?" He made a great pretense of surprise when she smiled uncomfortably at him.

"Now, Janie! You're eighteen, aren't you? You're so glamorous these days. And you won't keep me company? You make me feel awfully ashamed of myself. Dissolute!" He spoke to her in the wheedling tones of a host whose hospitality has been spurned, but Jane didn't know anything to do but smile at him. Then he clapped his hand to his forehead in a pantomime of surprise.

"Oh, Lord! What am I thinking of? Virtue is visiting us. Now you certainly won't catch Virtue swilling the devil's own brew!"

Jane regarded him solemnly and didn't answer, because Vince was talking about the Halloween party she had come to in this house, and at which she had been so happy until she had caught on to the fact that she and her parents had somehow stepped out of the bounds that delineated appropriate behavior in society. But she had never understood what her parents had done, and she looked at Vince without sharing his amusement.

The day of that party had been a day that Jane had put away in her mind in parentheses, bracketed by lesser moments, as a fleeting definition of her parents' marriage. Early on that morning she had stopped and stood in the bathroom door while her father was shaving and her mother was sitting in her brilliant red robe on the edge of the bathtub smoking a cigarette and gesturing as she spoke, so that her billowing sleeves followed her quick hands in a diaphanous accentuation.

Jane had known right away that they would have a good day, because there was that current of animation and pleasure running between Claudia and Avery. They were filled with a glistening and elusive exuberance that puzzled Jane but was mesmerizing, also. She could only grasp the essence of their good humor now and then, and not with language; it was her instinct that informed her in this case and led her along into the same high spirits. When this temperament settled over her household for very long, Jane was relieved and agitated at once. She would have liked to know that pleasure. No couple could be as delighted with themselves as her parents sometimes were. No other two people she had ever seen were capable of enjoying each other so much, now and then, and oddly enough when her father didn't have a single drink and her mother's affability overcame her melancholy disorientation, Jane sometimes fell into a brooding sense of dissatisfaction with everything around her. But on the morning of the Halloween party she was pleased to see her parents' enthusiasm, because she was so excited herself.

"But I can't think of anything to go as," Claudia was saying when Jane stopped at the door. "Maybe someone out of Greek mythology. That would be easy enough to do with sheets. I think we have enough white sheets. And sandals." She settled back to consider this, bracing herself comfortably by putting both hands on the rim of the tub, and the puff of her sleeve slowly settled around her wrist perilously close to her burning cigarette.

But Avery had stopped in the middle of shaving and was staring at himself in the mirror. He put his razor down on the counter by the sink. "Now, wait," he said, still looking directly at his own reflection. "I think I know what we can do. Now just wait a minute." He slipped his arms out of the sleeves of his T-shirt so that the body of the shirt hung around his neck. He studied himself carefully in the mirror, leaning forward to peer closely at his own face. Then he took hold of his T-shirt at the back of his neck and stretched it up to cover his hairline and ears and circle under his chin.

"A wimple! Look! It's perfect." He turned around to face them, and he looked absolutely unlike himself. The shirt was taut across the top of his head and the upper part of his lean face, and then it draped in soft folds beneath his chin and onto his shoulders. It robbed his face of that sharp charm that he possessed, a quizzical look of irony, and he seemed unusually benign and sweet natured in a dim-witted way. Both Claudia and Jane laughed.

"That's wonderful! That's just wonderful!" Claudia said, and even Avery's smile, which always curved up a little more on one side of his face than the other, was transformed into a simpleminded, beatific beaming. Claudia was entranced and immensely pleased. She got up and walked all around him to see how he looked from every angle. "Okay, okay. That's great. I've got to see how it'll work for me," she said. "I know what we can do. Now just stay right here for a minute!" And she left the room and came back with one of Avery's T-shirts for herself, a navy blue scarf, and Avery's academic robes that the university had bought in his graduate school's colors for him to wear during processionals in the years he was teaching. Avery's robe was a dark blue almost the color of the scarf. The hood was scarlet and gold, but Claudia undid the buttons that attached it. "Some nuns dress in blue, don't they? I think so. They must. There's that ad on television with a nun riding a bicycle, and she's wearing blue, but it's brighter than this." She reached up to fix the scarf over Avery's head as a veil. "I wonder how they keep these things on. I'll pin it somehow. This blue will be all right, don't you think? I'll have to go in black if I can borrow an undergraduate robe. Avery, you'll have to call the custodian and see if he'll get one out of storage. I think this will be all right. I think this will be exactly right!"

They spent the day assembling these disguises. Jane went everywhere with Avery, because he was such a pleasure to be with when he was benevolent with cheer. They picked up the black robe Claudia wanted and went to K-Mart to buy a black scarf to go with it, but they couldn't find one. All the scarves were printed in brilliant designs, but Avery was undaunted and on the alert in every direction. He was delighted when he spotted a revolving rack of sunglasses. He rotated the stand slowly and considered the glasses with great concentration, and finally selected two pairs with plain, octagonal wire rims. Standing right in the aisle he twisted the frames gently until he could remove the plastic lenses. "Janie, nuns wear these sort of glasses, don't they?" He asked her, but he was going to buy them anyway.

"I've never seen a real nun," Jane said. "I can't remember if the nuns in TV shows wear glasses or not. But what should I go as? I don't think I can go as a nun, too. We have to go as a family. I mean we have to dress as a group. Something that all three of us could be."

Avery still worked with the wire frames of the glasses, holding the four abandoned lenses in his palm, but he looked startled. He was clearly taken aback and didn't say anything for a minute until he had adjusted the frames to his satisfaction, then held them out to show Jane. He had bent the frame of each eyepiece into a shape that was pointed at its center but then curved outward on either side to the bottom edge which went straight across.

"Gothic arches," he said, and he put on a pair so she could see how they would look. The points of the arches reached the middle of his eyebrows; it was a nice effect. He was abstracted, though, and forgot to take them off.

"The child of two nuns . . . let's see . . . what two nuns possess. Not chastity. That wouldn't be any good, would it? That would be pretty predictable. What about virtue? That would be right, don't you think? You think that would work?" He looked very concerned as he studied her through the empty wire-rimmed glasses.

"Oh, yeah. That's good," said Jane, although she wasn't sure about this idea at all; she wasn't sure she understood it.

He took off the glasses and folded down the ear pieces with care, leaving the price tag on for the check-out girl. "We could do that with a white sheet. We need a ribbon, though, and some paint. Gold." Her father was lost in his idea, and she followed along behind him while he bought three yards of stiff wide purple ribbon and two yards of plain black cotton fabric for Claudia's veil. He finally found some metallic gold paint in the craft section next to the macrame materials.

That evening after Avery had brought home dinner for them all from the drive-thru at Burger Chef, he and Claudia fashioned a flowing white robe for Jane from a twin-sized sheet. From shoulder to waist, Miss America style, they pinned the purple ribbon on which Claudia had painted in the shiny gold paint *OUR OWN RE-WARD*. At the party that night, when Jane and Diana were by themselves, Diana pressed her about this costume, but Jane was disdainful.

"I'm Virtue, Diana. If you don't understand it you just don't have any sense of humor. Virtue is its own reward, you see!" She was so snappish that Diana just nodded. She and her family had dressed as Mouseketeers, with Mickey Mouse hats from the dime store. Another family had come as Little Orphan Annie and Daddy War-bucks, and they had dressed their four-year-old daughter as Sandy, the dog, but they had taken her home early to stay with a sitter. Some people had not dressed in costume at all. There was a man in a leopard-printed bathing suit with a woman in a sarong, and Jane finally figured out that they were Tarzan and Jane. All in all, though, she thought her own parents had come up with the most interesting costumes.

She and Diana sat in on the grownups' party for a little while, and Jane watched the couples dancing and thought that her parents looked wonderful and exotic swaying across the room together with their robes flowing around their legs and their veils swinging behind them. When Avery had come to get Jane to dance with him, she had been thoroughly glad to be connected with her father and her mother. She listened to her father being clever and pleased with the things he said. When Maggie said to him that his costume was ingenious, but whatever had made him think of it, he had grinned at her wholeheartedly.

"What could be more appropriate? I've taken the veil to save my family from disgrace. Now I can confess and go to heaven! It's your costume that is ingenious, Maggie," he said. "I wouldn't have thought of it. You look just right. You're the quintessential Mouse-keteer!"

Across the room her mother had taken off her veil and wimple, but she was still wearing the glasses with her hair fluffing around her face as she laughed and gesticulated. Claudia was elated, too; she and Avery were alight with energy, and in any corner where they were not the party palled and went limp. That's how it looked to Jane.

Later in the evening, however, Maggie had come to find Jane and had leaned down to her in an attitude of worried affection. She was still wearing her mouse ears, and her short hair spiked out around the edge of the black felt cap in a way that exaggerated her look of concern. "Janie, why don't you sleep over with Diana tonight?" She had said, leaning forward in a sort of insistent entreaty. That particular night Jane didn't want to be away for even one second from her glowing parents, and she gazed at them across the room longingly, because she didn't want to insult Maggie, either.

"Well," she said, "I have to get up really early in the morning to practice my violin. I have a lesson at ten o' clock."

Maggie had shifted her position slightly, straightening up and then bending protectively over Jane again with her arm across Jane's shoulders. But her voice was more brusque; her intention was more determined. "Look, Jane, you really should spend the night here. Sweetie, your father's had a lot to drink." She looked straight at Jane, but Jane held her face utterly still; she didn't let her expression change in any way, but she was shocked. Maggie had spoken to her so matter-of-factly, as though she could ever have the right to make such a comment. Maggie had spoken to her as if Jane were just anyone and as if her father were just anyone. Just someone Maggie happened to know. But Jane was learning early in her life that in order to like most people she had to ignore most of what they said and did.

"It's really nice of you to ask me," she had said, "but I'm afraid I can't stay over tonight." Jane's intention had remained firm, but she had been as overwhelmed then as she was now, sitting in Vince's study and being cheerfully teased about her costume—teased in a way that she suspected was now somehow an indictment of her whole family. The emotion that began to creep over her as she listened to Vince's banter was almost like the disheartening pang of homesickness. She was touched suddenly by a loss of hopefulness, and since she counted on the Tunbridges to be her measure of all things normal, all things in their right proportion, it was essential to her that she evade this encroaching disillusionment. She was restless sitting there with Vince in his study, having to listen to anything he might say, and she suggested to Diana that they go upstairs.

They found Celeste sitting cross-legged on her bed, surrounded by books and loose papers and notebooks, talking on the phone and making notes, and Jane and Diana stood in the hall idly eavesdropping on her until she spotted them out of the corner of her eye.

"Hey! You two!" She covered the mouth of the receiver with her hand. "Hey, in just a minute how about playing just *one* hand of canasta? Or we could do a hand of bridge again if I can get Mark or Maggie to sit in." Celeste loved to play cards and was currently trying to interest Jane and Diana in learning bridge. Jane had once heard Maggie say to Vince that Celeste might ruin her grade point average if she didn't play less bridge. "Or we could play Michigan rummy. We could play that three-handed. Just one game. I promise." Celeste's bedroom was vast and was furnished like a living room, with her great-grandmother's desk, a reading chair and a long couch. Jane had been there the afternoon Celeste and her friends had brought in the eight-sided game table and four wooden chairs that were set up at the foot of her bed. Maggie's whole expansive expression had drawn in with irritation, but she hadn't said anything to Celeste; she had just gone on about her business.

When Celeste turned back to the telephone, Diana led Jane away, because she knew that Jane would rather do anything Celeste wanted of them instead of whatever Diana could counter with and she hated card games with her sister. Eventually Celeste did search out the two girls in Diana's room, but by then Diana had interested Jane in the idea of glamour. She was pinning Jane's hair up, unsuccessfully as it happened, but Jane was pleased enough with the new image of herself without hair falling straight down in neat panels on either side of her face. She didn't pay any attention to the clumps of hair pinned tenuously on top of her head with a bristling of hairpins. Celeste helped them devise disco outfits for themselves out of odds and ends from her own wardrobe, and Diana put a Pointer Sisters' album on her stereo:

I want a lover with a slow hand.

I want a man with an easy touch . . .

Celeste looked over at them. "I know that's a song you're not supposed to understand."

"Oh, we don't," Jane said. "We don't understand a word of it!"

They danced in front of Diana's long mirror for a while, believing that they looked like the best dancer, the black dancer, on Solid Gold. When they were bored with that they moved on to Maggie's room, where she had set up her easel to catch the north light. She was working with her pastels, and Jane stood behind her and watched, but Diana strayed around the room, trailing her hand across the dresser to touch the little bottles of perfume, Maggie's silver brush and comb, a pair of leather gloves left lying out; she lounged disconsolately against a windowsill, not especially interested in what her mother was doing. Jane would have liked to have the right to browse through Maggie's room like that, trifling with all of Maggie's possessions. It wasn't possible for Jane to retain any suspicion of or disappointment in Maggie when she was in Maggie's company. From Jane's point of view, Maggie, more than anyone else she had ever known, had the irresistible allure and completely charismatic quality of unalloyed competence. Competence under any circumstances. It was what Jane so admired; it was what she, herself, aspired to.

Maggie had organized the girls to pose for her, so for a little while Diana sat back on Maggie's chaise lounge with her legs drawn up while Jane sat at its foot leaning against Diana's knees for support. Maggie was working in quick strokes with charcoal, and before she handed the finished sketch over to them she sprayed it with fixative and let it dry.

Jane took the sketch and laid it down on the coverlet of Maggie's bed to study it. She was entranced by her own earnest stare, drawn in with firm lines next to a softer more hesitant rendering of Diana's sweeter face.

"Look at this!" she said. "Just look at this! I look more like Maggie than you do," she said to Diana. And it was true, because Jane had both height for her age and some grace, and she was fair, although not in the same pink and freckled way that Maggie was so blonde. Both Maggie and Jane were tall and thin, so that their joints—their knees and elbows—appeared to be just marginally broader than their fragile arms and legs. Maggie was not especially pretty. She had a faintly simian look and a rather alarming smile that stretched her mouth too far into a grimace that bared her large straight teeth. But Jane was pleased as she looked at the sketch, because she had always thought that Maggie looked exactly the way Maggie ought to look, and she wasn't at all sorry to think that she might look that way, too. It delighted and hugely flattered her that Maggie had wanted to draw her picture.

When the girls finally drifted out of Maggie's room, just as Jane crossed the threshold into the wide upper hall, she experienced a momentary ecstasy of inclusion. She had a sudden piercing feeling of familiarity that made her want to open out her arms and receive every nuance of that sensation, which she perceived as something of actual substance that radiated from the walls, the pictures, the dark wood floors, the people. At the very moment when she stepped out of Maggie's room, she had a sudden apprehension of the history of the house, its present, and its future. As she moved along the hall, she did raise her arms just a fraction before she remembered not to, and her aborted gesture was like the flap of wings. For the few seconds Jane was possessed by this phenomenon, she was following Diana down the hallway, self-consciously aware of her own footsteps in her wooden heeled clogs as they clattered across the floors of all the Tunbridge forbears and future generations.

*   *   *

By late day Jane and Diana sat in the dining room eating potato chips. They curled onto their chairs with their legs tucked under them and leaned their elbows on the table. They were delicate with the greasy chips, carefully lifting them to their mouths with the tips of their fingers and making two bites of the large ones while they looked out at the rain that had begun to fall. It was an odd rain that didn't streak down out of running clouds sweeping over the region. This rain was pendulous and globular, drop by drop, falling over the porch with a sound like cooked peas hitting the porch floor with a pulpy splash outside the shadowy room.

Maggie came in and joined them at the table without interrupting their silence. The rain fell, and Maggie ate a potato chip and sat listlessly spellbound also by the peculiar downpour. Each drop contained too much; it was an unpleasant sound all around them, a natural obscenity. Maggie took a handful of chips and moved to the French doors.

"Umm. This looks bad. It's turning to ice."

But Maggie went away to start dinner while the girls set the table, and the weather wasn't important when the whole family sat down to eat together. At the Tunbridge's house it seemed to Jane that everyone was the same age, and in her mind there was no sweeter equality. Tonight Vince was irritable, and Celeste was quiet and sulky with fatigue from having spent the day studying. But these were pale passions, nothing to conceal. Jane had never seen any member of this family really angry, and she thought that the knowledge of anger was her own secret shame. By age eleven she had already met in herself the height of any anger she would ever feel again. She hadn't revealed it, of course, because she still had only the status of a child, but occasionally she was relieved of it vicariously by one or the other of her parents if either one of them happened to say to the other exactly what Jane was thinking. What she suspected, though, was that her fury was a shabby emotion, because it could not be controlled, and everything about this household indicated that a modicum of restraint was the order of the day.

By the time Jane and Diana went to bed, Jane was sated with fellowship, and she wasn't sorry to be left alone in the small, flower-papered bedroom that she had chosen as her own for when she slept over. It was known by all the Tunbridges as "Jane's room." She didn't mind being separated from Diana, whose own room was down the hall, because Maggie said it was barbarous to deny people privacy while they were sleeping. They had such a big house, she said, that it was ridiculous to crowd people together as though they must live in dormitories. Sleep was a solitary undertaking, a time to muse and dream alone, said Maggie. And after spending a day in communion with that family, Jane didn't think that Maggie's ideas were at all unusual or precious. She wouldn't have known how to think any thoughts like that about Maggie, and if the two girls had slept in the same room they would have been far more likely to awaken each other and the entire family too early on the following Sunday morning.

At eleven o'clock Jane put on her pajamas and brushed her teeth and said goodnight to Diana. She got into bed and under the covers that Maggie had turned down for her sometime during the evening and began to read one of the selection of books that were always left on the bedside table for her along with a glass of ice water. But she fell asleep within four pages of the first volume of *The Book of Three*. She had climbed into bed and settled back among her pillows without responsibility of any kind in this vast houseful of grownups, and that was a powerful soporific.

*   *   *

Jane woke up early, just before dawn, and she woke up alarmed. She lay still for a while listening for the reason she had awakened. She was too young to care if she fell asleep again, but she did care to calm herself; she did want to lapse back into that same soothing state of mind in which she had gone to sleep the night before.

Finally she sat up and pulled the down comforter around her shoulders like a cape and crossed the floor barefooted to the window to open the curtains. She was still just waking up, and her coordination was slumberous in spite of the shock of the cold floorboards and rarefied air. Overnight all the objects in the room had become just fractionally clearer to the eye, easier to discern in the crystalline atmosphere, but her attention was too lethargic to take this in. She struggled with the drapes, trying to fasten the tie-backs with one hand while holding the quilt around her with the other. At last she dropped the quilt on the floor so she could use both hands, and she settled the tie-backs around the drapes and hooked them in place with exasperation.

She looked out the window with only a drowsy interest, but when she took in the dark panorama of the bluff and the river and the meadow to her right, she moved backward just a scant step, and then she moved forward again to peer out of the glass in earnest. She stood perfectly still staring out for several minutes, but she could not organize the scene before her into any landscape she could recognize.

The river roiled sluggishly wherever it had not crusted over, and the railroad tracks were furzed with ice. In the meadow nothing moved. The trees did not tremble, and their bright fall leaves hung glazed and heavy from the branches. The meadow itself, through which she had made her way the day before, was smoothed over with ice, sleek and undulating and foreign. She made no sympathetic association to any bit of the earth she gazed out upon, because what she saw exceeded anything she might have imagined. The landscape was icebound, desolate, and bruised where it mirrored the barely lightening sky. It slowly came into her thoughts that her parents would not possibly be able to weather such an extremity of climate, and Jane knew that she ought to do something, but she didn't know what would be expected of her.

She got dressed and made her bed and packed her backpack before anyone else in the house had awakened, and she sat on the edge of the bed looking out at the mysterious accumulation of ice and tried not to anticipate anything at all. But she was puzzled the same way she had been the morning her mother had come in and curled up in Jane's bed with her after both of them had spent a sleepless night appeasing, avoiding, and enduring Avery's violent raging about the house. Her mother had put her head down on the pillow next to Jane so that her fluffy hair wisped across Jane's cheek and got into her mouth. On that morning her mother had chatted in whispers as though anything at all could possibly awaken Avery, who was sprawled asleep in a living room chair.

"You know," her mother had said, "I think it's perfectly understandable that children do the things to their parents that they do. I was reading about a thirteen-year-old boy who climbed up on top of the refrigerator with one of those huge cast iron skillets," she said. "He knew his father was going to come home drunk, and he waited for hours. Of course, when the man walked through the door the boy hit him as hard as he could with that skillet and just killed him." Claudia had paused to think about it, and she had turned onto her back and pulled Jane's blanket up to her chin. "I don't really think that's murder, though, do you? Well, they aren't even trying him for murder," she had added thoughtfully. "They're calling it self-defense. Don't you think that's probably fair?"

Jane hadn't responded at all to that. She had tried to sort it out but had never succeeded. She was fairly certain that her mother didn't want her to bash her father's brains out with a skillet, but she was just as certain that there was something that her mother did want her to do to make their lives easier. And yet, as far as Jane could see, she was without any power whatsoever.

This morning, however, as she stared at the ice, she did understand why, after all those nights when she and her mother had taken long drives straight toward St. Louis on the interstate to be out of Avery's way, her mother always turned around and came home in the end. When Avery had thought of removing the distributor cap early in the day so that they couldn't forsake him, and when her mother had taken the precaution of going to an auto supply house to buy an extra one in case he should do that again—then Jane had finally asked her mother why they had to go back.

"I don't see why we have to go home," Jane had said. "I mean, why can't we just go to a hotel like Dad does when he really gets mad?" She was curled up in the back seat of the car while her mother had stretched her legs out on the front seat. They had just driven around town for a while that night and finally parked on a street near their house while they waited until they thought Avery had gone to sleep.

"Dad usually stays in a suite at the Oakwood, too, and it's really nice. We could just go there." Jane adored being with her father when he was away from her mother and when she visited him in the nice rooms of a motel. Whenever he moved out, he and Claudia channeled information to each other through Jane, and they set up a pattern so that Avery would meet her twice a week at her music lesson at Miss Jessup's, and sometimes they would all three go back to his motel for dinner. Avery would order all sorts of things from room service, because Jane loved to have her dinner arrive on a trolley underneath a silver dome that kept it hot. And even Miss Jessup would become lighthearted as they unveiled one surprising dish after another. Then they would settle down in the room to watch TV until it was time for Jane to go meet her mother in the lobby. Her parents didn't like to see each other during times like those. Avery had only stayed away two or three weeks at a time, but they had been the nicest times Jane could remember, and she didn't see why she and her mother couldn't try the same ploy.

But when she suggested it, Claudia had shaken her head forward and swung her face toward Jane in a pale orbit over the car seat, moving her hand in front of her to stave off any other question. Jane had been surprised to see that her mother was both angry and shocked.

"Don't be silly, Jane. What in God's name do you think would happen to your father? Where in the world would we even want to go? What do you think he would do?"

All Jane had been able to decide then was that her mother must love her father, but at last she understood that that wasn't all there was to it. She had never been sure, anyway, that being in love was the right idea to have about her parents. And this morning Jane knew all at once that she was looking out upon the world the way it was for her parents. It was a place in which there was no refuge for either one of them except the other. Now she needed to be home, but she thought that when she did get home her father would have left them again. She didn't think he would stay until she could get there, and she didn't know how long he would be gone this time.

CONTRIBUTORS

Will Baker: "Chiquita Banana Muy Bonita," p. 99 (*MR* vol. 12, no. 2, 1989). Baker is the author of two critical books, two novels, and two volumes of nonfiction, *Backward* and *Mountain Blood*.

Russell Banks: "Sara Cole: A Type of Love Story," p. 1 (*MR* vol. 7, no. 3, 1984). Banks has written eleven books of fiction, most recently *Success Stories*, which included "Sara Cole," and the novels *Continental Drift*, *Affliction*, and the forthcoming *The Sweet Hereafter*. "Sara Cole," his most anthologized and translated story, was reprinted in the Pushcart Prize anthology and *Best American Short Stories* and is being adapted for television.

Stephanie Bobo: "Recognizable at a Distance," p. 105 (*MR* vol. 11, no. 2, 1988). This was Bobo's first story publication and won the William Peden Prize in Fiction.

Paul Bowles: "The Eye," p. 22 (*MR* vol. 2, no. 1, 1978). Bowles has published many books during his long and distinguished career. "The Eye" was reprinted in *Best American Short Stories* and proclaimed the best story of the year by the *New York Times Book Review*. It appeared in Bowles's collection *Midnight Mass*.

François Camoin: "Lieberman's Father," p. 206 (*MR* vol. 5, no. 1, 1981). Awarded the William Peden Prize in Fiction, this story was included in Camoin's collection *The End of the World is Los Angeles*, which won the Associated Writing Programs Award in Short Fiction. He is also the author of *Benbow and Paradise*, *Why Men Are Afraid of Women*, and *Deadly Virtues*.

Ron Carlson: "At the Hop," p. 48 (*MR* vol. 8, no. 3, 1985). Carlson has published the short story collection *The News of the World* and two novels, *Betrayed by F. Scott Fitzgerald* and *Truants*. "At the Hop" was cited in *Best American Short Stories* and reprinted in *Editors Choice*.

Raymond Carver: "A Serious Talk," p. 245 (*MR* vol. 4, no. 1, 1980). A well-known and influential practitioner of the short story until his early death in 1988, Carver wrote several award-winning collections, including *What We Talk About When We Talk About Love* (which contains "A Serious Talk" under another title), *Will You Please Be Quiet Please,* and *Cathedral.*

Alice Denham: "The Professional Thief," p. 156 (*MR* vol. 10, no. 2, 1987). Denham has published two novels, *My Darling From the Lions* and *Amo.* "The Deal," was made into the movie *Quizas,* which won a Silver Plaque at the Chicago Film Festival in 1989.

Robb Forman Dew: "The Secret Feather," p. 299 (*MR* vol. 7, no. 3, 1984). Dew won the American Book Award for her novel *Dale Loves Sophie to Death.* "The Secret Feather," which is part of her second novel, *The Time of Her Life,* won the William Peden Prize in Fiction.

Jim Hall: "Poetic Devices," p. 164 (*MR* vol. 4, no. 2, 1980). "Poetic Devices" appeared in Hall's collection *Paper Products.* He has published two novels, *Under Cover of Daylight* and *Tropical Freeze,* and another, *Bones of Coral,* is scheduled to come out in 1991.

Amy Hempel: "Today Will Be a Quiet Day," p. 30 (*MR* vol. 8, no. 2, 1985). Hempel's two story collections are *At the Gates of the Animal Kingdom* and *Reason to Live,* which included "Today Will Be a Quiet Day." This story was one of her first publications and was reprinted in both the Pushcart Prize anthology and *Best American Short Stories.*

Linda Hogan: "Aunt Moon's Young Man," p. 226 (*MR* vol. 11, no. 1, 1988). Hogan is the author of *Seeing Through the Sun,* which won the American Book Award of the Before Columbus Foundation. She has also published a novel, *Mean Spirit.* "Aunt Moon's Young Man" was reprinted in *Best American Short Stories.*

Wally Lamb: "Astronauts," p. 121 (*MR* vol. 12, no. 2, 1989). "Astronauts" was Lamb's first story publication. It has been reprinted in *Streetsongs: New Voices in Fiction* and in the Pushcart Prize anthology. It also won the William Peden Prize in Fiction.

Naguib Mahfouz: "Tales from Alleyways," p. 252 (*MR* vol. 8, no. 2, 1985). Mahfouz has won the Nobel Prize for Literature, and is the author of many novels currently available in translation in the United States. *Palace of Desire*, the second novel in his Cairo Trilogy, has recently seen print in an English version. "Tales from Alleyways" is from *Fountain and Tomb*.

David Zane Mairowitz: "Hector Composes a Circular Letter . . .," p. 283 (*MR* vol. 10, no. 1, 1987). Residing in France, Mairowitz is the author of *Wilhelm Reich for Beginners*, and his radio plays are regularly produced by the BBC. "Hector Composes a Circular Letter . . ." was reprinted in the Pushcart Prize anthology.

Kevin McIlvoy: "Second Hands (1970)," p. 219 (*MR* vol. 10, no. 3, 1987). McIlvoy has published the novel *The Fifth Station*. "Second Hands" earned special mention in the Pushcart Prize anthology.

Kathy Miller: "The Boys From This School," p. 261 (*MR* vol. 10, no. 1, 1987). This intriguing piece was Miller's first story publication.

Kent Nelson: "The Rangold Consortium," p. 138 (*MR* vol. 9, no. 3, 1986). Nelson is the author of the story collection *The Tennis Player* and two novels, *Cold Wind River* and *All Around Me Peaceful*.

Michael O'Hanlon: "Crooner's Party," p. 270 (*MR* vol. 8, no. 1, 1984). This story, O'Hanlon's first publication, won the William Peden Prize in Fiction and earned special mention in the Pushcart Prize anthology.

David Ohle: "Bagatelle," p. 59 (*MR* vol. 7, no. 2, 1984). Ohle is the author of the novel *Motorman* and coeditor of a book of "oral hippie tales" scheduled for publication in 1991. "Bagatelle" earned special mention in the Pushcart Prize anthology.

Ninotchka Rosca: "Epidemic," p. 70 (*MR* vol. 8, no. 3, 1985). Rosca was born in Manila where she worked as a journalist until she was arrested in 1972 after martial law was declared. She is the author of four books, including *State of War,* a novel that has been released in seven countries.

Bob Shacochis: "Hunger," p. 36 (*MR* vol. 3, no. 3, 1980). Shacochis won the American Book Award for his first collection of short fiction, *Easy in the Islands.* "Hunger," a part of that highly acclaimed debut, was his first published story and was reprinted in *Missouri Short Fiction.* He is also the author of the story collection *The Next New World.*

Robert Thompson: "Under the Swaying Curtain," p. 173 (*MR* vol. 5, no. 1, 1981). "Under the Swaying Curtain" was reprinted in *Missouri Short Fiction* and received special mention in both the Pushcart Prize anthology and *Best American Short Stories.* Before his untimely death, Thompson's fiction also appeared in *Harper's, The New Yorker,* and *Kenyon Review.*

Barton Wilcox: "Ferguson's Wagon," p. 78 (*MR* vol. 10, no. 2, 1987). This was Wilcox's first published short story. It earned special mention in *Best American Short Stories.*

Connie Willis: "Cash Crop," p. 187 (*MR* vol. 7, no. 2, 1984). Willis has won four Nebula Awards for short fiction and two Hugo Awards. Her novel *Lincoln's Dreams* won the John W. Campbell Memorial Award for Best Science Fiction Novel. "Cash Crop" was reprinted in *The World's Best Science Fiction.*